Timecrack

By

William Long

New Generation **Publishing**

By the same author
An Unexpected Diagnosis
A collection of Irish short stories

Acknowledgements

For all their support and encouragement during the writing of Timecrack, I must thank my son, Ryan, for his enthusiasm and helpful comments on the manuscript; and my daughter, Alex, equally enthusiastic, for her original contribution and suggestions on the drawing of the Timeless Valley map. Also, not least by any means, I must thank Vi, my wife, for her endless patience and understanding while I worked through the days and late evenings to finish the story.

Every writer needs a good copy writer and I was fortunate to have Rachel Malone, at Author Press, for her invaluable advice and editing of the book.

And I must extend my appreciation to Tamian Wood at www.BeyondDesignInternational.com and Ramah at www.cartographersguild.com for the speedy completion of the map design at such short notice

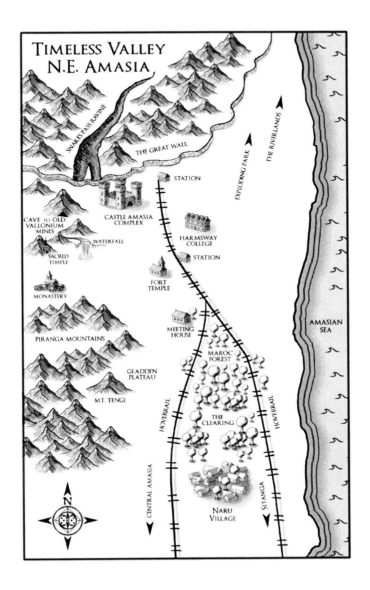

Contents

Part One

Through the Timecrack 9

Part Two

Timeless Valley 75

Part Three

The Legend of Arnak 153

Part Four

The Stone 261

For my grandsons
Finian and Lukas

Part One

Through the Timecrack

Chapter One

The Pyramid

The boy pointed to the eastern side of the pyramid that dominated the early morning skyline. It was partly obscured by the strange blue cloud that had suddenly appeared after the last lightning strike.

Dr Malcolm Kinross glanced down at the boy. 'I see it, Manuel.'

But what the blazes is it? he wondered.

A big man, broad-shouldered and deeply tanned from years of working on digs throughout Mexico, Kinross was fit for his fifty-two years. But he gritted his teeth as a sharp pain shot through his right leg, making him shift his weight onto the aluminium walking stick. Leaning heavily on the handle to ease the ache in his knee, he surveyed the damage done to the campsite. The risks of working through the Yucatan's hurricane season were well known, but nothing could have prepared him for the devastation that lay before his eyes. It was like a scene from a First World War battlefield.

At the height of the storm, lightning bolts had struck the pyramid's flat top and what was left of its once golden column, long since stripped of the valuable metal by ancient raiders. Tons of stone facing blocks had been sent tumbling down onto the camp below where the mestizos slept in their tents. They never had a chance. Several of them now lay dead, their bodies crushed like thin eggshells, while the rest who survived the avalanche of stone fled into the jungle, vowing never to return.

Only Manuel, along with Lucy, had stayed behind to help Kinross try to cover the excavations with tarpaulin and plastic sheeting, but it had been a wasted effort. The trenches were half-filled with muddy rainwater and lay across the dig like sinking boats, with yet more pebble-sized drops of rain falling, threatening another deluge.

'Malcolm ... what are we going to do?'

The voice, shaking and frightened, made Kinross look down at his wife. She was on her knees, arms held tightly across her chest, like a shield against what might come next.

They were on a large slab of honey-coloured stone, its wheel-like shape covered with mysterious symbols they had yet to understand. It had been discovered inside the remains of a temple, complete with columns and pediment, once the dig had been cleared of the undergrowth that had hidden it for centuries. Their work had shown that the temple with its wide marble steps, and the pyramid several hundred yards away, had been constructed on two sides of a large square. It was an incredible find by Kinross; nothing like the temple with its Greek-style architecture had been discovered before in the depths of the Yucatan jungle.

As far as he could tell, the stone – the Transkal – had been positioned in the middle of a large room, somewhere inside the temple. It had yet to reveal its purpose, but from the carved images and central trough sculpted into its surface he thought it might be some sort of sacrificial site. Over two feet in height and twelve across, he had named it after his late friend and former head of the department of archaeology at Cambridge, Sir Archibald Transkal, his mentor during his time at the college. And now they were on the stone that had kept them free from the river of mud that coursed its way through the campsite during the night.

'I don't know, Lucy, but we're finished here for the time being, that's for sure.'

He could see that she was suffering from one of her headaches again. Her natural, silvery-blonde hair was lying mud-spattered against her skull, and her deep-set blue eyes, dull with pain, betrayed her exhaustion. They were both ready to drop, having tried over the past few hours to save some of the pottery sherds and coins they had so patiently excavated near the temple. What they had saved now lay spread out on the stone, a pathetic reminder of how little they had managed to rescue before the torrential rains had forced the collapse of the trenches.

Lucy was groaning. A low, whimpering, child-like sound that warned Kinross she was slipping into a trance, but there was nothing he could do. It was a worrying condition that happened sometimes in her sleep. At other times, like now, she would unexpectedly stiffen and withdraw into another world. A world that might last minutes, or perhaps longer, and then she would recover, claiming she had 'seen' things – not dreams, but real events that very often included their two boys, Archie and Richard.

For a brief moment, he thought of the boys at Grimshaws, back in Ireland. Would he ever visit the school again? Would he see them again? *Damn it! Damn this storm!* He gripped his walking stick more tightly and watched Lucy as she slowly closed her eyes, but there was little he could do and nothing to be gained by thinking the worst. He knew he would have to keep a clear head if they were to survive this disaster.

'Señor Kinross! See there!'

Manuel's words were almost drowned by an almighty roar of thunder directly above them. Lightning crackled again as it lit up the eastern face of the pyramid, exposing large gaps where the huge stone blocks, already weakened by centuries of neglect, had broken away

'Look, Señor – *Chac*!'

The boy was pulling at Kinross's belt and pointing towards the blue cloud. It had drifted away from the pyramid, but now it contained, at its very core, a pulsing bright light, and it seemed to be coming their way.

Chac was one of the most ancient Mayan gods. As a bringer of rain and maize, Chac was still worshipped by Mayan farmers, especially during times of drought, but also a god to be feared as a bearer of thunderbolts and destruction.

'I don't think so, it's only –'

But Manuel wasn't listening. At the sight of the blue cloud approaching, with its yellow inner light getting brighter by the second, he leapt into the sea of mud surrounding the stone. His little legs buckled and nearly gave way as he struggled through the thick sludge to reach the edge of the jungle, but he made it, glancing only briefly over his shoulder to see the cloud he believed to be Chac.

With a sense of sadness, Kinross watched him disappear into the trees, thankful that the young boy who had been like a puppy around his legs for so long had made it safely out of the mud. He turned to see that the cloud was almost upon them. He was mystified by it, but he could do nothing about it. His leg had stiffened and he could hardly walk, let alone make his way through the mud. And Lucy was in no fit state to move; she had settled into a trance-like state and was as still as death. All he could do was watch and wait as the cloud slowly enveloped them like some great heavenly cloak.

*

Hidden by an old tree stump and a screen of dense undergrowth, Manuel lay flat on the ground, afraid to raise his head in case the great god, Chac, might see him. He had no idea how long he lay there, but eventually his curiosity got the better of him. Crawling to the side of the tree stump he carefully parted the long wet grass to get a better view of the campsite.

The stone was deserted. He didn't know what it was, the villagers simply referred to it as the 'Big Stone', but he had known since he was little that, like the pyramid, it was a special place. His eyes scanned the campsite searching for some sign of life. It had stopped raining and the blue cloud was gone, but so were Dr Kinross and his wife.

It had come true – the warning given by old Mateo, the shaman in his village, the day Dr Kinross had arrived looking for workers to help him excavate the area around the ancient pyramid. Mateo, who rarely spoke to anyone, had been troubled and had warned Kinross and the villagers:

'Beware the anger of the Gods. Those who would take from them, they also will be taken.'

The young mestizos had ignored the old shaman. They said they were good Catholics and no longer listened to such nonsense. Besides, they would be well paid for their labour, and was this not more important to their families? Now some of them lay dead, and the doctor and his wife had disappeared.

As he prepared to leave the sacred grounds, Manuel prayed that the gods would not be too unkind to the doctor and his wife. Little did he know that Malcolm and Lucy Kinross had embarked on a very strange journey that few would have believed.

Chapter Two

Aristo's Journey

A young man who would understand what was happening to Malcolm and Lucy Kinross was also in a difficult situation, except that he was *looking* for the blue cloud and so far he hadn't found it.

Aristo felt his heart begin to beat more rapidly as he watched the great rhino-like beasts feeding on the leaves of the large flowering plants that grew along the edge of the riverbank. He couldn't believe what he was seeing. They were dinosaurs, with thick, greyish-green leathery hides and massive heads dominated by three fearsome-looking horns. At the back of the head was a large plate-like frill with bony tips that covered the neck like a huge collar. He guessed they were plant eaters, but that didn't mean they were not dangerous. These incredible beasts were over thirty feet long, nearly ten feet tall, and each one probably weighed at least ten tons. If he got in their way, there wouldn't be much left of him to make a decent sandwich.

God! Just my luck to land in the middle of nowhere with a bunch of dumb dinosaurs!

He shook his head in frustration as he lifted his left arm to switch on the Timecrack Tracking Unit. He was careful to leave it on silent mode as he shielded the display window with his right hand, in case it glowed. *If only it would!* The dinosaurs probably wouldn't see it at this distance, but he wasn't about to take a chance on giving away his position before a timecrack fully materialised. Who knew how these beasts would react if they were startled by a strange flashing light.

The TTU, as it was usually called, was built into the sleeve of his tracker suit, with a back-up unit in the other sleeve. He looked closely at the grey neutral display, hoping to see some sign of blue edging into the lower quadrant. *Please ... go blue!* But no matter how hard he wished, the display remained grey.

Leaving the TTU switched on in silent mode, Aristo positioned himself on the ledge to get a better look at the lie of the land. He had fallen onto the ledge earlier, but luckily he had suffered no serious injury. The metallic fibre suit he wore had protected him from the worst of the fall.

Only a short time ago he had been scouring the edge of the forest for edible plants and berries to supplement his emergency rations, when, without warning, the ground had started to tremble and the sound of large boulders smashing their way through the trees had frightened him. Fearing an earthquake, Aristo had run for his life along a narrow path, hardly caring where it led.

With the earth growling and heaving like an angry sea and giant conifers uprooting all around him, Aristo felt something touching him as it crashed to the forest floor behind him. He looked over his shoulder and saw that a tree had narrowly missed him. He sprinted blindly along the rough track hoping to find solid ground and shelter from the rocks now hurtling down the mountainside.

Ever since he had arrived in this strange, forbidding world several days before – *Old Earth* days, he had to remember – Aristo had only been able to make headway through the forest by travelling on trails made by the dinosaurs. The lush vegetation, with conifers screened by thickets of broad-leafed ferns, created an impenetrable barrier through which only the huge beasts could trample their way.

Suddenly the ground heaved and burst open beneath his feet with such force that he was catapulted through the air, head over heels, to land on a flat inclined rock covered in green slimy moss. Slithering down the face of the rock he fell onto a wide rocky ledge overlooking a great plain.

Aristo picked himself up and checked his green – now somewhat greener – camouflage tracker suit for any tears or damage to the complex life-support system that had been woven into the special metallic fibre. Everything seemed to be in working order, but he felt stiff and sore from the fall. After the almost impossible hike through the thick forest he was exhausted and needed to rest.

His olive skin, usually smooth and fresh, was smeared with dirt, and his golden curls, greasy and unkempt, lay flat against his brow. His greenish-grey eyes, despite his tiredness, were still sharp and alert for any sign of danger. It was an instinct that had always been a part of him.

As a seven-year-old youth in the city state of Sparta in Ancient Greece, Aristo had been taken from his parents to be subjected to a brutal thirteen-year programme that had been designed to turn Spartan boys into future warrior-citizens, to be feared and grudgingly respected by their enemies. Unfortunately, at the age of fourteen, none of his early fighting and survival skills had been able to prevent him from being taken by a timecrack.

It had arrived when he was fighting with a group of other boys on a hillock near their training camp. The evening light was fading, and so determined had Aristo been to beat the bigger boy he was wrestling he hadn't seen the blue cloud descending on them. It was only when he looked around that he realised the rest of the group had fled back to the camp. Before they had time to even think about following them, the cloud had swept over the hillock, sucking the two boys and everything else in its path up into a crazy swirling mist.

Aristo had lost consciousness and remembered nothing of that journey, he only knew that he had awakened in a strange land, alone, for there was no sign of his fighting companion. The other boy had completely disappeared, as was often the case when people were taken by timecracks, and which was exactly what the scientists back at Mount Tengi were trying to rectify with Aristo's current trip.

But here he was - lost again!

He was twenty years old now (measured in New Earth years), the youngest ever recruit to the Timecrack Research Programme, with everyone hoping he would be the very first traveller to make a successful return to the chamber at Mount Tengi. Unfortunately, the technicians had landed him in the wrong place at the wrong time and outside the return trip coordinates. Now his only way back was to find a timecrack, but so far there hadn't been any sign of one materialising.

He yawned and rubbed his eyes, checking the TTU again for what seemed to be the hundredth time. He needed to get some sleep before attempting to go any further. Stretching out on the ledge he settled into a recess in the rock and closed his eyes.

*

Awakened by the sound of thunder in the distance, Aristo watched as a bolt of lightning zigzagged across the horizon. It left him with a desperate feeling of loneliness in this vast and frightening place. It was the time before humans, a land roamed by dinosaurs and other unknown beasts yet to be discovered. He was just beginning to realise that he was probably the only person on the planet.

Reaching into one of his thigh pockets he extracted a food concentrate packet that would expand with his drinking water, satisfying his hunger, if not his palate. Water had not been a problem, as there were mountain streams throughout the forest all running down to a wide river not far below. *If only he had some Sticklejuice!* But Dr Shah had vetoed that, saying it wasn't practical to carry any extras on a timecrack journey; only the absolute essentials would be allowed. He finished his meal with a high-energy Actotab; at least it would help to revitalise him and dispel the poor mood that threatened to overtake him.

It was a short time later when he saw the dinosaur herd moving slowly along the riverbank towards dense scrub at the bottom of the mountain. The sight of so many dinosaurs nearby took his breath away, but he contained his excitement and kept a watchful eye on the herd. Although he had heard wild screeches in the treetops and other sounds in the forest that he couldn't identify, the dinosaurs were the first sign of life he had actually seen since his arrival in this strange world. After a few minutes quietly watching the huge beasts, he noticed a track about ten feet below the ledge where he lay. It seemed to lead to the river where some of the herd had stopped to drink. Probably a trail made by smaller animals, and a path, he decided, which he could use to leave the ledge.

Suddenly he sensed a change in the TTU. He looked at his left sleeve – *Yes!* A thin blue band had appeared on the display. It was not very bright – but it was definitely there! Aristo knew that as the blue band gradually spread across the display it would change to yellow and glow so brightly it would be impossible to view without a filter. By that time it wouldn't matter; he would be directly in the vicinity of a timecrack and at the mercy of its force. Considering the situation he was in now, not even Dr Shah or the technicians could predict with any accuracy what would happen next, but when the timecrack appeared it would be his only chance to return to Timeless Valley.

Thick, threatening black clouds were gathering on the mountain above him. The ground was trembling again and small rocks were falling onto the ledge, skittering over the edge onto the path below. By the river, the dinosaurs were snorting and grunting as if annoyed that their feeding had been disturbed. They tossed and twisted their mighty heads, the wicked-looking triple horns stabbing the air, listening to the sounds from the mountainside.

The TTU was sensitive to atmospheric changes up to a radius of nearly a mile, and Aristo was aware that any movement on his part would have to be carefully monitored, otherwise he might lose his position and be out of range when the timecrack materialised.

The herd was moving again and Aristo decided to move with it. He knew that animals were more sensitive than humans to the energy fields that accompanied timecracks. Atmospheric disturbance was a clue to their imminent arrival, and he could see that something was happening near the dinosaurs. He looked at the TTU and saw that the blue band was approaching the yellow sector. It would happen soon – but where?

It was getting dark as he made his decision to leave the ledge and make his way down to the narrow track. The mountain tremors were becoming more violent and Aristo soon found he was jumping every few feet as cracks opened up in the trail before him. Dense rotting vegetation and large twisting roots slowed him down, and by the time he reached the plain the herd had moved farther away from the mountain.

He glanced at the TTU and saw that the blue band had reached the yellow quadrant. It was glowing so brightly he had to use the filter.

The timecrack was here!

Aristo almost jumped out of his skin as a blinding white flash of light struck the herd, followed almost immediately by a deafening thunderclap. The terrified dinosaurs scattered, several of them charging towards Aristo as he made his way across the plain. The tracker suit was slowing him down, but he had to move quickly and hope that he wouldn't be too late.

He almost missed it. The sky was black with storm clouds and he only just made out the blue mist that was forming by the river, but it had started to glow... and now its centre was turning yellow!

Lightning struck the herd again, and the mountain roared as great fissures opened up sending boulders and trees down onto the plain. It was as if this world was coming to an end. Two of the dinosaurs, maddened by the lightning strikes, had separated from the rest of the herd and were now charging blindly into the glowing bluish-yellow mist. Aristo watched them warily as he dashed from the opposite direction, entering the timecrack as it threatened to disappear as quickly as it had arrived.

Inside the blue cloud the sound of the timecrack was like a thundering waterfall and the yellow light so intense it hurt his eyes. He felt himself being sucked into a passage of blinding brightness. The last thing he saw as he adjusted the headband filter was the strange sight of two great triple-horned dinosaurs spiralling away from him down a very long tunnel.

Chapter Three

Highway Pueblo Motel

Seventy million years later, an unholy row was taking place between two boys in a motel room in New Mexico. Archie Kinross had just lost patience with his younger brother when he returned to the room to discover that Richard hadn't even got out of bed.

'Get up, Richard, it's time to go!' yelled Archie, trying to pull the bedclothes off Richard's bed.

'Go away – I'm tired.'

The muffled voice came from a hump-like figure that had completely disappeared inside the bed sheet. Resisting all Archie's attempts to remove it, Richard was striking out with his fists like a ghost gone berserk.

'C'mon,' said Archie, 'I'm tired too, but we have to get ready to see Uncle John.'

'No – I'm not going!'

'Look, Richard, Marjorie will be waiting for us – so let's go!'

Like a magician opening his magic cabinet to reveal his missing assistant, Archie suddenly grabbed the bed sheet and whipped it away to expose Richard standing in the middle of the bed.

'Give it back!' screamed Richard.

Archie couldn't help laughing at the, thin angry figure bouncing indignantly up and down on the bed. Bright blue eyes glared furiously at him through long, fair hair that rippled across a slim angular face. They were quite different in appearance and temperament in nearly every way. Archie at sixteen, was three years older and taller, stockily built, with brown eyes and brown curly hair, and not so short tempered.

Ever since their parents had gone missing in Mexico, Archie had become more protective of

23

Richard, but for the moment he was keeping his distance, at least until his brother decided to give up trying to punch him. Richard was hard to handle when he really got mad, especially if he thought Archie was trying to boss him around.

He couldn't blame Richard for being tired and irritable. Neither of them had had a decent night's sleep since leaving Grimshaws, their boarding school outside Enniskillen in Northern Ireland, four days earlier. What with delayed flights and missed connections between New York and New Mexico, the journey had exhausted the two of them. Especially for Archie, having to listen to Richard moaning about something every five minutes. If they hadn't had Miss Peoples, one of the new tutors at Grimshaws, with them to help with all the paperwork that was needed to get into America, Archie felt he would have been driven mad. When their uncle, Professor John Strawbridge, had phoned the school looking for a paid volunteer to look after them, it was Miss Peoples who had jumped at the chance. As she explained later to Archie:

'It's a wonderful opportunity to see New Mexico *and* meet your famous uncle!'

Just as well, thought Archie as he reflected on all the problems and delays they had experienced getting to Las Cruces and the Highway Pueblo Motel.

Although Richard was as thin as a rake, he had a ferocious appetite, so when Archie threatened him with no breakfast, Richard finally, but reluctantly left the bedroom.

Miss Peoples – or, as she had suggested that while they were away from Grimshaws, the boys should call her Marjorie – had given them some money for the vending machines situated in the motel foyer, and now Archie was standing in front of one of the machines wondering what to select.

'I want a Coke – and some of those,' said Richard, pointing to a crowded display of pink, green and yellow sticky-looking pastries, stacked in little white plastic trays.

'I don't know…' muttered Archie, flicking a strand of hair away from his forehead.

'C'mon, Archie, I'm *starving*!'

To keep the peace, Archie reluctantly put some coins into the slot, made a selection and gave Richard what he wanted. They went outside where, although it was early, the New Mexico sun was already unbearably hot.

'Phew, I'm burning here. Let's sit over there in the shade,' said Archie, pointing across the driveway.

Opposite the motel entrance was a small garden bordered by a low stone wall, with several tall soaptree yuccas overlooking a wooden bench where they could sit and wait for Marjorie.

'I wish this place had a decent restaurant,' said Archie.

Having decided against the dubious offerings provided by the vending machines, he was beginning to feel his stomach rumbling with hunger.

'I don't care – these are great,' said Richard, sucking sticky crumbs off his fingers into an already stuffed mouth.

Watching Richard demolish his so-called breakfast, Archie shook his head in despair at his young brother's eating habits. To avoid watching him eat, he cast his gaze around the pink, native Indian-style building that formed the bulk of the Highway Pueblo Motel. Uncle John, with whom they had always spent some part of their holidays for as long as he could remember, had arranged that they stay here for the first night until a driver came to collect them after breakfast.

As he enjoyed the early morning sun, Archie thought how different this place was from Ireland. Grimshaws was set in the beautiful lakelands of Fermanagh, and the outdoor sports had more than made up for the unpredictable rainy weather. For a time, while their parents explored the jungles of the Yucatan, they had attended one of the European International Schools in Mexico, but after their disappearance, Uncle John had sent them back to Grimshaws.

He had never thought of his parents as famous archaeologists until they had gone missing, and when reporters started arriving at the International School trying to interview them, he knew mum and dad must be something special. Uncle John had explained how excited their parents had been when traces of a lost pyramid in the Yucatan had been discovered, but in a world obsessed by wars and disasters the press and media hadn't really shown much interest in a lost pyramid – not until after Malcolm and Lucy Kinross had mysteriously disappeared. Three months later, when there was still no word or sign of what had happened to them and with reporters still pestering them at the school, Uncle John had decided it would be best to send the two boys back to Ireland to complete their education at Grimshaws, before going on to university. They never talked about it, but Archie was fairly certain that his uncle thought his parents were dead.

Richard tugged at Archie's T-shirt and asked, 'Can I have another Coke? I'm really thirsty.'

'Take it easy with that stuff. You're better off with water,' said Archie, trying to ignore him.

It was very hot, and Marjorie had warned them to dress properly and drink plenty of fluids, but Archie was sure she hadn't meant copious amounts of Coke.

She arrived shortly afterwards carrying a backpack. Handing over a bottle of sunscreen lotion, she gave them an appraising look.

'Morning, boys, it's going to be a scorcher, so make sure you use plenty of this – I've more in my backpack when you need it.' She nodded approvingly, as she looked them over. 'You should be OK in those outfits.'

Archie and Richard were both wearing khaki shorts and yellow T-shirts printed with GRIMSHAWS across the chest, and she had managed to pick up bush hats to protect them from the sun. Especially, she warned them, later in the day when they crossed the desert landscape of White Sands on their way to see Uncle John.

Reaching for the sunscreen, Archie stared at Miss Peoples as if he had never seen her before. Her crinkly red hair, instead of being tied up in a bun at the back of her head, was now loose around her shoulders and, like the boys, she wore sunglasses and a bush hat. A short-sleeve, open-neck, white cotton shirt and a blue, split denim skirt exposed her lightly tanned skin. Gone was the image of long black robes, dark stockings and flat brogue shoes.

'Good morning, Miss... er... Marjorie... You look... er... different...' said Archie, feeling strangely flustered.

'Well, it was good to get out of those travelling clothes, Archie, and I don't think my school gown would have been appropriate here, do you?' said Marjorie, grinning at the look on his face.

'Er... no... I suppose not.'

Sitting on the wall, Richard wiped his mouth clear of crumbs.

'Will we get to see the Space Shuttle, Marjorie?' he asked.

'All in good time, Richard, Professor Strawbridge said he would make arrangements to visit the shuttle sometime during our visit.'

At that moment, a gleaming red pickup truck entered the motel driveway and stopped at the entrance to reception.

'Hey, take a look at that!' said Richard, jumping to his feet.

That was a '99 Dodge Ram Sport Pickup, and it was huge. It was so high off the ground, with no running board, Archie reckoned you would need to take a running leap to get into it.

That is one terrific machine, thought Archie, leaving the bench to take a closer look. The driver's side cab door, printed with EFTF in black letters inside a gold circle of small stars, opened and the driver waved to them.

'Are you folks the Kinross people?' he asked.

The voice sounded to Richard like a cowboy's drawl. He joined Archie at the open door of the cab and looked up to see a man wearing a white Stetson, old worn denims and a blue checked shirt, looking down at them.

Richard was so surprised, he blurted out: 'Are you a *real* cowboy?'

The man, his face deeply tanned and with a mouth framed by a drooping brown moustache, laughed out loud.

'Only when I'm on a horse, son.' Tapping his large leather driving seat, he said, 'This is a sight more comfortable than a saddle, I can tell you.'

'Hi,' said Marjorie. She stood by the boys and looked into the cab. 'Are you Mr Winters from the Facility?'

'That's right, ma'am, just call me Chuck. The professor sent me to collect you first thing – before it gets too hot. Come on round and climb aboard.'

The boys didn't need a second invitation. Chuck opened the passenger door and they rushed around to climb in, but the cab was so high off the ground they couldn't make it the first time and Archie fell back onto Richard. Archie tried again and managed to get hold of the front passenger seat. He was about to haul himself up when he felt Richard thump him on the back.

'Stop hitting me!' yelled Archie.

'I want up front – you always go up front!' shouted Richard, making a grab for the back of Archie's T-shirt.

'No I don't–'

'Hey, take it easy, pardners.' Chuck decided he'd better interrupt them before they started swinging punches at each other. 'I tell you what – why don't you take turns up front?'

Archie caught Marjorie's eye as she nodded in agreement.

'OK, OK, I'll go in the back,' he muttered, feeling annoyed at having to give in to one of Richard's tantrums.

Marjorie climbed in beside him, smiled and mouthed a silent, 'Well done'.

'Chuck, what about our things?' she asked.

'No problem, ma'am, I'll call later to collect anything you need. In the meantime, I have to pick up some equipment for the professor, and that'll take up most of the truck space back there.'

Chapter Four

White Sands

Nearly an hour later they were heading east on Highway 70 towards the White Sand Monument. Travelling through hundreds of square miles of dazzling white landscape and nothingness gave little clue to their eventual destination.

'What's that?' asked Richard, pointing to something that scurried across the road.

'A bleached earless lizard,' said Chuck. 'It's one of the few things that can live out here in the desert. Except for some grass and yucca out on the edge of the dunes, there's not much else.'

Marjorie began to wonder why anybody would want to come and work in such a desolate place. As if in answer to her thoughts, Chuck explained to the boys that test missiles were fired here and that twice a week the road was closed to all traffic.

'NASA has a lot of test programmes around here, and the Space Harbor is the main training centre for the space shuttle pilots, as well as a landing site.'

'That's what I want to be – a shuttle pilot!' declared Richard.

'Well, the professor is a pretty important man around here; maybe he can fix it for you,' said Chuck, smiling.

'Chuck, why does Uncle John need all that equipment?'

Archie had been wondering exactly what it was that his uncle did out in the middle of the desert. It was something Uncle John had never discussed on his visits to the boys and their parents, as if it were a secret project he couldn't talk about.

They had stopped at a warehouse outside Las Cruces to collect four, large wooden crates marked TEST EQUIPMENT, now stacked in the back of the pickup, and Chuck had taken his time making sure the crates were well secured. He stroked his moustache with his thumb and forefinger before answering.

'It's a good question, Archie, but I can't rightly tell you the answer to that. All I can tell you is that he's been having a lot of strange problems with that machine of his lately.'

'*Machine*?' said Archie, his curiosity piqued.

'*Strange*?' said Marjorie, equally as curious.

'Yes, ma'am, his new machine has been causing him a lot of headaches these past few weeks. It seems there's some interference that keeps creeping in, but the test equipment back there should sort it out.'

'What kind of machine is it?' asked Archie.

'Oh, you'll have to ask the professor that when we get there.'

Archie had the feeling Chuck didn't want to elaborate, and for a while nothing more was said, all of them absorbed in their own thoughts as they gazed at the empty white desert from the air-conditioned comfort of the pickup.

*

Chuck turned the Ram Sport off the highway onto a narrow road with fine white sand blowing like talcum powder over a hard-packed gypsum surface.

A large white sign bearing the same gold logo enclosing the letters EFTF stated:

ENERGY FIELD TEST FACILITY
ENTRY PROHIBITED
U.S. GOVERNMENT PROPERTY

Ignoring the sign, Chuck drove on for another mile when, suddenly, they all heard a dull, whirring whumph-whumph sound somewhere overhead.

'Hey, look over there!' said Richard, excitedly.

Swooping to a point about fifty yards to their right, a sleek black helicopter, its main five-blade rotor fanning effortlessly, hovered like a huge hawk ready to descend on its prey. With its rear rotor fully encased in the tail and showing no undercarriage, the angular fuselage had the futuristic look of a stealth aircraft. The helicopter, displaying a US army emblem, held its position near the pickup, low-flying over the sands, just as a series of *bleeps* sounded in the console next to Chuck.

'What's happening?' asked Archie.

'It's a Comanche attack helicopter, one of the latest types they use here,' said Chuck. 'Nothing for us to worry about.' He reached into the console between the front seats for a microphone attached to a two-way transmitter. 'Hi, Spot Two, Chuck here,' he said, after flicking on the switch.

'OK, Chuck, just checking in.' The Comanche pilot came in low and close and stared at them for a few seconds. 'Your package all clear?'

'Yep, the package is Purple Three and all clear,' answered Chuck.

'OK, you are clear to go.'

'What's a Purple Three?' asked Richard, mesmerised by the sight of the helicopter flying so near to the pickup.

'That's the security code for this trip – you three and the cases back there,' said Chuck, switching off and replacing the microphone in the console.

'Security code?'

'That's right. If we hadn't used the right code and cleared, they would've forced us to stop.'

'Would they have shot us?' Richard's eyebrows were raised, his imagination fired up by the prospect of the Comanche helicopter shooting them to smithereens.

'Would–'

Richard's next question was suddenly drowned by the noise of the Comanche as it roared directly overhead. It soon left them behind as it sped towards a fence that could be seen some distance ahead on the horizon.

A short time later, they reached a high metal-mesh fence that seemed to stretch forever in both directions across the white sands. An imposing metal gate held by two stone pillars displayed a yellow and black sign that warned:

AFTER ENTERING THE COMPOUND
SWITCH OFF THE ENGINE AND
LEAVE THE VEHICLE

The gate swung open to allow the pickup to enter a secure enclosed area. At the far end they could see another gate that would allow them to exit the compound. They stopped next to a wooden one-storey building where several soldiers stood outside on a sheltered veranda. Some, armed with pistols, stared at them through reflective sunglasses, another, holding a clipboard, approached the pickup.

'Hi, Chuck, good to see you – been demoted to driver again?' asked the grinning soldier, taking some documents that Chuck handed him.

'You know me, Brady, whatever the professor says, I do!' replied Chuck, smiling and adjusting his Stetson as he leaned out of the window.

Sergeant Brady allowed them to stay in the pickup with the engine and air-conditioning running while he checked the documents.

'Don't we have to get out?' asked Richard, feeling a little nervous as two of the soldiers started inspecting the crates and underneath the pickup.

'Special treatment for guests of the professor,' said Chuck, winking at Marjorie, who by now was getting very restless stuck in the back of the cab.

'This place seems to be run like a prison, is all this really necessary?'

'Well, ma'am, I suppose it does seem a bit like that, but the work that the professor is engaged on is highly classified, and this particular facility is under *extra* strict security. So, I'm afraid, you will see a lot of this sort of thing around here.'

After ten minutes, Sergeant Brady handed the documents back to Chuck and waved him on.

'You're cleared. See you later.'

'Thank goodness for that!' exclaimed Marjorie, shifting impatiently in her seat.

'Don't worry, folks, we're nearly there. You'll soon be able to get a cool drink and a bite to eat in the canteen,' said Chuck, as he took the pickup through the second security gate.

Accelerating the Ram Sport into top gear he covered the last couple of miles in a few minutes. When he finally slowed down, Archie and Richard were amazed to see the size of the building that loomed up in front of them. It was a gigantic, white and blue, hangar-like structure that would easily have towered over St Paul's in London.

'Hey, look at that – it's *huge*!' cried Richard.

He was almost out of his seat, straining to get a better view. As usual, his curiosity was getting the better of him, but he couldn't help wondering what they might see inside.

'We're here, folks – and there's the professor,' said Chuck.

He drove them over to an imposing entrance of four, very tall, tinted glass doors that opened automatically onto wide marble steps as a busy stream of people walked in and out of the building. Standing at the top of the steps was a well-built man with stooped shoulders and rugged features, a misshapen nose giving testimony to his younger days as an Irish rugby international. Running his hand through thick sandy hair turning grey, he was frowning and seemed deep in thought.

'Uncle John! Uncle John!' the boys echoed, jumping down from the pickup and then running up the steps to meet him, leaving Marjorie and Chuck to follow.

Startled, he glanced down, allowing his glasses to slip to the end of his nose. He grinned as he saw the two excited young boys about to charge into him.

'Archie! Richard! You're here at last!'

Reaching out with two powerful hands he grabbed them and held them tightly against his deep broad chest.

'It looks as if you've got your hands full, Professor,' said Chuck, turning towards Marjorie. 'By the way, this is Miss Peoples.'

'Delighted to meet you, Miss Peoples. I'm deeply indebted to you for looking after the boys.'

'Not at all, Professor Strawbridge, considering all the delays we had, they have been marvellous.'

'Uncle John – I can't breathe...'

Richard couldn't believe how strong his uncle's arm was – it felt like a vice. They all laughed as the professor let the boys go.

'I'm sorry, Richard – I'm just so glad to see you both here.'

The boys removed their bush hats and sunglasses, as the professor stood back to look at them. He ruffled their hair, seemingly reluctant to stop holding them.

Archie had the feeling that Uncle John was thinking about their parents. That he missed them as much as he and Richard did. It was nearly eighteen months since they had all spent a wonderful Christmas holiday together in Mexico, little realising what was ahead of them.

'Right, let's get out of this heat and go over to the canteen,' said Uncle John. 'I'm sure we could all do with a cold drink.'

'I have to unload the crates, Professor, so if you'll excuse me, I'll see you folks later.' Nodding towards Marjorie and the boys, Chuck climbed back into the pickup and drove towards a loading bay at the end of the building.

Following their uncle, Archie and Richard, with Marjorie trailing behind them studying the surroundings, the group made their way along a paved path to the canteen. It was a modern, tinted glass and concrete structure situated in an extensive landscaped garden of large white boulders. Yucca plants in all sorts of stunning shapes and sizes bordered the path on both sides, with Native Indian wooden carvings set against dune grasses, placed throughout the garden, creating an unusual soothing effect.

'This is beautiful, Professor. I never expected to see anything quite like this in the middle of the desert.'

Marjorie had stopped to take a closer look at a small ornamental pond that had been formed in the middle of the garden.

'Yes, it is unusual, but as many of us spend most of our time here at the Facility, it was felt that it would be nice to have somewhere restful to relax. I'm glad you like it.'

Inside the cool, airy and spacious canteen they made themselves comfortable at a table with a panoramic view of the garden and the desert sands. They ordered a light lunch of grilled spicy chicken and salad, served with iced fruit drinks, followed by large banana splits. The meal was so delicious Marjorie felt able to relax for the first time since arriving in America, without having to worry about what Archie and Richard might be up to. She waited until the boys and the professor had finished their drinks before posing the question that had been niggling at her.

'I hope you don't mind me asking, Professor Strawbridge, but is all this security because of what *you* do here?'

Archie saw the surprise in his uncle's face at Marjorie's question, but he too had wondered about what his uncle actually did here. After the threatening appearance of the stealth helicopter and then the armed soldiers, he was beginning to think that Uncle John was working on some kind of secret weapon. Maybe that's what's inside the huge building, he thought.

The professor looked curiously at the young woman who had asked such a direct question. The filtered sunlight streaming through the tinted glass walls made the golden tones in her hair shine like burnished brass. She was certainly very attractive, and he could see that the boys were fond of her, but as a lifelong and confirmed bachelor, he had always been a little nervous in the company of women, young or old. He guessed, rightly, that this young woman wouldn't be fobbed off with his usual response of pretending not to hear the question.

'Well, Miss … May I call you Marjorie? Good. Well, to answer your question … If you look around, you will see there are dozens of scientists, technicians and engineers here apart from myself. There are also many more at the Facility, all of whom are working on a project of immense national importance – *that* is why we have so much strict security.'

Marjorie suspected he was being modest about his own role in whatever the project was, but she decided not to pursue it. After all, if it was top secret, he was hardly going to tell her very much about it – was he?

'I can see that ... it's just that, it's all so ... overwhelming,' she said.

'Yes, I agree that it can seem that way at first, but tomorrow morning I'll take you on what Chuck calls the "Ten Dollar Tour".'

'What's that, Uncle John?' asked Archie, enjoying another iced drink.

'That's Chuck's description of the restricted tour of the Facility that we give to VIP parties that visit us from time to time.'

'Is Chuck a cowboy?' asked Richard. He was still curious, wondering what a cowboy would be doing in a place like the Facility.

'Not really, Richard,' said Uncle John. 'Believe it or not, he's one of the most important people around here. He's the head of a government security team based at the Facility, and he's one of my closest colleagues – I couldn't do without him.' He stood up, pushing his chair away, obviously not wanting to say much more. 'Now, if everyone's had enough, I'd better get you settled in. I've arranged for you to stay next to my place in the civilian quarters not far from here. Chuck will bring your things round later.'

The professor's house was in a beautifully landscaped development, and located next door was a complex of several guest apartments. Further along, they could see a sign over the entrance to a health club and swimming pool. Nearby was a bowling alley next to a cinema advertising an old Arnold Schwarzenegger movie.

'I'm sure you'll like your accommodation. We have visitors from all over the world who come here to see what we're up to, so we try to make them as comfortable as possible while they're here.' The professor hesitated, looking a little guilty as he explained to them: 'I'm sorry to leave you to your own devices, but we are scheduled for a full-scale test of some new equipment tomorrow, and I need to be on hand this evening to make sure everything runs smoothly.'

The professor told them the preparations would go on all night and as director of operations he had to be there. However, he would meet them in the morning for breakfast and afterwards he would take them on the tour.

Chapter Five

The DONUT

Archie patted his stomach as if he was ready to burst. 'I'm stuffed! Do they always have such big breakfasts here?'

'You shouldn't have eaten so much,' said Richard, his mouth still full of grilled steak and sausage. 'Mum always said you didn't know when to stop.'

'What! That's not true! Anyway, that's a bit rich coming from you–'

'OK, OK, boys, take it easy.' Marjorie was getting used to nipping these arguments in the bud, and she wasn't about to let one start now. 'They tend to serve generous portions in America, but it doesn't mean you have to eat everything that's put in front of you.'

It was early morning and they had just left the canteen after helping themselves to an enormous breakfast. They were walking slowly towards the Facility with the professor, and he was about to tell Marjorie something of his work. He waited until Archie and Richard quietened down before explaining the importance of what he was doing.

'You see, *most* of what we do here is highly classified, but I can tell you a little of what we are trying to achieve. Broadly speaking, we're looking for an unlimited source of energy to meet the world's present and future requirements. As you may know, the demand for energy is increasing daily and at an accelerating rate as more countries such as China and India expand their economies. We are, in fact, using up all known oil and other valuable energy sources more rapidly than has been appreciated until now. Now the danger is that we are approaching a point when these resources will no longer exist, and nuclear energy is still proving to be unacceptable in many parts of the world.' He said nothing for a moment to let them think about what he had just said. As they approached the Facility he pointed towards the sun. 'If only we could harness a fraction of its energy, we would have a limitless source of power.'

Marjorie looked sceptical. She glanced towards the sun, shielding her eyes with her hand.

'I've read about that sort of thing before, Professor, but is it *really* possible?'

'I believe it is. For over twenty-five years I have devoted my life to this Facility and accomplishing just that.' The professor walked beside her, shading his eyes to look at the sun, then continued: 'We may well be on the threshold of a major discovery – hence the security you asked about.'

They arrived at the entrance to the Facility where he ushered them into a large reception area. Inside, one of several security guards welcomed them from a booth containing an array of monitors that surveyed various parts of the building.

'Good morning, Professor,' said the guard. 'I have your guests' tags ready.'

The professor nodded and took the ID tags he had arranged the day before, and passed them over to Marjorie and the boys.

'Just clip these on and follow me.'

He led them though a turnstile and walked to a metal door at the end of the room. He keyed in some numbers and placed the palm of his hand on an illuminated panel next to the door. The door slid silently to one side to reveal a long narrow corridor.

From somewhere above them a high-pitched metallic voice announced: *'Please enter.'*

Richard experienced a strange fluttery feeling in his stomach as he stepped, hesitatingly, into the corridor.

He didn't know what it was, but something about the Facility made him feel strangely apprehensive. He was about to say something, when Archie shoved him forwards.

'Get a move on, Richard.'

'OK, OK, I'm moving, stop pushing!'

'Quiet, boys!' scolded Marjorie, turning to stare at them.

'Sorry, Marjorie,' said Archie, nudging Richard again.

They waited before being allowed to proceed through another metal door at the end of the corridor. Uncle John explained that each of them were being scanned by a hidden security identification process before the metallic voice would confirm their entry to the next room. After a few seconds, their IDs were confirmed and they walked through to a scene that made Archie and Richard stop and gasp in amazement. Nothing could have prepared them for the size of the room in which they now stood, even the size of the exterior belied what they saw before them.

The corridor had opened onto a wide terrace with a guardrail overlooking a vast cathedral-like interior with walls that plunged into the bowels of the earth. Above them the walls soared to a vaulted ceiling covering a complex so big that the place reminded Archie of an ant colony, with countless men and women going about their various tasks taking the place of worker ants. A large number of them, dressed in yellow coloured overalls, were sitting in front of rows of computer screens on a terrace several levels below them. Technicians in blue overalls, carrying odd-looking pieces of equipment, swarmed along the inner metal catwalks which circled a gigantic tyre-shaped cylinder as it rose up out of the depths of the room.

'Is that the *machine*?' Archie was spellbound as he watched the people below him go about their duties. 'I've never seen anything like this before.'

'It's gi ... normous!' said Richard. He was whispering, as if the machine was a great sleeping beast that might come awake at any moment.

The terrace gave the group a commanding view of the heart of the Facility and a network of catwalks criss-crossing the centre of the cylinder, where more technicians could be seen talking to a man wearing a red overall.

'What in heaven's name is it?' asked Marjorie.

'The technicians call it the DONUT – aptly named I think,' replied the professor, smiling, 'but what you see is only a fraction of the Facility. The rest is several levels below ground – this is just the tip of the iceberg.'

'Professor Strawbridge!'

The man wearing the red overall had called out as he dashed along the catwalk to join them.

'What is it, Ed?' asked the professor.

'It would look as if our problem has returned, Professor. One of the technicians has reported seeing some blue smoke on one of the lower levels.'

'Not again! What about the new test equipment – can't it help us trace the source?'

'Not so far,' said Ed. He was wearing an ID tag that described him as a Facility Engineer, and he looked upset at having to report a fault. 'Besides the smoke, everything appears to be perfectly normal.'

'This is frustrating, but unless I have a confirmed source, I will *not* abort the test.' The professor turned to Marjorie and the boys to explain. 'During the past few months every time we've attempted a full-scale test there have been reports of blue smoke near the DONUT, but when we investigate, there's never any sign of smoke or fire. It is totally mystifying.' He shook his head and turned back to his engineer. 'Ed, keep an eye on the monitors and call me immediately if anyone spots *anything* unusual. I'll take our guests across the catwalk to the visitors' centre for refreshments then I'll head down to the lower levels. If –'

Before he could finish, the professor heard someone shouting. He turned round to see Marjorie supporting Richard. He was slumped against the guardrail and had gone deathly pale as if he were about to faint.

'Is he all right?' he asked Marjorie.

'Yes, I think so.'

Richard straightened up. He pushed Marjorie away, looking a little embarrassed at the concerned faces around him. He mumbled: 'I'm OK.'

'Let's get him over to the visitors' centre. I think a cold drink might help,' suggested the professor.

They left Ed on the terrace and proceeded across the catwalk, with Archie and Marjorie both keeping an eye on Richard as they did so. He seemed to have recovered from whatever it was that had troubled him, when suddenly he stopped again to stare down into the centre of the DONUT.

'What is it now, Richard – are you feeling sick?' Archie peered down over the guardrail to see what it was that had caught his brother's attention. 'This is like being on the edge of a volcano. I hope it doesn't erupt,' he said jokingly.

'Maybe it's going to … *look*!'

Richard pointed below the catwalk to a small cloud of blue, swirling, smoke-like mist rising up from the centre of the cylinder. The professor and Marjorie rushed to the guardrail to have a look.

'What is it, Professor?'

'I don't know, Marjorie, but it must be the problem I told you about. I've never seen anything like it before.'

He stared down at the blue mist that was growing larger and rising rapidly every second. Its centre had started to glow with a bright yellow light that made them turn their eyes away.

'Whatever it is, I think we'd better get off the catwalk!'

They were too late. A deafening explosion and a blinding flash of light engulfed them. Archie suddenly found himself twisting and turning in mid-air inside a brightly lit tunnel, with the others tumbling around him. He saw them disappearing, one by one, into the mist, before he closed his eyes against the brightness of the light.

When he opened them again he was on his hands and knees and his head ached, but that started to ease as he rose, a little unsteadily, to his feet.

As Archie looked around, he was astonished to find that he had ended up in the middle of a forest glade, alone. The Facility and the others had, somehow, disappeared. And he was slowly becoming aware that someone, somewhere beyond the trees, was screaming, and that it sounded very much like Richard.

*

At the Facility, Chuck Winters rushed into the control room of the DONUT to find that nearly everyone was running around in a state of panic.

'Ed, what the hell is going on?'

'I don't know, Chuck. One minute the professor and the girl with the kids were up on the catwalk – the next, they were gone!'

'What do you mean? Gone?'

''I can't explain. The blue smoke appeared again, and then there was an almighty explosion – but the strange thing is, there's no sign of any damage.'

Chuck looked at Ed as if he might be losing his mind. The engineer was clearly agitated as he pointed towards the catwalk.

'Chuck, I'm telling you ... the professor and the others have completely disappeared!'

Chapter Six

Orbiter 3

Nearly two centuries later, two more brothers, in quite a different time and place, were also in trouble. As much as they disliked thinking about it, they had to face the unpleasant fact that they would receive a *very* long term of imprisonment once they reached Earth.

They had recently been deported from Mars, where they had worked and planned to overthrow the Mars Mining Consortium, but like many criminal schemes, their plans had been flawed, and they had unsuspectingly walked into a trap.

It was the year 2182 and the Cosimos had just disembarked from the interplanetary spaceship, *Destiny,* shortly after it docked with the *Orbiter 3* space station. Under guard, they were escorted to one of the station's holding rooms and locked in while final preparations were made for their journey to Earth.

A few days earlier, one of the brothers had been dismissed by a hastily convened group of senior officers, their decision still ringing in his ears.

'Major Anton Cosimo, you have been found guilty by your fellow officers of betraying your position with the Military Space Command and the Mars Mining Consortium.

It is, therefore, the decision of this Tribunal that you are to be returned to Earth forthwith for sentencing by a military court. Your brother and co-conspirator, Sandan Cosimo, who took advantage of his position with the Mars Mining Consortium and aided you in your wicked plan to divert their funds to your own pocket, for a purpose that is not yet clear, will also be returned to Earth to be tried by a civilian court.'

As he remembered the words of the tribunal, Anton felt his brother pull on his sleeve.

'Blast you! See where all your scheming and planning has landed us!'

'Stop your whining, Sandan, you were happy enough to take your share when things were going well.'

'Yes, like you, but now look at us – we could end up in a desert prison for the next twenty years!'

Sandan groaned, and held his head in his hands as he visualised confinement in one of the notoriously congested prisons in the middle of the Sahara.

Anton Cosimo glared angrily at his brother. It was always the same with the fool; when his plans were running smoothly, Sandan would be first in line to take whatever profits he could, but as soon as trouble appeared he would carp incessantly that they would be caught. Now they were, and it was Sandan's fault.

'You damned idiot! Did you not realise that the Consortium was bound to have another auditor making checks on your work?' hissed Anton.

'It wasn't my fault. I meant to update the records, but I was delayed. How was I to know they carried out secret audits on my accounts?'

'You should have known! Now my plans are in ruins because of your incompetence!' roared Anton. He stood in front of his brother with a fist raised, as if ready to strike, but suddenly he turned away, his mind churning with frustration.

Sandan kept quiet. He knew better than to argue with Anton when he became angry. Although they had been through a lot together, and in some ways they were very close, Anton still frightened him. Physically, they were quite different. Anton was tall and might be described as handsome, but his pale hawkish features, thin nose and narrow-set eyes, especially when he smiled, gave him the appearance of a benevolent executioner just before the blade struck. He was a cruel and dangerous man whose greatest pleasure was to destroy those who might oppose him. By contrast, Sandan, his half-brother, was short and brutish, his face dominated by a flat wide nose and large yellowing teeth, leaving him little in common with Anton except the coal-black hair they had inherited from their Romany mother.

She had been killed during the New European Wars and, as they had never known either of their fathers, they had been left at an early age to fend for themselves. During those terrible long years, it was Anton who had led them throughout Europe, scheming and planning, always desperately seeking a way to improve their poverty-stricken lives. He stole anything and everything they needed to stay alive, showing little or no mercy to anyone who got in his way. Eventually, his notoriety for such acts came to the notice of one of the many rebel groups spread throughout the territories that were attacking and stealing weapons from the government supply depots.

One of the rebel groups appreciated Anton's ruthlessness and skill in obtaining supplies, and soon he was offered an alliance that he readily accepted, but he had ideas beyond the theft of weapons and food. He knew the rebels would be hunted and contained in their strongholds for many years to come, and he had no intention of being caught with them. It wasn't long before he joined the other side, betraying the alliance that would lead to the massacre of the rebels by government forces.

Anton's treachery was rewarded by a safe passage out of the War Zone and a junior military commission, the senior commanders being of the very sensible opinion that it would be better having such a heartless individual working for them than against them. In due course, like many others before them, they soon regretted their action, for Anton always made it his business to learn the weaknesses of such men, enabling him to take advantage of them. It surprised some, but not Sandan, when Anton quickly achieved the rank of captain and transferred to the Military Space Command.

Sandan, on the other hand, had not been acceptable for military service, but during the early years at government headquarters on Earth he had been allowed to live near Anton while obtaining whatever work he could. It was only later when he was transferred to carry out clerical duties for the Mars Mining Consortium that he unexpectedly discovered he had a way with computers and figures. In time, he progressed, and eventually gained a permanent position with the Consortium, where he dealt with the accounts of the mining camps now established across the red planet.

Five years after Sandan arrived on Mars, his brother was posted to a minor security command responsible for several of the mining camps. It had long been suspected, by some, that Captain Anton Cosimo might be part of an armaments supply ring selling weapons to the rebels in the New Europe Territories, but there had never been any proof of such dealings. However, suspicion was enough, and promotion to major with a posting to one of the less desirable commands away from Earth was deemed sufficient to neutralise his activities. Only later, when it was much too late, was it realised that this move had been to Anton's advantage.

In its desperation for new sources of minerals and energy, Earth's ruling government had granted open licences to any large corporation that possessed the enormous resources needed to pioneer and explore the

Solar System. Unfortunately, no one had foreseen that this unrestricted policy would lead to widespread chaos and squabbling amongst the mining groups over their legal rights. And with so many arguments and disputes taking place, it had been the Government's decision to leave it to the local security forces to settle them. This, of course, suited Anton very well. With command of his own security force he was now in the perfect position to put his own treacherous plans into action.

Knowing that Sandan was now the senior records officer for the Consortium, with responsibility for supplies and accounts, Anton had soon persuaded him – with the point of a stiletto tickling his throat – to start diverting money and documents into his hands. His vision of an interplanetary mining syndicate that would dictate supplies and terms to Earth's fuel-starved industries still recovering from the European wars, would soon be a reality – or so he had thought.

'But for your stupidity, the mining camps – and the Consortium – would have fallen into my hands. Think of the power that would have given me!' growled Anton.

As he vented his fury on Sandan, Anton thought of the endless scheming and effort that had gone into his plans, now wasted because of his brother's carelessness. All he had needed was access to the Consortium's funds to pay his rebel contacts on Earth to persuade them to join him in taking over the mining camps. Although, years ago, he had betrayed his alliance with one rebel group, he knew well enough that there were thousands more who would rally to his side, provided he could promise them the riches they craved, for that was all they really wanted. Now, instead of being at the head of a mighty and united rebel army, he found himself trapped like a rat in a metal cage aboard the space station.

*

Commander Croft was proud of *Orbiter 3*. It was a rare materials research unit, and in the thirty or so years it had been in orbit above the Earth, it had received countless spaceships depositing their cargoes of precious mineral samples for commercial evaluation. But never in all that time had he been obliged to put up with rogues such as the two now held in one of the holding rooms.

Normally, prisoners and undesirables were rocketed straight to Earth and dealt with there. However, on this occasion some damned fool on Mars had sent them under guard on a spaceship that wasn't even going to Earth! Now *he* would have to deal with them. Well, he would make sure they didn't stay on *Orbiter 3* a minute longer than necessary.

Arriving at one of the holding rooms that usually only held valuable ore samples for further analysis, the commander nodded to one of the guards to open the sealed door. With the guard in tow, he entered the room and saw the prisoners sitting on metal sample containers, and noted that neither of them bothered to stand or acknowledge his rank. He ignored the insult and got straight to the point.

'Gentlemen, I am Commander Croft, and it is my rather unexpected duty to look after you until I can arrange –'

'You needn't babble on about your duty, Commander Croft,' interrupted Anton, smirking at the commander's obvious reluctance to speak to him. Standing up to face Croft, he said 'I am well aware of your position, as well as my own. So, if you would make the necessary arrangements as soon as possible to get us off this antiquated station, I would be very grateful.'

'*Antiquated*! You ... you would be *grateful*!' spluttered Croft. He was about to order the Cosimos to pay more respect to his rank, but Anton had turned his back on him, while Sandan, still sitting, held his head in his hands. He said, instead, 'Well, if you're in such a hurry, we'll just have to see what we can do for you.'

Returning to his quarters, he used the intercom to summon one of his officers.

'Lieutenant Karkov, how soon can we prepare a Robopod for launch?'

'As soon as we complete maintenance. We will be ready within the hour, Commander, but I wouldn't advise a launch just yet,' said Karkov.

'And why not?'

'Sir, as you know, we have received a report about unusual sunspot activity and it may well affect spacecraft on re-entry. Extreme weather conditions on Earth are predicted over the next forty-eight hours.'

'Yes, I know all about the sunspots, Karkov. Increase the radiation shields and prepare a Robopod for immediate launch.'

'Sir, I must repeat, it will be –'

'Lieutenant, that's an order!'

After Karkov left, the commander smiled to himself. He was well aware of the potential hazards facing spacecraft returning to Earth during solar flares, nevertheless, he strongly disapproved of having the Cosimos aboard his space station. The report he had read earlier about their activities on Mars had convinced him they should have been sent to rot on Phobos instead. Well, let's see how they enjoy their trip back to Earth. Yes, a rough ride on their way to a long prison sentence, he thought, is exactly what they need.

*

53

The great outer wheel of *Orbiter 3* spun silently in space more than two hundred miles above the Earth. Its rim contained the docking bay for the Robopods and it was here that Lieutenant Karkov waited patiently for the prisoners to arrive from the holding room.

The Robopod, a small, six-person pilotless shuttle, was designed to ferry crew and small cargoes between the Earth Command base and the space station. It could also be used in emergency situations, so it hadn't taken him long to get one ready. Only two passengers this trip; unusual, but he wasn't going to question orders – not with the mood the commander was in.

As Karkov considered just how risky the flight might be during the solar flares, the prisoners suddenly appeared with the guards on the launch deck.

'About time,' he said. 'Our launch slot is nearly ready and we need to commence the checklist.'

'Sorry to keep you waiting, Lieutenant, but as you can see, we were required to change into something more suitable for the journey,' said Anton.

Karkov, tall, slim and smartly attired in his Space Command uniform, observed that the prisoners were now dressed in the standard black crew overalls, but without insignia or rank. The flight documents he held in his hand gave names, titles and other information, including the charges against them, but Major, if that was still his rank, Cosimo seemed indifferent to the seriousness of his position. If anything, he acted as if he was about to take command of the Robopod. Any doubts he had held for the Cosimos' safety were soon dispelled as the major continued to stare at him, making him feel distinctly uneasy. This is one dangerous customer, thought Karkov. The commander's right; the sooner these two are off *Orbiter 3* the better.

He turned around as the holocube on a metal pedestal next to him bleeped a warning that an image was about to be displayed.

'Lieutenant Karkov, is everything ready?' demanded Commander Croft, his head and shoulders appearing in the holocube.

'We are on schedule, sir, although the geomagnetic storms forecast for the area is still in place.'

'What storms?' cried Sandan, terrified at the thought of being in danger in the spacecraft.

'Shut up, Sandan!' snapped Anton. 'They're only trying to frighten us. If we ever cross paths again we will deal with them then.'

Croft's ghost-like image shimmered in the holocube as he spoke.

'I doubt very much that where you're going, you will be dealing with anybody, Cosimo, but your journey should be an interesting one. Lieutenant Karkov, proceed with the launch.'

Double automatic doors hissed open as the commander sent a signal to the launch deck, allowing the group, including the guards, to move into the docking bay. The doors closed behind them as they walked towards a rectangular pit where metal steps led down each side to the exposed interior of a Robopod. Two of the seats were raised to pit floor level to permit easy access to the cabin.

'Please go to either side and take a seat,' instructed Karkov. 'As soon as you are seated the rest of the procedure is automatic. The seats will retract, the hatches will seal and you will be on your way.'

'There is no one else?' asked Sandan, looking around him.

'Just you two,' said Karkov, grinning at Sandan's obvious nervousness. 'Commander Croft has awarded you the privilege of travelling on your own. However, he is assured you will be met on landing by the appropriate authority. I am sure you understand.'

'Oh, we do, Lieutenant, and we will not forget *your* part in this.'

Anton's voice was filled with venom, making Karkov shiver as if someone had just walked over his grave. With the guards behind him, he quickly left the docking bay. Using the holocube he informed flight control he had completed his checklist.

'Thank you, Lieutenant. Launch will take place in ten minutes,' confirmed the flight controller, his image fading from the holocube.

Not soon enough, thought Karkov.

*

In the Robopod, Sandan was in a near state of panic after the pit floor above them closed, effectively sealing them outside the space station.

'I don't like this – this thing is too small to survive a storm!'

'Calm yourself, Sandan. I suspect Commander Croft was in a hurry to get rid of us, storm or no storm, but Space Command has never lost a Robopod, and I don't expect this to be the first.'

'It's all right for *you*, you're trained for this sort of thing,' complained Sandan, gripping the edge of his seat. He felt a jolt as the Robopod came alive with lights flashing on the panel in front of him. '*What's happening?*'

'What did I just say? I told you to be calm! We have just separated from the space station.'

At that moment they experienced an abrupt surge, pushing them deep into their padded seats as the thrusters ignited, shooting them away from *Orbiter 3.*

Soon, they were hurtling towards the distant Earth, its bright blue surface broken by the outline of the continents under drifting clouds. As they travelled through the inky blackness of space, Anton worried about their landing and how they might make their escape. He had no plan yet, but he knew Sandan was right about one thing: they must avoid being sent to a Sahara prison from where escape was known to be impossible.

An hour later, they entered the upper atmosphere where the Robopod was buffeted by the forces of re-entry. The Cosimos, quiet now, watched through the narrow viewing panels as the colours of the Earth were rapidly replaced by the fiery orange-red of their blazing descent.

Anton glanced across at Sandan and saw that he was petrified by the re-entry. Good! Let the fool suffer for his incompetence – if it wasn't for him, we would not be here, he thought. Suddenly, the Robopod lurched to one side, then the other. *What was that? Has something hit us? Something must be happening outside the spacecraft*! He pushed his thoughts to one side and stared at the viewing panel in front of him. The flaming colours of re-entry had started to change to a strange, ghostly, glowing blue; something he had never witnessed before.

The Robopod was diving and turning like a corkscrew, twisting their bodies inside the restraining straps of their seat harness as they fought to stay in an upright position. They must be caught in the geomagnetic storm Karkov had warned Croft about, thought Anton. It was as if they had entered a whirlpool, whirling and plunging, deeper and deeper to the bottom. There was nothing Anton could do except curse his misfortune and the fool of a half-brother who had brought him here.

Fearful they would be destroyed, Anton continued to stare at the viewing panel, mesmerised by the strange blue light, changing slowly now to a brilliant yellow, so intensely bright he had to close his eyes.

After a time, which might have been several minutes or several hours as he had no way of telling, he gradually opened his eyes. His senses registered little, except for a slight numbness in his limbs. He could feel no movement from the spacecraft; everything was deathly still. *What's happened?* He wondered. *Have we crashed?*

He looked across and saw that Sandan was unconscious, but neither of them seemed to have come to any harm. On landing, the hatches had opened automatically, allowing him to climb slowly out of the Robopod onto the fuselage. He saw that they were perilously near the edge of a ravine in a place he did not recognise; but more importantly, there was no sign of the reception committee Karkov had warned them about.

Anton smiled. Perhaps fortune is beginning to favour me again, he thought.

Chapter Seven

The Exploding Park

'*Help! Help meee!*'

Archie could hear Richard's screams getting louder as he tore at the brambles and branches that crossed his path. The forest was damp and thick with rotting vegetation, making it impossible to make any quick progress through the trees that stood before him. He swore as he scratched himself again on a thorn bush before stumbling back into the clearing where he had landed after the explosion. Confused and desperate, he looked around to see if there was another way through.

Further down the clearing he spotted a break in the trees. He ran towards it. It was a narrow opening that might take him to where he thought he heard Richard's voice. He couldn't hear him anymore, but he kept on running, hoping everything was all right. Suddenly, he was out of the forest and facing a vast grassy plain. He stopped dead in his tracks when he saw something that shouldn't be there.

Dinosaurs! Two dinosaurs – and Richard was standing on the back of one of them!

Archie rubbed his eyes and looked again. The bright yellow light of the explosion had blinded him temporarily and he couldn't be sure if he was seeing properly, but there they were, standing before him near a huge black rock, as motionless as two great statues. He had read a lot about dinosaurs when he was younger and he recognised them as triceratops.

A short distance away from the black rock, he saw Uncle John near the dinosaur. He was shouting something at Richard, who was holding onto the big bony frill around the dinosaur's neck. Marjorie was crouching behind the rock, fearful of making a move in case the dinosaurs saw her. Wasting no more time, Archie sprinted across the grassy plain towards Uncle John.

Richard saw him coming and yelled at the top of his lungs.

'*Archieee! Get me down from here!*'

Marjorie, startled by his sudden appearance, stood up and started waving both arms frantically.

'Archie, don't go over there, it might charge!'

Archie ignored her and kept on running. He was almost breathless by the time he reached his uncle, grabbing his sleeve. 'We have to get him down – we can't leave him up there!' he yelled.

The professor gripped him by the shoulder, obviously relieved to see Archie, but this wasn't the time to ask questions about what had happened to him and where he had come from. That would come later.

'I know, Archie, but while we've been here that great ugly beast hasn't made a move. Neither of them have moved an inch. I've been trying to get Richard to slide down its back so I can catch him, but he's too frightened to let go.'

Richard was beginning to panic. He had just felt the dinosaur move for the first time since he had landed on it, and now, as he looked over to the other dinosaur, he saw it lumbering in his direction.

'Archie, it's coming over here!'

Richard was right. It was as if the huge beasts had been stunned and shocked, but now after standing motionless for so long they were on the move.

*

While Archie and Uncle John endeavoured to find a way to get Richard off the dinosaur, a lone figure was staggering around on an old deserted road like a drunken man trying to find his way home.

Aristo rubbed his eyes, adjusting to the change in light after travelling through the timecrack. He stood still for a moment to regain his balance and started stretching his limbs to relieve the stiffness. After his journey to Old Earth, it seemed as if every muscle in his body was aching. He looked around and saw that he was standing on the remains of the Old Brown Road, now mostly overgrown with weeds and wild rambling bushes. It was the ancient trading route that ran through the heart of the Exploding Park. A distant boom, like the sound of thunder, made him laugh out loud.

'*Yes*! *I made it!*'

He threw his hands up into the air and laughed again. He was back! He was actually back in the Exploding Park! Wait until Dr Shah and Benno Kozan discover that he had returned. They had been reluctant to let him go, knowing how dangerous it would be; nevertheless, he had qualified and pestered them until they had agreed to let him make the journey. Nobody had ever returned from a *planned* expedition through a timecrack. But he had done it!

A thunderclap sounded the opening of another timecrack. He wasn't startled or surprised; it happened all the time, it was how the park had got its name, from the New Arrivals landing through timecracks, throughout the centuries.

He wasn't sure which part of the park he was in. There were no signs or markers on the road, but it didn't really matter; there were Lancer patrols in the park that would pick up the signal from his tracker suit. He switched on the signal unit and started to walk slowly along the Old Brown Road.

Aristo hadn't walked very far when he heard sounds coming from the other side of the trees. Cries?

Screams? He couldn't tell, but he decided he'd better take a look. He left the road and made his way along a newly formed track leading into the forest. It looked as if something large had bulldozed a path through the trees leaving familiar deep impressions in the soft earth. He heard another scream, forcing him to move more quickly until he came out of the forest onto the grassy plain, presenting him with the unexpected spectacle of a group of people pointing and yelling at two dinosaurs.

They were probably New Arrivals and, unbelievably, one of them had ended up on the back of one of his two companions from Old Earth. *God!* It was a young boy! His friends were trying to get him down, but their shouts and screams were more likely to stampede the huge beasts.

Aristo felt he had better do something – but what?

The Fourth Lancers patrolled all sectors of the park, but something could happen to these people long before they got here. There was nothing else for it. He withdrew the paragun from the holster strapped to his thigh and set it to full phase. It was a non-lethal weapon only meant to be used in self-defence, but it could discharge a force that would disable any human or animal for thirty minutes – what it would do to a dinosaur he had no idea.

Making his way along the edge of the trees he found a position that would place the black rock between him and the dinosaurs. Crouching low, he ran through a patch of tall grass towards the rock just as the dinosaurs began to move.

Marjorie was the first to see him.

'Look, there's someone coming!' she shouted.

Archie and Uncle John turned round to see a strange slimly built figure approaching them, carrying some sort of pistol-like weapon in his hand. He was dressed in an unusual green overall that looked to Archie like a spacesuit.

Aristo called out as he ran towards them. 'Stay behind the rock; I will try to get the boy.' They were so surprised to see him that they neither moved nor said a word as he ran past them towards the dinosaurs.

He was less than twenty feet away when he fired the paragun at the first beast carrying Richard. Aristo had calculated that if he aimed at the large eyes the force would reach the brain and stun the dinosaur. Unfortunately, it had the opposite effect and only enraged it to make a charge at Aristo, forcing him to turn and run as fast as he could. Archie and the professor ran with him until they were able to take cover alongside Marjorie behind the rock. The dinosaur ran past them, its great body heaving and snorting, with Richard still on its back screaming for help.

'Get me off this thing!' he yelled.

Marjorie and Uncle John were horrified by what had happened and both started yelling at Aristo at the same time. 'What have you done? Who are you?'

'My name is Aristo ...' He was out of breath and he didn't know what to say to these people. 'I'm sorry ...'

Archie glared at him. He was about to run after Richard as the second dinosaur thundered by, when Aristo grabbed him by the shoulder and pointed.

'No. Stay here, look, the Lancers have arrived!' said Aristo.

To his amazement, Archie saw a group of flying machines coming in over the trees in their direction. They flew in low over the plain to approach the rock, circling in formation like animals in a hunting pack, before taking up position just above their heads. There were eight of them, each scarlet torpedo-like machine flown by a pilot wearing a red and black skull helmet with a tinted visor. To Archie they had the appearance of medieval knights from a bygone age.

The leading machine had lightning marks that zigzagged along its fuselage, distinguishing it from the others. Its transparent canopy slid back to reveal the pilot, who pushed the visor away from his face. He was a dark-skinned man with deep-brown eyes that twinkled when he saw Aristo.

'You made it!' he called out, grinning widely. 'We picked up your signal, but how did you manage –'

'Later, there's no time to explain now,' said Aristo.

'What's happened here?'

'Captain Hanki, a young boy is on one of the dinosaurs,' said Aristo, pointing in the direction of the dinosaurs now heading towards distant woodland. 'We have to get to him before he gets killed!'

Hesitating only for a second, Hanki, his eyes raised in disbelief, lowered his machine to ground level.

He said, 'Aristo, you'd better come with me.' Then into his helmet mouthpiece, he spoke to the other Lancers still in formation above him. 'Lieutenant Akee, Malok, look after these people, we're going after the boy.'

'I'm going too.' Archie stood in front of Aristo with his hands clenched tight. 'He's my brother – I *have* to go!'

Aristo realised the boy blamed him for stampeding the dinosaurs, and was afraid something else would go wrong.

He nodded to Hanki.

'Let him come, we might need him.'

'On your head be it, but we're wasting time,' declared Hanki. Speaking to another Lancer, he ordered, 'Han-Sin, you bring the boy.'

Lancer Han-Sin lowered the machine to the ground and gestured for Archie to take the rear seat. He climbed onto a step on the side of the bodywork and clambered in awkwardly to reach the seat. As soon as he settled in he was surprised to discover the pilot was a young woman.

'Quickly, put on the helmet – it's below your seat,' she said. 'Good. Now press the green secure button in front of you and we will be away.'

Archie pressed one of several buttons on a glowing display panel and was instantly secured to his seat by a thin flexible harness that slipped over his shoulders.

The helmet radio startled him when Han-Sin spoke.

'Are you secure?'

'Uh … yes …'

Suddenly, without further warning, they shot off, and in seconds had caught up with Captain Hanki's machine.

Soon they were no more than ten feet from the dinosaur carrying Richard. Archie could see that he was hanging on grimly to the great bony frill with both hands. Rigid with fear, he was attempting to stay upright as his feet jerked up and down on the thick leathery hide. He watched as Captain Hanki attempted to bring his machine alongside the beast's awesome horned head, then realised Aristo was calling him on the radio.

'Your brother's name – what is it?'

'Richard, his name is Richard.'

Both machines now had their canopies fully retracted, and Aristo was trying to reach Richard by stretching out of the cockpit until he could almost touch his shoulder.

'*Richard! Give me your hand!*' he shouted.

Archie could see that his young brother was terrified and wouldn't let go of the frill. Suddenly, the dinosaur lurched away from Hanki's machine, causing Aristo to fall back into his seat.

Han-Sin and Archie both knew they had to act quickly. The dinosaurs were heading straight for the forest and would crash through the trees, giving them no chance to follow – even if Richard managed to hold on.

Swiftly and smoothly, Han-Sin guided her machine as close to the side of the dinosaur as she dared. Pointing to a narrow step on the side of the fuselage she called to Archie.

'Press the secure button again to release your harness, then try and get him onto the step. I'll get as near as I can, then you can pull him into the cockpit. Hurry, we don't have much time.'

She flew so closely to the dinosaur that the machine was in danger of being hit by the beast's bony frill. Archie released his harness, enabling him to lean out of the cockpit and reach Richard.

'*Richard, let go and give me your hand!*' he yelled.

Richard was so surprised to hear Archie's voice he turned and reached out his hand. It was as if a terrible spell had just been broken, allowing him to release his grip on the dinosaur's frill. Archie stretched as far as he could to catch him under the arms, hauling him onto the step, and then with a great heave, hauled him into the cockpit.

'Well done!' cried Han-Sin, banking the machine sharply to starboard to avoid flying into the trees. 'Now, let's get back to the others.'

Archie could hear Captain Hanki and Aristo laughing and congratulating him, obviously relieved by his success, but he was in no mood to listen to them.

As they turned away from the forest Archie watched in disbelief as the dinosaurs tore through the trees ripping them apart as if they were matchsticks. When he looked down at the small curled-up figure lying at his feet, he realised just how close they had come to losing Richard.

Chapter Eight

The Lancers

Exhausted and hardly able to keep his eyes open, Archie sat with his back against the black rock. So much had happened to them that he could hardly take it all in. He looked up and gazed at the peach-coloured clouds drifting across a fading blue sky, thinking that daylight here had a soft warm glow that was almost dreamlike. This wasn't a dream though, *something* had happened to them. Somehow, they had travelled and landed in another place ... another country, perhaps ... *another time* ...   Had they gone back into the past, *to the time of the dinosaurs*?

As far as he knew, there hadn't been any humans during the dinosaur age, certainly not men and women who flew fantastic flying machines, at least, not in any books he'd ever read. Yet here they were, with strange people who spoke their language and had come to their aid when they were in trouble. He didn't know what to make of it. He wasn't frightened, just very tired and confused, and wondering if they would ever find a way to get back home.

He looked at Richard. He was standing in front of Archie, staring up at the rock, his eyes transfixed as if something about it had disturbed him. Archie had seen that look before when Richard would call out and wake up from one of his dreams and then stare at the ceiling.

'What are you staring at, Richard? What is it?' When he didn't get an answer, Archie gave a sigh of exasperation, got up and shook him by the shoulder. 'Richard, wake up!'

'It's the rock ... I've seen it before ...'

'What do you mean, you've seen it before?'

'Back at the Facility … I saw it in the dream …
when we were on the catwalk.'

'That wasn't a dream, Richard, you were feeling ill
– it was probably a hallucination.'

'It wasn't a … a whatever you call it. I saw it. It's
the same rock.'

'How do you know it's the same?'

'I dunno, Archie … I just do.'

It was all very strange, but it reminded Archie of the
times back at Grimshaws when Richard would
suddenly wake up in the middle of the night and tell
him about a dream he'd just had. Richard would swear
he had been a part of the dream, and Archie would
laugh at some weird and wonderful story he would tell.
But this was different. They were actually here in this
place, wherever it was, and Richard was claiming he
had seen it before.

Archie didn't know what to think, but before he
could say anything, he heard Uncle John calling their
names. He looked across to see him standing with
Marjorie, Aristo and the Lancers. He was waving to
them and seemed to be unusually excited by something.
They walked over and joined the group.

'Archie, Richard, I hardly know how to explain …
It's amazing what's happened to us!'

'Uncle John, what's wrong?' Archie looked
nervously at his uncle, worried by what he had to say.
'What *has* happened to us?'

'It seems, Archie, we have travelled through a …
well, a timecrack … and ended up here,' said Uncle
John, smiling and shaking his head in disbelief.

'Where's here?'

'The Exploding Park … so called, apparently,
because of the noise timecracks make when they open
up.'

'What are timecracks, Uncle John?' asked Richard.

'Well, Richard, they're like wormholes … or secret tunnels … tunnels that connect our world with this one, but they only open up when a great deal of energy is generated, such as an electrical storm or, as in our case, when we were testing for a new energy source at the Facility.'

'But can we go back?' asked Archie.

'I don't know how we're going to manage that. It would appear that Aristo here is the only person to have travelled *both* ways through a timecrack.'

Archie suspected by the look on his uncle's face that he wasn't overly concerned about getting back; his excitement at arriving in a new world was too obvious for that. Maybe it's because he's a scientist and he likes to discover things. Well, thought Archie, maybe he can discover a way to get us back.

Marjorie didn't seem too concerned either. She was standing beside Aristo and smiling, giving the impression that she was thoroughly enjoying the whole experience, in spite of their encounter with the dinosaurs.

'Aristo says we will be taken to a place called Castle Amasia where New Arrivals – that's us – are examined before admittance to the valley,' she said.

'Valley?' said the professor.

'Timeless Valley,' said Aristo. 'It's where our people live and work. You will see the city of Fort Temple and many other places there, but first we must go to the New Arrivals' Centre at Castle Amasia. Some of the Lancers will take us there, while the others drive the dinosaurs to the wild animals' sector.'

'*Wild animals?*' Richard looked around, wondering what other fierce beasts might be lurking in the tall grass. 'Where are they?'

'Not to worry, young one, my Lancers will round-up any wild animals in this area.' Captain Hanki had walked up behind Richard and placed a hand on his shoulder. 'You were very brave, but there will be nothing to fear on our journey to the castle. All the dangerous animals are contained in the Riverlands, which is a long way from here.'

Although only five and a half feet tall, Hanki was the tallest of the Lancers, and his authority was clear as he ordered the Lancers to their flying machines.

'Han-Sin, Teekoo, Ree-Tan, we will take these people to meet Brimstone. Lieutenant Akee, you and the others will find the dinosaurs, take them to the Riverlands and then return to barracks.' Hanki walked over to his own machine, and then turned to the boys. 'Archie, please go with Han-Sin, and … Richard, perhaps, you would like to ride with me?'

Lancer Han-Sin and Captain Hanki flew up front in close formation, allowing Archie to see Richard's grinning face through the glass canopies that now enclosed their cockpits. Richard waved excitedly while Archie studied the sleek lines of Hanki's machine and wondered what made it fly, as there was no obvious sign of an engine.

'Han-Sin, what sort of machines are these?' asked Archie.

'Spokestar Specials,' answered Han-Sin. 'This is the Mark 6 version with the latest laser lance, which is very useful when we have to deal with the bigger animals in the park.'

'Do you have to kill them?'

'Yes, sometimes it is necessary to kill if there is great danger, but usually our weapons function at the non-lethal level.'

'Why are they called Spokestars?'

'All our machines, including the monorail that runs through the valley, were designed and built at the Spokestar factory. In fact, Henry Spokestar may have come from your part of Old Earth, but that was nearly two hundred years ago and, unfortunately, he died last year.'

'Last year? But … that would have made him over two hundred years old!'

'Yes, Archie, you will find that people live much longer in Timeless Valley than they do on Old Earth.'

Archie's eyes widened. He couldn't imagine such a place.

'What's Timeless Valley like?' he asked, studying the landscape they now flew over.

'It's a beautiful place, with much to see–'

Archie's helmet earpiece buzzed as he heard Hanki's voice. 'That's enough, Han-Sin. The New Arrivals will be fully briefed at the centre. Please keep an eye on the road; we have spotted Arrivals in this area before.'

'Yes, Captain.'

Executing a sudden dive, Han-Sin swooped to an opening in the forest that revealed the overgrown remains of the Old Brown Road. Long disused, it had been built with local stone nearly ten thousand years ago by New Arrivals to the Exploding Park. Over the centuries it had been improved and maintained as a trading route for the scattered tribes of Arrivals who had made their homes there, but as the frequency of timecracks increased, many of the Arrivals had moved on and built new settlements in the valley beyond.

As they followed the line of the ancient road, sometimes crossing rivers and small mountain ranges, Archie saw lonely stone ruins dotting the landscape, but there was no sign of life of any kind.

'Han-Sin, do we have much further to go?' he asked.

They seemed to have been flying for hours; nightfall hadn't arrived, but Archie could hardly stay awake.

'Not long, Archie, another six hundred miles and we will be there.'

'*Six hundred*?'

'Yes – less than two hours and we will be at the castle. If you wish to sleep, please do so. It takes time for New Arrivals to adjust to our day and night periods.'

He didn't understand any of this, but Archie was too tired to care, and soon he was fast asleep as Han-Sin banked the Spokestar to fly through a deep mountain pass.

*

On and on the Lancers raced; Han-Sin keeping an eye on the road while Captain Hanki and the other Spokestars flew above in close formation. She wasn't expecting to see anything in this particular sector, but timecracks were unpredictable, and Hanki was a stickler for being prepared for the unexpected. The road frequently disappeared into an endless green sea of mighty oak trees, tall slender pines and great spreading maples, all draped with thick twisting ropes of clinging vines that clung to the trees as if a giant net had fallen on the forest.

'Do you see anything, Han-Sin?'

Hanki's voice made her glance up at his Spokestar directly above. She was virtually flying on autopilot, knowing that New Arrivals had not been found in this part of the park for nearly five hundred years.

'No, Captain, not a thing. It's hardly likely that we will,' answered Han-Sin, wondering if it was a serious question, or was he just checking her for alertness?

'Maybe so, but it is no reason not to be vigilant. Keep your eyes open for anything unusual.'

'Yes, Captain.'

Not quite a reprimand, she thought. He's just asserting his authority in front of the others. Not that she minded; he was her father and she understood he must not be seen to show favouritism.

They flew on without incident and two hours later, Archie woke up to find they had stopped. He rubbed his eyes, looked around and saw that they were hovering in close formation with the other Spokestars over a small hillside.

'Why have we stopped?' asked Archie, stretching out of his seat to get a better look beyond the nose of their Spokestar.

'A patrol is coming out.'

As she spoke, Han-Sin turned her machine broadside to give Archie a clear view of the open countryside and, as she did so, she pointed to a sight that made Archie whistle softly.

There, in the distance, stood a magnificent castle, its weatherworn stone rising proudly to the sky in a silhouette of towers and turrets. Shielded by a massive rampart of brown rock, the castle was partly shrouded in a thin grey mist, out of which Archie saw another group of gleaming Spokestars ascending into the evening sky. Except for the flying machines, it might have been a scene from a medieval painting.

'That's really something!' said Archie, not realising the others could hear him.

Captain Hanki nodded silently, knowing that the first sight of Castle Amasia was an awe-inspiring, sometimes frightening, prospect for all New Arrivals.

Part Two

Timeless Valley

Chapter Nine

Castle Amasia

Teekoo brought his Spokestar to a halt at a position just above the east wall of the castle. He engaged the autohover and watched silently as Hanki descended to the white landing-square, followed by Han-Sin with Archie, then Ree-Tan with the professor. On landing, a ground crew rushed forward and immediately took charge of the Spokestars, ready to prepare them for the next patrol.

Sitting quietly behind Teekoo, Marjorie felt slightly apprehensive as she looked down on the castle. So much had happened, so quickly, she hardly had time to think about what the future might hold in store for them.

As Teekoo started his descent into the vast courtyard, Marjorie studied what lay below. Surprisingly, although the castle had the appearance of a medieval structure from the outside, this part of the interior was quite different. It was getting dark now and the courtyard was illuminated like a sports stadium by spotlights positioned high on the grey granite blocks of the castle walls. The whole area had the appearance of a small modern airport, complete with landing strips and a control tower backing onto several hangars. Just beyond the courtyard, she could see a network of narrow cobblestone streets and houses with steep, slate rooftops next to spires that reached upwards like stalagmites into the night sky.

A loud alarm and the sudden flashing of a bright orange light in the cockpit startled Marjorie into grabbing the edge of her seat.

'What's wrong, Teekoo?' she called out, alarmed that something was about to happen to them.

'It's the emergency Keep Clear warning,' said Teekoo. He had been keeping in touch with ground control during the Spokestar's descent. Now he responded to the warning from the control tower by quickly pulling a hard turn upwards away from the courtyard to resume his position above the wall. 'I'm sorry, Miss Marjorie, but we will have to wait a few more minutes until the landing-square clears.'

'I don't understand – what's going on?'

'I'm not certain, but something has happened to Lieutenant Akee and his patrol on their journey to the Riverlands. Two more patrols are being sent to investigate, so we will have to wait until they leave, but don't worry, we'll land soon.'

While they waited, Teekoo explained that this part of the castle housed the Fourth Lancers squadron and the maintenance workshops for the Spokestars. Marjorie detected a hint of pride in his voice as he told her a little of the Lancers' background and their place in Castle Amasia.

'Is the castle very old?' asked Marjorie, watching as more Spokestars left the courtyard.

'Yes, it is. No one knows for certain how old, but there are traces of original occupation going back at least seven thousand years. At one time, the castle used to be the centre of a thriving community, but that was before the plague.'

'The plague?'

'Yes, Miss Marjorie … It was at a time of exceptional timecrack activity when many New Arrivals came through, some bringing the Old Earth sickness with them. There was no way of stopping the disease, and in less than a year nearly half the population died.'

'That's terrible. What happened to the rest of the people?'

'It was a dark period in our history. The people were forced to leave their homes and find safety deep in the valley beyond the Great Wall. It's how the city of Fort Temple was founded; a beautiful place you and your companions will see in due course.'

Intrigued by Teekoo's story, Marjorie could see now that the castle had been built as part of a huge fortified wall that stretched out of sight across the valley. She looked to the far end of the courtyard where a brightly lit building caught her eye. It was the headquarters of the Fourth Lancers, said Teekoo, and it had become a scene of hectic activity as Lancers in their smart black and red uniforms dashed down wide steps to rows of Spokestar Specials parked nearby on one of the landing strips.

Within minutes, like rockets in a brilliant fireworks display, the sleek scarlet machines, noselights flashing, had zoomed beyond the castle walls on their way to discover what had befallen Lieutenant Akee and his patrol.

*

In the courtyard, the professor held his arms tightly around his nephews' shoulders as the last of the Spokestars disappeared into the night.

'Wow! That was fantastic! I wonder if they'll go after the dinosaurs?'

The professor smiled as he saw the wonderment dance in his young nephew's eyes.

'I don't know, Richard, but I hope they keep them outside the castle walls.' He winked at Archie and said, 'Anyway, I think we've had enough excitement for one day, don't you?'

Archie nodded, not really knowing what to say.

'And now I think it's high time we got ourselves sorted out!'

Archie and Richard glanced at each other, wondering what their uncle had in mind to do. They trailed behind him as he strode over to the steps of the Lancers' headquarters where, standing on the top step with another Lancer, Captain Hanki was looking grim-faced as he watched the patrols leave the castle.

'Captain Hanki – may I enquire what is going to happen to us?'

The professor's voice boomed unexpectedly loud across the courtyard, causing the Lancers to turn their gaze to the tall, heavy-set figure walking towards them.

'I'm sorry, Professor Strawbridge, but we are waiting for Lancer Teekoo and your friend, Miss Peoples, before you proceed to the New Arrivals' Centre. As you saw, they had to wait during the emergency.' Hanki's attention was drawn to the landing-square. 'Ah, they are coming in now. You must excuse me, Professor, I need to speak to Lancer Teekoo.'

As Hanki made his way to the landing-square, Archie and Richard dashed past him to greet Marjorie as she climbed out of the Spokestar. She hopped onto the ground and looked around the courtyard as she spread her arms and chuckled.

'Well, boys, what do you think of all this?' she said.

'I think it's brilliant,' said Richard, stroking the polished skin of the Spokestar as if it were a young colt. 'I would love to fly one of these someday.'

Archie shrugged. 'I don't know … it's all pretty weird … isn't it?' His eyes wandered to the high walls of the castle, like a prisoner contemplating escape. His expression saddened Marjorie and she moved closer to put her arm around his shoulders.

'I think I know what you mean, Archie, but I'm sure we'll all feel a lot better once we get a decent night's sleep. Maybe then we can find out what we're going to do about getting back home again.'

'I don't think we can go back. Uncle John says Aristo is the only person ever to have travelled *both* ways through a timecrack,' said Archie.

He'd also overheard Captain Hanki tell Aristo it was a miracle he had made it alive, but he didn't want to frighten Richard by saying so out loud.

'Well, we'll just have to wait and see. Look, there's Aristo with your uncle talking to someone. Let's go over and join them.'

Marjorie put her other arm around Richard and ushered the two of them across the courtyard. As they approached, they saw a tall, black-skinned man, attired in a black business-style suit with a colourful floral-patterned shirt and matching cravat, standing in front of Aristo, with a hand on his shoulder.

He was saying, 'This is the breakthrough we needed, Aristo – but there is so much more to be done, and Dr Shah is impatient to hear from your own lips all that happened on your journey.'

'I know, sir, and I will make my report as soon as I can, but first I must take these people to the New Arrivals' Centre,' said Aristo, indicating Marjorie and the boys as they joined the company. He smiled and introduced them to Benno Kozan.

'Professor Strawbridge,' said Kozan, 'you and your friends must forgive my poor manners, but Aristo's return has made me forgetful. All of you must be exhausted, so I will leave you with Aristo until we meet at a more opportune time, after you have settled in.' Apologising again, he left them, his tall, commanding figure striding purposely towards the Lancer headquarters, up the steps and into the building.

Aristo watched him, seemingly lost in thought, then he quickly turned to the group.

'If you'll follow me, I'll take you to the centre now.'

He led them to the far end of the courtyard and into a maze of narrow cobblestone streets. They passed by ancient walls that had shed large patches of once golden-brown plaster into untidy heaps of rubble along the deserted streets. Old street lamps cast a dull, yellow glow over the stone-built houses and shops. Long empty, the doors and windows of old buildings were boarded with rotting wood, giving evidence of years of neglect. Weeds grew profusely in every nook and cranny, suggesting that nature would eventually reclaim this part of the castle.

It was a depressing sight, and Marjorie shivered as she accidentally touched a stone wall, slippery with damp and lichen.

'What is this place, Aristo?' she asked, wiping a hand on the side of her shirt.

'It's the oldest part of the castle and, as you can see, no one lives or works here anymore.' He pointed to the weatherworn wooden signs, decorated with indistinct lettering, above some of the boarded-up doors.

'There used to be many businesses here that traded with the tribes in the valley, but after the plague only a few were prepared to stay and save their livelihoods. They and their descendants stayed for many centuries, but they too eventually decided to move to the valley and the cities where most people now live and work. This area was occupied up until only a hundred years ago by a small number of businesses who tried to carry on the ancient traditions, but now they are gone.'

Marjorie explained to the professor and the boys what Teekoo had told her of the plague, and as they passed the dark empty buildings, Archie tried to imagine what it must have been like. He had read in school about the Great Plague that had ravaged London. Had it been the same here? Did the people have horrible sores all over their bodies? Were they left to rot and die in the streets? he wondered. He shivered at the thought of what might have happened here, all those years ago.

They continued on their way through more deserted cobblestone streets, while Aristo explained that, normally, they would have flown directly to the New Arrivals' Centre, but Captain Hanki had needed to land at headquarters first to confirm an urgent message he had received during their journey to the castle. Apparently, something serious had happened to Lieutenant Akee's patrol, so Aristo had offered to take over from Hanki and escort them to the centre by way of a route through the Old Town that hardly anyone ever used now.

'There is a main road to the centre, but this is more direct,' he said, quickening his step.

They walked for another fifteen minutes, to arrive at a massive carved stone arch that stood proudly over a heavily-studded door lit by a single lamp. Aristo reached out with both hands to twist a large iron ring, encrusted with age-old rust, just above the lock. The door groaned as it swung open to reveal a large, central mosaic square surrounded by a well-kept lawn. They followed Aristo along a paved path set into the lawn to reach a magnificent multi-storey edifice that dominated the square.

Marjorie stepped forwards to gaze upon the ornate architecture. She could see archways and decorated pillars on every level rising to support a huge golden dome, reminding her of the great mosques she had seen on her travels on Old Earth.

'It's stunning, Aristo. What is this place?' she asked.

'This is the New Arrivals' Centre – and that, is Brimstone,' said Aristo.

He inclined his head towards an unusually tall figure standing in the portico. Next to him was a curious-looking little man hopping up and down as if he were treading on hot coals.

'Who is Brimstone? Is he the man in charge here?' asked the professor.

'Yes and no,' said Aristo, mysteriously. 'He is more than a man, but you will see for yourselves. Please follow me and I will introduce you.'

Aristo approached the tall figure.

'Good evening, Brimstone, I have brought the New Arrivals.'

'Yes, Captain Hanki informed me of their coming.'

A little over seven feet tall, Brimstone towered above Aristo as he inspected the group. His face-skin blended smoothly with the grey metal that covered the rest of his head. Wearing a knee-length tunic of silver-blue silk, held neatly at the waist by a thin silver chain, his outfit was completed by black leather trousers tucked into calf-length boots, giving him the appearance of a warlike Cossack.

His ice-blue eyes glinted sharply as they swept across the New Arrivals. As if recording every feature in his memory, he nodded to each of them before passing to the next in the group. In spite of his height and fierce looks, Brimstone's voice was unexpectedly gentle. It was calm and reassuring, not at all threatening, as the arrivals half-expected from his appearance.

'It is good to see you, Aristo; I congratulate you on your safe return. You may leave now, if you wish. I am told Dr Shah is anxious to meet with you as soon as possible.'

'Yes, I must go, but I will return at the end of the evaluation period if I may,' said Aristo, then he turned to Marjorie. 'Perhaps, I can show you Fort Temple when you have finished here?'

'I don't know what's going to happen to us here, Aristo,' said Marjorie, her face flushing slightly, 'but I'm sure *all* of us would like that.'

Aristo nodded, looking a little embarrassed, and agreed that, of course, was what he meant. He left, assuring them that they would be well looked after while in Brimstone's care.

'Welcome to Castle Amasia,' said the tall figure. 'My name is Brimstone, the Castle Protector. The name of the castle is derived from Nicolo Amasia, who spent his life exploring our continent, which is also named after him. During your stay here you will be evaluated and processed as required by our laws –'

'What do you mean, *processed*?' demanded Uncle John, a steely edge to his voice the boys rarely heard.

'Do not be concerned, Professor Strawbridge, you will be protected and cared for, but it is necessary that all of you submit to our tests.'

'What *sort* of tests?'

'You will all be required to undergo a medical examination to ascertain your body condition, and assessed for treatment if you are found defective. Your suitability for citizenship of Fort temple will also be gauged. If you do not qualify, you will be transported to a suitable community within the valley or beyond.'

Archie didn't like the sound of maybe being found *defective* and possibly transported. Isn't that what they used to do to convicts in England in the old days? Obviously, Uncle John didn't like the sound of it either, judging by the way he stared at Brimstone.

'And what if we don't want to be *processed* or *gauged* for citizenship?'

'You must understand, Professor Strawbridge, that there is no alternative to this procedure. It is in your best interests to co-operate fully. However, you should not interpret that as a threat, but as a preliminary step to your new life in Amasia.'

Their new life in Amasia.

Suddenly it dawned on all of them that their presence in this new world was expected to be permanent. Marjorie looked at the professor, watching as his face expressed realisation at what Brimstone had just said. Although he had adopted a no-nonsense approach so far, he was now showing concern and, possibly, she guessed, feeling guilty that their journey through the timecrack had occurred in the Facility.

'Don't worry, Professor, whatever it takes, I'm sure we will find a way back,' said Marjorie, although she was not entirely convinced they would.

While his uncle and Brimstone continued to talk about their situation, Richard moved away to get a better look at the strange little man hopping up and down behind Brimstone's back, muttering words that none of them could hear. Richard could hardly keep from laughing out loud at the little man's comical antics, behaving as if he were a performing clown in a circus.

Brimstone's head swivelled one hundred and eighty degrees to look down at the little man who was now tugging at his tunic.

'Finbar! Be still! You will attend to your duties shortly.'

If Brimstone's head had fallen off, they couldn't have been more astonished. His face and behaviour had been perfectly human, and they had been too preoccupied by what he had to say to appreciate the rest of his appearance. Now that they could see the back of his head they were stunned into silence.

It was Archie who finally voiced their thoughts.

'He's a robot!'

Brimstone's head spun round to its normal position, and for a brief moment he scanned Archie's face before speaking.

'You are incorrect, Archie Kinross. I am an Androt, but at present such information will not concern you; however, if after evaluation you qualify for citizenship you will learn of me, and much more.'

'How … how do you know my name?'

'All of you wear name badges. How else would I know?'

Archie glanced down at his T-shirt and saw that he was still wearing his ID tag from the Facility. He had forgotten they were still wearing the same clothes since the explosion at the DONUT, not realising how dishevelled they must look. He wasn't thinking very clearly, and he knew he would have to sleep very soon. Unable to prevent himself from yawning, Archie pointed to the Centre.

'Will we be staying there?'

'Yes, it is time for all of you to rest. Until you adjust to New Earth time you will need two sleep periods a day. Finbar will advise you on this, and now he will take you to your sleeping quarters where you will find food and fresh clothing.' Brimstone looked down on the little man still tugging at his tunic. 'He is impatient to join his friends at the tavern in Fort Temple, so that he may drink with them.'

'Ach, ye great big hulk, I should've been away long before this.'

Finbar, obviously in a temper, shook his fist at Brimstone, who seemed unaffected by his behaviour.

'Enough, Finbar! On your return from Fort Temple tomorrow you will escort these people to the clinic for their first medical examination. Please do not be late.'

Turning to the professor, he said, 'Now, if you will excuse me, I must attend to other matters.'

He left them, to make his way across the mosaic square towards the archway to the Old Town.

Archie and Richard watched him walk away, and then looked at each other, not knowing what to think. Before Archie could say anything, he heard the little man speak.

'Look at the creature. He'll spend the night plannin' how he's going to restore another part of the castle, an' keep us all runnin' around until he does it!'

Finbar pulled at the lapels of his brown woollen jacket and hitched up matching trousers that threatened to slip away from a small round belly. His dark brown eyes, black curly hair and ruddy complexion, gave him the rustic look of a farm worker, which was what he had been before the arrival of a timecrack on the stormy coast of a lonely Irish island, years earlier. He cast a curmudgeonly look over his shoulder as he led them into the Centre.

'Anyway, it's no matter. Ye'd better be followin' me – I've been here long enough!'

They left the portico and entered the Centre where a large entrance hall met a wide marble staircase leading to the first floor sleeping quarters. The professor and Marjorie followed Finbar as he led them to their rooms at the end of a long corridor, hung with gold-framed landscapes of the castle and Timeless Valley. He told Archie and Richard to wait for him at the head of the staircase.

'Grown-ups an' young people are separate. I'll take ye to yer rooms in a minute. I hope ye can look after yerselves, for I'll not have the time to do it.'

'I think we can manage, thank you, Mr Finbar,' said Archie.

'I'm not a mister. I'm Finbar the Guide, if ye want my proper title, not that anyone ever uses it.'

While they waited for Finbar to return, Archie and Richard watched the entrance hall as other people entered and left the Centre.

'I wonder who *they* are?' said Richard, gazing at two unusual-looking men approaching them from the bottom of the staircase.

They wore colourful robes of yellow and green trimmed with silver thread, and tooled snakeskin boots decorated in gold. Their faces were long and deeply tanned, with golden hair flowing over broad shoulders that hinted at great strength.

When the men reached them, Richard was startled to hear one of them speak.

'We are Vikantus, master builders to the Castle Protector, and you are?'

He hadn't thought they could hear him, but one of them stopped and made a short bow. The man smiled and nodded when Richard told him their names.

'You are both very welcome here. My name is Targa; please ask for my assistance if ever you need it.'

After the men left, Archie stared at Richard in astonishment.

'What was that all about?' he asked.

'Didn't you hear? He said he would help us whenever we needed him.'

'I never heard him say a thing. Richard, you're acting very strangely lately. What's going on?'

Before Richard tried to explain, Finbar joined them, shifting from foot to foot impatiently, complaining that he didn't have all night to get them settled in.

'Finbar, who are those men?' asked Archie. 'Richard says they spoke to him, but I never heard a word they said.'

'They're Vikantus. Ye'll see plenty of them around while Brimstone restores the castle to the way it used to be. They've been here these past hundred years or more workin' in the valley, an' he'll have them workin' on the Old Town for another hundred. But there's a strange thing – they're mutes, so they don't speak to anyone, except themselves - an' Brimstone, when he tells them what to do.'

Finbar shook his head at Richard, as if he had been imagining what he had heard.

'But he *did* speak to me!' insisted Richard.

Finbar wasn't listening. He quickly made his way along the corridor, beckoning Archie and Richard to follow him. As they watched his little figure hopping along in front, they couldn't help laughing at his comical mutterings about how Brimstone didn't appreciate him.

'I've my own friends to see at the tavern, an' by the time I get there they'll be leavin'! Only last week, I missed them when *His Lordship* made me stay to look after a horde of Japanese workers that couldn't be helped.'

'What do you mean, Finbar? Why couldn't they be helped?' asked Archie.

'Ach, it was a terrible sight. The poor devils were blown sky-high through a timecrack by an awful explosion – they said it was like the sun itself had exploded during their war with the Americans. I don't know what they meant, but their injuries were a terrible sight. Most of them died before we could help them.'

'Is there anyone else here now?' Richard thought that the centre was so big it could accommodate hundreds like themselves and the Japanese workers. 'I mean ... like us?'

'So far this week just yerselves. The Japanese – what was left of them – left yesterday for Sitanga, the factory city.' Finbar tutted at the memory of it, and then stopped at a highly polished rosewood door with a gleaming brass handle. 'Here ye are, this'll be yer room for the next few days. Ye'll find a selection of clothes in the wardrobes – somethin' in there should fit ye. An' there's food and drink on the table to keep ye goin' until yer called.'

Finbar ushered the boys into a large room containing ten beds with a wardrobe beside each one. A long oak table in the middle of the room held silver platters of fruit, cold meats and cheese. Two jugs of iced drinks on a silver tray stood nearby, but neither Archie nor Richard were interested in food or drink. At the sight of the beds they both felt desperately tired. Without saying another word they each chose a bed near a tall window overlooking the mosaic square, and promptly collapsed on top of the bedclothes. Within minutes of Finbar leaving the room, they were fast asleep.

*

Aristo hurried along the hallway past the recreation rooms to the main door of the Lancers' headquarters. Benno Kozan had arranged with Captain Hanki for him to have a room to shower and change into fresh clothing before leaving to meet Dr Shah. The tracker suit and equipment had been packed into a sealed case, and would be sent to the scientists for a detailed examination to see how well it had functioned going through the timecrack, and its operation on Old Earth.

Feeling refreshed, and dressed in a khaki overall, he was anxious to get away as quickly as possible, knowing Dr Shah would wait up for him despite the late hour, to hear a report on his journey. He walked through the main doors onto the top step, where he joined Benno Kozan talking with Hanki and Teekoo. He could see from Teekoo's face that something was terribly wrong.

'I'm very sorry, Teekoo,' said Benno, placing a hand on the Lancer's shoulder. 'They can't get very far, but it will be difficult to search the ravine in the dark.'

'Is something wrong?' asked Aristo. Teekoo was his friend and he was disturbed to see him so upset.

'I'm afraid so.' Hanki's voice trembled as he tried to contain his rage. 'Teekoo's cousin, Suntee, has been reported injured, perhaps … dead. Lieutenant Akee has seen his body at the bottom of Snakespass Ravine. It looks as if New Arrivals may have attacked Suntee and stolen his Spokestar!'

Chapter Ten

Snakespass Ravine

'*Stay down!*'

'What is it, Anton?'

'Look!'

Anton pointed to a strange craft approaching the copse where they now lay hidden. It passed silently overhead making them crouch lower in the grass until it flew over the ravine, coming slowly to a halt as it surveyed the area below.

'It sees the Robopod,' whispered Sandan. 'Do you think it's looking for us?'

'I don't know. We may have landed a long way from Military Space Command's reception committee, but there will be others to take up the hunt.'

Earlier, after the Robopod had smashed a path through young trees and tall yellow grass, Anton had discovered they had only been saved from crashing into a deep rocky ravine by a thick screen of thorn bushes. These had started to uproot under the weight of the Robopod, leaving only minutes to spare to drag a panic-stricken Sandan to safety before the Robopod plunged to the bottom of the ravine.

They had made their way into the copse fifty yards away, where they lay hidden while Anton pondered their next move. Where to go? Anton had no idea where they were. Africa, the Americas? He couldn't tell, but sooner or later, they would have to find a way out of this place.

'What will we do?'

Sandan's voice betrayed his nervousness as he gazed upwards, fearful of the red flying machine hovering above them.

'Be quiet,' hissed Anton. 'We'll have to wait and see what he does next.'

He studied the strange craft, a type and design unknown to him. As it flew over the ravine he suspected it might land to take a closer look at the Robopod. If so, he had an idea on how to deal with it.

*

As Lieutenant Akee's patrol headed eastwards to the Riverlands, herding the dinosaurs in front of them, Lancer Suntee noticed the path of broken trees near Snakespass Ravine. He examined the forest canopy closely, the evening light revealing a scar-like break that might have been caused by another craft.

Before altering course to investigate, he radioed Akee.

'Lieutenant, it looks as if something may have crashed down there. I think I should take a closer look.'

'Affirmative, Suntee, let me know what you find. We will continue to the Riverlands. Rejoin us as soon as you can.'

Suntee acknowledged, and then broke away to make a pass over the ravine. Descending to a lower position near the rim he saw the Robopod wedged between rocks at the bottom of the steep ravine wall. Just as he decided to check for survivors he spotted something – or someone – moving away from the trees.

*

Hidden in the copse, Anton and Sandan watched carefully as the strange machine approached until it was almost level with the trees. The pilot was so near, Anton could see the markings on his helmet. The machine and the identification symbols on the fuselage

94

were unknown to him, but he had tested many types of craft during his early years with Military Space Command, and he felt that this machine would not be too dissimilar to the last one he had flown.

'He's coming around again – what will we do?'

'Fear not, Sandan, this could be our opportunity to leave this place.'

'But he may be armed –'

'Quiet! He will cause us no harm if you do as I say.'

'What do you want me to do?' asked Sandan, suspiciously.

'My plan is simple, and requires little of you. All you have to do is fall down and lie still. Do you think you can manage that?'

'What good will that achieve?'

'Just this: I want you to stagger to the edge of the ravine, and then collapse as if you are injured. When the pilot leaves his machine to investigate – as he will do – he will be distracted. Then I will deal with him.'

'How?'

'Whatever is necessary to ensure we do not become guests of a Sahara prison. I take it you agree?'

Anton's eye's narrowed to cruel slits as he waited for Sandan's response.

Sandan nodded, knowing he had little choice but to agree to whatever Anton had in mind.

'Good. Now go!' urged Anton, pushing Sandan away from the copse into the open. 'Let him see you fall!'

Stumbling across the flattened grass and loose rocks towards the ravine, Sandan overacted his part, but finally he dropped flat on his face when he heard a shout:

'You – stop!'

Anton shook his head in disbelief at Sandan's drunken-like run, but smiled as he watched the pilot leave his machine to chase after Sandan, just as he had predicted. He waited a moment then left the cover of the trees, picking up a large rock with both hands before creeping up behind the pilot.

Suntee kneeled down to turn the fallen figure over, but as he did so, he heard a sound behind him. He turned quickly, but it was too late. All he had time to see, before he was struck down, was a tall man dressed in black holding a rock over his head. He cried out:

'No – *aaah*!'

'You've killed him!' cried Sandan.

He stood up, horrified by what Anton had done. He stared at the body, sickened by the blood seeping slowly onto the grass. Anton's blow had been so vicious it had split the helmet, pulling it away from Suntee's head.

'Shut up! We have to leave here quickly. There may be others in the area who will be looking for him. Get a hold of his feet and help me take him to the edge.'

Suntee's body was small and light, so they had no difficulty throwing it far out into the ravine, but Sandan was terrified by the thought of it being found.

'Anton. What will we do if they find him? What have we done?'

'What was necessary and, I must admit, Sandan, *you* played your part to perfection. Now, let's see if I can get us out of here.'

Anton dashed to the Spokestar and climbed onto the step below the cockpit. With the machine on autohover he knew the power-unit (whatever that might be) hadn't been shut down. He lifted himself into the cockpit and studied the controls: right and left moulded handgrips for direction and height; central thumb-buttons for speed and autohover. A child could fly this, thought Anton, examining the other panel buttons in front of him. A scanner displayed the machine's position near the ravine. Excellent! This would help him chart their escape. Daylight was fading, so he made his decision to fly westwards following the sun.

He looked out at Sandan, who was obviously overwhelmed by what they had just done, but there had been no other way, and he couldn't let him weaken now when others might arrive at any moment.

'Get in, Sandan! It's time we were away from this place.'

'Where can we go?'

'I don't know, but we must find somewhere we can hide for a while. At the very least, we need to find out exactly where we are, then food and drink would be very welcome.'

Checking that Sandan was secure, Anton closed the canopy and had a quick look around the area to see if they were clear, before pointing the Spokestar westwards.

*

'Lancer Suntee … Can you hear me? Lancer Suntee … Please respond.'

Akee was worried; it was not like Suntee not to keep in touch, and after an hour of radio silence he knew something was wrong. After another few minutes he made his decision to return to the ravine.

'Malok, Zantay, I'm going back to find out what has happened to Suntee. Continue as planned. I'll contact you within the hour.'

It was twilight by the time Akee reached the ravine. He flew over the copse following the line of flattened grass to where some thorn bushes at the edge of the ravine had been torn from the soil. Suntee was right; it did look as if something had crashed here. He made several passes before deciding to land to take a closer look.

Leaving the Spokestar on autohover he walked slowly across the site to the track of scarred earth that led to the edge of the ravine. He almost missed the helmet lying in the grass behind a large rock. Picking it up, he shuddered as he fingered the wide split and traces of blood that could only mean one thing: Suntee had been injured. But how? *Where was he?*

Akee had a bad feeling as he retraced his steps to the Spokestar with Suntee's helmet under his arm. As soon as he gained height he scanned every square foot of the crash site without finding anything else, and it was only when he flew into the ravine he saw the wreckage of the Robopod – and something else he had hoped *not* to see.

It was with a heavy heart he switched on the emergency channel and spoke.

'Lancer Headquarters, this is Lieutenant Akee reporting. I have an emergency...'

He continued to report as he descended towards Suntee's body.

*

The Spokestar was even easier to handle than Anton expected. Although they were flying in darkness now, the powerful noselight and map scanner enabled him to hold a steady course through the ravine. He was desperately tired, and his concentration was waning to the point where he knew they would have to land soon and find food and shelter before daylight. Sandan was right, of course; they would be in danger once the machine and the pilot were reported missing. After that it would only be a matter of time until the body was found – then the hunt would be on.

Sandan had remained quiet since the death of the pilot, shocked by what he had witnessed, no doubt, but it had been necessary. The pilot would have told others, preventing their escape, and Anton had no intention of ever being caged again.

What was that?

Anton's eyes were drawn to an orange blip that had suddenly appeared on the scanner, and then another, until more than a dozen blips seemed to be in line behind them. They were being tracked and, by the look of it, whoever they were, they were gaining rapidly.

'Sandan, prepare yourself. We're being followed, and I don't know if we can lose them.'

'I knew it! You should never have killed him! It will be the end of us!'

'Shut your whinging mouth! They've yet to catch us, and I'll be damned if they do!'

Anton took the Spokestar lower into the ravine, hoping that they would be less visible to their pursuers. They were flying dangerously close to the treetops growing out of rocky outcrops. Twisting and turning to avoid them, Anton saw three more blips appear on the scanner *ahead* of them. He saw something else too. Some sort of barrier, perhaps a wall, seemed to be looming up behind the blips. He realised he would have to gain height to avoid it, whatever it was.

*

What Anton didn't know, was that Captain Hanki, Han-Sin and Teekoo were patrolling the Great Wall, having learned that Suntee's killer was probably heading through Snakespass Ravine towards the wall.

Hanki had given the order to all Lancers to put their lances on full-phase lethal status. This was rare, but he was not going to risk another Lancer's life pursuing a ruthless killer. He and Teekoo were stationed near the Great Wall, while Han-Sin had taken a position farther down the ravine, with orders not to intercept, but to report as soon as she saw any sign of Suntee's Spokestar.

Hanki saw a blip appear on his scanner, warning him that something was approaching the wall, but just as quickly, another blip appeared on what seemed to be a collision course. *Damn!* Han-Sin was engaging, despite his order not to.

'Han-Sin! Break away now! Do not engage!' he yelled, but either she didn't hear him, or was ignoring him.

He realised she was trying to force the other machine down before it gained height, allowing it to escape from the ravine.

But the fugitive also understood what Han-Sin was up to, immediately pulling upwards to avoid being trapped, and then aiming his machine at the underside of Han-Sin's Spokestar, just before she could take evasive action.

Han-Sin was too late. She was caught in the beam of the noselight rising towards her. Seconds later, her Spokestar bucked wildly out of control as it was struck from underneath. She had not anticipated such a suicidal attack, and before she could regain control she found she was being forced into a jagged outcrop of rock directly above her head. The Spokestar smashed into the rock, ripping the canopy and fuselage apart, throwing Han-Sin wide, like a flimsy rag doll, onto a crowded bed of tangled evergreen shrubs at the side of the ravine.

'*No!*' Hanki screamed.

He had arrived to see his daughter's Spokestar shatter into pieces against the rocky outcrop. Shocked, he watched as her attacker, seemingly unharmed, climb rapidly and disappear into the darkness. Fearing the worst, he descended to see what had happened to Han-Sin. Opening the emergency channel, he called repeatedly.

'This is Captain Hanki to all Lancers. Han-Sin is down – *I repeat*, Han-Sin is down! I'm going to investigate. Lancer Teekoo, you are the nearest, pursue the fugitive and fire at will. This order applies to all Lancers. Bring down the fugitive at all costs!'

Teekoo heard the fury in Hanki's voice and shook his head in despair at this latest disaster. His anger at his cousin Suntee's death now turned to an all-consuming rage he could barely contain. His only thought now was one of revenge as he watched the blip on his scanner turn south-west towards the old vallonium mines at the end of the Great Wall. The fugitive was heading into the Piranga Mountains, and if he made it, they might never find him. *No! Not if I can help it.* Checking his lance was on full-phase, Teekoo set the Spokestar on an intercept course that would place him between Suntee's killer and the Pirangas.

*

'This is madness, Anton. You nearly killed us back there!'

'Would you have preferred us to be forced down and captured? Not to mention that they might wish to exact some sort of punishment for the death of their friend.'

'*You* killed him! We could have taken him prisoner and forced him to help us. Now we will be hunted down like animals and destroyed!'

'Perhaps, but we are not in a position to take prisoners, and if we do, it will be at a time and place of *my* choosing. Understand this, if nothing else, Sandan: I have a mission to fulfil, and *no one*, or *anything* will be allowed to stand in my way – is that clear?'

Sandan grunted and said nothing more. He heard the cold menace in his brother's voice and knew it would be wise to keep silent.

The sudden appearance of a bright light startled them and Anton instinctively pulled away from it.

Whssst!

Something flashed over the canopy and struck the ravine wall. Rock exploded all around them, hitting the Spokestar like large hailstones.

Anton had been distracted and caught off-guard by Sandan's whinging; he had taken his eyes off the scanner and now they were under attack! He corkscrewed the Spokestar to avoid the line of fire that was trying to lock onto it, bringing old battle skills into play that brought back memories of past wars and hard-won victories, when no one could outfly him. That was then, though, and now he was uncertain if this machine even had a weapon.

The scanner warned him of the barrier ahead, the noselight picking up part of the huge wall as it loomed up in front of the Spokestar. He had no choice but to climb, leaving him vulnerable to their attacker.

Whssst!

He heard another shot pass over the canopy.

Crackkk!

They were nearly over the wall when, suddenly, he felt the machine shudder violently – they had been hit! The canopy had split open and, as they dropped into the black void, all Anton could hear was the roar of the wind and Sandan screaming behind him.

It seemed like an eternity before they hit the ground, with Anton striving to keep the machine upright and level. Miraculously, the Spokestar stayed in one piece as it finally skidded to a halt near the bottom of the wall. The canopy had blown away and Sandan was scrambling wildly to leave the cockpit, while Anton sat back, as if in a daze, amazed that they had survived yet another crash. Neither of them seemed to be hurt, and he wondered if this was a sign that he was meant to live to fulfil the destiny he dreamed of.

He looked upwards to the night sky and saw there was no sign of their attacker, but he frowned as he stared at the stars that glittered high above the mountains. Wherever they were, this world boasted a sky he did not recognise.

'Anton, we have to get out of here!'

Sandan was right; whatever his destiny might hold, they first had to make their escape. He released himself from the cockpit and jumped to the ground.

'We'll head up into the mountains; it'll be more difficult to find us there. Let's go. Quickly!'

They had no sense of time as they climbed. Bone-weary and weak with hunger and thirst, they trekked a rocky mountain path until, almost dropping with exhaustion, they found they could go no farther. By starlight they could see the mountainside was dotted with a succession of dark caves stretching away into the night. Anton chose one of the larger ones hidden below the treeline and, to his relief, as they entered the cave he heard the sound of running water cascading into a stream that ran deep into the interior.

'We'll rest here tonight. In the morning we'll decide our next move.'

Sandan nodded wearily, not caring what tomorrow might bring. He dropped to his knees by the edge of the stream, drinking thirstily, and then cleared some loose stones from the side of the cave where he lay down and promptly fell into a deep sleep.

Before joining him, Anton looked back along the path they had taken. There was no sign of anyone following them, but he knew that by daylight their hunters would soon pick up the trail. The cave was well screened by a ridge of pine trees and a few straggling thorn bushes, but the ridge would offer little protection against determined pursuers. It was obvious that they would have to be well on their way before sunrise. These people were resolute, and whoever they were, they would not give up easily.

As he lay down near Sandan his mind churned with questions.

Strange soldiers in a strange world – who are they and where have we landed?

Chapter Eleven

Evaluations

'I'm telling you, Richard, if we don't do something soon, this place will drive me nuts!'

'What can we do? Old Kripps –'

'*Doctor* Krippitz,' corrected Archie. 'It's not Kripps, and he's not that old.'

Richard shrugged, not caring one way or the other.

'Well, anyway, he said it was very important to carry out the extra tests before we leave the castle.'

'It's all right for you,' said Archie. 'You're getting all this special attention over those peculiar dreams of yours. He seems to think you're ... well ... *different.*'

They were lying sprawled out on the lawn beside the mosaic square enjoying the bright sunshine, while men and women, dressed in a variety of strange clothes (although probably not so strange to the people wearing them), strolled in and out of the New Arrivals' Centre. People-watching, Marjorie called it, when they'd sat there yesterday having lunch, but Archie had quickly become bored and today wasn't much better.

It was late afternoon, and Richard had just returned from the Evaluation Clinic after another series of tests. Ever since old Kripps – as Richard insisted on calling him – had discovered that Richard could communicate with Targa the Vikantu, he had insisted on personally carrying out more investigative tests to find out the extent of Richard's ability. Richard had told him about the dreams and the headaches he had experienced in the past. And that he *had* talked to Targa, even though Archie hadn't heard him.

Krippitz said he believed him, but that it was very rare for anyone, especially someone so young, to have such ability. He explained that only Brimstone, and a holy man who lived in a small village deep in the valley, were known to be able to communicate with the Vikantus, without actually writing anything down on paper.

Archie didn't really begrudge Richard getting special treatment, but his own evaluation tests had finished yesterday, and that seemed ages ago. Brimstone had told him that he should amuse himself until everyone else's tests had been completed. Amuse himself – doing what? he wondered. It would probably take another day before they were finished with Richard, and he'd hardly seen Uncle John or Marjorie for more than a few minutes. It was all very well, but there was nothing to do, or anyone of his own age with whom he could talk to or pass the time.

It wasn't just Richard and the tests. It was the days – *they were so long.* Although they used a twenty-four hour clock, the valley's time wasn't the same as on Old Earth. Somehow … it was much longer … it was as if time had been … *stretched.*

After the first day, they had all been advised to take a midday break and sleep for a few hours until they adapted to New Earth time. Although the others seemed to manage it, Archie found it impossible to keep his eyes closed for more than a few minutes at a time. His mind was just too alive with questions about what was going to happen to them after they left Castle Amasia.

'I'm sorry, Archie, but Kripps says it's really important to do these extra tests,' said Richard, suddenly sounding very superior.

Archie burst out laughing; he couldn't help it, but he had to laugh at Richard's face – he looked so terribly serious.

'OK, OK, I know it's important; it's just that I was getting fed up being on my own. Look, let's go and see if we can find Uncle John and Marjorie, they might be in the dining room.'

They crossed the lawn to the end of the portico where a glass-panelled door took them through into a large room that reminded Archie of the smoking lounges he used to see in old photographs of London's grand hotels. Seated in brown leather sofas, below a crystal chandelier suspended by a long brass chain, were Uncle John and Marjorie talking to Brimstone.

'Ah, boys, you're just in time,' said Uncle John. 'Brimstone was about to explain the results of the evaluation tests. It seems we're to travel to Fort Temple tomorrow.'

Archie stared at the back of Brimstone's head, the grey ribbed metal a contrast to the human-like skin of his face. Acknowledging Archie's presence, the head quickly swivelled to greet him.

'Please join us.' His voice soft and soothing, Brimstone gestured to two high-backed chairs by a marble-topped table in front of him. 'I hope you and Richard have had a pleasant stay so far.'

Richard was fascinated by the way Brimstone's head worked, but Archie thought it was sick to see someone's head back to front. It was just like the plastic toy space-soldiers he used to play with when he was small. He used to twist the legs and heads in opposite directions for fun, but this wasn't nearly so funny.

'Uh … we're fine … uh … sir,' said Archie, feeling as if he had been caught off guard.

'You may call me Brimstone. Now let me present all of you with the results of your evaluation tests and what is proposed for your future in Timeless Valley.' Turning his head to Richard, he said, 'Dr Krippitz would like to carry out more specialised tests with Richard, but it will not affect what I have to say.'

He waited until Archie and Richard had settled into their seats before continuing.

'You will be pleased to know that your medical assessments show all of you to be in excellent condition, and your personal profiles indicate that you will be eligible, in due course, for Timeless Valley citizenship. Accordingly, the following recommendations have been made, which I hope will meet with your approval. Professor Strawbridge, Dr Shah is looking forward to meeting with you to discuss a position at the Timecrack Research Unit. Is that acceptable?'

'Indeed, it is.' The professor smiled and nodded enthusiastically. His initial misgivings of what might happen to them in this new world had, by now, worn off, to be replaced by scientific curiosity at what Dr Shah was trying to accomplish at the TRU. 'He was before my time, of course, but I've read of his work back on Old Earth, and his work on timecracks here is intriguing. I would very much like to meet him; but I can hardly believe he is here!'

'He certainly is here, Professor, and you will meet him soon. Now, I must ask if Miss Peoples is ready to meet Miss Harmsway?'

'Who is Miss Harmsway?' asked Marjorie, wondering what was in store if she said yes.

'She is the headmistress of Harmsway College, founded by her great-grandfather, Samuel Harmsway. You mentioned your work at Grimshaws on Old Earth, so it seemed appropriate to introduce you to the possibility of a position at the college. Do you agree?'

It seemed to Marjorie that she didn't really have any choice, besides which, her early apprehension had disappeared, and she was intensely curious to find out more about Timeless Valley and its inhabitants.

'Absolutely. When do I go?'

'As soon as Richard has completed his tests with Dr Krippitz, he and Archie will accompany you to Harmsway College. They, of course, need to continue their education, and arrangements have been made to admit them to the college.'

'And where will we live?' asked Archie.

He was feeling annoyed that *his* opinion hadn't been requested about going to this Harmsway place. Not that it would make any difference, but he couldn't help thinking they were all being pushed into something they knew nothing about.

Brimstone looked at him as if he had read his thoughts.

'You will stay at Harmsway, as will Miss Peoples – that is, if she confirms her position there.' He hesitated, and then glanced at all of them. 'Of course, to refuse a position or citizenship is possible, but that would be foolish.'

'And why would that be?'

The professor's voice had hardened, as if he perceived a threat.

'Do not be concerned, Professor Strawbridge; it is simply because all of you have revealed talents and skills that would be most welcome in Timeless Valley. You should understand that not everyone is offered citizenship. In fact, many New Arrivals are sent to other regions of Amasia that might be considered less attractive.' Brimstone stood up and looked at each of them in turn. 'However, all of you are perfectly free to leave the valley if you wish to settle elsewhere.'

The professor pushed himself up from the sofa and gazed steadily back at Brimstone. It was strange dealing with a non-human, whose actions were probably programmed, yet behaved in every way like a normal human being. His instinct was to trust him, but he knew he shouldn't let his enthusiasm in finding out more about Dr Shah's work obstruct his responsibility for the boys and Marjorie.

'As we have no knowledge of Amasia, we are hardly in a position to make a realistic choice on where to settle, are we? My main concern for the present is to see that everyone is well looked after, and as for the future ... well, I think we will leave the permanent decisions until later.'

'As you wish, Professor,' said Brimstone. 'Tomorrow morning, Aristo will take you to meet Dr Shah, and in the afternoon the boys and Miss Peoples will be escorted to Harmsway by Finbar. Richard will have finished his tests by then.' He arose from his seat, ready to leave. 'Also, I should tell you that as accepted citizens of Amasia, the language translation chips you received during your clinical assessments are now active.'

While he tried to take in all that Brimstone had just explained, Archie reached reflexively for the little implant that had been inserted into the back of his neck. It had been a painless procedure and he could find no trace of it under his skin. They had all objected at first, not knowing what was involved, but when it was explained that they would be living among many races with diverse languages, they had to admit it made sense.

Before Brimstone left, his icy-blue eyes brightened, as if a switch had just clicked, and locked onto Richard for a few moments, then without another word he left them and strode across the room to the portico door.

Richard watched him leave, giving Archie a sharp dig in the ribs.

'He spoke to me ... He said to be careful ...'

'Ow, stop that, Richard!' Archie rubbed his side, taking a step back. 'What are you talking about?'

Richard waited until Uncle John and Marjorie walked a few steps ahead of them towards the dining room next door, before whispering to Archie.

'Brimstone, he spoke to me … he said … "Be careful with your power, it is not given to everyone" … What did he mean?'

'How would I know? I can't hear him when he speaks to you!' Archie felt exasperated, but he knew it wasn't his brother's fault. He put his arm around Richard's shoulder and told him not to worry. 'I don't know what he meant. Let's forget it and go get something to eat, I'm starving.'

Marjorie turned and waved to them to hurry up.

'C'mon, slowcoaches – there's steak pie on the menu today.'

Archie suddenly found himself on his own as Richard dashed for the door. At least he's not too worried about his appetite, he thought.

*

The following morning, Richard's final test was underway. He was reclining in a deep padded couch, very much like a dentist's chair, with a soft plastic helmet encasing the top of his head, which was connected to dozens of thread-like cables that snaked across the floor to a series of wall-mounted screens. The nurse, Shona, who had prepared the helmet, explained he was undergoing a trance test that would enable them to see his dreams while he was asleep.

'Are you feeling relaxed, Richard?'

Shona's voice sounded hollow and far away, but Richard could see that Krippitz was nearby, doing something to the helmet. He was a tall, thin man with black and silver spiky hair and a hooked nose that supported glasses with thick round lenses. Richard thought he looked like a frightened parrot with his head bobbing back and forth. He nodded as he tried to tell Shona how he felt, but he found it difficult to say anything. His eyelids felt thick and heavy, and soon her voice had disappeared into a black void that left him suspended in a womb-like world.

'He's gone under, Dr Krippitz,' said Shona, checking a monitor linked to Richard's left arm.

'Good. Let's get started. I'll watch the screens.'

'Richard, can you hear me?'

Shona spoke softly, almost as if *she* were also going into a trance. Each word she uttered dropped slowly into Richard's subconscious like small pebbles into a pond, each sinking gently to the bottom.

Small and attractive, with coffee-coloured skin, Shona Kelly hailed from Jamaica, and had lived with her parents in a small apartment outside Kingston, near the hospital where she worked. Next to nursing, yoga was her passion, and every week for over five years she had run free evening classes in the local church hall for anyone interested in relaxation techniques. The psychiatric patients from the hospital especially had benefited, but no one with any sort of problem had ever been turned away, so it was no big surprise when she eventually took a break from the endless routine of work.

It was only because her mother had arranged a surprise two-week holiday in Florida, and wouldn't take no for an answer, that Shona finally agreed to the break. She'd refused to go at first, claiming that her patients couldn't do without her for so long.

'Nonsense!' her mother had shouted. 'And what about *us*, Shona, are we not entitled to some consideration?'

She had pointed out that none of them had had a holiday for years, so Shona had relented, knowing that her mother was probably right. Little did any of them realise that their plane would never make it to Florida.

As they flew unconcernedly to their destination, a storm of unexpected ferocity had spread throughout the Caribbean, forcing their flight far off its planned route. The pilot had fought desperately to stay on course, but one of the worst storms he had ever experienced had worsened, ripping open a timecrack that plunged the plane through a blue cloud, taking it and all its passengers into a new world. And in time, it would become just another statistic in the ongoing mystery of the notorious Bermuda Triangle.

Shona rarely thought of her old life in Jamaica, for she had enough to think about dealing with the constant flow of New Arrivals through the Evaluation Clinic. The traumas that many of them experienced travelling through timecracks were enough to keep her fully occupied, without worrying about the past.

Shona dimmed the lights and made a final check on the connections to Richard's helmet.

'Everything is fine, Dr Krippitz, we can proceed now. I'll guide him through the first few questions until we get some reaction on the screens.'

'Look, something is happening already!' said Krippitz.

'Shh! He must only hear my voice, otherwise he may become confused.'

'Yes – yes, but look!'

*

At first, only two of the screens were flickering, showing fragments of scenes outside the clinic, but within moments, all the screens had burst into life. One showed Archie and Marjorie standing in the portico talking to Finbar; another displayed the professor sitting at a desk, studying what seemed to be a drawing, while others revealed glimpses of strange-looking patterns for a few seconds before breaking up. One in particular lasted a little longer: it showed a group of men standing on a wall overlooking the sea, but before Krippitz could make sense of what he was watching, the image faded from the screen. He shook his head, as one by one, the images disappeared.

'This is amazing! He is able to see events beyond his own environment. These are not dreams – they are actual happenings! I wonder if he can choose what he *wants* to see.'

Soothingly, and taking her time, Shona asked a few more questions.

'Richard, can you see anyone else?'

Krippitz looked at the screens, but they stayed blank. Anxiously, he waited for a few moments, and then nodded to Shona.

'Ask him if he can see Brimstone.'

Richard must have heard him. Suddenly one of the screens lit up, displaying a picture of Brimstone and Targa standing near the Great Wall. They were examining one of several huge stone blocks that lay at the bottom of the wall where they had fallen centuries ago. Brimstone straightened and gazed upwards, as if he had seen something. He turned to Targa standing beside him and they both nodded silently.

The picture shimmered and disappeared, and in its place a message read: *Targa and I thank you for your thoughts, Richard.*

That's OK ... I was asked ...

Richard shifted restlessly in his chair, and the words faded, leaving the screen blank.

'He's coming round,' said Shona, 'I think we should finish now.'

'Incredible! The boy has the ability to see *and* communicate at great distances, using only his mind!'

Krippitz was elated. *The software I have spent years developing actually works*, he thought. *I can view and record telepathic thoughts!*

Shona detached the cables and removed the helmet, allowing Richard to awaken naturally before he left the chair.

'Well, Richard, that wasn't too bad, was it?'

Krippitz watched carefully as Richard rubbed his eyes, glancing around the room as if he were uncertain of his whereabouts. He realised the boy could be the key to unlocking one of the great mysteries of how the human brain and the mind worked. For years he had observed Brimstone and the Vikantus communicate telepathically, but neither had been prepared to reveal how this was done, in spite of his repeated requests to interview and examine them. Now he had Richard to work with, and who knew what he might learn.

'I feel sleepy ... and my head hurts,' said Richard.

'That will soon pass. Now, tell me, can you remember anything of your dreams while you were asleep?'

Krippitz was not ready to explain that the 'dreams' were, in fact, actual events in real time.

'I saw Brimstone ... but it was kind of fuzzy ... He was standing with Targa beside a big rock ...'

'Excellent. Did you see anything else?'

'No ...'

'Dr Krippitz, maybe it would be better to let Richard rest awhile before he answers any more questions.'

Shona feared that if they pushed too hard, more harm than good would be caused, and she didn't think Richard had fully recovered from his trance.

Irritated by Shona's intervention, Krippitz looked at her sharply, as if he might reprimand her, but thought better of it.

'Perhaps you're right. He has been here long enough, and I'm sure he has better things to do than listen to me asking a lot of questions, eh? In a few days, after you have settled in at Harmsway, you will come back and visit us?'

'I suppose so,' said Richard, wondering if it meant more tests.

Although it had been pretty exciting stuff at the beginning, and he did enjoy all the special attention he had received, it was starting to bore him, and now it was leaving him tired and headachy.

Thumppp! *Thumppp*!

A loud hammering on the clinic door interrupted them.

'Who is it?' called Shona, walking over to open the door.

'Ach, it's me – who else would it be?'

Finbar was hopping from foot to foot with his little fists bunched up ready to strike the door again just as Shona opened it.

'Weren't ye expectin' me? Sure, haven't I to take the boys to Fort Temple?'

'And no doubt you will be paying my father a visit?'

Shona was referring to the tavern her parents owned, where Finbar was known to spend a little too much of his free time. Her Irish father, who had come through the timecrack with Shona and her mother, had been a merchant seaman on a container ship. After arriving in Jamaica he had never left; not only fulfilling the ambition of many an Irishman to own a pub, but unique in that he repeated the feat in another world, in Fort Temple. He was fond of Finbar, probably because they shared an Irish background – and, of course, Finbar could tell a story or two and sing some of the old folk songs that her father enjoyed so much.

Another talent Finbar enjoyed was *not* minding his own business. Listening outside other people's doors was hugely entertaining, and it never ceased to astonish him what people got up to when they thought no one was looking or listening. Not that he understood half of what he heard, but he liked to think that knowing some of their secrets gave him an advantage over them.

Whatever it was he heard when he had paused outside the clinic door, it had got Dr Krippitz into a rare old state of excitement; something to do with Richard being able to see inside people's heads – *whoever heard the like of it*! Now that would be a story to tell his friends in Kelly's tonight.

*

Late that afternoon, Marjorie and the boys stood with Finbar on the hoverrail platform waiting for the next railcar to arrive.

Nearby, a group of off-duty Lancers were engaged in a heated discussion, with one of them shaking his fist in the air, so that no one could ignore what he was saying.

'We should not be here! *Every* Lancer should be in the Pirangas hunting those mad dogs!'

'What is he talking about?' asked Archie.

'He's angry they've not been allowed to join the hunt for Lancer Suntee's killers,' said Finbar. 'Aye an' I think he's right – it's a terrible thing that's happened. They should all be out there 'til they catch them.'

By now, practically everyone in Castle Amasia and Fort Temple had heard of the tragic events that had taken place at Snakespass Ravine. It was a worrying time, for the death of a Lancer and the lucky escape by another, was a reminder to the citizens of the valley how vulnerable they were to disease and undesirables coming through the timecracks.

'I thought there was only one fugitive,' said Marjorie.

'So did everyone else, but the trackers say there are two of them in the caves. An' if ye ask me, they'll never catch them if they get any deeper into the mountain. I can tell ye, when they were still diggin' in the old mines, many's a one got lost in there an' never came out again.'

Finbar went on to explain that the mountains held vallonium, the main energy source for the valley and Amasia, but the mining operations near Snakespass Ravine had closed down years before, leaving miles of tunnels and deep shafts that would never be used again.

Richard felt a shiver go up his spine as he thought about what it must be like to be trapped in a dark place with no way out. He remembered the time when two Spanish boys at the school had locked him in an old tool cupboard in a deserted garage, far enough away from the main building so no one could hear him shouting and screaming to get out. It had been stupid to fight back and call them names – they were just too big and powerful – but they had been calling him *el hombre de nieve,* the snowman, because of his fair hair and light skin, and he'd just had enough. They'd dragged him to the tool cupboard and squeezed him in with a lot of old oilcans and greasy rags, and locked him in. It was only the next morning when the teachers discovered he was missing, and that Archie couldn't find him, that they had carried out a search and found him fast asleep in the cupboard.

Now he thought of the fugitives lost somewhere in the caves with no chance of escape. It would be a horrible way to die; trapped in the dark with nothing to eat or drink. Maybe that's what the Lancers will decide to do; just seal the caves and never let them out.

Richard hated thinking about such things, but he couldn't shake the feeling that *he* too could end up trapped in a cave, with no hope of escape.

Chapter Twelve

The Hooded Figure

'Look, it's been there for the past few minutes – it must be in contact with trackers on the ground!'

Anton had been watching a scarlet Spokestar only a short distance away, hovering less than two hundred feet above the mountainside. The morning sun's rays filtered through the high branches of the pine trees into the cave, and now that it was daylight he knew the hunters would soon pick up their trail.

Suddenly a flock of birds, disturbed by horrible cat-like screeches and excited voices calling to each other, broke from the trees and flew past the Spokestar.

'Quickly!' hissed Anton. 'They have found our tracks – we must leave here *now*!'

*

For the next hour or so, a pale ghostly light lit the way as they stumbled and crawled their way through tunnels where pieces of rock had fallen from the roof, creating pyramids of rubble that made it almost impossible to get through to the other side. After a long torturous passage through yet another narrow tunnel they arrived at an opening carved out of the rock wall. Two large stone slabs supported another to form an arch in which both of them could stand upright, giving them space to stretch their limbs and look around.

Anton entered and saw that it was a large chamber that had been blasted out of the rock; a place cluttered with a variety of workmen's tools. Sledgehammers, picks, chisel, shovels, and tools not familiar to him, lay derelict on the floor near upturned empty boxes marked with explosive symbols. In the middle, a rock-boring machine fitted with a corkscrew ram straddled a narrow-gauge track that disappeared into a tunnel in the far wall. Obviously an abandoned mining operation from long ago, the whole place had a forlorn, ghostly feel to it, in spite of the light being a little brighter in here than the tunnel they had just left.

It was only because of the unusual glow cast by countless pinpricks of light scattered throughout the rock face in the tunnels, like a billion tiny stars in the night sky, that they had been able to see the way ahead. The light in here was stronger, emanating as it did from vein-like streaks in the rock. Anton approached the chamber wall and examined the rough cut edges of the veins more closely, touching them carefully, unsure if they would cut or burn him.

'What is it I wonder?' said Anton, dusting the rock with the end of his sleeve. 'It has a phosphorescent effect, but I think it is a material unknown to us.'

'Can we eat it?' asked Sandan, not caring if his sarcasm offended his brother.

He wasn't the slightest bit interested in Anton's preoccupation with rocks, not with his stomach churning and growling with hunger. He was exhausted, and he knew he couldn't go much farther without something to eat. Even capture by their hunters, who might feed them, would be better than this hellhole.

At least while in the cave they had been able to eat the wild berries that grew in profusion on the mountainside.

Curiously, though, the berries had had a strange effect that neither he nor Anton had experienced before. The large orange-coloured, strawberry-shaped fruit possessed a sharp tangy taste that temporarily revived their morale and energy, only to leave them despondent and listless afterwards. Fortunately, the mountain stream water was clear and refreshing, and it had helped Anton to wash away the worst of the berries' aftertaste, but Sandan's hunger had made him eat too many and now he felt worse than ever.

'No, we cannot, but I believe this rock is something very special,' said Anton. 'I've never seen anything like it, not on Earth or Mars.'

'This is madness! We could die in here, and you are inspecting *rocks*!'

'Shut up! We are not dead yet, and your whining every few minutes is not going to help –'

'*Aarghhhh*!'

Sandan's horrible cry and the fear in his wide-open eyes, made Anton whip round to see what it was that had frightened him so much.

For a brief moment Anton felt strangely unsettled, for he was not a man easily alarmed, but what he saw made him step back until he stood side by side with Sandan. Although his eyes had adapted to the strange light, it was difficult to see anything in detail, except for the black shadowy apparition that had stepped straight out of the rock wall.

'In God's name, protect us!'

Sandan, terrified by what seemed to him to be a creature from the depths of the mountain, had dropped to his knees, hiding his head in his hands, suddenly seeking refuge in a religion he had forsworn a long time before.

'Who are you? What do you want of us?' demanded Anton, stepping forward, his fists ready to strike if the strange figure threatened them.

'Do not be frightened; I mean you no harm. I have come to help you,' said the figure. The voice was muffled by a scarf that covered the lower half of the face, leaving only dark eyes partly hidden by a wide cowl, above a dark-coloured robe that trailed on the tunnel floor.

The strange figure, which Anton guessed to be a man, perhaps a crazy old cave hermit living in the mountain, spread his arms outwards to show that he was unarmed.

'Why would you help us? Where have you come from?'

'I can answer your questions, but before I do, we must leave this place quickly. You have done well to escape the Lancers so far, but their trackers are close, and they will not give up easily, especially when it is the killers of one of their own whom they seek.'

Sandan, a little recovered, stiffened, about to deny that he had killed anyone, but Anton grabbed him by the shoulder and pulled him to his feet.

'Don't say anything. He seems to know enough about us already. Besides, we really have no choice but to follow him, do we?'

The stranger nodded and beckoned them to come with him. Anton and Sandan approached cautiously to the spot where they first saw him appear and, as they watched, he slipped back into the rock wall. Anton moved closer and saw the cleft into which a man might go if he were slim enough, but could Sandan?

As he contemplated what lay beyond the narrow opening, Anton heard a horrible screech somewhere behind them that made his skin tingle.

'Come ... you must not waste time!' called the stranger, stepping into the opening. 'The trackers and the hunting cats are nearly here!'

'Go, Sandan! I'll push you through.'

Before Sandan could object, Anton stepped behind him and with a mighty shove pushed him into the opening.

'Aahh! I'll be crushed in here!' Sandan cried, finding himself stuck fast against a jutting rock.

'Give me your hand,' insisted the stranger, from the other side. 'I will pull you through.'

With one pulling and the other pushing, part of the rock crumbled, allowing Sandan to fall through the break. Anton followed with less difficulty, and discovered they were in a wide passage brightly lit by what he would come to know as vallonium lamps.

'Quickly, move away from the opening.' The hooded figure placed his hands on a great, man-sized wheel-shaped rock, and with a heave it travelled along a shallow channel until it came to rest against the space through which they had just entered. 'We are safe now, no-one can enter here while the stone is in place.'

Anton nodded his approval, relieved that they could make their own pace now, and not that of their hunters. He looked around and saw that the passage was man-made with unusual patterns cut into the rock face stretching in both directions as far as the eye could see.

'What is this place? Who are you?' asked Anton.

'I am Lotane, a prince of the Arnaks.'

'A prince of ...?'

Lotane held up his hands to ward off any more questions.

'Later. We have a long way to go, but you will learn in due course the purpose that has brought you here.'

Strange words, thought Anton, but he sensed that Lotane would say no more until he was ready. No matter, he could wait a little longer before making his next move.

*

For more than a mile they walked, every step taking them further into the mountain along an ancient passageway where the still musty air had hardly been disturbed for generations. Finally, they came to a halt before a set of steep wide steps that had been chiselled out of the dark brown rock. Anton and Sandan watched as the hooded figure, Lotane, ascended the steps to reach a heavy wooden door set back into a small cave-like depression.

'How much farther, Lotane?' called Anton, turning to have a look at his brother.

Sandan's face was wet with sweat, and his ragged breathing was laboured to the point of exhaustion.

'If we continue much longer, I will have to carry this ugly brute when he collapses!'

Lotane, on the top step, gestured for them to follow him.

'Come, my friends, we are here. On the other side you will be able to rest.'

Ignoring Anton's cruel tongue, Sandan staggered past him and painfully climbed the steps to join Lotane at the door. He walked slowly through to see a sight that made him whisper in astonishment at what lay before him.

'Where are we?'

They were in a huge cavern, the ceiling hundreds of feet above them. Large boulders lay scattered, like fallen soldiers on a battlefield, across a tiled floor that stretched out to a deep chasm spanned only by a narrow stone bridge. It wasn't a proper bridge, but a long flat pillar that had fallen away from the ruins of a collapsed building near the edge of the chasm. To their left, daylight and fresh air entered the grotto through numerous openings in the side of the mountain, and beyond the bridge the remains of a paved road led to what once might have been a large market square. Overlooking other ruined buildings was a majestic edifice, partly covered by a landslide of rocks and shale, where mighty stone columns once stood, now fallen from their plinths. In the middle of the structure, unaffected by the landslide, were great golden doors that lay open to a wide terrace and marble steps that curved gracefully downwards to the square.

'We are approaching the Sacred Temple of Arnak. I have had rooms prepared there where you can rest, and there is sufficient food and drink until I return.'

'Until you return?' queried Anton.

'Yes, I must leave you for a little while, but do not worry, you are quite safe here. No-one but the disciples of Arnak know of this place.'

Anton shook his head.

'No, I need to know more before you leave. We are lost in a strange land and you talk of things I know nothing about.'

Lotane hesitated for a moment then moved to a long marble bench untouched by fallen rock and gestured that they sit beside him.

'Perhaps you are right. I should tell you something of what has happened to you.'

He told them of timecracks and new universes. He told them of the Exploding Park and New Arrivals, and of the continent of Amasia and its people. He described the role of the Lancers from whom they had fled and how they were his people's mortal enemies. There was much more to tell, of course, but they would have to wait until he returned from work to which he must attend.

Anton's eyes narrowed as he listened to Lotane's story.

'You are trying to tell me we are in another world ... another dimension?'

'Yes, my friend, and you have already proven yourself to be a worthy adversary of the Lancers. It is a long time since they have met their match, and I and my followers have need of skills such as yours.'

'That may be –'

'Please, say no more. Both of you must rest now. I only need to know your names, and then I must leave, but I will return soon and tell you of my Lord Arnak and what must be done to restore his kingdom!'

As he spoke, Lotane's eyes betrayed a fiery zeal that made Anton doubt his sanity.

'Come, let me show you something,' said Lotane, leading them to the side of the cavern where there was a cave with a small opening, just tall enough for Anton to stand in and welcome the cool fresh breeze that swept in from the outside.

The cave overlooked a great valley of open fields and wide mountain terraces with rows of bushes that carried heavy clusters of the strange berries they had discovered and eaten. Tiny robed figures worked in the fields, while others tended the terraces just below a large brownstone building that rose from the side of the mountain, its walls lined with small cell-like windows.

'This place and far beyond has come to be known as Timeless Valley,' said Lotane, 'but it is truly the land of the Arnaks, and someday soon, it and the Sacred Temple we now stand in will be restored to us.'

He stood with his left arm stretched out, pointing towards the valley. Like an ancient biblical prophet, thought Anton.

Lotane's eyes were ablaze as he continued.

'The Salakins are our enemies – and the Lancers are Salakins, so we will fight them together!'

His muffled voice had started to rise, but he suddenly stopped and then quickly stalked away from Anton and Sandan, back into the cavern.

This mad creature is a religious fanatic, thought Anton, but the uncertainty of what might happen to them made him hold his tongue.

Could it *really* be that they had entered another dimension? If so, then his conviction that he had a destiny to fulfil must be true. To have voyaged so far and to have endured so much seemed to Anton to be a vindication of all that he believed, but did his destiny lie in this new world, or would he have to find a way to return to Old Earth?

As Anton considered their situation, he looked across the valley and saw in the distance a yellow bullet-shaped train speeding towards a tunnel in the mountain. He watched it until it disappeared from sight, and then turned to make his way to the Sacred Temple.

Chapter Thirteen

The Railcar

'Finbar, how long will it take to get to Fort Temple?' asked Marjorie.

'Ach, this contraption is so fast ye hardly have time to think. We'll be there in no time at all,' said Finbar.

They were seated together, opposite Archie and Richard in a comfortable railcar as it sped along the hoverrail towards the city. The off-duty Lancers occupied some of the other seats, with one of them still talking loudly about the hunt for the fugitives, to the annoyance of some of the other passengers. It made no difference to Archie, who was thoroughly enjoying the ride after being cooped up in Castle Amasia.

'Don't you like the railcar,' asked Archie, grinning as he watched the little man's feet tapping the floor nervously.

'It's all right for them in a hurry – an' there are too many of *them*, if ye ask me.' Finbar scratched his nose as he thought about it. 'I'd rather have my horses from the oul country, but there's not much chance of that.'

He sounded so mournful that Marjorie felt sorry for him.

'What happened to you, Finbar? Did you come through a timecrack on your own?'

'Hah! It was a night I'll never forget. Wasn't I mindin' my own business, headin' home to the cottage, after a night with the lads in the village when the storm broke. It was as if the divil himself had come out of Hades itself to take me!' Finbar shook his head at the memory of it. 'I've been here nigh on a hundred years, an' there's still no sign of anyone goin' back.'

Archie stared incredulously at Finbar as he told his story. He was still finding it hard to believe that everyone here was *so old*.

'But isn't that what happened to Aristo? Don't they have a machine to send people back?'

Although he had overheard Benno Kozan talking about the problems encountered during Aristo's journey, he wondered what Finbar might know. He suspected that the little guide had a pretty good idea about a lot of what went on in Timeless Valley. And he couldn't help thinking that there must be a way back that no one had yet discovered. Maybe if Uncle John was going to work with Dr Shah to find it – and *maybe* with all his knowledge about energy research at the Facility – they would find the way even more quickly.

'Ach, so they say, but they'll have to make it work a lot better than it did for Aristo. I don't fancy endin' up with the dinosaurs like he did!'

Finbar grunted as if that settled the subject, and made it clear he had nothing more to say on the subject. He twisted himself into a more comfortable position, with his feet landing on the seat beside Archie.

Neither do I, thought Archie, but sooner or later they had to find a way to travel back to Old Earth safely. He didn't want to be stuck in Timeless Valley when he hadn't yet discovered what had happened to his parents back home. Deep down, he *knew* they were still alive, and he would never, ever, give up until he found them. Although he didn't know how, he had a feeling Richard's visions were going to help.

He turned to look at Richard, who had been sitting quietly, staring through the window, not saying a word.

'Are you OK, Richard?'

'Yeah … I was just looking at the mountain … I thought I could see a hooded man in a cave up there.'

Richard still sounded a bit sleepy, and nobody said anything until Finbar broke the silence with another grunt.

'Ach, he's dreamin'! He's been watchin' the monks up at the monastery gatherin' stickleberries on the terraces, an' they're all hooded, aren't they?'

Archie looked out at the brownstone building perched on the side of the mountain. Finbar was right; there were hooded figures on the terraces collecting and tossing berries over their shoulders into wicker baskets strapped to their backs. But he wondered if Richard had 'seen' something. He no longer doubted that Richard did experience visions, strange as it might seem to others.

He ignored what Finbar said, and asked: 'What are stickleberries?'

'Stickleberries? For makin' Sticklejuice — what else?' said Finbar, wondering about their ignorance of one of life's great pleasures. 'Ach, ye've never tasted anything like it. The monks make it up there at the old monastery then export it all over Amasia as a valley tonic — but it's the stuff in the barrels ye want to try. It's as good as any brandy ye'll find anywhere!'

Finbar obviously had a liking for Sticklejuice, but Archie couldn't think of anything he was less likely to try. He looked at Richard again and saw him still staring back at the monastery.

'Hey, wake-up, sleepyhead! Finbar says we should try the Sticklejuice — what do you think?'

'What?'

Richard looked startled. He obviously hadn't heard a word that had been said.

'Never mind' said Archie, deciding it would be better to leave him alone until they reached Fort Temple.

Suddenly, the compartment lights came on as the railcar entered a tunnel.

'Hah, we're nearly there,' said Finbar, bouncing up off the seat to make his way to the sliding doors. 'Follow me, an' don't be gettin' lost!'

A few minutes later the railcar slowed and came to a halt at a crowded platform. The doors slid open and as they stepped out they were immediately pushed and shoved to one side by the oddest mixture of people Archie had ever seen.

Dark-skinned Salakin tribesmen wearing long, saffron-coloured woollen coats, breeches tucked into leather boots, their hands resting on fierce-looking knives held by a broad belt, muttered greetings to their kinsmen, the Lancers, as they passed by. Tall, golden-haired Vikantus in their colourful robes smiled silently as they boarded the railcar, and a dozen or so New Arrivals still wore clothes that hinted at their origins on Old Earth.

'Where are all these people going?' wondered Marjorie, out loud. She shoved her way through the crowd alongside Finbar and the boys.

'Ach, who knows? Salakins back to their villages, others to Sitanga or Port Zolnayta – could be anywhere,' said Finbar.

He was more impatient than ever, his little feet moving as if on springs and his elbows working like pistons clearing a way through the crowd until they reached the end of the platform.

A sign over the metal exit gate proudly proclaimed:

WELCOME TO FORT TEMPLE

THE CITY OF SAINTS AND WARRIORS

'I don't think we qualify,' joked Archie, 'maybe we should try somewhere else –'

'Ye can stop yer bletherin', I'll not have us runnin' late,' interrupted Finbar, clearly not in a mood for jokes or pleasantries.

Marjorie raised her eyebrows and winked at the boys.

'OK, Finbar, you're the guide – show us the way.'

Giving her a sour look, Finbar shrugged and shook his head at their nonsense, and took them through the gate into the city.

Chapter Fourteen

Harmsway College

The first thing Archie noticed as they left the hoverrail station was the crazy mix of buildings that lay spread out before them.

Huge, golden onion-domes across the city skyline gleamed in the bright sunlight, competing with the tall glass pyramids that reflected streams of puffy white clouds drifting across a brilliant blue sky. Bright red pagodas with their gold and green terraces supported dozens of large, stone jars filled with a profusion of colourful plants. There was even a windmill on a far-off hill with its great wooden blades turning in the gentle breezes that swept down from the mountains and through the city. Every nation and culture from Old Earth seemed to be represented here, thought Archie, a little wistfully.

The station, situated on the side of the mountain, offered a panoramic view of Fort Temple, from the cobblestone streets that ran higgledy-piggledy all the way down from the station until they joined a wide, tree-lined boulevard in the centre of the city. Adjoining the boulevard was a large square where he could see people standing in queues, waiting to board several buses below different destination signs.

It was a crazy hotchpotch of a city that had evolved over nearly five thousand years, with many of its citizens the descendants of the people who had fled the plague and the fall of Castle Amasia. The quaint two-storey houses and tradesmen's shops that lined the streets were just like the ones they had seen on the way to the New Arrivals' Centre, except that people now lived and worked in them.

'It's … breath-taking! Archie … Richard … isn't it fabulous?' Marjorie could hardly contain herself at the thought of exploring such a wonderful place. 'Look! Over there – it looks just like the Eiffel Tower!'

The tower, like many other similar structures that had been reconstructed in Fort Temple, was near enough an exact replica of the original on Old Earth, giving the city and its inhabitants a curiously cosmopolitan feel. Thousands of years of continued occupation had left its mark, with the ruins of old churches and minor temples scattered across the landscape. Many of its people still wore robes in a style that dated back to the days when the ancient tribes ruled the area, long before Timeless Valley received its name.

Archie raised his eyes at Richard. *What are we supposed to say? That everything is fantastic?* Marjorie seemed to be treating everything as a big adventure, like an expedition to the Himalayas or some sort of journey to a long lost city. Archie couldn't afford to think like that – not while his parents were still missing, and not before they had found a way back to Old Earth.

It was Finbar who answered her, brusquely.

'Ye'll have plenty of time for sightseein' later. We've a bus to catch, so let's be goin'.'

Rushing ahead, he led them into one of the old cobblestone streets, past shops selling all manner of goods. There were shoemakers, booksellers, herbalists, pottery shops and tailors, just to mention a few; and in the middle of the street, a little man smaller than Richard was selling strange wolf-like cubs with hairy coats that looked like wood bark.

'The Rooters rear them in the Screamin' Forest – nasty bad-tempered brutes ye want to stay away from, if ye ask me,' warned Finbar, skipping around the little trader.

Ignoring Richard's plea to explain what he meant by the strangely named forest, Finbar marched them down to the square past an open-air cafe advertising thick dino burgers with chips. A few doors away a nightclub offered exploding cocktails and all-night entertainment. Next to it, they came to a halt outside a brightly painted, emerald-green tavern with a sign above the door that declared it was:

KELLY'S TAVERN
'A NEW DIMENSIONAL EXPERIENCE WITH THE BEST FOOD & STICKLEJUICE IN THE VALLEY'

Small metal tables with green tablecloths and gold-coloured chairs decorated with shamrocks and Irish harp designs had been pushed across the pavement, effectively barring their way.

'What's this, Kelly?' shouted Finbar, to a big heavy-set man standing with his back to them. 'Are ye not satisfied with the premises ye have that ye need the whole street as well?'

Kelly, who was scratching what little carrot-red hair he had left, was staring at a curious sight: at least half a dozen of his chairs and tables were jammed together into the space where the glass in the window used to be.

'Finbar, you wee rogue!' Kelly turned round and grabbed Finbar by the shoulder, pointing to the window. 'Look at what your Russki friends did to my place last night!'

'*My* Russki friends? What the divil are ye talkin' about, ye big wallop?' demanded Finbar.

'The Russian whalers who were in the clinic the other week. Our Shona told me about them. She said they were a bad lot, and she was right!'

'Russian whalers? They should've been in Port Zolnayta a week ago,' said Finbar. 'Brimstone posted them to a ship just in from the Icefields – sure wasn't I there when he did it?'

'Well, you can see for yourself where they were last night!' roared Kelly, his puffed-up red cheeks nearly at bursting point. '*And* I can tell you, I'll be taking it up with the Council of Elders to see that Brimstone takes better control of the New Arrivals that he lets into the city!'

'Ach, ye great windbag, ye can tell him yerself when next ye see him,' said Finbar. 'I've no time to be stoppin' here when I've my duty to attend to. I'll be in tonight, so I'll be expectin' my usual seat.'

Before Kelly could say another word, Finbar turned abruptly, leaving him to sort out the problem of what to do with his window. He gestured to Marjorie and the boys to follow him.

'Let's be goin', the bus'll not wait.'

'What was all that about?' asked Marjorie, as they walked to the square. 'It looks as if a riot took place back there.'

'Ach, Kelly probably robbed the whalers blind, seein' as they were New Arrivals, an' then the juice got the better of them an' they objected. Hah, I'd have given my right arm to see Kelly tryin' to sort them out,' cackled Finbar. 'It must have been a great commotion there last night!'

'Where did they get the money from?' asked Archie, as the thought occurred to him. 'Old Earth money isn't any good here, is it?'

'Weren't ye told?' said Finbar, shaking his head again at their ignorance. 'Dependin' on yer evaluation at the clinic ye get an allowance until ye can earn yer keep. Ye'll get whatever yer entitled to at Harmsway.'

'Finbar, that man Kelly mentioned the Council of Elders,' said Marjorie, trying to keep up with him.

'What are they? They sound terribly important if he's going to complain to them about Brimstone.'

'Will ye never stop askin' questions?' answered Finbar, scratching his chin. 'It's like a parley-ment I suppose ye'd call it. It's them that make the rules for runnin' the valley an' whatever else they've a mind to do. They represent the three cities an' all the villages in the valley from here to the sea, an' beyond the wall to the Riverlands. Probably linin' their pockets most of them, if ye ask me.'

Shaking his head at what the Elders might be up to, Finbar brought them to the first of the bus stops at the side of the square below a sign:

THE FREEBUS
FINAL STOP - HARMSWAY COLLEGE

'Hey, look at that, it's an old double-decker!' said Richard as a red omnibus pulled in beside them.

'Yeah, it is,' said Archie, stepping on board the open platform at the back of the bus, 'except it doesn't have any wheels and it doesn't have a driver!'

'Yer right,' said Finbar. 'Henry Spokestar said ye didn't need drivers; he said there were more accidents with them than without them.'

He boarded the bus ahead of them as a female voice announced:

'Welcome to the Freebus. Please state your destination.'

'Harmsway College,' shouted Finbar, unaware that the bus welcome system didn't need him to shout so loud.

The Freebus looked the same as the double-deckers Archie had seen in old postcards of London. But that was on the *outside* – inside, it was quite different. Besides not having a driver or wheels, there were also the floating seats; as far as Archie could tell, there were no structural supports – the seats just ... well, floated!

At the front of the bus Archie noticed a plaque that read:

THE FREEBUS
PRESENTED TO THE CITIZENS OF FORT
TEMPLE
BY THE SPOKESTAR CORPORATION IN
MEMORY OF ITS
FOUNDER: HENRY SPOKESTAR.

'Y'know, this Spokestar guy must have been a brilliant engineer. This bus is amazing!' said Archie.

Both boys chose window seats as they watched other hover vehicles entering and leaving the square.

'Indeed he was, young man,' said a voice with very precise tones, each word selected and polished as if a pearl of wisdom was being gifted to the recipient.

Its owner, wearing a black suit with a short shoulder cape, allowed his seat to swivel until it was facing Archie and Richard. If he had been standing he would have stretched to over six feet; instead, he lay back in his seat with one leg crossed over the other, a monocle over his right eye, and carefully stroked a well-trimmed silver moustache with long slender fingers.

'The man was a genius and, *yes,* he was probably the greatest engineer in Amasia's history. Unfortunately, he is no longer with us, but his Unified Antigrav Principle will be his everlasting legacy – as you are now experiencing on this bus.'

Neither Archie nor Richard said a word. They just sat in silence as the Voice (Archie couldn't think what else to call him) continued to regale them with facts and figures on the wonderful achievements of Henry Spokestar.

'His factory in Sitanga is the most interesting place you could hope to see. In fact –'

'Uh, excuse me …uh, sir … but … who are you?'

Archie had heard enough. He had been on the bus for half an hour or more and he'd hardly seen the city they were passing through, and he didn't want to hear any more about the theory of the Uni Anti thingamajig, or whatever the heck it was called. Richard had the right idea; he'd pushed his nose up against the window and simply ignored what the Voice said, and Finbar had conveniently gone to sleep soon after the bus had left the square.

'Ah, yes, of course ...' the Voice stumbled, for the first time, obviously not used to being interrupted, 'you are quite correct, young man; I have not properly introduced myself.' He sat up straight and said, 'I am Major Ramstiff, Head of the Department of Orientation at Harmsway College, and ... ah ... I see you are with Finbar the Guide. No doubt he is escorting you and your friend to the college.'

'*Humphhh!*' muttered Finbar, opening one eye, and just as quickly, closing it again.

Archie reckoned that Finbar had heard Major Ramstiff's boring monologues before, and had decided going to sleep was the best option. Richard was still glued to the window and Marjorie, wisely, had taken a seat near the front of the bus to get a better view, so he was the only listener. What suddenly worried him was the major's announcement that he was the head of some department. Did that mean he was going to be one of Archie's teachers?

Oh, no! Maybe it would be a good idea to show some interest in what the major is talking about, thought Archie. There was no point in getting on his wrong side, especially, if he *was* a head of something at Harmsway.

'Er ... Major Ramstiff ... what *exactly* is Orientation?'

The major sat in his floating seat, polished his monocle with a navy, polka-dot, silk handkerchief, and took a closer look at the boy sitting in front of him who had asked such a sensible question.

'Very good. Yes indeed, after all, at what better point can one start than your very question?'

Major Ramstiff was in full flow. He proceeded to explain that Samuel Harmsway, the founder of the college, had established the Department of Orientation over four hundred years before, when he realised that New Arrivals were wandering around Amasia in aimless confusion, unaware that they had penetrated a timecrack, and were trying, sometimes for years, to find towns and places that did not exist.

'For centuries, thousands of poor souls were passing through timecracks and then going off in different directions only to find themselves in very difficult, if not dangerous, circumstances. Needless to say, many of them didn't survive the experience.' The Major polished his monocle again and made a sweeping movement around the bus with his arm. 'This is a wonderful country full of opportunities for young men like you, but it is not without its risks, especially for the unwary who are untutored in its customs; hence the Department of Orientation.'

He replaced his monocle and peered at Archie like a one-eyed goldfish, to see if he understood. Archie nodded, remembering how easily their experience in the Exploding Park could have ended more disastrously than it did. Suddenly, a thought occurred to him.

'Do all New Arrivals end up in the Exploding Park, Major Ramstiff?'

'Sadly, they do not. If only they did, it would be easier to keep track of them. No, a small number do end up elsewhere, depending on the strength of the timecrack, or, at least that's what the scientists at Mount Tengi tell us.'

'And does everyone go to Harmsway?' asked Archie.

'My goodness, no! Only the children selected to stay in Fort Temple, and those adults who choose to pursue their careers here. All the rest are dispersed according to Brimstone's evaluations. We are really quite exclusive at Harmsway, you know!'

'Stein's Museum of Interdimensional Art'

They were interrupted by the welcome system as the bus stopped outside an extraordinary building made up of glass cubes and spheres, each connected to the other by a series of spiral stairways enclosed inside stained glass tubes.

Several passengers Archie hadn't paid any attention to before now left their seats to exit the bus. They looked like students, most of them carrying art portfolios. He watched them enter the unusual-looking building as Major Ramstiff continued to explain.

'You see, not everyone is qualified to stay here. You should appreciate that you are quite fortunate to be accepted for –'

'What's Interdimensional Art?' asked Richard, suddenly taking an interest in the strange-looking building into which the students were going.

The major stared at the smaller, fair-haired boy who had just had the temerity to interrupt him. Unlike the older boy, he thought, not as well mannered. Ah, well, we'll see about that at Harmsway, he decided.

'I'm told it's about discovering new art forms in a multidimensional universe. A very creative discipline, they say, but it's not really to my taste,' he said sniffily. 'Later, when you graduate from Harmsway, you will have a choice of the arts at Stein's, or the sciences at the Vallonium Institute …'

When we graduate! We won't be here that long, Major Ramstiff! thought Archie. Not while mum and dad are still missing. Somehow we're going to find a way back to Old Earth and discover what happened to them.

As the major droned on with more facts and figures about the valley, Archie's mind churned with possibilities about how they might return to the Facility or Grimshaws – anywhere – as long as it was back home. After a while he dozed off into a dreamless day-sleep until he awoke with a start as the bus made a sudden turn to leave the main road.

The bus passed through a massive set of black iron gates that gave entry to parkland on the edge of a great lake. The road meandered for several miles before approaching a river spanned by two, narrow stone bridges, one leading to the college, the other out. As they crossed the inward bridge, Richard suddenly sat up and gripped Archie's arm. He pointed through the window.

'*Look*!'

Archie looked and his mouth dropped when he saw what Richard was pointing at. On the far side of the school playing fields was a sports arena surrounded by several tiers of bench seats, which meant they couldn't actually see the pitch, but it didn't prevent them from seeing the players. A team of boys, outfitted in strange sports gear, were playing in mid-air! They were zooming back and forth swiping at a small tennis-sized ball using baseball-style bats, but with flat ends.

'What are they doing?' cried Richard.

'… and the Harmsway estate is now administered by the Council of Elders – what's that, my boy?'

Major Ramstiff was still talking, apparently unaware that Archie had been asleep for the past half-hour, and he would have happily continued his monologue if he hadn't been interrupted.

'Those boys ...' said Archie, now wide awake, but not knowing how to describe what he saw.

'Oh, the boys are playing zimmerball. That will be one of the house teams practising. Now, as I was saying ...'

The major told them nothing more about zimmerball, much to their disappointment, but insisted on boring them with more facts and figures about Amasia until, thankfully, the bus drew up in front of a large building near a carved stone archway.

'*Harmsway College. Final Stop*,' intoned the welcome system.

Finbar was the first to leave the bus. He called impatiently for the others to follow him through the archway into a large quadrangle.

Marjorie took her time, as something was nagging her, something about the building. When she reached the quadrangle she turned and looked back, giving a little gasp of delight when her eyes took in the great archway with its five tiers of double columns.

'It can't be!'

'Ah, I take it you know Oxford then?' said the major, coming up behind her, watching her confusion turn to recognition.

'Know it? I *graduated* there and this is the college quadrangle!' Marjorie's eyes were wide open as she took in the splendour of the seventeenth-century architecture. 'How did it get here? Surely not through a timecrack?'

'Of course not! It's a replica of the original building. The Vikantus built it to Samuel Harmsway's specifications, but it wasn't finally completed until some years after his death. It's not entirely accurate, I'm afraid, but near enough. It was his way of maintaining a link with Old Earth and his time at Oxford.'

While Marjorie continued to stare in amazement at the archway and the adjoining buildings around the quadrangle, Archie felt Richard jerking his sleeve and motioning towards a figure about to join them.

'I wonder who that is? She looks like a witch.'

If Miss Harmsway had been wearing a proper witch's hat instead of a black headband studded with pearls, which held back thick silver hair that fell to her shoulders, it wouldn't have looked out of place with the black robes she wore. As she approached the New Arrivals, the steely look in her green eyes and the crisp manner of her stride suggested she might be a very formidable lady.

'Welcome back, Major Ramstiff. I hope you enjoyed your trip to the city? Ah, I see our friend Finbar the Guide has brought the Kinross children to us.'

Archie frowned at the word *children*, but she continued.

'And you will be Miss Peoples? I am delighted to see you here; your assistance will be much appreciated, my dear. Oh, Finbar, will you see the boys to their rooms before you leave? Perhaps they would like to day-sleep before they do anything else and, maybe, Miss Peoples, you would like to rest as well? Yes, of course, and now just a few words before we part, on the subject of school regulations...'

Archie could only gape while Miss Harmsway rattled on and on about what you could and couldn't do, hardly taking a breath and seemingly oblivious to the incredulous looks of Archie and several other new students who had also just arrived on the Freebus.

'I do hope I have made myself quite clear – *where is that boy going?* Please tell him not to wander while I am speaking!'

Miss Harmsway directed a long stick-like finger in Richard's direction. He was walking towards a massive stone slab sitting in the middle of the quadrangle, and didn't hear Archie calling after him.

'*Richard!*'

Richard paid no attention and climbed up onto the slab. By the time Archie reached him he had closed his eyes and was standing still in a shallow trough in the centre of what seemed to be a great stone wheel. Its outer rim was decorated with twelve weatherworn animal and human-like figures, which led in segments to the trough that had been carved in the centre of the stone.

Oh no! Not again! Richard had gone into another trance and Archie didn't know what to do about it. It was occurring so frequently now he was worried that something serious was happening to Richard, although in the past he had seemed perfectly all right when he came out of a trance.

Archie ran over and climbed up onto the stone slab. He put his hand gently on Richard's shoulder.

'Wake up, Richard! *Please* ... wake up!' pleaded Archie.

'He has the second sight, that one!' said Finbar.

He and the others had followed Archie and were standing around the stone looking up at the two boys, just as Richard opened his eyes.

'What's wrong? Why is everyone staring at me?'

Richard's voice was shaky as he rubbed his eyes and looked around the quadrangle. Archie led him to the edge of the slab and they jumped down.

'I dunno. You suddenly left us to come over to this thing.'

'Archie ... I heard voices ... one of them sounded like mum's ...'

'I'm telling ye, he has the second sight –'

'Oh, be quiet, Finbar!' said Miss Harmsway. 'I would be grateful if you would keep your Celtic superstitions to yourself. The boys probably need their day-sleep, so perhaps you would be good enough to show them to their rooms in Prade House before you return to Castle Amasia.'

Dismissing Finbar with a wave of her hand, Miss Harmsway excused herself and said she would see them later at supper in the main hall. As she left the quadrangle, her black robe swirling around her, Major Ramstiff spoke quietly to Archie, as if he didn't want anyone else to overhear what he said.

'It's interesting that your brother should have his little ... *episode* ... on this spot.'

'Why, what's so special about it?' asked Archie suspiciously, turning to see if Richard was listening, but he was walking around the huge slab examining the carvings.

'It's actually quite rare and is thought to have special powers,' said the major, tracing his fingers across the stone. 'Father Jamarko at the old monastery is something of an expert on these things, and he believes the stone is an ancient sacrificial dish that was used by one of the tribes who lived here thousands of years ago. He's also convinced that another stone lies in the ruins of the temple somewhere below the monastery. He's been searching for it for years.'

'The temple?'

'Yes, the Sacred Temple to be precise. The city of Fort Temple is named after both it and a fortress that was built at a later date on the site where the monastery stands today.'

Archie looked at the strange symbols that had been carved into the stone so long ago.

'But what did you mean by Richard having something to do with it?'

'Well, I'm not really sure, but Father Jamarko believes the stone was used in religious rituals to appease a god known as Zamah – one can only imagine how they carried out their sacrifices! However, and this is the interesting part, he says the stone was always placed where Zamah's followers believed it would be at its most powerful. So powerful, in fact, that it induced a trance in the sacrificial victim. Others, like the scientists at Mount Tengi, say there is evidence that a stone might well be found over extensive vallonium deposits.'

Richard rejoined them and Major Ramstiff refrained from saying anything more about the mysterious stone wheel. He left, reminding them to be on time for their first class in the Department of Orientation.

Archie watched him leave the quadrangle, his mind more alive than ever and churning with questions about Richard and the stone.

Chapter Fifteen

Kelly's Tavern

If there was one thing that Finbar couldn't abide, it was old women trying to tell him what to do. He'd had enough of that as a boy growing up in a small village on an island off the coast of Ireland. Besides his mother, there had been plenty of aunts, neighbours and his teacher, all of them old women who had been too fond of giving him advice on how to behave, or worse still, some chore he had to carry out before he could have any supper.

'I tell ye Kelly, old interfering women are a great pain to any man,' said Finbar, enjoying his third twenty-year-old Sticklejuice with all the appreciation of a man who thinks he's had a long hard day.

As soon as he had seen the Kinross boys settled in, he had left Harmsway and made his way directly to Kelly's Tavern. His favourite seat in a snug at the end of a long mahogany bar had been empty and he'd curled into it like a lazy cat, as if nothing, bar an earthquake, would shift him for the rest of the night.

He looked around the room and nodded appreciatively. Kelly had managed to restore the place to its usual smoky, smelly atmosphere in spite of the Russki trouble the previous evening. The window was boarded over and a heavy, velvet curtain had been drawn across it so that it wouldn't spoil the appearance of the place.

The tavern was crowded now with regulars and visitors, and Kelly was doing his best to serve them while trying to hear what Finbar was saying.

'What are you complaining about now, you miserable rogue?' bellowed Kelly, from across the bar.

'Ach, that old woman at Harmsway, she would have ye chasin' yer tail if ye let her,' grumbled Finbar, taking another long sip of Sticklejuice.

'Now, don't be too hard on Miss Harmsway, she does a grand job at the college. It's the envy of the rest of Amasia, and there are not too many men who could run it as well as she does.'

'Ye may well think so, Kelly, but she has the look of the witch about her, an' she had the nerve to say I was superstitious!'

'You're complaining about the kettle calling the pot black!' exclaimed Kelly, laughing. 'So what was it, did her black cat cross your path?'

'Not the divil of it!' said Finbar, his voice getting louder as the twenty-year-old Sticklejuice loosened his tongue. 'I told her that the boy had the second sight, an' yer own daughter, Shona, knows the truth of it!'

'What are you raving about, you old fool?'

As none of Finbar's friends were in the tavern tonight, Kelly thought it best to humour him for a few minutes, so he listened while Finbar related the event concerning Richard on the big stone in the quadrangle at Harmsway, shortly after they had arrived at the college.

But Kelly wasn't the only one listening to Finbar's curious tale. A little earlier, two swarthy-skinned men, one fat and the other thin, had made their way to the bar, and as Finbar became louder in the telling of his story, the closer they moved to the snug.

'Innkeeper, another drink please!' called the thin one.

'Sorry, gentlemen, I was a little preoccupied with my friend in the snug,' said Kelly.

'Yes, I couldn't help but overhear. Is your friend a guide? If he is, we might be able to use his services while we are in Fort Temple,' said the thin one. 'Perhaps he would care to join us for a drink?'

'He's not a city guide, but he might be able to help you, and as for a drink, I've never known him to refuse one!'

Kelly poured the drinks and led the two men to the snug where Finbar was muttering to himself, his little feet hopping as restlessly as ever.

'Finbar, these gentlemen have very kindly bought you a drink,' said Kelly. 'They insisted on buying you the fifty-year-old juice, and you know there's little enough of it left in the cellar.'

Finbar's face creased with delight as he recognised the rare honey-coloured juice placed in front of him.

'Kelly, ye divil, I thought it was all gone!' He clutched the glass like a precious jewel and looked closely at the two men standing there. Ugly as sin, Finbar thought, but their generosity was not to be ignored, especially if they could afford the fifty-year-old. 'Sit down, gentlemen, and tell me what it is I can do for ye?'

'My name is Nitkin,' said the thin one, 'and this is my friend, Anakat. We are visitors to the city, and Mr Kelly mentioned that you are a guide.'

'Aye, I'm a guide all right, but I'm in the employ of Brimstone at Castle Amasia, not the city, so I'm afraid I'm not much use to ye.'

'No matter. Allow me to buy you another drink; you may be of more help than you realise.'

Nitkin was not an attractive man. His yellow crooked teeth and twisted nose did little for his sallow appearance, and when he smiled, not many people realised he was doing so. Unfortunately, his ugly nature matched his appearance, and he would just as quickly have strangled Finbar as buy him a drink. He hated New Arrivals with such venom that even his fellow

Arnaks, including his companion, Anakat, were worried that his temper might inadvertently betray their real purpose during their travels in Timeless Valley (or Hazaranet as they preferred to call it).

As two of Prince Lotane's spies, it was essential that they act discreetly while obtaining information that might be useful to their master. And Anakat realised that the little man they now plied with Sticklejuice had a curious story to tell, which could be of great interest to them.

Nitkin agreed. Curbing his natural instinct to reach across the juice-stained table and throttle the old fool, he continued throughout the rest of the evening to ply Finbar with more of the rare beverage until he fell into a drunken sleep. But by that time, Nitkin was satisfied he had dredged from Brimstone's guide all that he could about the boy with the second sight.

'A tiresome business, Anakat, but our master will be well pleased when he hears the news that we bring him.'

Part Three

The Legend of Arnak

Chapter Sixteen

The Sacred Temple

'Long before Nicolo Amasia discovered the continent that came to bear his name, more than two hundred tribes roamed across the land, known then as Hazaranet. Two of the largest and most important tribes were the Salakins and the Arnaks. They were descended from the Zamahonites, an ancient people who paid homage to a fierce demanding god they called Zamah.

'The Zamahonites were a savage warlike race and they ruled Hazaranet with an iron fist, showing no mercy or quarter to anyone who stood against them, but one day it came to pass that their enemies joined forces and attacked the kingdom. After a battle lasting many months, the invaders entered the city of Ka and killed the rulers and the high priests. Those who were not put to the sword were sold into slavery and sent to the far corners of the land, never to be heard of again.

'It is said that in their despair, the remaining Zamahonites cried out, asking why such a terrible thing had happened to them, and that Zamah answered by saying that it had been too long since the Ritual Sacrifice of a Shamra child

'The message was well learned by the succeeding tribes of Hazaranet and, in particular, by the Salakins and the Arnaks. They now ruled the kingdom together, a land that was rich in wildlife and mineral wealth, shared equally by the two tribes. It was also a land where strange happenings and terrible events took place, a land where mysterious beings arrived in thunderclouds from the heavens and spoke of other worlds. It was during such times when Zamah had to be *appeased that sacrifices became commonplace, but the Ritual Sacrifice of a Shamra child was still a rare event in Hazaranet.*

'And so it was, in the city of Ka, that when the people of both tribes heard that a sacrifice was about to be offered to Zamah, they would gather at the temple in the early hours of the morning before sunrise. Quietly, and fearfully, they would watch the twelve priestesses, dressed in white purple-hemmed dresses, take their places at the rim of the stone. As the victim was brought forward and placed in the central trough, some in the crowd would shout blessings, hoping that the ritual act would bring good fortune to Ka. As the eastern sun arose above the temple, the High Priest, wearing a brilliant golden robe, would move slowly to the centre of the stone, aware that the eyes of the crowd were upon him. Raising a double-handled stone sword, he would plunge the blade into the chest of the hapless victim, crying out: "Almighty Zamah, spare us the fate of the Zamahonites!"...'

*

'Ritual sacrifice? What damnable nonsense are you listening to now, Sandan?'

Anton's voice was loud in the lofty atmosphere of the cavern and it startled Sandan as he sat with Lotane on a marble-topped bench near the steps of the Sacred Temple.

'Anton – you're back!'

Sandan worried every time his brother ventured into Fort Temple. He feared Anton would be caught and that he would be left to cope on his own in this strange new world.

In spite of his fears – or maybe because of them – Sandan would sit and listen whenever Lotane chose to

156

visit them and tell of his tribe's history. Sandan, although a highly skilled administrator trained to be unbiased and clear in his thinking, was, nevertheless, a deeply superstitious person, much in the same mould as his Romany mother had been. Glad though he was that Anton had returned safely, he was disappointed not to hear more of Prince Lotane's story about the plight of the Arnaks.

'Ritual sacrifice!' Anton repeated the words and shook his head at the thought of such barbaric practices. All he had heard was the tail-end of Lotane's story, but he was annoyed that Sandan was taking such rubbish seriously. 'Can you not find other ways of spending your time, Sandan, than listening to such fairy tales?'

'Be careful what you say, Cosimo,' snapped Lotane, his hooded face muffling the anger in his voice. 'The history of my people is sacred, and someday soon the Legend of Arnak will come to pass.'

'Of what use is this to us?' demanded Anton. 'My only interest is in the glittering rock you call vallonium. I would like to learn more of its properties, and, in due course, how we might return to our own world!'

It had been ten days since their escape from the Lancers, and while they stayed hidden in the temple, Anton spent much of his time studying the unusual rock formations that produced the sparkling light. He had explored the deeper tunnels that led into the centre of the mountain and was amazed to find that the only illumination came from the rock itself.

He had also visited the Vallonium Institute and learned that the rock had been mined for thousands of years as a fuel for campfires, but it was only within the last two hundred years that a new secret chemical process, now controlled by a man called Benno Kozan, the institute's director, had led to a better understanding of the rock's limitless energy potential.

Visitors and students to the institute's public lectures were told that although the mysterious rock had, so far, only been discovered in Timeless Valley, it might well exist elsewhere.

Perhaps on Old Earth, thought Anton ... and if it did, imagine the power that would give him, for he would use the process to deal with the Consortium on *his* terms.

The question was: how would he obtain the secret process?

Anton knew that without Lotane's help, he and Sandan were trapped in this world. It was thanks to Lotane, who had provided him with the traditional sand-coloured trader's robe, which enabled him to travel freely throughout the city. It was the ideal guise, as there were hundreds of such traders from all over Amasia, many of them strangers to the authorities and the Lancers.

He had agreed to help train Lotane's Arnaks at a place called the Darklands for the day when Lotane would call them to arms, but that was a promise easily broken to a madman hell-bent on pitching his followers into a battle they were unlikely to win.

Yesterday, he had heard the gossip in Fort Temple's boulevard cafes that someone called Aristo had made the return journey through a timecrack. Somehow he would find a way to do the same, but in the meantime he would have to be tolerant of Lotane's fanatical ambitions.

Regretting his remarks, Anton was about to apologise when Lotane forestalled him.

'I understand your impatience, Cosimo, for I suffer from the same affliction, but I can assure you, it is in both our interests to wait for the right moment before we act. The Ritual Sacrifice is important to the Arnaks – without it we are lost!'

'I am sorry, Prince Lotane, if my clumsy words have caused you offence,' said Anton, bowing slightly to show humility. 'You are right, of course; I have become impatient and ungrateful. Please accept my humble apology.'

Sandan stared at his brother in surprise, for Anton never apologised to anyone for anything. Taking advantage of Anton's change of heart he turned to Lotane and asked: 'The Legend of Arnak – what is it?'

Prince Lotane nodded, and walked towards the great golden doors of the temple. He stood quietly for a moment, then spread his arms out wide as if to encompass the whole of the cavern.

'It is fitting that you should ask, for it is here at this very place that the legend began. It is written in the sacred scrolls that the people came in their thousands from all over Hazaranet to be here on the very day that the High Priest would read the proclamation that would condemn a temple priestess to death...

*

'Rumours abounded everywhere; people crowded together in little groups in the large square and on the wide marble steps that led to the temple. Never, in any of their lifetimes, had they heard of such a thing, and yet, the unthinkable was about to happen.

' "Who is she?" asked an old woman, hugging her robes to keep out the early morning chill.

' "I hear it is Verena, youngest daughter of the Chief Elder, Han-Beth of the Salakins," said a young woman carrying a small child clutched tightly to her bosom.

'Some in the crowd gasped when they heard this news. They knew that the Salakins and the Arnaks each provided the temple with their youngest daughters, six from each tribe, to be trained in the holy rituals dedicated to Zamah, but none thought that it would be a daughter of the Chief Elder who had broken her vows.

' "She'll suffer the stoning!" declared a fat red-faced man, to the horror of those standing nearest to him. "It's the only punishment for such sacrilege!"

' "But what did she do?" asked a stranger, newly arrived in the city.

' "She broke her vows and took a lover, that's what she did!" bellowed the fat man, making sure that all around him could hear his indignation.

'And so the gossip and rumours continued until, suddenly, there was a deathly silence that descended upon the crowd like an invisible cloak. The High Priest had just appeared on the uppermost step of the Sacred Temple in front of the golden doors. Behind him came a beautiful young girl, her sad brown eyes set in a pale face, partly covered by long black hair that fell to the shoulders of a dull red dress.

' "She wears the stoning robe," whispered the old woman, to no-one in particular, "and look, her father, Han-Beth, follows!"

'A murmur like the sound of falling leaves rose steadily among the people as they recognised the Chief Elder and his daughter, Verena, but they fell silent when the High Priest raised his hands to the sky.

' "People of Hazaranet, hear the words of Almighty Zamah, for he is greatly offended by one of his servants. She is Verena, daughter of Han-Beth, and she is brought here this day to hear the decision of the temple Elders. Such is her crime that only one punishment is acceptable to Zamah. Hear, people of

160

Hazaranet, that it has been decreed that before the sun sets, she will be taken to unholy ground outside the city wall where she will suffer death by stoning ... ".'

*

'But what about her lover, what happened to him?' interrupted Sandan, now totally absorbed by Lotane's story. 'Who was he – was he punished too?'

'His name was Lotane the First, son of Lord Arnak,' said Lotane, smiling, waiting for their reaction.

'The same name as you?' enquired Anton.

'Yes, I am directly descended from him. The firstborn son in each generation has been so-named since that time.'

'But what happened to him?' persisted Sandan, anxious to hear more of the story.

Lotane was patient, for he understood Sandan's curiosity. The history of this land was not that of Amasia, but of Hazaranet and its ancient tribes. It was a story of sacrifices and divided loyalties, and ultimately, of tragedy and revenge. It was a story that had to be told – and one that should be heard...

*

'When Lotane the First's father, Lord Arnak, became suspicious of his son's too close relationship with Verena, he prepared him for a diplomatic mission that would send him to one of the smaller tribes at the farthest reaches of the kingdom.

'While his son was away, Lord Arnak made it his business to question, not altogether too gently, the other temple priestesses about Verena's secret meetings with his firstborn and favourite son. When the terrified priestesses confirmed his worst fears, Lord

161

Arnak went into a terrible rage and blamed Verena for seducing his son into an unholy affair. He went directly to Han-Beth and demanded that he deal with his daughter in the manner prescribed by temple law.

'Verena confessed willingly to her father of her love for Lotane, thinking she might be released from her vows, but with a heavy heart Han-Beth knew that, although he was the Chief Elder, he could not do so. He had no choice, but to let the law take its course. So the stoning of Verena took place, and the manner of her death reached the ears of all the tribes in every part of Hazaranet.

'Verena's punishment was not enough for Zamah, for that very night he sent torrential rains that flooded the narrow streets of the lower city. Worse still, he made the mountain directly above the temple tremble like a waking giant until its rocks tumbled into the city, smashing through the thin brick walls of the houses where many of the men, women and children were killed as they slept.

'The people were distraught, and in their confusion they screamed out, wanting to know what it was that Zamah required. Was the stoning of Verena not enough?

'Her father, Han-Beth, knew that it was not. Only the Ritual Sacrifice of a Shamra child would satisfy the wrath of such an angry god, and in the entire kingdom there was only one child known to him as Shamra: that child was Rodin, the youngest son of Lord Arnak. Reluctantly, he made his way to the upper terraces where the palaces and the villas of the high-born were situated, as yet untouched by the disaster that had destroyed much of the lower city.

'Lord Arnak received the Chief Elder who, in recent days, seemed to have aged beyond his years, and listened to what he had to say about the Shamra. He knew only too well of the ancient practice of Ritual Sacrifice, which had not been offered up to Zamah for over one hundred years.

' "You know, My Lord, that it must be a Shamra child, a boy not yet thirteen years, who has the gift of dreams; one who can see the other world is believed to be a son of Zamah," said Han-Beth.

' "Yes, I know it well, and only Rodin, my youngest son, has such a gift. It has long been my fear that Zamah would demand his return to the other world – and now that day has come"

'So it was decided that the sacrifice would take place on the next holy day in two days' time. There was no more to be said. The two men sat in silence, thinking only of the dreadful events that Zamah had visited upon their children, but such are the ways of men and their gods that they had no idea that an even greater disaster was set to visit the city of Ka.

'At the same time, returning to Ka, with his father's business concluded, Lotane the First heard the whisperings from the roadside travellers fleeing the catastrophe that had befallen the city. Fearful of his anger, they pleaded ignorance and told him no more.

'Suspicious of what he had heard, and needing to learn the worst, Lotane rode at great speed to Ka, only to discover that much of the lower city was in ruins and that the mountain splitting itself asunder now threatened the Sacred Temple. When he learned of the death of Verena at the hands of the Elders he went into a blind, all-consuming rage, swearing he would destroy them and the temple.

'When his followers joined him, they attacked the temple and dragged the Salakin Elders, including Han-Beth, into the square near the sacrificial stone, and hacked them into bloody pieces. It was not long before the Salakins heard of the massacre and, enraged, they *vowed to hunt down and kill every Arnak they could find until the rainswept streets ran red with their blood.*

Inevitably, war broke out between the tribes. Lord Arnak was killed in his palace, and his sons, Lotane and Rodin, fled with their remaining followers to a distant territory, which they named Arnaksland, but in time became known to the Salakins as the Darklands.'

*

'So the Shamra child was never offered to Zamah?' said Sandan.

He was fascinated by Lotane's story. It appealed to his mystical Romany background, and he wished he could learn more about the mysterious Arnaks.

'No, my namesake was heartbroken, and he could not bear to lose his brother as well as Verena and his father,' said Lotane.

'Then, I take it, this happened?' said Anton, pointing to the temple ruins behind them.

'Yes, after the floods, Zamah destroyed the mountain and sent its mighty boulders to cover the temple so that it would not be seen by men again. It has lain hidden for over four thousand years and only a select few have ever found this cavern.'

'And this legend ... whatever it is, do you really maintain that it will come to pass after four thousand years?'

Anton was amused to think that such myths could be believed, but he kept a serious face to avoid causing further offence.

'It is but an instant in the eyes of Zamah,' said Lotane. 'My people have waited patiently for the coming of a Shamra child, to make amends for my ancestor's understandable error in not offering the sacrifice. The Legend of Arnak says that when a

Shamra child is sacrificed on the stone, Almighty Zamah will restore the Sacred Temple to the Arnaks – then we will drive the Salakins back to their villages and we will once again control the land of Hazaranet!'

The man is mad, thought Anton, to think that an ancient, barbaric practice would be sufficient to enable primitive tribesmen to take over a modern city like Fort Temple and the rest of the valley, all of which was patrolled by squadrons of Lancers. He had not met any of Lotane's followers yet, but with his knowledge of the long years of warfare in the New Europe Territories, he knew they would hardly be a match for the Lancers and their Spokestars.

He kept his opinion to himself. After all, he needed Lotane's help, and it would not do to upset him before he had formulated a plan to obtain the secret process from the Vallonium Institute.

Anton's thoughts were unexpectedly interrupted by the sound of someone slamming the heavy tunnel door. He looked across the chasm and saw two men, dressed like himself in traders' robes, enter the cavern and walk across the collapsed pillar bridge. One of them, a thin-faced ugly creature called out.

'Master! I have good news!'

'Nitkin! Anakat! You are most welcome, especially if you are able to confirm the news you gave me recently,' said Lotane.

'Yes, My Prince, I can indeed! Since my first meeting with the guide known as Finbar, I have met with him again to obtain more information about the boy,' said Nitkin, glancing suspiciously at the two strangers sitting with Prince Lotane.

'Come, my friends, I want you to meet Anton and Sandan, who fought bravely and escaped the Lancers, killing one of them and destroying two of their Spokestars. We have need of such men, and if your news is indeed worthy then our day of reckoning with the Salakins draws near.'

Lotane made the introductions, with Anton taking an immediate dislike to the two Arnaks, but he sat quietly while Nitkin described his latest meeting with Finbar.

'With his fondness for the valley juice, the fool talks quite readily about the boy. He says Dr Krippitz at the Evaluation Clinic has conducted many tests and is very excited by what he has discovered so far.' Nitkin hesitated, wanting to make the most of the moment, stretching out the last bit of news for his prince to savour. 'He says, he has heard the boy can communicate with the other world!'

'Almighty Zamah!' cried Lotane. 'If this is true then our time has come! His age – is he still Shamra?'

'Yes, My Prince, I believe so. He has not reached manhood.'

Lotane smiled, knowing if the boy had reached manhood he would not be acceptable to Zamah.

'It *is* good news, Nitkin; you have done well so far. Now you must find the boy and bring him here as soon as you can. I will start the preparations for the Ritual Sacrifice.'

Anton listened carefully as Lotane walked away with his arm draped around Nitkin's shoulder. He could hear no more, but he was astonished by what had been said.

This unknown boy might hold the key to contacting Old Earth – perhaps, even returning there. And yet, if he had read Lotane and his friends correctly, they were proposing to *sacrifice* him! Not that he was worried about the boy's life – he had taken many lives in his time without a moment's concern – but if this boy possessed special powers that could help him return to Old Earth, then he needed to keep him alive. Once he obtained what he wanted, Lotane could do as he wished with the boy.

Only one thing bothered him, and that was Sandan's obvious infatuation with Lotane's legend. He would have to keep an eye on him, and make sure that he didn't hamper his plans again.

Chapter Seventeen

Zimmerball

As far as Archie was concerned, two hours cooped up in one of Major Ramstiff's Orientation classes listening to the ancient history of the Zamahonites, Arnaks and Salakins was a real bore. His mind had gone numb halfway through the class; after that he couldn't take in anything that the major said. It just seemed pretty pointless having to learn stuff that he would never use.

At least he and Richard could look forward to a free afternoon away from the college to visit Uncle John at the Timecrack Research Unit – which was bound to be a lot more interesting than Orientation. They hadn't seen him since just after they'd arrived, over four weeks ago, and Archie was really looking forward to finding out what sort of work he was doing at the TRU with Dr Shah. It would be great to skip the afternoon classes, and, anyway, Uncle John had said it was very important that they meet. He had made the arrangements with Miss Harmsway for Archie and Richard to meet him as soon as possible.

It was the lunch break and Archie was sitting on one of the middle-tier bench seats that surrounded the Harmsway sports arena. He was watching a practice game of zimmerball between Prade House and Sohead House, while waiting for Richard to turn up from another session with Dr Krippitz.

'Hey, Archie, what's up? You look as if someone's stolen your lunch!'

Archie looked over to see Jules Stein hovering three feet in the air near the guardrail, a short distance away.

Jules switched off his wrist-control, allowing the Zap boots to lower him to the blue-coloured bounce pitch. Tall, slimly built and with thick brown hair that covered most of his brow, he possessed film star looks and moved with the confidence of someone who was a House Captain *and* a key player for the Harmsway zimmballers. Not only that, but his father was an Elder, and one of the most powerful industrialists in Sitanga.

Archie liked him, it was Jules who had taken himself and Richard under his wing and helped them settle in shortly after they arrived at Harmsway.

'What is it, Archie?' said Jules. 'Are you feeling OK?'

'Oh, I dunno,' said Archie. 'It's just that I'm a bit fed up with the orientation classes, and there hasn't been much of anything else.'

'Yeah, I know what you mean. I'm third-generation myself, so I grew up with it,' said Jules. He was dressed like a downhill skier, but with more padding to protect against accidental hits and falls. He dropped the helmet he was carrying and continued. 'Most of the New Arrivals feel the same way at first, but the way things are, it's a good idea to have a grasp of some history and stuff. It'll probably give you a better understanding of what's going on in the valley, especially with some of the things that have been happening lately.'

'What do you mean?' asked Archie.

'Well, you'll know from your class that there hasn't been too much love lost between the Salakins and the Arnaks. The two tribes get on well enough with each other most of the time, but in recent years there have been Arnak extremists stirring it up when they get the chance.'

'Like what?'

'Like street protests, like threatening letters to some of the Council Elders, including my father. But it has gotten worse lately, with some of the more extreme fanatics causing explosions and small fires in Fort Temple itself. So far, the Lancers have managed to contain them, and nobody has been hurt, but it might be only a matter of time before someone is seriously injured.'

'But what is it they want?'

'They're nutters. They say that according to some old legend they're going to take over Fort Temple and kick the rest of us out! I tell you, they're a bunch of crazies,' said Jules, unstrapping his Zap boots. 'Anyway, if I were you, I'd find something a bit more active than orientation.'

'What do you suggest?' asked Archie, although he had a pretty good idea what Jules had in mind.

'You look pretty fit,' said Jules, 'why don't you try out for the zimmerball team?'

'You must be joking! For one thing, I don't know anything about it, and from what I've seen so far, I wouldn't last five minutes out there!'

'It's not a game for wimps, for sure, but it's a simple enough game to learn. I tell you what, c'mon down to the pitch and try the Zaps on – what size do you take?'

'Seven ...'

Archie hesitated, thinking it might be better if he made an excuse and left, but Jules didn't give him a chance to say no.

'Near enough. I've a second pair in my bag.'

'Do I need a ... suit?' enquired Archie, not sure what to call the outfits the zimmballers wore.

'No, you won't need one – I just want you to get a feel of the Zaps.'

After securing their boots with zips and Velcro straps, they stepped inside the guardrail where Jules handed Archie a wrist-control band.

'Wear that, and don't switch it on until I tell you. You'll see the face has four segments with breaks in between, OK? Right, each segment is a fifteen-minute playing period followed by a five-minute rest. The rests are important because the play period can be pretty intense and we don't want any accidents, OK? Anyway, it's important to know how long you have in each period, because five or more net scores in any play period gets the team an extra five points. Each net score is worth five points. Right, stay with me and we'll try a couple of moves.'

The Zaps felt heavy and Archie had to make an extra effort to lift his feet as he walked across the bounce-pitch. He looked at the guardrail and saw the black poles with red lights flashing on top all around the perimeter. He had noticed them before, but didn't know what they were. He asked Jules.

'It means the force-field is on and the Zaps are active. We play from three feet above the pitch to a maximum of twenty feet. OK, switch on.'

Archie looked at his wrist-control and pressed a red button. Suddenly his feet left the ground and he had the sensation of going up in a lift. He stopped automatically at the three foot level, with Jules hovering beside him.

'This is fantastic!' yelled Archie.

'Right,' said Jules, 'this is our base playing position. Neither the Zaps nor the zimmerball can go below this point. The force-field allows us to play up to twenty feet, but it takes a lot of practise to reach that stage.'

'What happens below the base position?'

'Try it'

Jules pushed down on Archie's shoulder, causing him to lose his balance.

Archie felt himself sinking as if he had just dropped into a pond of jelly then, without warning, he popped up again, his arms flailing wildly until he fell over and hit the bounce-pitch. He felt embarrassed; he was now in the ridiculous position of lying almost on his back, but with his feet hanging in the air as if his heels were caught on a ledge.

'*Aaoowww*! That hurt!

'Oh, it's not that bad, Archie,' said Jules, laughing. 'The bounce-pitch prevents serious accidents, but if that had happened in a game, you would have just given away ten points to the other side. Here, give me your hand, it's the only way you'll get up – you can't do it on your own, so it's a good reason for staying on your feet!'

Archie reached for his hand, but fell back again with his feet still above his head. He swore as his elbows hit the bounce-pitch.

'Bugger it! Why can't I just switch the Zaps off?'

'Of course you can, but if you did that during a match you would be disqualified. OK, let's try again. It's a seven-a-side game, with three reserves,' Jules explained. 'The nets at each end are at the ten foot level and the idea is to hit the ball into the net for five points. Simple enough, Archie, but a lot of the points come from forcing your opponent off-balance so he touches the pitch. As I said, he loses ten points for that. Get the idea?'

They spent another fifteen minutes with Archie learning the basic moves, floating slowly from the base position up to the ten foot level.

'We'll not go any higher at this stage, but you're getting the hang of it,' said Jules.

Archie wasn't so sure about that. Every time he descended to the base position, he hit it too hard and fell over for the umpteenth time. He felt as if he had just rolled down the side of a mountain.

Helping him up again, Jules suggested they call it a day and try again at the next practice session.

'Thanks for the lesson,' said Archie, feeling up and down his arms for any broken bones, 'but I'm beginning to think orientation mightn't be so bad after all.'

*

While Archie waited at the sports arena, Shona Kelly was watching Richard devour another portion of the Hungry Dragon's speciality: Deep Fried Dinosaur Tails in a spicy Stickleberry sauce piled so high they were in danger of falling off the large clay platter.

They were sitting in a cubicle decorated with golden pagodas and snarling dragons, in one of Fort Temple's famous Chinatown restaurants. When Shona had first discovered the place she couldn't help thinking that no matter where you went – even another dimension – you would always find a Chinese restaurant, or for that matter, an Irish pub like her father's.

'Where *do* you put it?'

Shona gazed in astonishment at the remains of the half a dozen dishes he had already consumed.

'Ummm … ummm … mmmm!'

Richard had his eyes closed, and his mouth was so full of spicy tails he couldn't say a word.

'I think you've had enough, Richard, and I did promise Aristo I would get you back to Harmsway in time for him to take you and Archie to see your uncle.'

Richard could only nod. He licked some sauce from his lips while Shona sighed as she watched his soft doe-like eyes flash with irritation – she could see he didn't like being told what to do. It seemed that only his brother, Archie, had any influence over his unpredictable moods, and even then, at times, Richard would ignore him and disappear into his own special world. He was a good-looking boy: his fair hair, bleached blond by the hot valley sun, was growing long in the fashion currently favoured by Fort Temple's young set; but, more mysteriously, his pale blue eyes, deep within, sometimes seemed to flicker strangely, enhanced by that peculiar quality that only he possessed.

Dr Krippitz had told Shona he was now convinced that Richard could 'see' into other worlds, but making contact was the problem. He was trying to find a way to harness Richard's visions, or, 'sightings' as he preferred to call them, but, so far, he'd had no success during Richard's tests. The trouble was that the sightings were fragmentary and always broke up after a few seconds, not allowing them to develop any form of communication with the other world. It was so frustrating getting these tantalising glimpses of Richard's visions, but he seemed to be unable to hold on to them for more than a brief moment or two before the monitors went blank.

Not totally unexpectedly, Richard had announced he was getting fed up with the whole business and didn't want to do any more tests, but luckily Shona had found a way to stop him dropping out too soon. It was on a visit to Harmsway that Archie had told her of Richard's passion for Chinese food, so when she told Richard of the Hungry Dragon's lunchtime special where you could eat as much as you wanted for the price of one meal, he had caved in. Of course, she reminded him that he had a special dispensation to skip the Orientation classes while he did the tests.

The only problem was that the owner of the Hungry Dragon didn't appreciate Richard's appetite and was threatening to discontinue the special offer. He'd never had a customer like Richard before, and he made it plain he didn't want any more like him. As Shona paid the bill, he glowered at Richard, hoping to put him off coming back to the restaurant.

*

'Hey, look at Archie!' Richard pointed to his brother who was lying on his back struggling to get onto his feet above the bounce-pitch. 'What's he trying to do?'

'It looks as if he's got himself into a predicament,' laughed Shona.

They had just arrived at the sports arena as the zimmerball practice was coming to an end. Jules Stein was helping Archie to his feet, but he kept falling over until he switched off his Zaps.

'You're supposed to play the game on your feet,' called Richard, leaning on the guardrail, 'not on your back!'

'Very funny,' said Archie, pulling off a Zap boot. 'I'd like to see you do any better.'

'I bet I could, no problem.'

'Do you really want to have a go, Richard?' offered Jules. 'The Zaps'll be a bit big for you, but you're welcome to try.'

'OK, I will,' said Richard, sounding more confident than he actually felt.

Jules handed him the boots and helped to secure them.

'Here's your wrist-control. Just stay beside me, switch on when I tell you and you'll be all right.'

Richard grinned nervously and moved clumsily after Jules onto the pitch. The Sohead team had left, leaving only two Prade House players at the ten foot level practising long shots by hitting the zimmerball into the net below them. Otherwise, they had the pitch to themselves.

175

'Right, Richard, let's see what we can do.'

They switched on their wrist-controls and immediately ascended to the base position. Jules stayed close to Richard to help him keep his balance.

'OK, move your feet as if you are about to climb a flight of stairs and then –'

Jules broke off and stared. Richard was like a ghost with his face drained of blood. His eyes had closed, then suddenly opened, but they were like small black stones – unseeing, as if he was blind.

'Are you feeling all right?' Jules reached out and shook Richard's shoulder, but he was as stiff as a plank and hardly moved a muscle. 'I think I'd better get you down again.'

Holding Richard by the waist, Jules switched off both their wrist-controls and dropped to the bounce-pitch.

'Be careful! He's in one of his trances!' Archie shouted to Jules. He dashed onto the pitch, followed closely by Shona, who was shocked to see Richard in a trance outside the properly controlled conditions of the clinic.

Shona touched his face, but he didn't respond. She could see that his skin colour was paler than normal, much more so than in the clinic.

'I think we had better get him to the college hospital and let the doctor have a look at him; I don't like the look of this.'

'What's happening here?' Aristo joined them on the pitch. He had just arrived to collect the boys to visit their uncle at the TRU when he heard Archie shouting. 'Is there a problem?'

'I don't know, Aristo, he suddenly froze and he hasn't said a word since,' said Jules, glancing down while he held Richard's arm.

'He'll be OK,' said Archie, quickly. 'He's been in these before and he usually wakes up after a couple of minutes.'

He wasn't so sure this time. Richard had a faraway, zombie-like expression on his face that he hadn't seen before.

'Maybe so, but I think we should get him over to the hospital and let the doctor have a look at him,' repeated Shona, a little anxiously.

'Hold on for a minute,' said Aristo, 'I have an idea. Jules, do me a favour, tell the players to leave the pitch then go to the power-box and shut down the force-field. Stay there until I call you.'

Jules removed his Zaps and ran quickly to a bright red kiosk at the end of the guardrail. Shouting a warning to the two zimmballers still on the pitch that he was shutting down the force-field, he opened the door with a key that only he and the zimmerball coach were allowed to keep during training sessions. The kiosk was the size of a telephone booth with a black on/off lever attached to a red box on the inside wall. He entered and pulled the lever to the off position, then went outside and waved to Aristo that the force-field was shut down.

As soon as he saw Jules's signal, Aristo turned quickly to see Richard's reaction. He watched closely and saw his eyes begin to brighten and then focus on Archie.

'What's up?' asked Richard.

'Richard, how do you feel?' said Aristo.

'I dunno ... a bit stiff ...' He stretched himself and looked around, suddenly realising that everyone was staring at him. 'It's happened again, hasn't it?'

Archie nodded.

'You were *really* out of it this time – we were beginning to get worried.'

'Archie ... *I was at the DONUT!* I saw Chuck Winters and I left him a message!'

'What do you mean – a message?'

Archie watched his young brother carefully for any sign that maybe he wasn't a hundred per cent ... normal. He didn't understand what the trances meant, but they seemed to be getting ... *deeper* ... as if, somehow ... Richard was actually in these other places.

'I was in a room with a whole bunch of computers – and I left a message on one of the screens!'

'You're saying you were *actually* back at the DONUT and you left a message – what did you say?'

'I said we were in Timeless Valley with Uncle John. It was really funny, Archie – Chuck was running around shouting at everybody, wanting to know where the message had come from!'

Aristo listened carefully, nodding as if he understood what Richard was saying.

'Look, Richard, I want to try something. The force-field is off at the moment, but I want to switch it back on again. You might go back into the trance – are you game?'

'I don't know if that's wise,' said Shona.

'Yeah, I don't think it's a good idea,' agreed Archie. He was worried that the trances seemed to be getting out of hand.

'It's OK, Archie, I'll be all right,' said Richard.

Aristo smiled. 'Good for you, Richard. We'll make this really brief, but I've got an idea what might be happening here.'

Jules was still at the power-box waiting for a signal from Aristo when he heard him shout:

'*Switch on!*'

As the force-field came back on they all watched carefully as Richard closed his eyes and then opened them again, looking blankly into space. He had gone back into the trance.

Aristo waited for a moment, keeping an eye on Richard.

'*Switch off!*'

Richard recovered almost immediately, with everyone staring at him expectantly.

'Did you see anything?' asked Archie.

'Sort of ... but it was all kind of ... mixed up.'

'It was probably too quick this time, but it's just as I thought,' said Aristo, 'it's the force-field that's triggering the trances. When I was playing here in my last year, we had a player who used to get these terrible headaches and see things – we thought he was hallucinating. It got so bad he had to give up zimmerball, which was a pity because he was one of our best players, but it was reckoned it was the force-field that was causing the headaches.'

'Did he experience any trances or sightings like Richard's?' asked Shona.

'I don't think so, at least he never said, but we both left Harmsway soon after and I never saw him again.'

'Well, Richard seems to be fully recovered now, so if you have no more fancy ideas you want to try, I'll be on my way,' said Shona. 'Dr Krippitz is expecting me back at the clinic.'

And he will be very interested to hear about this latest development, especially Richard's contact with the professor's Facility, thought Shona.

'We have to be going, too,' said Aristo. 'So if you're feeling OK now, Richard, it's time you and Archie went to see your uncle.'

Chapter Eighteen

The Meeting House

Aristo led the boys into an old, paved courtyard where delivery vehicles from a bygone age used to unload supplies of food and drink, and all the other goods deemed necessary for the running of the college. It was now a parking area reserved for Harmsway's visitors, and today its large, stone square-sets, rutted with the tracks of pre-hovercraft cars and carriages, were host to a variety of more modern, but distinctly odd-looking, vehicles from all over Timeless Valley. None seemed odder to Archie's eyes than the one he was staring at now.

'What is *that*?'

'I dunno. Let's take a look,' said Richard, running ahead to climb a set of metal rungs that led to an open cockpit in the nose of the massive vehicle.

Bigger than an army tank, it was the most unusual machine they had ever seen. Its large, slate-grey armoured panels, pockmarked with crater-shaped dents, resembled a lunar landscape, and with its nose encased in a huge, reinforced triangular fender like a small Antarctic icebreaker, it almost defied description. Yet the whole contraption, crouched as it was on six retractable landing-pads, looked incredibly like a giant insect ready to take flight at the slightest sign of danger.

Archie wasn't quite so enthusiastic and he hung back while Aristo walked around the machine inspecting each of the landing-pads.

'It's a beauty, isn't it?' said Aristo.

'Er ... it's ... I've never seen anything like it,' said Archie, which was true.

It was probably the ugliest-looking vehicle he had ever seen, and it didn't look particularly safe to ride in.

It was so big that Aristo had parked it in the middle of the courtyard to avoid any collision with the rows of smaller hovercraft nearby.

'The Lancers called it the Bonebreaker when they used it in the old days to herd the animals in the Exploding Park,' said Aristo. 'After a hundred years or so, they pulled it and two others out of service and replaced them with a squadron of Spokestars. I love flying it; it's a real workhorse.'

'What happened to it?' asked Archie, touching the bodywork, his fingers working across some of the dents.

'Oh, those happened before it could fly. Sometimes the bigger animals in the park would take exception to it and ram it. That's why they called it the Bonebreaker.'

Archie's spine tingled as he thought of being in it when one of the dinosaurs charged.

'What's it used for now?'

'When it came out of service, Dr Shah requisitioned it so he could move heavy equipment in it to the TRU at Mount Tengi. Old Henry Spokestar converted it to use a vallonium propulsion system, and I get to fly it most of the time when I'm not in training.'

He finished his inspection and urged Archie on board to join Richard, who was having the time of his life pretending to fly the huge machine.

'OK, get yourselves strapped in. It doesn't pay to keep Dr Shah waiting when he wants things done.'

Settling into a high-backed seat behind an old-fashioned steering wheel, Aristo engaged the propulsion system by pulling one of a row of levers set into the cockpit panel in front of him.

The Bonebreaker shuddered like a wet dog drying itself as it ascended, almost reluctantly, into the air. It wasn't as smooth as any of the other hovercraft Archie had been in so far, but he could sense its enormous power vibrating through every part and bolt. He began to appreciate what it was that Aristo felt about this old machine.

Little more was said as they approached its maximum cruising height, two thousand feet above the grounds of Harmsway College. Limited by its original design, the cumbersome machine couldn't fly much higher. Taking one final look to see that the boys were properly secured into their seats, Aristo set course for their meeting with Dr Shah.

*

Although they were sheltered behind a deep-set windscreen, Archie could still feel the cool fresh wind whipping around the cockpit as Aristo tried to stabilise the Bonebreaker in the turbulence of the mountainside air currents. Buffeted by a crosswind, the ungainly machine was proving to be a handful to fly, but Aristo wasn't concerned, and soon he was preparing to lower the landing-pads as he circled the campanile at one end of a huge, brownstone building overlooking an old graveyard.

'Ah, good, there's plenty of space for us down there,' said Aristo.

'Is this a church?' enquired Archie, impressed by the great flying buttresses that lined the side of the building.

'It used to be, but years ago when a fire destroyed most of the interior the Elders decided to restore it as the new site for the Meeting House. With few people attending any of the churches in Amasia it seemed ideal. Only the monks at the monastery in Fort Temple and some of the old tribes practise any sort of religion now. And so, with Fort Temple's rapid expansion, it was decided that the old Meeting House had become too small for the business that needs to be carried out.'

'Oh – but I thought we were going to see Dr Shah and Uncle John at the TRU?'

'Sorry, I should have mentioned it earlier; Dr Shah asked me to come here first. I don't know why, but he said it was important to be here before the end of the session.'

Aristo said no more; he knew they would find out soon enough. If Dr Shah wanted them here there had to be a good reason.

They landed on a rough expanse of grass beyond the graveyard, the landing-pads flattening large patches of nettles and wild flowers.

'It's the only place near the Meeting House they'll let me leave it,' complained Aristo, as they walked along a gravel path at the side of the building.

Archie and Richard went ahead, treading warily past weather-worn headstones, some were tilted at crazy angles, while others were embedded in the grass like postage stamps on a green envelope. One or two had collapsed in on the coffins where the ground had subsided.

'Be careful where you walk,' warned Aristo, 'it wouldn't be the first time that someone fell into one of these old graves.'

'Ooohh!'

Richard jumped back when his foot touched one of the large fallen slabs. He reached out for Aristo's arm to steady himself.

'It's all right, Richard, just stay on the path,' said Aristo.

Archie laughed as Richard leapt away from the slab, but he was reminded of the stone at Harmsway and the weird effect it had had on his young brother.

'No, there's nothing like that here that I know of,' answered Aristo, when Archie asked him.

There seemed to be no pattern to Richard's unusual behaviour, except that back on Old Earth it had only been dreams – up until the explosion on the catwalk at the DONUT. But here in Timeless Valley, Richard went into trances because of strange stone carvings and force-fields, or whatever they called them, and then there was Krippitz at the clinic with his tests.

When he was little, his father had mentioned his mother having dreams and headaches, and he had warned Archie not to bother her when she was 'asleep'. It was beginning to occur to Archie that Richard and his mother shared the same sort of gift – if you could call it that – of 'seeing' things and somehow being able to communicate with each other no matter where they were. It was like telepathy and mediums, sort of, but mediums only got in touch with the dead, didn't they? Richard was able to 'talk' to the Vikantus and Brimstone, even if they weren't there, and leave messages for Chuck on his computer – and they were all *alive,* so, if Richard had 'seen' mum and dad in his dreams … *then they must still be alive!*

Archie felt as if he had been hit by a thunderbolt. It suddenly dawned on him why Krippitz had been so insistent on carrying out so many tests with Richard. If the Vikantus and Brimstone could only 'talk' over short distances, yet Richard could get in touch with other worlds, then he had to be very special. So special, in fact, that he might be the one that would get them back home…

'Here we are,' said Aristo.

They stood facing the huge, arched doors of the Meeting House while dozens of serious-looking people, dressed in sober grey and black clothes, which made them look even more serious, streamed in and out of the building. Some carried half-open briefcases stuffed with paperwork, others balanced boxes of files – marked HIGHLY CONFIDENTIAL – stacked precariously one on top of the other, all of them desperately weaving a snake-like path through the crowd to avoid colliding with each other.

Once inside the narthex, the circular high-ceilinged antechamber, a tall, burly red-faced man sporting a thick walrus moustache advanced purposefully across the chequered marble floor to greet them. He was the commissionaire, dressed in a black and green, military-style uniform with bright, gold stripes on each sleeve. Hardly looking at them, he bellowed like a sergeant major addressing raw recruits on a parade ground, which, in fact, was what he had been back on Old Earth.

'Good day, gents! You're late! Dr Shah expected you here before he went into session.'

'I'm sorry, Trumpton, but we were –'

Aristo didn't get a chance to finish. The commissionaire turned abruptly on his heels and marched over to a wide, curving marble staircase near the entrance, snapping his fingers and indicating that they should follow him. A security guard kept watch beside a sign that read: VISITORS' GALLERY. He stepped aside and saluted as Trumpton swept past and called back:

'Follow me – no point in wasting more time!'

Archie nearly tripped over Richard's feet as they tried to keep up with Aristo following directly behind Trumpton, who was making his way up the staircase two steps at a time. They reached the floor above the entrance where a great stained glass rose window cast the last rays of dying sunlight onto the nave below.

'Seats have been kept for you down there at the front. Take them and Dr Shah will see you later.'

Trumpton indicated three numbered seats behind the guardrail where other visitors were leaning and watching the proceedings at the table below. Without another word he left them to make their own way down half a dozen steps to the seats, which gave a very good view of what used to be the nave of the church.

No longer were there pews filled with worshippers. In their place, dominating the nave, stood a very long black table, its surface worn with age and decorated with similar symbols seen on the stone at Harmsway. On each side of the table were six, high-backed, black wooden chairs finished in rich red velvet. Each chair was separated from the other by nearly twelve feet of space, which made some of the Elders dreadfully hoarse at the end of each session, as they shouted to be heard. Along the length of the nave small groups of personal attendants stood by marble columns waiting to be called by an Elder if needed, which was not infrequent, as files and mounds of paperwork were constantly in demand.

'Is this place never used as a church now?' asked Richard.

He gazed up at the high vaulted ceiling with its massive oak beams and ornate stonework, and thought that the interior still looked very much like a church. Tall stained glass side windows cast coloured beams of light into the nave, while around the table, below a large, brass chandelier holding vallonium lamps, the Elders in their traditional, long black robes debated and argued the affairs of the valley.

'No, Richard, as I said earlier, not many in the city practise religion, but those who wish to can go to the monastery where Father Jamarko still holds services. What you see here in the Meeting House are the Elders paying tribute to the old traditions by sitting at the ancient table which represents the old tribes, and by wearing the robes of Hazaranet. It is all meant to symbolise unity, but as you've probably heard by now, there are people in the valley out to cause trouble, and unity is the last thing they want.'

For the next hour Archie and Richard had to listen to the Elders debating all sorts of issues from increasing Stickleberry juice output for export to creating new identity cards for visitors to the valley. It was all mind-numbingly boring and Archie was almost settled into a day-sleep when the sound of a very loud voice shouting across the table below caught his attention.

'I've said it a hundred times at this table, and I will say it again!'

As he raised his voice, Julius Stein's fist struck the table so hard that an empty crystal goblet bounced into the air and shattered into myriad pieces as it struck the stone floor. His black, purple-hemmed robe swirled around him, displaying the ancient tribal symbols of Hazaranet richly woven in gold throughout the plush fabric. Like the other Elders, Stein's robe represented the ultimate authority in Timeless Valley, his being that for industry. To many of the visitors in the Meeting House, Stein might have been a mighty wizard casting a spell across the table.

The hushed gallery knew that this was the man who made terrible predictions about what would happen to Timeless Valley if the other Elders did not heed his dire warnings of invasion and war. Unfortunately, although they had nothing to do with anyone outside the valley, the recent disturbances by rebels and troublemakers were beginning to make people wonder if, perhaps, he was right.

'We are not investing enough in the defence of this valley,' continued Stein, 'and we will rue the day when we are caught unawares by our enemies! Make no mistake, our cities, mines and lands have long been coveted by those less fortunate than ourselves!'

Julius Stein was an imposing figure, even more so when he was angry, and he knew it. He was a handsome, well-groomed man, his brown hair long and edged with silver tips. His usual composure was disturbed, for he knew that if, on this final day of the session, he did not secure the extra funding he needed from the treasury, he would have to finance the factories out of his own pocket, and that would never do.

'And who are these so-called enemies, Elder Stein, who we should be so concerned about? Name me *one* who is ready to invade our territory?'

Yevi Valkov was the Elder for Trade and Development and he was worried about Stein's accusations affecting their trading relationships with other countries. He was determined no more money would be poured into Stein's factories in Sitanga, especially at the expense of more worthwhile projects – Shah's in particular. As he thought of the Timecrack Research Unit, he looked across at his fellow Elder and wondered what he would say in response to Stein.

'You may well ask, Valkov!' said Stein. He stared for a moment at the little bald figure seated directly opposite, then turned and gestured with an open hand towards the other end of the table to where a beautiful, tawny-haired woman sat, her high cheekbones tinted with purple powder, denoting a person as royal-born. 'If you had paid heed to the reports brought back to us by our ambassador, Elder Countess Flick, from her overseas missions, you would be better informed of the dangers we face!'

'Scaremongering!' retorted Valkov. 'We have all read the reports, and we are well aware there are those who are envious of our vallonium mines – but it does not mean they are going to invade us! This is just a ploy to direct valuable resources into the Sitanga factories. Let them pay for such investments out of their own profits!'

He was careful not to say Stein's factories – that might cause more trouble than it was worth – but it was obvious to all in the Meeting House what he meant.

'I agree with Elder Stein –'

General Branvin, a bullish man with long scars on both cheeks, was about to rise from his seat when he suddenly found himself interrupted by a long-standing opponent of his defence policies.

'Of course you would! You're the head of the armed forces! What else could we expect?' boomed a voice that could be heard clearly throughout the Meeting House.

Just at that moment, Archie felt Aristo's elbow nudging his side.

'Look, Archie – it's Dr Shah!' said Aristo.

There was an air of expectation and a murmur of rising voices around the gallery as visitors pushed and leaned forwards to get a better view of the man they had heard so much about, but rarely seen. Dr Shah was reputed to be a reclusive, dedicated scientist who rarely left his laboratory on Mount Tengi, having sworn to the other Elders that he would solve the problem of timecrack travel during his lifetime. And as everyone knew, lifetimes in Timeless Valley were very long indeed. It was not known exactly how much, but it was also widely rumoured that millions of dolans had already been poured into his project.

It had even been reported in the *Amasian Chronicle* that Shah had volunteered to be the first to test the timecrack chamber on Mount Tengi, but that was soon shown to be an absurd proposition, for who would run the TRU if he did not return? Unfortunately, the first twenty volunteers had not returned, which, of course, was a fact that Elder Stein constantly brought up at every session in the Meeting House.

Archie leaned over the guardrail and stared, for there was something unusual about Dr Shah.

'What's he sitting in?' asked Archie.

'It's a hoverchair. He was paralysed in an accident coming through a timecrack. The chair was specially designed for him.'

It was an amazing sight. Dr Shah had been sitting inconspicuously at the end of the table, well below the level of the other chairs, not saying a word. Now he elevated the hoverchair to a position slightly above the heads of the Elders, forcing them, especially Stein, to look up to him.

Archie was impressed, for Dr Emil Shah was a striking figure. He had a magnificent head of snowy-white hair that flowed around him like a horse's mane, and a thick moustache that drooped below his chin. His twinkly eyes and almost permanent smile had beguiled many an opponent into thinking he was a soft simple-minded man, until they discovered that, somehow, *they* themselves had been outwitted. It was hardly surprising, though, as he had been a renowned chess master since childhood and a war games tactician for the US government, as well as a leading scientist on secret research projects before his encounter with a timecrack.

'And might I say, Elder Branvin, your military success in the field during the troubles outside Port Zolnayta is to be commended. Although I suppose, as your forces outnumbered them – *the children* – by one hundred to one, it was not totally unexpected.'

Laughter broke out in the gallery at the widely reported incident involving schoolchildren playing with fireworks that had precipitated a military response from

General Branvin's forces. This was what the visitors had come to hear, not only the long drawn-out discussions on valley economics and endless politics, but the cut and thrust of powerful men seeking to consolidate their privileged positions, as well as seeking money for their respective interests.

Before a highly embarrassed and red-faced Branvin could reply, Stein spoke up.

'At least Elder Branvin did not lose any men in that battle, and I don't believe that we should commit more funds to dangerous projects that have no reasonable chance of success!'

More gasps of surprise and shouts of 'Shame!' broke out in the gallery.

'Fellow Elders, I fear we are straying from the agenda.' Benno Kozan, the Elder and Institute Director for vallonium supplies and research, was worried that the session was getting out of hand. It wouldn't be the first time these two had insulted each other, but nothing was to be gained by it. 'It would be appropriate if we could close this session on more cordial terms, and I am certain that the gallery, as well as the rest of the valley, would like us to get to the vote sooner rather than later.'

'Thank you, Elder Kozan,' said Dr Shah, 'you are right, of course, but for the record, I would like to correct an impression that has just been given by Elder Stein. I did not *lose* any men. *Volunteers* were sent through the timecrack chamber on Mount Tengi. They may be alive and well in the other worlds; I do not know, but they are not necessarily dead!'

'A rather dubious distinction, Elder Shah; however, as I understand it, you are opposing my proposals on the grounds that you want *more* money to send *more volunteers* through timecracks to an unknown fate. It's hardly a proposition that this table would wish to support.'

Stein's voice was treacly thick with sarcasm, but loud whispers around the gallery agreed that he did have a point. What would Elder Shah say?

'Elder Stein is correct, of course. I *am* asking for more money, but he, and everyone else in this house, must be aware of the enormous benefits that will be brought to Amasia, as well as the valley, when we bring this project to a successful conclusion.

'Although it is generally agreed that most timecracks take place in the Exploding Park, they do occur elsewhere, and unfortunately, along with the many New Arrivals now arriving on an almost daily basis, there are undesirables we have to accept into our society. The recent killing of a Lancer, if nothing else, should be a warning to us to take action.' Dr Shah hesitated for a moment, and then raised his voice. 'If only we could send them back —'

Before he could finish there was a sudden burst of applause from the gallery. Shouts of 'Yes!' and 'Send them back!' from some of the visitors showed where their feelings lay. It was a hot topic and Shah knew it was time to strike. He elevated his hoverchair until he was nearly level with the gallery.

'Elder Stein's household could not have received a copy of the *Amasian Chronicle,* for if they had he might have been better informed that someone *has* returned through a timecrack.' He allowed the laughter to stop before pointing to Aristo. 'He sits there among you, unharmed by his journey, and is living proof that we are on the verge of unlocking the door to success.' As the visitors strained to get a better look at Aristo, he continued:

'*And beside him is a boy who holds the key to that door*!'

Everyone was stunned. Loud whisperings and muttering broke out: What did Elder Shah mean? Who was the boy? Where did he come from? They looked to Elder Shah to explain what he meant, but he had nothing more to say, and he lowered the hoverchair to return to his place at the table.

Another Elder stood up, his right arm extended upwards to still the babble of the crowd

'As Father Jamarko's deputy, I am the acting Elder in his absence on behalf of the church. I propose we now put the requirement for more funds for either Elder Shah or Elder Stein to the vote. I know that Father Jamarko would not want to put his name to any increase for armaments, therefore, I pass my stone to Elder Shah.'

Father Haman was a pleasant-looking young man. His handsome features and reputation for hard work had made him a well-known figure at the Meeting House, as well as being an able administrator for the monastery. He hitched up his robe, which was a little too long, walked to the end of the table and placed a white stone in a small wooden bowl in front of Elder Shah. Each Elder possessed a similar bowl to receive stones when they put forward their own proposals. It was a very old system, but it worked very well.

The Elders nodded their heads in agreement to the vote. One by one, they placed their stones in either Shah's or Stein's bowl.

Above them in the gallery, Richard was perplexed.

'Why was he pointing at me and what did he mean about opening doors? He's scary – I thought he was going to float right over us!'

'No, his hoverchair can't go that high,' said Aristo. 'Anyway, I don't know what he meant by all that stuff. We'll probably find out later when we take him back to Mount Tengi.'

With the voting completed, the session had come to a close. The Elders now made their way to the changing rooms where they would leave their robes of office until next month's session.

'Well, I'm glad that's over,' said Aristo, getting to his feet. 'If there's anything that I hate, it's politics. I don't know how they stand all the back-stabbing and nonsense that goes on in this place. Remind me never to become a politician.' He looked behind as someone pushed to get past. 'OK, we'd better go.'

*

A short distance away in the opposite gallery two men in sand-coloured traders' robes studied Aristo and the boys as they left the gallery.

'So, that is the boy we're supposed to abduct,' said Anton, after the other visitors seated around them had left. 'How did Lotane know he would be here?'

'*Prince* Lotane has informers everywhere,' answered Nitkin. Angered by the outsider's disrespect for his master he almost spat the words at Anton. 'It would not surprise you if only you knew how many followers he has in the valley.'

Maybe not, thought Anton, but you and your crazy master may be surprised when I put my own plan into place.

Today's session had been very useful in helping Anton to identify the boy. And he now had the germ of an idea on how he might secure the secret of the vallonium process.

Chapter Nineteen

Mount Tengi

'I'm afraid my performance today was shamelessly opportunistic,' said Shah, 'but I really had no other choice if we are to secure the funds we need to continue our work at the TRU.'

He was watching Aristo secure the hoverchair to shackle points on the floor of the Bonebreaker. They were directly behind the cockpit in the open load bay where the TRU supplies were normally carried. Along one side of the bay on a metal bench were seated Benno Kozan, Archie and Richard, ready for the flight to Mount Tengi.

'Yes, you were on exceptional form, Emil,' said Kozan, 'I've rarely seen Stein look as surprised as when you introduced Aristo and the boys to the house!'

'Hah! The man is devious and I had to play him at his own game,' said Shah.

'What do you mean, sir?' said Aristo, getting to his feet, now that he had secured the last shackle to the hoverchair.

'What I mean is that we were on the verge of losing ten million dolans to Stein for a new weapons factory! I heard from Klinghorn himself that his directors would prefer to invest their money in a project that would show massive profits on exports. Exports he says! So much for rumours of invasion! Hypocrites – that's what they are!'

Elder Klinghorn, Chairman of Klinghorn and Yaxley, the valley's most prestigious bank, was known to be an avaricious man, but he was like the wind in the mountains: swirling and constantly changing direction, sometimes trapping the unwary climbers who had not prepared for the unexpected change in conditions.

'Klinghorn is a greedy man, but he is also a very practical man. He supports public causes when it suits him. Knowing, of course, that the same well-meaning people will invest their money with his bank if it is seen to be behind any worthwhile project that is beneficial to the valley – and *that* was the way to get his vote. I knew the people would be with me if I could show a way of controlling the undesirables arriving in the valley, for that is an issue they constantly debate. That is not my intention of course – Brimstone and Dr Krippitz do their jobs well enough, but it was a course I was prepared to take if we were to win the vote. And now I have it – even if it is only for six months.' Shah shook his head with impatience. 'Damn his deadlines!'

'No matter, Emil, you may well be closer to success than you think,' said Kozan. 'All the vallonium columns in the grid are now connected to the chamber, so you should have all the energy you need. If, as you suggested in the house today, Richard *is* the key to finding the final piece in the puzzle then we need to take very good care of him, for his contribution will be priceless!'

Benno Kozan's dark features warmed with a reassuring smile as he turned from Shah and spoke to Richard.

'Do not be too concerned about what we are saying, young one. You apparently have a very special gift, but it is something we will talk about later.'

Richard didn't say anything. He felt confused about all this talk that had him linked to being the key to something – *the key to what?* He supposed it must be connected to what he could see in his dreams – or sightings as Kripps called them – but how could they help with anything?

Looking at Dr Shah, with his lower body encased in the shiny metal capsule and his snowy-white hair blowing around his shoulders in the light breeze, Richard couldn't help thinking that he looked like God, or one of those *Old Testament* figures he'd seen in church books or religious paintings, except that Dr Shah was wearing a safari jacket, which wasn't really godlike. He even sounds like God; his voice loud and thundery, and a little bit scary, thought Richard. Leaning to one side he whispered to Archie.

'I wish we were back at Grimshaws – or even Harmsway. I don't think I'm going to like this Mount thingmy place we're going to.'

'Don't worry – it'll be OK when we see Uncle John,' said Archie, not altogether too convincingly, for like Richard he had his own misgivings on what lay ahead of them, but he said nothing more.

'OK, that's us ready to go,' said Aristo.

He left the load bay and went forwards through a narrow opening into the cockpit. Minutes later they were on their way.

Archie gazed out over the rear of the Bonebreaker and saw they were leaving the Fort Temple skyline behind them. The Piranga mountain range rose majestically above the city like a row of witches' hats against a darkening sky, while not far below, a wide river fed by meltwater from the mountains, was starting its long journey to the Amasian Sea over a thousand miles away.

Soon they were flying over a narrow two-lane road that speared its way through dense woodland with huge fingers of black vallonium rock poking through the forest canopy like lonely lighthouses in a choppy sea. An occasional Lancer patrol caught their attention, but beyond that there was no sign of life.

When Archie commented that he had hardly seen any other form of transport – like the planes and cars they had on Old Earth – Shah explained:

'It is different here in Amasia, Archie. Mainly for environmental, but security reasons as well, the Elders have decreed that only the Lancers, and other special groups such as our own organisation, are allowed to fly. But, as you have seen, the citizens have excellent transport systems, and they seem happy enough with that.'

After nearly two hours of travelling due west towards a sinking sun, Shah announced that they would shortly be at their destination: the Gladden Plateau, where they would spend the night.

'The Gladden Plateau? What's that? I thought we were going to the TRU?' said Archie out loud, to no-one in particular.

He raised his eyebrows and looked at Richard in case he'd heard something, but Richard just shrugged his shoulders and said nothing.

'We will visit the TRU tomorrow, Archie,' said Shah. 'We work there, but we don't live there. Our accommodation is based in the compound at Gladden and it is only a few miles from Mount Tengi, so it is quite convenient. I'm sure you will enjoy your stay there, for it is a beautiful place, but first we must all get a good night's sleep. It has been a long day for all of us, eh?'

The Bonebreaker suddenly banked and started to circle in a slow spiral, making Archie grip the edge of the metal bench. It was nearly dark now and he couldn't see very much except the shadowy outline of the trees below and the silhouette of a mountain not far away.

'Good! We are here! And that is Mount Tengi,' said Shah, pointing to the mountain,' but it is too dark – you will see it better in the morning.'

He's right, thought Archie, as they landed. He couldn't see anything, but he couldn't care less, for he was dog-tired and he just wanted to sleep.

*

The next day, Archie and Richard spent part of the morning wandering curiously through the outbuildings dotted around the compound. Some were occupied while others lay empty, like the old stone church where the roof had fallen in and had never been replaced, so that grass and thorn bushes now grew up through cracks in the cobblestone floor.

Earlier, Aristo had explained that the plateau with its magnificent views over hundreds of square miles of woodland and black rocky outcrops had been named after Nathaniel Gladden, a reclusive leader of a mysterious religious sect that had died out nearly two centuries before, leaving almost no trace of its existence.

Still remaining was the clapboard house where Gladden had once lived, and where, last night, because all but one of the bedrooms were fully occupied, Archie and Richard had been forced to share a huge four-poster bed. Archie hadn't been too happy about it, for he knew how Richard could kick and punch when he had one of his dreams, but there had been nothing else to sleep on except a lumpy old leather couch, and that hadn't looked too inviting with a couple of its springs ready to burst through the material. In the end, though, he had fallen asleep on top of the bedcover and Richard hadn't bothered him one bit.

Now, after spending an hour or so climbing through the old church, Archie and Richard raced each other across the sandy surface of the compound back to the house.

'Hey, look at this!'

Nearly out of breath, Richard collapsed beside an ancient-looking, brass telescope mounted on a tripod at the end of a veranda that ran the length of the house. Swinging it around, he pointed it over the treetops towards Mount Tengi, and then pressed his eye against the lens while he adjusted the focus.

'I wonder what that is ...'

'What? Let's see,' said Archie impatiently, gripping the barrel of the telescope and raising the level of the tripod to take a look. 'It looks like an observatory, but I can't tell what the black pillars are –'

'That's the timecrack chamber, Archie,' said an unexpected voice behind him. It was the professor in company with Aristo who had just joined them. 'That's where Aristo set off on his journey to Old Earth, and those black pillars you see are the vallonium columns in a grid that supplies power to the chamber. In fact, Mount Tengi itself, and all the black rock you see around here, is vallonium in its natural unprocessed state.'

'Uncle John!'

Richard dashed past Aristo and threw his arms around his uncle's waist.

'Well, that's quite a welcome!' said the professor.

'Hello, Uncle John,' said Archie, hanging back. He was feeling a little strange now that he was so close to the chamber that might get them back to Old Earth.

Sensing Archie's mood, the professor put his arms around both the boys' shoulders and apologised.

'I'm sorry it's been so long since I've seen the two of you, but the work I'm doing on Mount Tengi is so important that it's taking up every minute of my time.'

'Is Aristo going through a timecrack again?' asked Richard.

'As soon as I get the chance …' said Aristo, his voice drifting as he thought about how his last journey had ended.

'No, we're not ready for that just yet – as keen as Aristo is to go.' The professor smiled. 'Dr Shah and I have a lot more work to do before the chamber is used again.'

'What *sort* of work are you doing, Uncle John?'

'Well, Richard, the best way I can explain it, is that it is very much like the work I was doing at the DONUT.'

'That sounds … really important,' said Richard, still not really sure what his uncle was trying to tell him.

'Yes it is, but we have reached a point where we need to make a breakthrough – and you, Richard, may be able to help us achieve it. That's why you are here. You too, Archie.'

'Me? I don't understand – what can *I* do?' said Archie.

'Not to worry, Archie, all will be explained shortly, but before we get into that, what do you say we all have some lunch first?'

Not waiting for an answer, the professor steered the boys, with Aristo following, to the dining room at the other end of the veranda.

Archie's mood had lightened as he thought about what he had just heard. He had guessed that Uncle John was involved somehow with Dr Shah on the TRU timecrack project because of his work at the DONUT, and that they might be close to a breakthrough to get them back to Old Earth safely was brilliant news. But how could he help? It seemed obvious that they were going to use Richard's trances in some way to help with the project, but he knew nothing about them, except what Richard had told him, and it was only recently he had begun to believe any of it.

As he thought about it, Archie felt confused and he was becoming a little apprehensive about what was going to happen to them next, but he was also excited that Richard and he were actually going to *do something* to help them get back home.

While all these thoughts tumbled through his mind, he noticed that one of the house servants, standing by the doorway to the dining room, was staring intently at Richard, her dark-skinned face all screwed up like an old prune, as if she was trying hard to remember something important.

*

Anka was one of several servants whose work gave her access to every part of the house. She had been there for as long as anyone could remember, and some said she had been there in Nathaniel Gladden's time, but no one knew if that was true.

She was a small woman with narrow eyes, and a pointed nose that was almost hidden in thin folds of leathery skin, which made her look very old indeed. So old, said some of the other servants sneeringly, that she might have belonged to one of the ancient tribes of Hazaranet

Little did they know how close they were to the truth, for Anka was an Arnak and a devoted follower of Prince Lotane, whom she regarded as her lord and master. She was not one of those who compromised her faith to please the Salakins; only her master could make her do that, and this she would do gladly, without question, even if she had to work amongst those whom she despised as unbelievers and outsiders.

When he had contacted her yesterday to confirm that the boys had left the Meeting House with Aristo and Dr Shah, and that she must report all that she saw and heard concerning the young one and his brother, she had praised Zamah that Prince Lotane could still trust her to carry out such a task after so many years in his service.

Now, as Anka watched Richard pass by, she wondered what it was that made the boy so special that it warranted her master's personal attention.

*

'Sticklejuice! That's the stuff that Finbar drinks!'
Archie reacted as if the amber-coloured liquid in the crystal glass that had just been placed in front of him on the coffee table might explode. He'd seen how the drink had affected the little guide and there was no way he was going to try it.

'No! No! It's not the same thing, Archie,' said Krippitz. 'This is a non-alcoholic drink that the monks have produced for centuries as an after-dinner tonic, but now it is the most popular drink in Amasia – and one of the valley's top exports! Try it. I think you will like it.'

'Mmmm, it is good – it tastes just like Coke!' said Richard. He licked his lips and before the servant, Anka, had a chance to move the trolley away, he reached for a refill. She scowled at his poor manners and shuffled off to another part of the room.

'You're right, Dr Krippitz, it's not bad,' said Archie, after trying a sip, 'but what is it that Finbar drinks?'

'Oh, that is something totally different, and only supplied under licence to the taverns – although, I dare say there are others who do have access to it.'

Krippitz glanced meaningfully at Shah, and smiled.

'Well, now that we have dealt with the merits of the drinks trolley, perhaps we can get on with the business in hand,' said Shah, ignoring Krippitz's remark by swallowing the last drop of his own alcoholic version of the drink.

He was no longer in the hoverchair and was now settled comfortably in an armchair with a glass in his hand, his withered legs covered by a colourful, woollen rug.

After leaving the dining room – with the exception of Aristo, who had to meet the engineers on Mount Tengi to test a new version of the tracker suit – they had all retired to Shah's private lounge, where they now sat in an assortment of chairs around an ornate coffee table, its carved wood decorated with mysterious figures and symbols. They were there to listen to a presentation by Krippitz on the results of Richard's tests at the Evaluation Clinic.

Krippitz's work was now high on their list of priorities, for the tests had led to an idea – one that had developed out of a conversation between the professor and Shah, and one that both had agreed should be more fully explored. Now they and Benno Kozan, who would have a major influence in what would happen next if things went to plan, were eager to hear what he had to say.

'Carl, perhaps you would begin by giving us an overview of the tests you carried out with Richard and the conclusions you made. Then I believe Professor Strawbridge has something to say.'

Shah nodded to Krippitz to start then gestured to Anka, who was fussing around the drinks trolley, to refill their glasses.

Carl Krippitz was something of an enigma to Shah. There was no doubt that his work at the Evaluation

Clinic had been, and continued to be, highly successful. The screening programmes he had created to evaluate the New Arrivals were now well established procedure – there was no denying that – but his apparent obsession, with what might be best described as *paranormal* activities, was, in Shah's opinion, pure mumbo-jumbo. Yet here he was, about to listen to a presentation that might lead to a solution to one of the greatest challenges of modern science: interdimensional travel and the culmination of all his work at Mount Tengi.

For the next forty minutes he listened patiently while Krippitz spoke of his work at the clinic: about how the equipment and methods he had developed over many years now applied to a wide range of tests. He explained how they examined the myriad individuals that came to them and how they were evaluated, and also how the use of Shona's techniques involving hypnosis and meditation had proven so invaluable –'

'Yes, Carl, it's all highly praiseworthy, but could you get to the *point* as to why this meeting was called, before we all fall asleep?'

Shah yawned, making it clear how he felt. Krippitz's spiky hair seemed to stand on end as he adjusted his glasses to stare at Shah, whose interruption had caught him off guard.

'I'm sorry, Emil … but I thought it necessary to give *some* background to the tests we have carried out so far –'

'Yes, yes, I think we all understand that, but we have a limited timescale to achieve our objective – six months, in fact!'

Shah used his arms to shift his weight in order to make himself more comfortable in the armchair, making the rug slip to the floor. Richard instinctively left his seat to lift the rug and replace it over Shah's legs.

'Thank you, young man that is very kind of you. I'm afraid I'm not as mobile as I used to be,' said Shah.

'Can't you use your hoverchair?'

Richard was standing quite close to Shah, not finding him as scary as he'd once thought.

'Yes, I probably could, Richard,' said Shah, 'but you know … sitting in this old chair gives me a feeling of … normality. Do you know what I mean?'

'I think so – you'd like to be able to walk again?'

'Hah, the directness of youth,' chuckled Shah. 'It is very refreshing to have young company again!' He sat quietly for a brief moment before continuing. 'Yes, Richard, I would indeed, but it is not to be. Fortunately, my work does not allow me to dwell upon it.'

Glancing across to Krippitz, who was looking annoyed at being interrupted, he waved his hand, encouraging him to continue.

'Forgive me, Carl, for my rudeness. I'm getting impatient in my old age, but I do think that before these two boys reach the same age, they would very much like to see Old Earth again, eh?'

Everyone laughed, with Archie and Richard nodding their heads vigorously in agreement.

'Yes … Well, let me cover the main areas of interest with regard to Richard's unusual … let's say, *ability*, to 'see' current events at great distances. First of all, we considered Richard's dreams. We did this by monitoring some of his day-sleep periods, although he no longer seems to need such rest any more, as he has adapted quite well to New Earth time.' Krippitz nodded towards Richard. 'Unless we were prepared to monitor *all* of Richard's sleep-periods over a much longer time – and, as I have been reminded, unlimited time is something we do not have – we had to be satisfied with

Richard's recollections. Such dream recollections are subjective and notoriously unreliable, as virtually any interpretation can be put upon them. The only item of interest here is Richard's insistence that he 'sees' his parents in many of these dreams, but this is something I do not want to comment on at this stage.'

'But I *do* see them!' insisted Richard.

'Yes, I understand, but I'm afraid such sightings are not really very useful to us,' said Krippitz. 'What *is* interesting, though, are your trance experiences, and these are quite different from your dreams, as I'm sure you realise, Richard.'

Richard looked blankly at him, not really that sure what he was talking about. He was about to ask what he meant, but Krippitz continued.

'The main difference is your telepathic ability to communicate with others who also have this ability.'

'Like the Vikantus and Brimstone?' queried Kozan.

Krippitz turned in his seat to answer the question. Benno Kozan's very presence, even when he said little or nothing, was always a positive influence in any company. He was a member of the powerful Happanot tribe, whose holy men had been renowned for centuries as peacemakers and teachers to the scattered tribes of Hazaranet and their descendants. The Happanots were a peaceful people and their shamans, although still regarded as holy men with strange powers, now trained their young people to be useful and important citizens in the modern world of Amasia. So it was with Kozan, a successful lawyer who now sought to benefit all the people of Amasia through his position as Director of the Vallonium Institute.

'Only in that he can communicate with them, but Richard's ability is far greater than theirs,' said Krippitz. 'It is well known that the Vikantus evolved from a race that did not use language in the way that we know it, and that their telepathy is limited to much shorter distances – certainly, only in this dimension. As far as Brimstone is concerned we know even less. He and his two 'cousins', Sunstone and Firestone, as they are now known to us, arrived here, not from Old Earth, but from an unknown dimension. Apparently they were created on another world that we know nothing of, and besides the fact that they are virtually indestructible, all we can say about them is that they also have limited telepathic powers, and that they are excellent administrators. Unfortunately, despite my repeated requests for them to participate in tests to determine their powers, both Brimstone and Targa have refused to co-operate.'

'No doubt they don't like the idea of being treated like guinea pigs,' grunted Shah.

'Hardly guinea pigs!' protested Krippitz.

'No matter,' said Shah. 'As I understand it, we are here to determine *Richard's* power, so what have you concluded, Carl?'

Krippitz hesitated, while Anka cleared the coffee table and brought them fresh drinks and biscuits to nibble on, before he continued.

'The remarkable aspect of Richard's trances is the spontaneity with which they arrive. In every case there seems to be some kind of energy-trigger that induces the trance –'

'Like the zimmerball force-field!' said Archie, excitedly, trying to remember all the occasions he had witnessed Richard in a trance. 'And the Harmsway stone, and the time –'

'Exactly,' said Krippitz. 'Strangely enough, it would seem to confirm the old legends that the stones are sited over some kind of hidden energy source, such as vallonium inducing some kind of trance in our ancient predecessors.'

'That's the main reason why you did not go directly to Mount Tengi, Richard,' added the professor, who had been watching his nephew closely, wondering how he would react to all that Krippitz had said so far. 'The mountain is composed mainly of vallonium and we didn't know how such a massive amount of potential energy might affect you.'

'Oh … well … I feel OK, Uncle John; nothing's really bothered me here,' said Richard.

This wasn't exactly true because he was getting fed up with sitting listening to all this stuff about his trances or sightings, or whatever they wanted to call them. He'd far rather be outside with Archie exploring the rest of the compound, or whatever, but what really annoyed him was the old prune-faced woman who kept staring at him. Every time she attended to the coffee table she gave him a queasy feeling in his stomach.

'Good, that's very good,' said Krippitz, wanting to move on to his main theme, before there were any more interruptions. 'I think what we all want to know is how Richard's ability can be of use to us …' Krippitz glanced at Shah, expecting him to say something. He didn't, so he continued. 'Well, the most amazing discovery to come out of the tests was Richard's claim to have contacted Professor Strawbridge's Facility on Old Earth –'

'I did! I saw Chuck and left a message –'

'We believe you, Richard, of course we do. That is precisely why we are here today. It is your ability to contact Old Earth – and perhaps, other dimensions!'

Krippitz stopped for a moment, wanting all of them to reflect on what he had just said, and what it might mean to the timecrack project.

'Carl, when I announced to the Meeting House that Richard would be the key to our success, it was based entirely on an idea that Professor Strawbridge and I

209

shared shortly after his discussions with you at the clinic, but what I would like to know is, where do we stand *now?*' growled Shah, his earlier good humour deserting him as he tried to shift his weary body into a more comfortable position.

'Perhaps I should comment on this,' said the professor, raising a hand to stay Krippitz before he said any more. 'Over the past two weeks or so, I have carried out an in-depth study of the timecrack chamber and the vallonium power-grid – which, I must admit, is far beyond anything I could have conceived possible. However, I'm now in agreement with Dr Shah that we have the capability of sending a traveller into another dimension whenever we wish, although at this point we are only talking about Old Earth. The problem, of course, is pinpointing the *exact* time and place we want the traveller to arrive. Well, gentlemen, I believe we have the resources at the DONUT on Old Earth to resolve that problem, and that the *combined* forces of both facilities can send a traveller to any destination we choose!'

Archie gasped at what his uncle had just said.

'Do you really think we can go back home when we want to?'

'Yes, Archie, I do, but the crucial part of all this is that we need to establish a line of communication to the engineers at the Facility to enable them to line up the DONUT with the timecrack chamber.' The professor allowed his gaze to wander from Archie's incredulous face to rest on Richard. 'This is where we need Richard's help – we have to contact Ed Hanks, our chief engineer at the DONUT, to help us secure that connection.'

Suddenly it dawned on Archie, as it had with the rest of them, what the *real* problem was – could Richard repeat what he had achieved before? Could he contact the DONUT again? He looked at his young brother on whom so much now seemed to rest. Richard had dug his heels into the carpet and pushed himself away from the coffee table as if he didn't want to hear any more.

'Richard,' said Archie, 'do you think you can do it – get in touch with Ed Hanks?'

'I dunno … I … I've never really tried to *make* things happen before. They just *happen* …'

'Precisely!' said Krippitz, quickly. 'The tests we have carried out so far, and the past incidents that Richard has reported to us, have all been stimulated by *outside* factors. In other words, *he* has had no control over them.' He lifted his hands as if in supplication. 'What I have been endeavouring to discover through the tests is how Richard can take control over his own ability – this *power* that we know so little about.'

'And so, Carl, what do we do now?' asked Shah.

He was impatient now, knowing that Krippitz would talk all day about his work, but time was precious and he had to decide on what they should do next.

'There is little more that *I* can do at this stage, but I've discussed the matter with Benno Kozan, and he has a suggestion to put to Richard.'

Richard had taken to studying his feet for the last few minutes to avoid looking at the old woman with the horrible screwed-up face, who still seemed to be staring in his direction, but his head jerked up at the mention of his name. He was startled to find that Benno Kozan was also staring at him.

'What –'

'I was just saying, Richard, that after all you've heard here today, you might be surprised to know that there have been others who have experiences similar to your own. In fact, in my tribal homeland there is a holy man who helps my people understand such things.'

211

'Can he contact other ... places ... other worlds?' asked Archie.

His question was one of many that had been buzzing through his mind ever since Uncle John had said they could get back to Old Earth, but if Richard couldn't get in touch with the DONUT again, could anyone?

'I don't know, Archie. He is a very wise man, but it is not something he has ever spoken of,' said Kozan, casting his mind back to a time when he, too, was a young boy, who once sat at the feet of the great Shaman-Sing, and like Archie now, he had been full of confusion and unanswered questions. 'What I *do* know, is that he will help us find a way, if such a way exists; and that is why I would like you both to visit him in Naru, my home village – will you do that?'

Archie turned to Richard, who looked as confused and uncertain as he himself felt.

'What do you think?'

'I dunno – what do *you* think?'

'I don't think we have any choice. If we want to get back home.'

'Oh, by the way,' said Kozan, 'your uncle agrees, of course, but I've also secured Miss Harmsway's permission for you to take an extra few days leave from the college.'

'OK – we agree!' said Archie suddenly, convinced that besides being really important that they should go, anything would be better than sitting in Major Ramstiff's class. 'When do we go?'

'I need to confirm an escort, but it should be within the next day or so,' said Kozan.

'Good!' said Shah, waving to Anka to refill his glass. 'The sooner we get this business settled, the better.'

Chapter Twenty

Slashface

Three days after the meeting at the Gladden Plateau, Archie and Richard found themselves back at the Fort Temple hoverrail station, only this time they were on their own, waiting for Jules Stein who had volunteered to be their escort to Naru.

They were dressed in their new Harmsway College uniforms that Marjorie had insisted they wear for the journey.

'I'm not having nephews of Professor Strawbridge running around looking like vagabonds, especially when you're staying away overnight,' she had announced after breakfast.

She had then proceeded to fuss over them, making sure the smart dark-blue, denim-style jacket and trousers were a proper fit, and that the matching white T-shirts with the blue HC college logo had been properly ironed. Up until now, they'd had no choice but to make do with their old clothes and the several changes of plain T-shirts and trousers that were issued to all new students.

Marjorie hadn't been told – and she hadn't asked, but assumed it must be important – why the boys were going to Naru, but when she discovered they would be away overnight, maybe longer, she had immediately gone to the Harmsway tailor in Fort Temple and demanded that the uniforms be ready the next morning.

'The poor man was shaking when I told him that Miss Harmsway herself would be down to see him if they weren't ready – not true, of course, but I thought we'd all waited long enough for our outfits.' She'd winked and said, 'Just because I'm tutoring another class, doesn't mean I've stopped looking after you!'

She had also found them two shoulder bags for their overnight stuff including toiletries and fresh underclothes, and after a last minute inspection to check all was in order she had finally let them leave to catch the Freebus that would take them to the station.

Now they were standing at the back of the platform, behind a group of Salakin women chattering loudly about their forthcoming shopping trip to Sitanga , where they expected to pick up lots of bargains.

'Let's move down a bit,' said Archie. 'I don't know why women have to make so much noise about shopping – how can they get so excited about pots and pans?'

'I dunno,' said Richard, following Archie down the platform to a less crowded spot near the entry gate. 'Women are like that, I suppose. Look at the way Marjorie fussed around us this morning – I thought she'd never stop.'

'Maybe you're right,' said Archie, looking around the platform to see if there was any sign of Jules. 'Huh … look at that guy … it looks as if someone took a sword and slashed his face!'

'Where?'

'Over there – don't stare at him!'

Archie nodded towards four men wearing traders' robes standing a few yards away. One of them, a big man, had a long, thick cord-like scar that snaked a path from his brow down between his eyes, then over his nose and mouth into a cleft chin. He was carrying a long leather holdall that he set down on the platform. As he looked up, he caught Richard staring at him. Before Richard could look away, Slashface (as he now thought of him) gave a huge grin that exposed a mouthful of crooked yellow and black teeth.

'I told you not to stare!' whispered Archie.

'I couldn't help it – I've never seen a face like that before.'

Richard had turned away from Slashface, but he could still feel the big man's eyes boring into his back.

'Well, let's hope you don't end up sitting beside him,' said Archie, moving further away from the traders. He heard someone calling his name from near the gate and he turned around. 'Hey, Jules has arrived!'

They both waved to the tall athletic figure wearing the Harmsway uniform, carrying a large sports bag with a zimmerball bat strapped to the side. He yelled as he approached them.

'Hi, you guys, sorry I'm late, but my father called and I couldn't get away from the com. How are you both anyway?'

Archie told him they were fine, except that Richard seemed to be trying to pick a fight with one of the traders, nodding towards Slashface, who was talking to one of his friends.

'Ha, ha, very funny,' scowled Richard, looking around nervously, in case they could be heard.

'Holy snakes, he is an ugly brute!' said Jules, grinning at Richard's discomfort. 'I wouldn't want to take him on – by the look of him, he doesn't fight clean!'

Richard didn't appreciate their humour, and he wasn't prepared to listen anymore, so he just walked away, dropping his shoulder bag at Archie's feet.

'Where are you going?' called Archie.

'I'm going to get a drink,' Richard yelled back as he headed for a snack bar advertising Sticklejuice and sandwiches, at the end of the platform.

Archie and Jules watched him shuffle his way through a crowd of factory workers to join a queue at the snack bar. Marjorie had given each of them some

215

dolans to cover expenses during the journey, so Archie knew Richard was all right for money.

'I'm sorry,' said Jules, looking embarrassed. 'I didn't mean to make fun of him.'

'Oh, it's OK,' said Archie, 'he'll soon forget it. He just doesn't like my jokes!'

Fifteen minutes later Richard rejoined them. Having finished two bottles of Sticklejuice and a chocolate bar he seemed to be in a better mood, much to Archie's relief. A short time later they heard the dull swoosh of the Sitanga Express as it slipped into the station, the sliding doors of its four railcars opening as it stopped alongside the platform.

'C'mon.' Jules grabbed his sports bag and headed for the first railcar. 'I have the tickets.'

It suddenly dawned on Archie that he hadn't thought about tickets. He had just assumed it was like the Freebus that you got on and off wherever you liked. He supposed Finbar must have had tickets the last time they were on the hoverrail. He looked across to where the traders were and saw that they and Slashface were boarding the second railcar. Well, at least we'll not be sitting anywhere near them, he thought thankfully.

Jules inserted the tickets into a slot beside the sliding doors, where they were stamped and returned. With the boys in tow he made his way to a large curved window at the front of the railcar.

'Here, take these seats, you'll get a terrific view of the valley once we leave the station,' said Jules, putting their bags on a rack above the seats.

'How long will it take us to get to Naru?' asked Archie.

'It's about halfway to Sitanga, so I suppose around three hours will get us there,' said Jules, taking one of the front seats that afforded the passengers a panoramic view of the mountain on one side, and the streets of Fort Temple stretching away below them on the other.

The seats were divided by a central aisle, with the other seats occupied by the Salakin women, still chattering about their shopping expedition.

'Oh, heck,' muttered Archie, wondering if their incessant babble would last all the way to Naru.

He heard the warning whistle blow three times before the railcar doors finally closed to a raucous cheer from the Salakin shoppers. A few minutes later they had left the station far behind as the Sitanga Express quickly built up speed, skirting the edge of the mountain before dropping into the city suburbs and on into the open countryside.

*

Richard had sat quietly for the past half-hour, not saying a word, with his head tilted against the side window. With his fair hair obscuring his eyes, it was difficult to tell if he had fallen asleep – or, wondered Archie, was he … 'seeing' something?

The last time they travelled on the hoverrail they had passed the old monastery where Richard had spoken of seeing a hooded figure. Finbar had ridiculed him then, but now everyone knew differently, and Richard was being treated as something special – which he was – as he always had been, as far as Archie was concerned.

'Are you OK, Richard? You're not dreaming … or anything …?'

'Uh, no … no, I was just thinking about the holy man we're going to see.'

'What about him?'

'Uh, I dunno … It's just that we don't know anything about him. What's he supposed to do?'

'Don't worry about it,' said Archie, smiling. 'He'll probably just ask a lot of questions and then report back to Dr Shah what he thinks.'

'I suppose so,' said Richard, not sounding entirely convinced.

They settled back into their seats to enjoy the scenery while Jules pointed out different locations of interest including the Meeting House now coming up on their right. A few minutes later they swept past the great brownstone building and bell tower they had so recently visited and onwards to what looked like a major junction directly ahead. The Sitanga Express didn't slow down; instead they felt the railcar tilt as it forked to the left at the junction. They were going much faster now, literally flying above the hoverrail, giving both Archie and Richard the sensation of incredible speed as open fields and woodland blended together into a colourful tapestry.

'Port Zolnayta is over a thousand miles south on the Amasian Sea,' Jules announced, after nearly an hour. 'We're going south-east now past the Screaming Forest to Sitanga – Naru is on the other side of the forest.'

'The Screaming Forest?' said Richard, flicking his hair back and sitting up straight, his interest suddenly piqued by the strange name.

He remembered Finbar mentioning it during their walk through the streets of Fort Temple where he saw the odd-looking creatures for sale.

'Yeah, we're approaching it now,' said Jules, pointing to a line of tall trees in the distance. 'Well, it's really called Maroc Forest after the great maroc trees that grow there – because they don't grow anywhere else, I suppose – but everyone calls it the Screaming Forest because of the way the wind blows through the trees. It gets so bad at night they say that anyone who gets lost in there will go mad before the dawn. I don't know if it's true, but it's not a place where I would want to spend the night.' Jules shook his head at the thought of it. 'I was in there a couple of years ago with my father and his security supervisor when they were buying wolftans from the Rooters, but that was during daylight –'

'Wolftans? Rooters? What are they?' asked Archie, puzzled by the unusual names.

'I know! Finbar said they were bad-tempered brutes and that we should stay away from them!' said Richard, delighted to be able to tell Archie something he couldn't remember.

'I wouldn't worry too much about the Rooters, they're friendly enough, although they never say very much. As Richard says, it's the wolftans you want to watch out for. They run wild in the forest and the Rooters catch them when they're still young –'

'What for?' asked Richard.

'They rear them and train them as guard dogs, although, strictly speaking, they're really a rare species of wolf, and then they sell them to companies like my father's and to farmers to protect the land. They're really something – if you like that sort of thing.'

'What do you mean?'

'It's because their thick coats look like wood bark, and when they're lying still it's hard to tell you're not looking at a log of wood.'

'That's really weird,' said Archie.

'Maybe so,' said Jules, 'but when they're fully grown, they're really fearsome-looking with their six little ears and forked tails.'

'*Six* ears? You're kidding!' said Archie, trying to visualise a wolf's head with six ears.

'No, I'm not. It's because of their hearing that they're used for hunting and security work. They're supposed to be directly descended from the great wolves that used to roam Hazaranet millions of years ago.'

Archie was impressed by how much Jules knew about the wolftans.

'You know a lot about them, Jules.'

'I can thank Major Ramstiff for that,' said Jules. 'He wouldn't let me go to zimmerball practice unless I had written loads of essays on that kind of stuff. My father bought a few of them for the factories, so I've seen them close up – only with their handlers, of course!' he added quickly.

'Anyway, what is it about Naru that you have to go there? You know there's not very much to see there.'

There were shrieks of laughter from one of the Salakin women across the aisle, making Archie squirm in his seat as he tried to explain to Jules why he and Richard were going to see Shaman-Sing, the holy man, at his village.

'Well, I hope he can help,' said Jules, thinking of Richard's experience on the zimmerball bounce-pitch. 'Aristo said it was important when he asked me to escort you to Naru, but as I was going to Sitanga anyway it was no problem.'

'Are you going to see your father?'

Archie couldn't help comparing Jules with the man he had listened to in the Meeting House, thinking they weren't alike at all.

'Yes. He's arranged a tryout for me with the Sitanga Rangers at their headquarters.'

Archie looked at him blankly.

'They're the champions of the zimmerball league – and he's the chairman,' he explained.

'Oh …'

'He says they'll take me on after I graduate from Harmsway next year, but I know he's angling for me to go into the business instead of going on to university. The tryout is his way of getting me to Sitanga.'

'Don't you want to?'

'No, not really. I'd rather go on to the university and join Benno Kozan at the institute. He can't stand the thought of that –'

Jules suddenly stopped talking when they all heard a high-pitched scream from the rear of the railcar. They had been travelling for well over two hours now and had almost become used to the unending chatter from the Salakin women, but this was different. Another scream made Archie turn and look over the back of his seat to see from where it had come. What he saw at the end of the aisle made his blood run cold.

It was Slashface, and he was standing back to back with another man in the connecting doorway between the railcars. The leather holdall lay floppy and empty at his feet, with both the men now holding what looked like shotguns pointed directly at the passengers. A swarthy woman stood near him with her hands waving wildly in the air, screaming and crying for help.

'Shut your face, you stupid woman, or I will do it for you!' shouted Slashface, snarling and pushing her down into her seat with the shotgun barrel.

He advanced slowly along the aisle, his cruel eyes scanning the passengers until he spotted Jules, Archie and Richard at the front of the railcar by the panoramic window.

'You – the small one! Come here!' shouted Slashface.

He obviously means Richard, thought Archie, but why? Surely he can't be that annoyed because Richard stared at him? Just as he tried to think quickly about what they should do he felt the Express slowing down as if about to stop. Another woman, with her arm outstretched, pointed outside and started to scream. Now what?

'They've blocked the hoverrail!' yelled Jules, jumping to his feet. 'They must be Arnak rebels!'

Pandemonium broke out when some of the passengers saw that large boulders and long branches cut from the Maroc trees next to the line, blocked the hoverrail. Four men in long robes, gripping swords by their sides, were standing in front of the makeshift barrier waiting for the Express to come to a halt.

Slashface tried to force his way down the narrow aisle, but the panicking Salakin women, terrified by the thought of being assaulted by their ancient enemy, were trying to get past him. Angry and roaring, he demanded that they get out of his way.

'Move aside – or I will shoot!' He barged forwards, stepping over a woman who had fallen in the aisle. He pointed the shotgun at Richard and shouted to Jules and Archie. 'Bring the boy to me!'

Jules watched as Slashface approached, and then he did something that he would come to regard as probably the most foolish thing he had ever done in his life. He suddenly leapt forwards, grabbed the barrel of the shotgun with both hands and tried to wrest it out of Slashface's grip.

Booomm!

The sound of the shotgun was deafening in the confined space of the railcar. *Booomm*!

It roared again and the panoramic window-glass blew into a thousand pieces.

Jules fell to one side, a red stain appearing in the shoulder of his dark-blue jacket. Slashface shouldered his way past him and reached over to Richard cowering in the seat behind Archie.

'*Run, Richard – get out of here*!'

Shocked and confused by what had just happened to Jules, Archie was yelling at the top of his voice, not knowing or caring where Richard could run to, just as long as he escaped from Slashface. When Slashface's hand appeared in front of him trying to grab Richard, he knew there was only one thing he could do. He bit it as hard as he could and held on.

Slashface screeched in agony and fell back into the melee of women pushing and tugging to get out of the railcar. Someone had hit the emergency button to release the sliding doors, and the passengers were spilling out of the railcars onto a grassy embankment, ignoring the threats of the Arnaks still on board.

Archie tried to place himself between Slashface and Richard, but he found himself swinging from side to side as Slashface attempted to free his hand. He bit down even harder until he tasted the blood seeping through his lips. It made him feel sick, but now he was too frightened to let go.

'*Aaaahh!*'

The howl of pain made Archie look up, but he was too late. Slashface's disfigured face was contorted with rage as he brought the barrel of the shotgun down on his head. It was a glancing blow, but it was enough to make Archie open his mouth. He staggered back as Slashface hit him again.

Red sparks danced before his eyes, and then darkness descended as he twisted round to see what had happened to Richard. He was losing consciousness, but as his eyes filmed over, he could see that Richard's seat was empty.

Somehow in all the confusion, Richard had managed to disappear.

Chapter Twenty-One

Maroc Forest

Nitkin turned to Anakat and the other two Arnaks standing behind him at the makeshift barrier they had built earlier. His eyes blazed with anger as he ordered them to follow him.

'The fools have let the boy get away! Catch him before he reaches the forest!'

At the moment the Sitanga Express came to a halt, Nitkin had been ready to rush forwards with his men to help secure whichever railcar the boy was in, but he had been stopped in his tracks by the unexpected explosions that had blown out the window at the front of the railcar.

To his astonishment he had seen the boy climb through the window and drop to the ground, then stand still as if not knowing what to do next. Suddenly, the boy made a dash to the edge of the forest when one of the Arnaks appeared at the shattered window, shouting and pointing a shotgun at him.

'Don't shoot – he must be kept alive!' Nitkin screamed in frustration as he watched the boy dive into the forest. 'Follow him, you fools!'

He spurred his men to intercept the boy before he disappeared in amongst the trees. Yelling obscenities and brandishing their swords they forced their way through the crowd of fleeing passengers, who became panic-stricken at the sight of more armed Arnak rebels descending on them. Nitkin ignored them, rushing forward to confront Slashface and his men as they leapt from the railcar to the side of the track.

'Dogs! You have let the boy get past you!' snarled Slashface, holding a rag around his hand where Archie had bitten him.

'You forget yourself,' hissed Nitkin. 'Remember it was *you* who let him escape and now he has gone into the forest!'

He let the words linger, knowing full well the impact his words would have on the men and their fears of entering the forest.

Slashface had no love for Nitkin, and he showed his contempt by spitting at his feet. He stepped forward and gripped Anakat's shoulder, who shook with fear at what might happen next.

'You are an old woman, Nitkin. Give me this man and the others and I will find the boy,' growled Slashface, motioning to the others to join him. 'You can do as you wish. Stay here, or follow.'

Furious, but knowing he had no other choice if they were not to incur Prince Lotane's wrath for letting the boy escape, Nitkin followed the men into the forest. He was as apprehensive as any Arnak might be venturing into Maroc, the territory of the little people known as the Rooters, so named because of the homes they had made among the roots of the mighty maroc trees.

Long ago, in a more turbulent time, when the Arnaks and the Salakins had gone their separate ways, keeping an uneasy peace, the Arnaks had settled in a far-off land. There in a deep gorge they had carved a city out of the huge, dark grey marble walls they found in the quarries at the end of the gorge. To help them build their new city they raided villages far and near where they captured and enslaved entire families, leaving behind only those too sick or feeble to work. Those captured were the little people, whose only skills up until that time had been confined to hunting the rich wildlife on the grassy plains and fishing in the numerous rivers that flowed throughout the fertile land.

The little people's village huts were simple affairs constructed from mud, bricks and wooden roofs. They had no working knowledge of stone or marble; nevertheless, they were dragged from their homes – men, women and children alike – and forced to work in the quarries until they dropped.

The Arnaks were not a compassionate people, and they were not disposed to caring for those less fortunate than themselves, so they simply threw those who could no longer work, along with those who died from their injuries in the quarries, into the bottom of the gorge.

One day, when one of the Arnak overseers in the biggest quarry killed one of the little people for not working fast enough, the anger of the little people finally exploded. They attacked and dragged the overseer to the edge of the gorge and threw him in, while everyone cheered as he fell to the bottom. Their joy was short-lived, however, when they realised what they had done. The little people knew they had no choice now but to escape from the Darklands and the city they were building, or they might all be dead by the time the city was completed.

The uprising took the Arnaks completely by surprise and, although many of the little people died during the fighting that ensued, many others managed to escape to finally reach the vast forestlands where the great maroc trees grew.

In the centuries that followed their captivity and escape, the Rooters remained a peaceful people, but they possessed long memories of the suffering their ancestors had endured in the Darklands, so every year they held a festival of storytelling and feasting in the large clearing deep in the forest where they told many versions of the great escape. Many who listened to the tales, which became more vivid and outrageous with the passing of the years, would nod in sympathy at the dreadful deeds inflicted on the little people so long ago.

Naturally enough, the Arnaks were not especially welcome in the forest, but a few enterprising souls, interested only in trade, would sometimes venture in to purchase wolftan pups, and as long as they left before nightfall, they were tolerated.

It was with this knowledge that Nitkin entered the forest, trying to put to one side the stories he had heard about the Arnaks who had stayed too long in the forest and were never seen again.

He could only hope that the boy had not gone too far.

*

Richard kept his head down as the little man beside him pointed back along the path they had just left.

'Do not let them see you, young one. Whatever you have done, they are intent on finding you.'

'I haven't done anything!' whispered Richard, crouching as low as he could in the soft mulch between the thick roots of a maroc tree.

He was terrified that Slashface or the others would find him, but neither did he want to stay in this dark, frightening place not knowing what had happened to Archie or Jules. When Archie had shouted at him to run, he'd pushed out the rest of the shattered glass from the frame of the window and jumped. He had expected Archie to follow, but neither he nor Jules were anywhere to be seen.

After Slashface appeared at the window with the shotgun, Richard had run for his life towards the trees, expecting at any moment, to hear the roar of the shotgun behind him. There were several paths leading into the forest, but the one he took led him unexpectedly towards a little figure peeking out from behind a tree. He hesitated, but the little man beckoned to him to leave the path and join him under the cover of several thick bushes between the trees.

Richard's hand was stinging where he had cut it climbing through the window of the railcar, and he was holding it tight to his chest to stop the pain as he dived into the bushes. The little man noticed his discomfort and took a look at the cut. Suddenly he spat on it and pulled a broad dock leaf and its stem from a large, spreading plant beside him. He pinched the stem and squeezed the sticky sap into the cut with the spit until Richard felt the stinging feeling disappear.

'Soon be better,' he said, smiling at the look of surprise on Richard's face.

He must be one of the Rooters, thought Richard, beginning to feel safer now that he seemed to have found a friend willing to help him. The Rooter was small, less than four feet tall, with pale soapy skin that didn't see the sun very often. He wore a leather tunic and trousers, a mix of red, green and brown colours, which blended well with the bark and branches of the maroc trees.

'I am Beepoo,' said the Rooter. 'Who are you?'

'Richard – I'm called Richard.'

'*Reech*-ard … it is a strange name,' said Beepoo.

Suddenly he put a finger to his lips and looked over the root they were hiding behind. One of the Arnaks, a fat man wearing a coarse woollen robe, was sweating and breathing so heavily they could hear him clearly at fifty feet as he made his way along the path. Behind him, another man was sweeping his sword back and forth through the shrubs that hung over each side of the path, muttering and swearing as he did so.

'We must leave,' said Beepoo. He left the cover of the root on his hands and knees, gesturing to Richard to follow him.

Richard, frightened by the sight of the men with swords, jumped to his feet too quickly. He was spotted by the fat man who yelled at him to stop. Beepoo grabbed Richard's arm, silently pulling him onto the path, where they ran as fast as they could into the forest.

*

'There they are! I see them!' cried Anakat, excitedly, but within moments he had lost sight of them as they disappeared into the trees.

'What do you mean, *them*?' growled the other man.

Before Anakat could answer him, Slashface, Nitkin and the rest of the Arnaks came running towards them. They had heard Anakat yelling and hoped he had captured the boy.

'Where is he?' demanded Slashface. He gripped Anakat by the collar of his robe so tightly that he risked choking him. 'Why were you yelling?'

'They – they've gone into – *aaah*!'

Anakat felt the thick fingers on his robe squeeze even tighter.

'*They*?'

'Yes, I saw the boy with one of the Rooters – *please* … aaah!* You're choking me!'

Slashface had Anakat raised up on his toes, close to his face, so close that Anakat could smell the foulness of his breath.

'You fat fool!' spat Slashface. 'Your yelling probably made them run.' He released his hold on Anakat and turned to Nitkin. 'We will have to move quickly before it gets dark, or we will never find the boy.'

Nitkin had to agree with him, but he had no desire to go any farther into the forest, especially not with this madman and his shotgun, who seemed to be prepared to shoot anyone who got in his way.

'You're right, but some of us must stay to the rear in case the boy doubles back,' said Nitkin.

Slashface wasn't fooled. He knew Nitkin for the hypocritical coward that he was, but neither did he care. Whoever found the boy and brought him to Prince Lotane would be greatly favoured and rewarded, and he would not allow Nitkin, or anyone else, to deprive him of that pleasure.

'Do as you wish,' sneered Slashface. 'Stay to the rear with two men, but your fat friend comes with me.'

'No! I don't –' squealed Anakat.

'Shut up! Your sharp eyes found the boy once, you can again.'

Not wanting to waste any more time, Slashface pushed Anakat forward along the path with the shotgun in his back. He called to the man with the other shotgun and two others to follow him, leaving Nitkin with two men to stay behind.

During the confrontation between Slashface and Nitkin, neither of them, nor any of their men, noticed the figure crawling on his belly through the undergrowth on a path that ran parallel with theirs. It was only twenty feet away, but the path couldn't be seen because of the tall thick grass and the twisting maroc roots that seemed to spread in every direction across the forest floor.

As Slashface and his men made their way farther into the forest in pursuit of Richard and the Rooter, they were unaware they had been joined by Archie following a short distance behind them.

*

Earlier, in the railcar, Archie had regained consciousness to find himself lying on the floor between the seats. How long he had lain unconscious, he had no idea, but now he had a thumping headache that threatened to split his head wide open. He felt gingerly above his right ear and discovered a lump where Slashface had struck him. It was the size of an egg, or so it felt, and he winced as he touched it.

A low groaning sound made him look round. It was Jules – *he wasn't dead*! One of the Salakin women was tending to his wound with a piece of cloth torn from her robe, while an elderly man he hadn't seen before was taking off his woollen jacket to make a pillow for Jules's head.

'Will he be all right?' asked Archie anxiously, rising to his feet.

The woman looked at him and nodded, but said nothing. She tore another piece of cloth from the hem of her robe and packed it against Jules's wound.

'He has been fortunate,' said the old man. 'The flesh was damaged and he has lost some blood, but he will survive. He is a strong one and that will help him.'

'But shouldn't we get him to a hospital, or somewhere?' asked Archie, wondering how much the old man knew about medicine or first aid.

He watched Jules as he shifted restlessly, moaning softly every time the woman touched his wound.

'The emergency system will have triggered an alarm in Sitanga,' said the man, aware of Archie's concern, 'and they will send a Lancer patrol to see what has happened. They will look after him, do not worry.'

Archie felt a flood of relief that Jules was going to be okay, but it was short – lived when he asked about Richard.

'Have you seen my brother? I think he must have climbed through the window after Jules was shot.'

'If you mean the small boy who was sitting beside you,' said the woman, speaking for the first time, 'he went into the forest, and the evil ones were not far behind him.' She stared at him as if uncertain what to say next. 'He is in great danger. You must find him before they do!'

She said nothing more and turned to Jules to fix the cloth padding more tightly on his wound in an attempt to staunch the blood seeping through his shirt.

What does she mean? Of course, Richard was in danger. Anybody would be if someone was shooting at them; but did she mean something else? thought Archie. He stared at her, wanting to ask her what she knew, if anything, about the danger Richard was supposed to be in, but she ignored him and he guessed it must be the Arnak rebels she was talking about. He turned and went to the open door of the railcar and looked up at the dark grey clouds gathering above the forest. He stood for a moment, feeling the stinging wind on his cheeks as it gathered strength.

The woman was right about one thing: he had to find Richard, and before nightfall, if what Jules had said about the wind was true. What if there were wolftans nearby? He shook his head as he tried to rid himself of the image of what a six-eared wolf would look like. It was pretty scary, but he couldn't waste any more time thinking about it.

Jules moaned out loud, his eyes flickering open briefly as he regained consciousness. Archie took a last look at him, giving him a little wave, not knowing if Jules could see him, before leaping from the railcar onto a grassy embankment. He landed on his toes then fell forwards onto his hands and knees. He picked himself up, hesitating just for a moment before making a mad dash for the trees.

Approaching the edge of the forest, Archie could see there were several paths he could take, but one was wider and seemed well-worn. It forked after a few feet with a track to the right where the ground had been disturbed by heavy footprints. Maybe the Arnaks had come this way; he had no way of knowing, but he decided to follow it anyway.

The forest was a gloomy and forbidding place to enter. Shafts of remaining sunlight pierced breaks in the forest canopy, falling on the forest floor to create strange shadow shapes amongst the trees. A light breeze was building, and the rustling of leaves mingled with the sound of running water somewhere nearby. Archie shivered as he turned up the collar of his jacket to keep the chill out and pressed on.

'*Ouch*!'

He yelped as an overhanging branch sprung back and hit him on the head near his painful lump. For the past few minutes he had veered onto another track that had looked promising, but now he was forcing his way over tree roots and through spiky bushes that crowded the path in front of him, making it almost impossible to go any farther. It didn't seem likely that Richard or the Arnaks had come this way, but he was reluctant to retrace his steps now that he had come this far. It was when he paused for a minute to think about what to do next that he heard the sounds coming through the trees.

It was someone yelling.

He dropped to his knees then onto his belly, holding a hand over his lump to protect it from the low branches as he crawled slowly forward to a ridge of stones and grass beyond the bushes. The ridge was at the top of a slope overlooking another path where several men had stopped. Among them was Slashface, and he was holding a fat man by the throat, obviously threatening him. He seemed to be interrogating him, but his grip was so tight the poor man could hardly speak. Not terribly clever, thought Archie.

As Archie listened, Slashface suddenly released the man and turned to the other men to give an order. They were splitting up, but Archie had heard enough to realise that Richard was with a Rooter, and Slashface was going after him.

Chapter Twenty-Two

The Wolftans

An hour later, maybe more, Archie couldn't be sure, but he was struggling now to keep up with the Arnaks. He was hot and tired, and his head was throbbing as he tried to concentrate on not making any loud sounds. He knew that the sound of snapping twigs or loose stones and rocks kicked aside might warn the Arnaks that someone was following them.

With every step he took, he was trying so hard not to be heard that he only became aware of the strange growling sound when he stopped to climb over a fallen tree trunk. His neck hairs bristled as he turned slowly around to face the wolftan that had suddenly appeared behind him.

'*Yaaahhh*! *Go away!*'

Archie screamed so loudly that the wolftan retreated a short distance from the unexpected noise and stood still. It was only for a moment or so, but it was enough time for Archie to get to the lower branches of a maroc tree and climb to the safety of a wide cradle-shaped branch that would keep him out of sight of the vicious-looking beast.

After a minute, he chanced a peek over the edge to look at the curious creature now prowling and sniffing around the bottom of the tree. It was no bigger than the gatekeeper's Labrador back at Grimshaws, but its long narrow head with six little pointed ears twitching at every sound and an open jaw full of sharp yellow teeth did nothing to improve its appearance. Fierce green eyes gazed up expectantly as it circled restlessly, waiting for Archie to climb down again.

*

'What was that?'

One of the Arnaks stopped suddenly when he heard the scream.

'It sounds like the boy,' muttered Anakat, nervously looking around at Slashface.

'You may be right,' said a grinning Slashface, his mood lightened by the thought of catching the boy, 'and where do you think he is, my fat friend?'

'Over there.' Anakat pointed to a break in the trees behind them where they could see another path. 'I think it came from over there.'

'Good. You may prove your worth yet, Anakat. Quickly, move before we lose him.'

Slashface pushed the shotgun savagely into Anakat's back, motioning to the other Arnaks with the swords to clear a way for them. Hacking at the undergrowth and thorn bushes, the Arnaks forced a fast pace to the other path. Anakat hurried to take the lead before Slashface had a chance to hit him again.

Anakat was fat and cumbersome, but his senses were sharp, especially his hearing, and it wasn't long before he heard something moving ahead of him. When he suddenly came to a halt, Slashface walked straight into him.

'What is it now? Why have you stopped?'

Slashface strode forward, pushing Anakat out of the way to take a closer look. Anakat didn't answer. He pointed a shaking finger at a huge maroc tree where a young wolftan was growling softly and looking up at a boy clinging to a thick branch overhanging the path.

Slashface quickly took in the scene, brought the shotgun up to his shoulder, took aim and fired, all in one swift movement, before any of the Arnaks realised what had happened. The wolftan was lifted several feet off the ground, its head almost severed, spraying blood across the path as its carcass careered into the deep grass above a stony ditch.

'You. Get down here!' ordered Slashface, pointing the shotgun towards the tree. 'Now, or I'll blow you out of there!'

Archie was trembling as he climbed down from the tree, but he was determined not to show how frightened he was in front of the Arnaks. They formed a circle around him, preventing any chance of escape, but after what happened to the wolftan he wasn't inclined to make any attempt to do so.

Slashface studied him closely, pushing his damaged hand into Archie's face.

'You! You're the one who bit me!' he roared. 'Where is your brother?'

'I don't know… I'm looking for him, too.'

'Don't lie to me! You told him to run – where to?'

'I don't know – *hey*!'

Archie suddenly found himself lying flat on his back with Slashface's foot on his chest. He tried to wriggle away, but Slashface pressed harder, almost stopping his breath.

'Stay still! You are not going anywhere until you tell me where your brother is hiding.'

*

Beepoo frowned and gestured to Richard to hurry up. He couldn't understand, with the Arnaks so close behind them, why Richard had stopped. They had to keep moving until it was dark; only then would they be safe.

They had arrived at the river that led to the Clearing where Beepoo lived with his sister and the other Rooters; a place that no outsider ever came to unless they had been invited, and rarely did they stay after daylight if they valued their safety. Soon he and Richard would be there and he could let the forest deal with the Arnaks.

Richard had unexpectedly stopped behind him by the little wooden bridge they had just crossed near the waterfall. He was watching the water burst over moss-covered rocks, frothing and spitting as it dropped into a shallow pool several feet below, while directly above, shafts of fading sunlight pierced the forest canopy to fall on coloured pebbles, glinting like little diamonds just below the surface of the pool.

Despite Beepoo's insistence that they must hurry, Richard had spent the last few minutes staring into the pool, seemingly mesmerised by the sounds of the waterfall and the ever-changing patterns in the water. As Beepoo spoke to him, Richard closed his eyes and his mouth started to work as if he was trying to say something.

'What is it, Richard? Are you in pain?' asked Beepoo, his little pale face creasing with concern as he tried to understand what was wrong with his new friend.

Richard's eyelids were flickering, his head cocked to one side, as if there was a sound he was trying to catch: something, or someone, that Beepoo could not hear. Suddenly, his eyes snapped open and he called out:

'Archie! No, don't…'

His words trailed off when Beepoo touched his arm, startling him into looking around, momentarily making him uncertain of where he was or what he might have said. He had been dreaming … No … It wasn't a dream … He had *seen* Archie, and he was somewhere in the forest – with the Arnaks!

'Beepoo, we have to go back! My brother's in trouble. I think he's been caught by the men who are chasing us!'

'How can you know this?' said Beepoo, shaking his head disbelievingly. 'We cannot go back – it is too dangerous.'

'We must, Beepoo! I *know* Archie is in trouble. Please ... We have to go back!'

Beepoo thought it very strange that Richard should behave in this way. Only the shaman of the Happanots would say such things when he was asleep, and only he could see and know what other men did when they were far away. Richard was neither shaman nor a Happanot, so how could he know what was happening to his brother?

While he pondered this, Beepoo thought also of the men who pursued them. They must be the rebel Arnaks his people spoke of in hushed tones when they sat around the campfires discussing the affairs of the valley. It was said that such Arnaks wanted to return to the old ways and that they would cause death and destruction to all those who stood in their way, including their own tribesmen.

Why they would do such things he had no idea, for the Rooters had kept an uneasy peace with most of the Arnaks for centuries, but always with the memory of what had happened to their ancestors so long ago. Now the men in the forest meant to harm Richard, of this he was certain, and it might well be that they meant to harm the Rooters as well.

Beepoo nodded thoughtfully as he considered this possibility. He reached into a leather tube attached to his belt and withdrew a beautifully carved wooden flute with a finely crafted bone mouthpiece. He proceeded to play a series of notes that were long and piercing.

Eeeppp! *Eeeepppp*! *Eeeeeppp*!

They were so sharp that Richard was forced to cover his ears with his hands until the notes became shriller and so high-pitched that he could no longer hear them.

'What are you doing?' asked Richard impatiently now that Beepoo had stopped playing.

'If, as you say, your brother is in trouble, then we must go back,' agreed Beepoo, 'but we will not go back alone. I have summoned the wolftans to join us.'

'What! But aren't they dangerous?'

'Do not worry, Richard, they are my friends and you are safe with me. Now we must move quickly to meet them.'

Clutching his flute, Beepoo recrossed the bridge, rapidly retracing his steps along the path they had just left, with Richard close behind.

*

It was almost dark now and Anakat was getting restless. Slashface had sent two men, including one with a shotgun, after the boy and the Rooter, but that was nearly an hour ago and they had not returned. Anakat was of the opinion they would not be seen again, and said as much to the man who sat beside him.

'We should leave here before the wind gets stronger, we all know what happens after dark to those who outstay their welcome in Maroc,' said Anakat, fearfully.

'Do not let him hear you,' said the other man, nodding towards Slashface, 'or he will make you suffer long before the wind comes. He will not leave here without the boy, but he will happily leave you behind with that young one.'

Anakat glanced across to where Slashface was pacing angrily up and down in front of the boy they had discovered in the tree. The boy cried out in pain as he

240

was kicked again while lying on the ground. His wrists and ankles were bound with leather thongs and he was tethered like a goat to a tree root, while Slashface shouted abuse at him, demanding to know where his brother was hiding.

As he watched, Anakat shuddered at the thought of being trapped in the forest overnight with this madman. His imagination ran wild as he remembered the stories from his childhood of the wolftans that devoured Arnaks, and the Screaming Wind that drove men mad. He shouldn't be here and he blamed Nitkin for getting him into this mess, and he had no intention of staying any longer than necessary.

His chance to leave came when his companion got to his feet and entered the bushes to answer the call of nature. With both men occupied and not paying any attention to him, Anakat knew that this might be his only chance to make his move to escape before either of them discovered he had gone.

Wasting no more time, he slipped away and made for the break in the trees they had entered earlier. He was no sooner through when he heard the shouting and the loud boom of the shotgun. It was Slashface and he was shooting blindly into the trees after him! Panic-stricken, Anakat tried to run faster, but his weight was a hindrance and after only a short distance he collapsed to his hands and knees, gasping for breath, his heart thumping so hard it felt ready to burst through his chest.

With his hands spread flat on the ground and his head bowed low, Anakat didn't see the wolftans, but as they got closer, their foul, offensive odour quickly overwhelmed him. Raising his head slowly, worried by what he might see, Anakat was confronted by a sight that made him think he was looking at the guardians of the gates to the underworld, threatening him with hellfire and damnation.

Towering over him, as big as a young pony, the leading wolftan was snarling and drooling thick globules of saliva from its huge open maw. A long, reddish-grey tongue hung loosely between razor-sharp yellow fangs while a cloud of rancid breath drifted through the air between them. The wolftan moved a pace towards him, its luminous green eyes locked onto his terrified face.

The wind was gathering strength and the damp, musty smell from the wolftan's thick wood-like coat of matted hair, made Anakat feel even more nauseous. He screamed in terror and threw himself flat onto the ground, covering his head with his chubby hands, pleading to Zamah that these beasts from the underworld would not harm him.

'Get to your feet, Fat One!' commanded a voice from above.

Anakat lifted his head and opened his eyes. Confused and frightened, he stood up, wondering if Zamah had actually heard him, but what he saw was even more confusing, for sitting astride the wolftan was a Rooter, and behind him on another wolftan was the boy Slashface was seeking.

Richard watched the fat man stagger to his feet, obviously worried that Beepoo's wolftan was about to devour him. He couldn't blame him, for Richard had felt just as frightened when he first met the wolftans.

Soon after they had left the bridge, Beepoo had played his flute again, calling the wolftans to him as they approached the place where the Arnaks held Archie. When the wolftan pack arrived, Beepoo spoke in a language Richard didn't understand, the language chip implanted in his neck seemingly unable to translate what he said. Two of the large beasts lay on the ground, so that he and Beepoo could mount them. In spite of his nervousness, Richard enjoyed riding the powerful animal, its strange matted coat deceivingly soft and comforting to the touch, although the smell took some getting used to.

They had ridden quickly to reach the path Archie had taken, the wolftans picking up his scent and that of the Arnaks. A few minutes later they had heard the shotgun blast and Anakat's stumbling progress through the undergrowth. Now Anakat stood shaking like a leaf before them.

'Where is my brother? What have you done with him?' demanded Richard.

'He's back there,' squealed Anakat, 'but I had nothing to do with hurting him.'

'What do you mean? Who has hurt him?'

He never answered. A shot rang out and Anakat fell to the ground, his arms flung out wide in shock. The wolftans snarled and slunk aside as the body fell amongst them. Beepoo commanded them to stay still just as his keen eyes spotted Slashface with the shotgun, passing behind one of the maroc trees.

'I see him, Richard,' said Beepoo. 'Stay close to me – we will let the wolftans take the lead.'

As they approached Slashface he beckoned to them with the shotgun.

'Boy! Come here quickly – by yourself, or both of you will join that fat fool over there!'

Expecting Richard to come to him, Slashface moved away from the tree and stepped out onto the path, but in that brief instant he was astonished to find that he was on his own. He had made the mistake of forgetting he was at the mercy of the Rooters and that *they* were the masters of the Screaming Forest.

Beepoo had needed only that instant to command the wolftans to move to the cover of the trees, well out of sight of Slashface. Now they moved swiftly until they came to the tree where Archie was tied. The remaining Arnak fled for his life when he saw the snarling wolftans bearing down on him.

'Archie!' yelled Richard, leaping from the back of his wolftan.

Beepoo watched as the young boy dashed to his brother, but frowned as the wolftan he was riding growled and made its way towards something lying in the grass near a shallow ditch. He dismounted to discover the body of a young wolftan that he had cared for since its mother's first litter. It had strayed from him earlier that day when he had ventured to the edge of the forest to see the Sitanga Express pass by.

'Eena,' he cried softly, although no tears came from his eyes.

He would mourn later after he had buried his faithful companion, but first he would have to find the evil Arnak, who seemed to be cursed with the killing urge.

As it happened, he didn't have to wait. Beyond the tree root where Archie was tied, Beepoo saw the figure of Slashface step from behind a maroc tree to raise and aim his shotgun in Archie's direction.

Calling to the wolftan he had been riding, Beepoo commanded the great beast to attack Slashface.

Neither Archie nor Richard knew what was happening until they heard the terrible screech of fear as the wolftan turned away from the ditch and launched itself over twenty feet through the air to seize Slashface by the throat and drag him into the trees. His dreadful cries suddenly stopped and there was only the sound of the wind as it disturbed the distant treetops. It was the last they ever saw or heard of him.

By the time Richard managed to loosen Archie's bonds only two wolftans remained. The others had been despatched by Beepoo to rid the forest of the rebel Arnaks, so that they would never threaten the Rooters again.

'They will not return; the wolftans and the Screaming Wind will see to it that they do not,' said Beepoo.

He was sad and would say no more about it.

Eena was buried on a slope by the waterfall, as it had been her favourite playground. As for Anakat, Beepoo said that like the others he would be left to the forest. Shortly after, they mounted the wolftans, Richard by himself and Archie behind Beepoo, for the journey to the Clearing, the home of the Rooters.

Chapter Twenty-Three

Shaman-Sing

The Screaming Wind howled and shrieked as it smashed its way through the upper branches of the great maroc trees. Not even the earplugs that Beepoo had fashioned for Archie and Richard could totally block out the horrendous noise as the wind roared through the forest.

They had stopped earlier to pick some chamomile leaves, which Beepoo moistened in the river to form earplugs that Archie and Richard pressed into their ears. Beepoo apparently didn't need them; and the wolftans seemed unaffected even though the wind was screaming through the trees at such a pitch that they couldn't hear each other speak.

Falling leaves and particles of soil swirled around Archie's head like a cloud of locusts, preventing him from seeing more than three or four feet in any direction. His eyes had adjusted to the darkness of the forest, helped by the occasional breaks in the canopy that allowed starlight to penetrate, but now it was almost impossible to see where they were going. Only Beepoo's homing instinct and the sure-footedness of the wolftans were keeping them on the right path.

Suddenly Beepoo turned to Archie and pointed to a dull golden glow that had appeared some distance ahead of them. Like a lighthouse in a stormy sea it beckoned to them, offering a safe passage home.

Although Archie could still hear the wind above and behind him, it seemed to be easing in front, with the falling leaves dispersing sufficiently to reveal the path now widening towards a large open space.

It was the Clearing.

As they rode into it Archie could see that a ring of gigantic maroc trees, much bigger than any he had seen so far, enclosed it. Open to a night sky filled with a million strange stars it was like an oasis in the middle of the forest.

Two vallonium lamps mounted on stout wooden poles on either side of the path marked the entrance as Beepoo led the way past a large corral where twenty, or more, wolftans were being settled for the night by a Rooter wearing a long cloak. He gave Beepoo a friendly wave then turned away to the task in hand.

Archie pulled the earplugs out and threw them away, relieved to get the sodden leaves out of his ears. He listened for a moment, and then realised that the sound of the wind had diminished to that of a distant roar of ocean waves crashing on a faraway rocky shore.

They stopped in front of a maroc tree where a narrow pebble path led between great serpentine roots to a small door at the bottom of a flight of polished stone steps. Light spilled out over the steps from a circular glass window next to the door, revealing a cosy interior that promised a peaceful haven for the rest of the night; something that, after his experience at the hands of Slashface, Archie was in desperate need of, and, no doubt, Richard was too.

'Is this where you live, Beepoo?' asked Archie, noticing that all around the Clearing dozens of maroc trees had similarly lit windows, some with Rooters standing outside chatting and staring at the strangers who had just arrived amongst them.

The whole place had the curious effect of a small country village stuck in the middle of a vast forest.

'Yes, this is my home. I live here with my sister –'

As if she had just been announced, a young woman, with her dark brown hair tied back in a ponytail, called out to him. Wearing the typical reddish-green and brown colours of the Rooters, her dress flounced up to reveal leather trousers tucked neatly into a pair of little bootees, as she came rushing up the steps to greet them.

'Beepoo! You are safe! I was so worried about you – you have been away so long – and when they said you had summoned the wolftans –'

'Quiet, Anni! Do not babble so!' said Beepoo.

He then spoke in that strange tongue that the wolftans seemed to understand. He commanded them to lie on the ground, making it easier for them to dismount, before ordering the huge beasts to return to the corral where they would spend the night.

He followed his sister as she fussed around Archie and Richard like a mother hen, urging them down the steps and into the tree house. It was late and Anni could see that the boys were very tired and dirty, their clothes torn and stained. She said little more, knowing from the look on Beepoo's face that he would tell her what had happened in his own good time.

They entered a large room where the massive maroc tree's roots spiralled across the ceiling and down the earthen walls before plunging deep into the ground around them. A low, wooden table and chairs stood on a brightly coloured rug in the centre of the room. Overhead, a vallonium lamp cast its golden glow around the walls revealing doorways that suggested the house was bigger than it seemed from the outside. Over the centuries, previous inhabitants in each generation had tunnelled and excavated between the roots to create extra chambers for their families, but, as Anni explained, now that there was only Beepoo and herself living in the house, there was plenty of room for visitors.

She ushered Archie and Richard into separate cubicles, each simply furnished with a wooden bunk and a bedside table supporting a vallonium lamp. A peculiar familiar smell made Archie's nostrils twitch as he entered the cubicle and sat on the bunk.

'What's that ... smell?'

'Ah, that is the mattress,' said Anni, 'it is filled with wolftan hair, which is very soft, and I have added lavender and lemon, which is good for sleep.'

She smiled, pleased that Archie had noticed her efforts to make the bed comfortable. Archie smiled back, but he hadn't the heart to tell her that the wolftan stink was still quite overpowering.

*

The next morning, as she busied herself preparing the midday meal, Anni told Beepoo that Shaman-Sing had sent a message that he would arrive later that day to visit Archie and Richard.

'It must be very important for Shaman-Sing to make the journey so soon after his last visit,' said Anni. 'We do not see him more than twice a year and he was here only last month for his supply of medicinal herbs.'

'I know, but the men we encountered in the forest were intent on capturing the young one,' said Beepoo, 'and if Shaman-Sing wishes to see him then the boy must possess something very valuable that the Arnaks want.'

'The Arnaks?'

'*Rebel* Arnaks, not the ones we usually trade with. I have heard on my visits to Fort Temple that they are causing trouble, even with their own people, because they wish to return to the old ways. I have seen with my own eyes the evil they will bring to the forest.'

Anni shuddered at the thought of what the rebel Arnaks might do if they came back to the forest, for she had seen the bruises on Archie's body when she had taken his and Richard's clothes to launder and repair.

As assistant to old Nanan, the Rooter herbalist and physician, whose preparations and remedies were known and used throughout Timeless Valley, she had seen many injuries and wounds, but they were usually accidental, not maliciously inflicted by the hands of others.

That morning she had escorted the boys to the bathhouse and prepared the herbal compresses for Archie's bruises, but despite her protests he wouldn't let her apply them, seemingly embarrassed by a girl helping him. She had thought it odd, for the Rooters had no inhibitions about such matters, but she had finally relented when he promised to let Richard help him.

'And if I had not been there,' Beepoo continued, 'both of them would have been taken by those men.'

Anni nodded, knowing that it was her brother's fascination with watching the speeding Sitanga Express pass the edge of the forest every day that had placed him in such a position.

'It was well that you were there, Beepoo, but from now on you must be more careful,' she said. 'We must ask Shaman-Sing when he arrives what we should do to protect ourselves against these men if they come again. Now I must return to the bathhouse. The boys' clothes were in a dreadful state, but I have done my best to make them presentable for their meeting with Shaman-Sing.'

Beepoo frowned as Anni left the tree house. He would have to warn the other Rooters to be careful when they ventured into the forest, for who could say that other rebel Arnaks wouldn't make another attempt to capture the boy?

But Beepoo was not overly concerned. The Rooters had lived in Maroc for nearly four thousand years, and in all that time no unwelcome visitor had ever survived the wolftans or the Screaming Wind, to reach the Clearing. Only their invited guests – such as the Happonots and those with whom they traded – could enter the forest safely. Of course, unexpected visitors who also suffered at the hands of the Arnaks would always be welcome and would come under the Rooters' protection.

Anni was right: Shaman-Sing would be here soon, and it would be best to ask him what was to be done about the boys.

*

'*Ouch*! That's really cold,' complained Archie, 'and it stings like blazes.'

Richard picked another cloth compress out of the clay bowl containing the herbal infusion and placed it on Archie's shoulder, covering a nasty-looking bruise now turning yellow.

'He really gave you a kicking didn't he,' said Richard.

It wasn't a question; he could see for himself just how vicious Slashface had been.

'Yeah, he did, but I don't think we'll have to worry about him again,' said Archie.

They were silent for a moment as they remembered Slashface's horrible screams and the sight of him being dragged into the trees by the wolftan.

Archie was sitting on a wooden bench in the steam room while Richard stood beside him applying the herbal compresses just as Anni had shown him. She had left a cauldron containing a foul-looking concoction for the compresses outside the door, along with robes and towels for them to use while she saw to the cleaning and repair of their clothes.

251

A Rooter named Cal looked after the waterwheel that scooped and piped the river water into the bathhouse where it was heated by an old-fashioned wood furnace. He was a kindly old soul who insisted on helping by bringing fresh bowls of the herbal infusion into the steam room, but he groaned and shook his head every time he saw Archie's bruises.

'I wish he wouldn't do that,' said Archie, after Cal had left the room for the tenth time.

He was feeling a lot better; the lump on his head was nearly gone, and the aches and pains were beginning to ease as the herbal compresses took effect, but Cal's reaction to how he looked only served to remind him of Slashface's brutal behaviour.

'He's all right,' said Richard, soaking another cloth in the bowl.

'I suppose so,' said Archie 'but what I still don't understand is why Slashface was so anxious to get his hands on you. After all, neither of us ever saw or heard of him before, did we?'

'I dunno what it was all about,' said Richard. 'I'm just glad it's over.'

But is it? Archie wondered. Whatever the reason for Richard being hunted, there could well be others out there waiting to take up the chase. If so, they would need to keep their eyes open for any sign of danger. He thought about Uncle John and Aristo, and Captain Hanki and the Lancers, and how he might get a message to them. The more he thought about it, the more convinced he became that they had to get back to Fort Temple as soon as possible.

Anni brought their clothes back freshly cleaned and pressed. She nodded her approval as Archie and Richard left the bathhouse.

'Shaman-Sing has arrived and is waiting for you,' said Anni. 'He is a very important person, and it is good that you look your best when you meet him.'

They walked across the Clearing where children were playing with a ball. Others were racing each other to the river before jumping in, and some were climbing the branches above the tree houses. All around them everything seemed normal – it was only when Archie looked up he realised that something, somehow, seemed ... *different*.

Earlier, on the way to the bathhouse the sky had been unusually dark and Archie had made no comment on it then, but now it was nearly midday, and although it was much brighter, the sky seemed to be tainted a faint bluish-green colour. It was as if a filter had been applied to achieve a magical, soothing and calming effect over the Clearing.

'Anni, why is it ... I mean ... why does the sky seem to have a different colour here?'

Archie had stopped to stare upwards through the break in the trees as the daylight cast its strange glow.

'We have a name for it, which means *the protection.* One of our legends says that the ancient Amasian priests created it as a shield against angry gods, long before the Rooters came here. It is said that the gods cannot see the Clearing while it is in place.'

'You're kidding ... I mean ... you're not really serious, are you?'

'I do not know how it came to be,' said Anni, 'it has always been this way for my people. I think it is why our ancestors settled here. But Shaman-Sing says it is because the great maroc trees cast their light upon the sky.' She smiled as her eyes twinkled. 'I think, perhaps, that both explanations are true.'

Archie raised his eyes behind Anni's back as she walked towards the tree house.

'This place is *seriously* weird,' he murmured to Richard.

A Rooter with little stumpy legs waddled past leading a magnificent black stallion, its heavily embossed black leather saddle gleaming in the sunlight.

'Shaman-Sing is waiting for you,' grunted the Rooter, nodding towards the tree house. He stopped for a moment and gave the boys a sour look that made them feel uncomfortable. 'He must be another that's staying for the night. I wonder, Anni, if you have plans for any more guests?'

'If we have, Topol, you will know soon enough,' snapped Anni. 'Just be sure Shaman-Sing's horse is well rubbed down or you will have me to answer to.'

She stormed off with Archie and Richard running to keep up, leaving the little Rooter muttering to himself.

'I am sorry for Topol's rudeness,' said Anni. 'I am afraid he is like many of our people who worry about strangers staying overnight, for it is our custom that visitors only come to the Clearing during daylight and then leave before nightfall. Shaman-Sing is a valued friend of the Rooters and Topol should know that.'

'I'm sorry if we're causing any trouble ...' said Archie, 'we really didn't mean to come into the forest –'

'Do not concern yourself, Archie – Beepoo was right to bring you here. It is enough for us that Shaman-Sing wishes to speak with you.'

They went inside the tree house to find Shaman-Sing sitting with Beepoo at the table. Both were drinking from silver mugs Anni had placed there as a mark of respect for their guest.

'Anni, my dear, it is good to see you again and, if I may say so, your excellent sweet beer is as delicious as ever,' said Shaman-Sing, taking another sip from his mug.

'It is very kind of you to say so, sir,' said Anni, 'and you are very welcome, as always.'

'Good, good, and these are the boys I take it, whom I have come all this way to see?'

Archie and Richard waited while a stout black man stood up and walked around the table to approach them. He wore a black and gold cloak, partly open to reveal a three-quarter length leather tunic and knee-high riding boots. His head almost touched the ceiling and his broad shoulders suggested great strength, but it was his deep-set eyes and warm smile that drew Archie's attention.

He was a Happonot like Benno Kozan, reminding Archie of the first occasion he had seen Kozan; the evening they had arrived at Castle Amasia when Archie had been so struck by the aura that seemed to emanate from him. It was the same with Shaman-Sing, but he was much older, his thick, black hair now partly white, and, unlike Kozan, he favoured a neatly trimmed goatee beard. He stood in front of them, resting his hands on his belly, not saying a word. Just looking, sensing them, nodding to himself when he found something agreeable.

Suddenly he turned to Anni and Beepoo.

'Forgive me, but I think we will take a short walk to the river where we will sit for a while.'

'As you will, Shaman-Sing,' said Beepoo.

*

They found a quiet place in the shade of a maroc tree by a bend in the river.

'Let us sit here,' said Shaman-Sing.

He spread his cloak on the ground and sat down, his legs crossed and his hands resting on his knees.

Archie and Richard knelt in front of him. They glanced at each other, not knowing what to say, or what to expect.

'Do not be nervous,' said Shaman-Sing. 'I know we were meant to meet in Naru and that you have suffered at the hands of the rebel Arnaks, but thanks to Beepoo and his wolftans that is now past. Now, we have a great deal to discuss, but perhaps it would be best if we introduced ourselves properly, then we can tell each other a little about ourselves – *before* we get to the reason you were sent to me.'

He smiled and stroked his beard thoughtfully, looking at each of them as if to memorise their faces.

'Now, I would say you are Archie?'

Archie nodded.

'And you must be Richard?'

Richard nodded.

'Good. As for me, I am given the title, Shaman-Sing, because my tribe, the Happanots, regard me as a wise and holy man, but only time and events will prove – or disprove – their belief in me.' He suddenly laughed out loud. 'Some of my people say it is because I have lived so long, and they may be right. I am over three hundred years old, and that alone should make anyone wise, don't you think?'

Archie and Richard gawped, their eyes wide open, hardly believing that anyone could be so old.

'Do not look so surprised. It is not that unusual in Timeless Valley, and I am not, by any means, the oldest.' Shaman-Sing's eyes drifted for a moment, as if it was something he had not considered for a while. 'But enough of me, tell me about yourselves and why you seem to be in so much trouble.'

Archie looked at Richard, neither of them sure what to say or where to begin.

'Try the beginning, it is usually best,' suggested Shaman-Sing. 'Where you come from and how you arrived in Amasia, will be a good start.'

So Archie and Richard told their story. They spoke slowly at first, each taking it in turn, sometimes quietly then excitedly as they recalled more and more of all the incredible things that had happened to them.

Archie explained how their parents had disappeared in the jungles of the Yucatan. He told of the timecrack incident at the DONUT and of the journey through the timecrack with Uncle John and Marjorie, and their encounter with Aristo and the Lancers. It was as if a floodgate had opened. He felt so relieved to be able to talk to someone about all the thoughts that had been churning around in his head for so long that everything just poured out. He told Shaman-Sing every little thing he could remember, including all the events they had experienced at Castle Amasia, Harmsway College and Mount Tengi, right up to the attack on the railcar.

Shaman-Sing said nothing, he simply listened, and whenever Archie paused he indicated to Richard to continue.

Richard described his dreams as best he could, but like most dreams they were patchy and he couldn't make much sense of them. The trances were more difficult to recall – they just happened without warning, and when he recovered from them he found it hard to put everything together; but it felt as if ... *he had actually been there.*

'Richard, you said you were able to leave a message for Chuck at the DONUT,' said Archie, trying to help his young brother explain the more recent events to Shaman-Sing, 'and on the big stone at Harmsway, you said you heard voices – maybe mum or dad.'

'I know ... it's just that it all comes in bits and pieces ... it's kind of hard to explain ...'

'I understand, Richard,' said Shaman-Sing, 'dreams are very often simply fragments of remembered experiences. Sometimes they are just a manifestation of a very active imagination –'

'But it's not my imagination!'

Shaman-Sing held up the flat of his hand to ward off Richard's protests.

'Perhaps not, but what is of great interest to me is your observation of current events in more than one dimension.'

Richard looked at him blankly, not fully understanding what he meant. Archie understood. It was what Krippitz had referred to on their visit to the Gladden Plateau. Ever since then he had been itching to find out if Shaman-Sing could help Uncle John and Dr Shah contact the DONUT to get them back home. Could he do it through Richard?

'You mean ... like getting in touch with Old Earth?' said Archie, unable to contain his curiosity any longer. 'Can ... can *you* do it?'

The old shaman didn't answer immediately. He watched the sunlight play on the surface of the water for a minute or so then he stood up and walked to the river's edge. He beckoned to the boys to join him.

'When I was young I dreamed of many things and I saw many things, but my power was like the river – it flowed endlessly through me, and I had no control over it. Now it has gone: like the river it has disappeared into the great ocean.'

Archie was bitterly disappointed, and it showed. Had they come so far, suffered so much, attacked by rebel Arnaks, nearly killed, only to be told Shaman-Sing couldn't help them?

'Do not be upset, Archie. Benno Kozan has explained what is expected of me, and I believe we may have some success, but I warn you, both of you will have to submit totally to my will, do you understand?'

Not really understanding, they both nodded solemnly.

'Good, but what you don't understand is that Richard's power is greater than mine ever was. And that may well be why the Arnaks want him; somehow they have heard of his power and believe him to be a Shamra child.'

'What is a Shamra child?' asked Archie.

Shaman-Sing told them of the Legend of Arnak and the danger that Richard now faced.

'It does not matter that it is only a legend – it is what the followers of Lord Arnak believe, and nothing can change that.'

'But I am thirteen! And everyone thinks I look older!' said Richard.

He was scared, and he didn't like the way things were turning out. How could anyone know what age he was?

'It is not that simple, Richard,' said Shaman-Sing. 'The Arnaks seem to know a great deal more about you than you appreciate. And it may well be that it is your power to see beyond this world that is important to them. If so, they will believe what they want to believe when it comes to the legend.' He turned to Archie. 'It is good that you are here. You will help your brother in the coming days to fully realise his power –'

'But how? What can I do?'

'Love, Archie. Understand this, if you never understand anything else: love is the greatest power in the universe. It survives when all else is lost – nothing can destroy it. Through your love for your brother, he will gain great strength – remember this always. It will not be easy, but he has been chosen to follow a path that is, as yet, unknown to us, and we must do our best to help him follow it, wherever it leads.'

Shaman-Sing talked a little longer and then told them they would not go to his village, Naru – it would be safer to stay in Maroc for the time being – and when Richard was ready they would return to Fort Temple.

Archie looked around the Clearing. The children were still playing with their ball, and Topol was walking several wolftans along the riverbank. Nearby, another Rooter was sitting cross-legged on an old tree stump carving a wolftan flute while whistling a strange tune, the notes joining the sounds of the river to form a soothing refrain.

He felt safe here, but he wondered what would happen to them when they left the safety of the forest.

Part Four

The Stone

Chapter Twenty-Four

The Voices

'Zamah damn you for a fool, Nitkin!'

Prince Lotane, his face partly masked, was furious. He barely restrained his temper as he gazed down at the trembling man standing below him on the marble steps of the Sacred Temple.

'Not only did you lose seven valuable men at Maroc, but now I am told that the boy and his brother have returned to Harmsway and that they are guarded night and day by the Lancers!'

'But, Master, I have explained that the boy escaped from the railcar before it reached me. I do not know what happened ... there was shooting –'

'Shooting! Who authorised the use of such weapons?'

'I didn't –'

'Quiet, Nitkin, you only make it worse for yourself. You realise, of course, that when the son of one of the most powerful men in Amasia was shot, it made our task of taking the Shamra child almost impossible. General Branvin now has Lancers looking for us in every corner of the valley!'

Nitkin tried to speak, but Lotane waved him out of his sight.

Daylight was fading and the vallonium lamps that had been placed on the remaining marble pedestals near the entrance to the temple, cast a sombre glow across the floor of the huge cavern.

As Nitkin retreated into the shadows, Lotane knew that his time was short. Weeks had passed since the disaster at Maroc and the Lancers were everywhere seeking those responsible. His army was small, and the few modern weapons they possessed – stolen mainly from Lancer armouries and the vallonium mines – would have to be kept in reserve for the final battle. His greatest strength lay in his network of spies, but one such spy, working in the administration block at Harmsway, had sent him the disturbing news that the boy might already be thirteen and his next birthday would take place in another month.

He swore to himself it would not matter. The Arnaks had already sacrificed so much, surely Zamah would understand it was for the greater good of Hazaranet and accept the boy's sacrifice. But to appease Zamah he knew that the ritual must take place soon

*

Anton stepped out from behind one of the collapsed stone columns at the end of the terrace. He waited until Lotane had disappeared through the golden doors of the temple before making his way to the top of the marble steps.

Beyond the golden doors a huge, flat, honey-coloured stone wheel dominated the centre of a high-ceilinged room. Thousands of years old, it was the original Zahamonite stone. Different from other ritual stones , the sacrificial trough set deep in the centre of the stone had been shaped by ancient craftsmen from solid gold, while the unusual symbols that decorated the rim were outlined in gold and rare stones. The other stones were copies of this one, fashioned without precious metals or stones, but according to Arnak legend all were said to contain the power of past sacrificial victims.

It must be worth a king's ransom, thought Anton. Not that it mattered; it was not likely that anyone could ever steal it. Lotane had told him that it had taken more than a hundred men, hauling and pushing it on wooden rollers and ramps to move it from its original position in the middle of the square to where it now stood. Fear of it falling into the chasm when the cavern had been hit by fresh tremors had necessitated the move.

Sandan had drawn his attention to the ancient bloodstains and blade marks that covered the bottom of the trough, confirming the barbarous practice of human sacrifice in this place so long ago. Sandan's morbid interest in Hazaranet's primitive customs had one advantage, though: it kept him occupied and out of harm's way while Anton attended to the training of Lotane's rebels.

Turning away from the stone, Anton returned to the terrace. He thought about the past few days he had spent in the secret training camp situated in a hidden pass high up in the Pirangas, trying to instil some sort of discipline into the Arnaks. It was a ragtag army: a motley collection of young and old men, some from the city, but mostly peasants from the Darklands, driven by religious fervour and Lotane's promise of riches once the land of Hazaranet had been reclaimed.

Anton laughed out loud at the absurdity of it: primitive tribesmen pitted against professional Lancers, and an uprising that hinged on the sacrifice of a young boy.

'What are you laughing at, Anton?'

Startled, he saw Sandan approaching him from a doorway in the cavern wall. He was wearing a cloak with a cowl, similar to Lotane's, giving him a monk-like appearance.

'I'm happy, Sandan, I have just returned from the training camp, and what I saw there has convinced me that this business will soon come to an end,' he replied, not wishing to argue with Sandan about the idiocy of

Lotane's plans, as he knew his brother was sympathetic to Lotane's cause

'That is good news, Anton.'

'Yes, I thought you'd like to hear that.' Anton looked at him curiously and said, 'Tell me, Sandan, why are you dressed like a monk?'

'It was Prince Lotane's idea. He said that if I wished to see the monastery, I could wear this cloak and enter by the old passage that leads into the cellars. I have just come from there.'

'You visited the monastery and no one paid you any attention?'

'No. There are many visiting monks, and I was made very welcome –'

'You were made welcome? By whom?' asked Anton, now a little worried that Sandan's behaviour might have attracted unnecessary attention to their presence here.

'By Father Jamarko, the old priest carrying out excavations and research into the history of the monastery. He is a remarkable man, Anton, and he told me a little of what he has discovered. Unfortunately, he was very busy with the students from the college –'

'Students from the college? Which college would that be?'

'Harmsway – the students visit the monastery every week.'

'Do they, indeed? Now, that is very interesting,' said Anton, scratching at the dark stubble on his chin. After sleeping rough in the mountains for the past few nights he felt in need of a shave and a hot bath, but Sandan's words had proved refreshing. 'Thank you, Sandan. I think I might pay the monastery a visit myself.'

*

'Kinross, could we have your attention please?'

Major Ramstiff's voice forced Archie's gaze away from the classroom door. Han-Sin had just popped her head in to indicate she would be waiting in the hall for him.

'I realise that after your little adventure in Maroc, events here must seem painfully dull, but I do have a class to run.'

'Sorry ...'

Archie heard the sniggering behind him and he felt his face beginning to flush as the whispering started.

'It looks like he needs a caretaker – or is it a nurse?'

It was Barron Cruet, a Canadian New Arrival who had landed in the Exploding Park a few weeks earlier than Archie. A lanky, greasy-haired seventeen year old, he already had a reputation for smuggling illicit alcoholic Sticklejuice and cigarettes, and anything else on which he could turn a profit, into Harmsway. He'd had it in for Archie, ever since Archie had stopped him selling some of his stuff to Richard and some of the younger boys who didn't know any better.

'Shut up!' hissed Archie, turning in his seat to face Cruet, who quickly looked away.

'*Quiet!*' roared Ramstiff, rising to his feet from behind a large oak desk. 'I would be grateful that when you *are* with us, Kinross, you would engage your mind with the work in hand. Perhaps an extra paper would help you settle down. Stay behind after class and we'll see if you can pay attention to that!'

Archie groaned inwardly. He had arranged to see Richard at the zimmerball match between Prade and Vale. It was the first inter-house game of the season, and as Richard and he both belonged to Prade he had been looking forward to seeing it. Now he was probably going to miss the whole game.

Ever since Archie had arrived back at Harmsway from Maroc, Cruet had been goading him over Han-Sin and Teekoo's presence at the college. *'Not able to look after yourself?'* or *'Want someone to hold your hand?'* were his usual taunts. Archie couldn't have cared less, for Cruet was nothing more than a pest, but now he was getting him into trouble with Ramstiff.

Twenty minutes later Major Ramstiff dismissed the class, and Cruet, with the rest of the students, stampeded through the door in a mad dash to the sports arena. Archie watched them leave, flushing angrily when Cruet turned and smirked, gesturing with two fingers stuck up in the air.

After he finished the paper – *Describe a New Arrival's First Impression of the Amasian Educational System* – Archie handed it over to Major Ramstiff who, without looking up from the large leather-bound book in which his nose was buried, took it and promptly dumped it into the wastepaper bin.

Archie's mouth dropped; it had taken him well over an hour to write on a subject he knew absolutely nothing about, and Ramstiff hadn't even looked at it.

'But, sir –'

'What is it? Can't you see I'm busy? I thought all you boys would be at the inter-house game?' said Ramstiff, waving him away dismissively with the back of his hand.

He hadn't looked up once, and didn't notice when Archie stuck his tongue out at him.

*

'It's not bloody fair!' moaned Archie, walking alongside Han-Sin towards the sports arena.

He told her about Cruet, who had been giving him a hard time over having an escort every day, and to cap it all, the time wasted on a paper that Ramstiff didn't even read.

'I wondered what had happened to you,' said Han-Sin, 'but don't concern yourself with Cruet, it's just juvenile behaviour.'

'I know Cruet's a twit … it's just that … Look, I don't mean to be rude or anything … but do you really have to be around so much? I mean … couldn't you be… less obvious?'

Han-Sin couldn't help laughing at the look of pleading on Archie's face.

'I can't make myself invisible, Archie, but I do know what you mean. I promise you, I'll do my best to be … as you say, *less obvious*, but you have to understand that after what happened at Maroc we can't afford to take any chances. Both your uncle and Dr Shah are adamant that Lancer Teekoo and I stay with you and Richard at all times, so I'm afraid you'll have to put up with us for a little while longer.'

She looked curiously at the young man beside her; his tousled brown curly hair and brown eyes along with strongly chiselled features, were quite attractive, but there was a serious side to him which made him look much older than his sixteen years.

'I don't know what's going on, Archie,' said Han-Sin, 'but with the latest rebel outrages in Fort Temple recently, I'm not letting you out of my sight.'

Han-Sin hadn't fully recovered from the crash at Snakespass Ravine where she had been lucky to escape alive with nothing more than cuts and severe bruises. Understandably her father, Captain Hanki, had been reluctant to let her return to any sort of active duty, but with the ongoing rebel disturbances taking place throughout the country she knew he was dangerously short on manpower. When Brimstone came under pressure from General Branvin to use every available

Lancer to find the rebels who had shot Julius Stein's son, her father had been left with little choice but to yield to Han-Sin's repeated requests to let her do something useful.

Hanki had assigned her to partner Teekoo, who was still brooding over his cousin Sun-Tee's death, with instructions to keep a close eye on the boys until further notice. Teekoo had objected at first, calling the duty a 'babysitting tour', but when Hanki had threatened to lock him up for refusing a direct order, he had reluctantly accepted.

'I know how you feel, Teekoo,' Hanki had said. 'We all feel bad about Sun-Tee, but I will not tolerate insubordination – so just get on with it!'

Han-Sin and Archie arrived at the stadium to see a crowd of boys and girls carrying Prade House banners, streaming out of the exits cheering and screaming:

'*We love Prade*! *We love Prade*! *We love Prade*!'

A small group of supporters broke away from the crowd, running towards them. Richard was in front.

'Where have you been?' he called out 'We won! *Prade won*!'

'Don't ask,' said Archie, huffily. He looked up to see Teekoo's Spokestar hovering just above the top tier of seats at the back of the arena. 'Let's get out of here, I'm starving.'

With Han-Sin walking behind at what she hoped was a discreet distance, and Teekoo somewhere overhead, Archie and Richard joined the crowd, pushing and shoving their way through to reach the main dining hall.

After every inter-house match it had become the practice for the winning team to choose the courses for the evening meal. It had also become a challenge for each house – Prade, Flint, Sohead and Vale – if and when they won, to outdo the other in the selection of the courses. Most agreed tonight's offering had been one of the best ever. With wild boar hamburgers, giant turkey steaks, fresh Piranga salmon and pickled dinosaur tails, enormous piles of vegetables and all sorts of potatoes including chips, roast and mash to choose from, nearly everyone was stuffed to the gills – except Richard, of course.

Archie pushed his half-finished plate of Stickleberry ice cream and apple tartlets towards the middle of the table out of temptation's way.

'That's it – I've had it.'

Richard was shocked.

'Aren't you going to finish those?'

'I don't believe it,' said Archie, staring at his brother in amazement. 'After second helpings of everything else, you want to eat mine as well! Where do you put it?'

Richard ignored him and reached for a tartlet.

As at the other tables in the dining hall, there were twelve students sitting at the table. They were mostly New Arrivals, and one of them, Ulrika, a big-boned girl with her hair tied back in a ponytail, offered her plate to Richard.

'Would you like mine, too?' she asked.

Two other girls squealed with delight, and everyone burst out laughing as Richard reached for it.

'Stop that!' snapped Archie. 'You're making a fool of yourself!'

His chair screeched on the old wooden floor as he pushed it away from the table. He stood up and without saying another word, he stormed down the dining hall to the open oak door that led into the corridor. Behind him he could hear another roar of laughter as Cruet at another table made some comment as he walked by.

Han-Sin was talking to Teekoo outside the door as Archie brushed past her.

'What's wrong, Archie?' she called after him.

'Nothing's wrong. I'm just going outside – is that all right?'

'Of course. Just wait and I'll –'

Han-Sin didn't get a chance to finish. Archie had gone through the main doorway and down the steps into the quadrangle leaving her open-mouthed, just as Richard suddenly dashed past, pushing his way between her and Teekoo.

'I wonder what's up with those two?' said Teekoo.

'I don't know,' said Han-Sin, 'but we'd better keep an eye on them.'

Richard ran across to the side of the quadrangle to where Archie was standing below a huge marble statue of Samuel Harmsway. Directly opposite, in the middle of the quadrangle, was the stone, its shadowy shape blending into the fading light.

'Archie, I'm sorry ... please don't be angry. I know I was being greedy, but I just couldn't help myself ...'

Archie suddenly felt ashamed of himself. His young brother was trying to apologise – and for what, because he had a big appetite? So what if he had – it didn't show; there wasn't a spare ounce of fat on him. He didn't know how Richard managed it, but he seemed to burn up calories faster than he could breathe, but deep down Archie knew it wasn't just Richard's eating habits that bothered him. It was ... *everything* ... It was not knowing what was going to happen to them. Timeless Valley was an exciting place, and probably the rest of Amasia was too, but it wasn't home – not that they had had a proper home for a long time. That was it really ... *they didn't have a home* ... and, more importantly ... *they didn't know what had happened to their parents.* There was never a day when he didn't think about them, and he knew that until he found out where they had disappeared to, he would never truly rest.

Now there was the problem of the rebel Arnaks. He realised they were in danger, especially Richard, although it didn't seem to worry him too much. Until Krippitz was ready to prepare Richard to try and get in touch with the DONUT again they would have to put up with Han-Sin and Teekoo hanging around them all the time, no matter what Cruet and the others thought, but he itched to do something *now.*

'It's OK, Richard ... it's me who should be saying sorry. I shouldn't have let the others get to me.' Archie smiled and shook his head. 'I'll have to learn to relax the way Shaman-Sing taught us, but I don't find it that easy, and if you're hungry – then just eat!'

Richard grinned, delighted that Archie was in a good mood again, but then he frowned and scratched the back of his head as if he had a problem.

'It isn't that I'm really hungry – it's just that I seem to ... feel the need to eat more all the time ...'

As Archie listened to Richard trying to explain why he ate so much, it became obvious it was something to do with the dreams and the sightings. It was as if he possessed a great fire deep inside him that needed more and more fuel to keep it burning. Sometimes when he was asleep or in a trance, Richard said he could feel so much energy coursing through his body he felt that he could reach out and touch the stars.

'But, Archie, it's when I hear the voices ... and when I try to tell them that I can hear them ... that I really flake out.'

'What do you mean? What voices?'

'Well ... it's really like *one* voice in a large crowd ... like in a football stadium and there's someone shouting at you, trying to tell you something, but you can't make them out. Sometimes … I think maybe it's mum trying to contact me …'

Archie was quiet for a moment. It was beginning to dawn on him what Richard must have been going through for the past few months – and he hadn't been paying attention. It wasn't as if he didn't know what had been happening. He just hadn't taken it seriously or understood it properly.

'Richard, I've just thought of something.'

'Like what?'

'Do you remember when we first arrived at Harmsway and you said you thought you heard mum's voice when you were on the stone?'

'Yes … I think so.'

'Well, I'm sure you did, and I think we should try again.'

'But … how?'

'I think we should come down here later tonight, when there's no one about, and put into practice what Shaman-Sing taught us at Maroc.'

Chapter Twenty-Five

The Quadrangle

Afraid that someone might hear him, Archie held his breath as he padded slowly along the upper corridor past the other dormitories where the muffled sounds of snoring could be heard. He had waited until he was certain that the five other boys in his own room were no longer awake before slipping out of bed, tiptoeing to the door and out into the corridor.

It was shortly after midnight as he made his way to the top of the wide stairway that led down into the large hall and the main doors. The lamps had been turned down low, creating an eerie glow that reflected off the heavy gold frames that held the portraits of a series of stern-looking men and women. They were the past masters and mistresses of Harmsway, and their eyes seemed to follow Archie as he started to hurry along the dimly lit corridor.

'And where do you think you are going?' called a voice out of the darkness of a nearby doorway.

Archie nearly jumped out of his skin when he looked over his shoulder to see a figure emerging from the shadows. It was Han-Sin, and she didn't look too pleased to see him.

'Oh, it's you – you scared the wits out of me!' whispered Archie, feeling relieved it wasn't one of the masters.

'Little wonder if you spend your time sneaking around in the middle of the night,' snapped Han-Sin. 'What *exactly* are you up to?'

'I'm sorry … I've arranged to see Richard outside –'

'What do you mean – *outside*? Do you realise what time it is?'

'Yes, I do,' said Archie irritably, wishing that she wouldn't ask so many questions. 'Look, I can explain, but ...'

He hesitated, suddenly feeling at a loss for words. He looked away, trying to avoid her eyes. How could he explain to Han-Sin that he was going to try and help Richard get in touch with their mother by meditating on a great big stone slab in the middle of the quadrangle, that he had to find out if their parents were still alive, and if they were, what had happened to them? How could she possibly understand that Richard's power might be the only way of reaching them?

Han-Sin waited. She sensed Archie's confusion and felt sorry for him. She decided not to press him any further; he would tell her in his own good time what was troubling him, and until then she would be patient.

'OK, let's go outside before we wake up the whole of Prade House,' said Han-Sin. 'Where did you arrange to meet Richard?'

'He's in the junior dorm down below – we agreed to meet at the Harmsway statue at midnight.'

'Well, it's well past that now, we'd better go.'

She led the way as they crept down the wide staircase to reach the main doors. Old Mankin, the doorkeeper, a wizened old Salakin who could hardly hear or see, would be on his nightly caretaking tour of the college buildings. It would take him ages to return to his cubicle by the doors, so they had little fear of being seen. So much for security, thought Han-Sin, as they left the building.

As they approached the statue they saw Richard looking out from behind the large marble plinth. Like Archie, he was wearing a navy-blue college night-cloak, pulled tightly around him to keep out the cold night air.

'What kept you? I've been standing freezing here for –'

Richard rushed towards Archie, but he pulled up when he saw Han-Sin.

'Sorry, Richard, it's my fault,' said Han-Sin. 'I found Archie on his way to this mysterious assignation and stopped him.' She smiled at his puzzlement and put a hand on his shoulder. 'So, perhaps you two will put me out of my misery and explain what this is all about, *before* Teekoo turns up to relieve me. He'll be here in a couple of hours, and I can tell you he's a lot less patient than I am when it comes to strange goings-on in the middle of the night.'

Report them to Miss Harmsway, supposed Archie, not that he really cared what Teekoo thought. This was too important. He had to try it, no matter what happened, but just for a moment he had a feeling of regret. After all, he had dragged Richard out of bed and into the quadrangle with only a vague idea of what they were going to do, and there was no way of telling what the consequences might be.

Richard had probably guessed from what he'd said earlier – about hearing mum's voice when he was on the stone – what he was planning, but at this moment Richard looked as if he wished he was back in his warm bed.

'I'm sorry, Han-Sin, I know you have to look out for us … but, to tell you the truth, I just didn't think about telling you.' Archie shrugged, glancing at Richard again. 'Even Richard didn't know what I wanted to do.'

'Yeah, I did; you want to get in touch with mum,' said Richard, rubbing his hands together to keep them warm. 'It's OK – I think we should try, but could we do it soon? I'm frozen out here.'

Archie nodded, relieved that Richard understood, then he told Han-Sin about their time in Maroc Forest and what Shaman-Sing had taught them.

'You see, I didn't think too much about what was happening to Richard before now. I just thought it was all dream-stuff that happens to lots of people, but Shaman-Sing explained that although everyone has dreams that might mean something, what Richard has is very special, and very few people ever get that sort of power. He said Richard had to learn how to control it and use it wisely, because he might not always have it.

'While we were in the forest with the Rooters he taught us how to meditate. It's a bit like going to sleep, but Shaman-Sing says it's a way of seeing things more clearly, especially for Richard if he goes into one of his trances. Anyway, I thought we might try the stone again to see if we could get in touch with our mother. I know it sounds weird, but something happened to Richard there before, and Shaman-Sing said there are special places where there's a lot of hidden energy that can make things like that happen.'

'I see, but what happened to your parents?'

'We don't know exactly. They were archaeologists working in Mexico back on Old Earth, and something went wrong at the site they were excavating. It might have been an earthquake or flood, or something, nobody's really sure. The search teams spent weeks looking for them, but they'd disappeared without a trace ... A bit like us I suppose.'

If they were taken by a timecrack, they may have come here, thought Han-Sin; if not here, then somewhere else. The valley was full of New Arrivals who had been unexpectedly taken away from their old world and into this one, but not everyone ended up in the Exploding Park. There were those less fortunate souls who arrived in other parts of Amasia that were not so welcoming.

As a Salakin, she was familiar with the stories and legends that had been handed down through the generations from parent to child, but like most modern young people she discounted them as myths. They were just stories that some of the old ones liked to tell around the tribal campfires of the homeland.

Of course, there were some Arnaks – like the rebels causing all the trouble in the valley – who believed in the most famous myth of all, the Legend of Hazaranet; a ludicrous belief that someday they would overthrow the government of the valley and regain the land of Hazaranet. She recalled the story of the Shamra child from her childhood. Suddenly a ridiculous thought occurred to her. Could it be that the rebels who had tried to capture Richard thought *he* was a Shamra?

'And you think Richard can actually get in touch with your parents?' she asked, her curiosity aroused

'Yes, I wasn't sure before, but I am now,' said Archie. 'We've got to try it, Han-Sin.'

'OK – this could get me into trouble, but I'm willing to let you try. Both of you should be in bed, so we can't spend too long here – and I want to be back inside before Teekoo arrives.'

*

A New Earth full moon lingered in the sky. Its light, filtered by drifting clouds, fell on the great grey stone walls of the college library that lined one side of the quadrangle.

Han-Sin stood in the shadow of one of the buttresses, her arms folded tightly in an effort to stay warm, thinking that she had been stupid to agree to this. If her father ever found out that she had encouraged the boys in this crazy escapade he would throw a fit. She quickly put the thought out of her head and watched closely as Archie and Richard clambered onto the stone.

Richard moved on his hands and knees towards the trough in the centre, while Archie positioned himself with his back to the edge. They sat cross-legged facing each other, not moving, but quietly still, prepared for whatever might happen. After a couple of moments, they reached out and joined hands as Shaman-Sing had instructed them. In spite of the cold night air, the stone below them felt strangely warm, as if it was in the path of the sun, rather than the moon above.

'Do you feel anything?' asked Archie.

'No, not yet.'

Richard closed his eyes and let his mind relax as Shaman-Sing had taught him back at the Clearing.

'*Do not force it,*' he had said, '*let the spirit of the universe come to you. Remember, Richard, the mind is the universe within, but you are also part of the universe without. Understand that your world and all other worlds are connected. It is a journey you have already taken many times, and you will again*'.

*

He opened his eyes again. Everything was still and deathly silent. Black, slow-moving clouds shrouded the moon, making it hard to see anything in the darkness. Then the stars appeared again, distant at first, faraway and untouchable, but as Richard watched, one grew closer, its light sparkling like the brightest crystal. He felt it now, drawing him slowly into its orbit. He knew he had made this journey before, but it was so much clearer now, and Archie's presence close beside him gave him the strength to stay a little longer.

Archie also felt the change. He was calm and peaceful, as when in Maroc Shaman-Sing had helped him reach this point, but something was different. Richard was moving towards a bright star and Archie was making the journey with him. He could see and hear what Richard could see and hear, as if they were one sentient body.

They were falling now, but he wasn't frightened – just intensely curious as to what they would find. Suddenly they passed through the brightness and it was dark again. Archie looked around; he couldn't see Richard, but he knew he was there … somewhere in the blackness around him. He felt as if they had been plucked out of the sky and dropped into the deepest darkest ocean, and now they were suspended in its vast murky depths.

In the inky darkness it was impossible to see anything, but slowly the blackness began to fade into misty green and grey clouds swirling around him, until … very slowly … they parted to reveal a … city … a city of stone-built buildings on an island in the middle of a raging sea.

He called out: 'Richard, where are we? What is this place?'

There was no answer, no sound of any sort. Archie felt strangely uneasy. Had Richard continued the journey into the city by himself, leaving him in limbo until he returned? What if he didn't return? What if he was harmed?

It was then Archie heard the voice. A faint whisper at first, but as the picture before him enlarged, the voice – a woman's voice – grew louder, repeating a name over and over again, until finally it faded away again.

'Richard … Richard …'

The voice disappeared and a strange scene formed before him.

A group of dark-skinned people stood near a railtrack that ran alongside the edge of a large, stone-paved square. They were held back by a squatly-built figure wielding a whip as two men, dressed in tunics and trousers, pushed a wagon full of rubble towards a wall at the end of the square. Unknown to Archie, they were slaves being escorted to the great seawall that protected the city from the sea.

He sensed that the crowd were jeering at the men, while the guard cracked his metal-tipped whip over their heads, causing one of them to stumble as he pushed the wagon.

Everywhere, from the buildings to the seawall, traces of a previous flood could be seen where the water had left its dirty tidemark before retreating back to the sea. Lazy spirals of sea mist drifted above a huge temple that lined one side of the square. Part of the temple pediment had fallen away from the building when two support columns at the end had collapsed across the temple steps. Beyond the temple, on the other side of a steep gorge, stood a great, flat-topped pyramid with its golden column rising through the mist.

The city of Copanatec had been built on a peninsula that jutted into the sea, connected to the mainland by a spit of rocky land and a series of great stone bridges. For centuries the city had proved to be an impregnable citadel, its citizens protected by the bridges and the sea against would-be conquerors. But huge land and underwater forces had in time become their enemy, attacking and driving the coast ever further back until Copanatec became truly an island, no longer a part of the mainland, and leaving them totally isolated.

And in more recent times the danger to the city and the people had increased a hundred-fold, with volcanic forces rumbling deep below the surface of the sea causing even greater waves to wash over the city.

Copanatecs had managed to keep the surging waters at bay by using forced labour – men taken from the villages on the mainland, or strangers unfortunate enough to stray onto their shores – to raise and reinforce the seawall, but the waters were now so high that flooding was a constant threat.

As he watched the strange scene unfold, Archie heard a familiar voice.

'*Richard, is it you? Can you hear me?*'

This time the voice was strong and clear, and Archie knew it to be his mother's.

'Mum!' he cried out, but she couldn't hear him.

He was in a place she could not reach: only Richard could answer her. Desperately, he cried out again.

'Richard, can you hear her? For heaven's sake, say something!'

He couldn't tell if Richard had heard him. But he sensed that his brother was somewhere near when he spoke, but unlike Archie's, Richard's voice sounded very grown-up, calm and soothing, untouched by the strangeness of it all.

'Yes, Mum, I can hear you. Where are you?'

'*Richard, thank God! Is it really you? Your voice sounds so strange ...*'

'Mum, it's really me, and Archie's here as well, but he can't speak to you. We're using a special stone to reach you, but I don't know how long we can stay here. Please, you must tell me where you are, so we can try again. What about dad? What's happened to him?'

'*We are in a place called Copanatec, Richard. I've no idea how we got here or where it is – but you found the Transkal stone at the pyramid? How did you ever –*'

Her voice suddenly disappeared.

Richard called out: 'Dad – what about dad? '

Her voice returned: '*I'm not sure. He's kept somewhere else ... I don't know where...*'

The scene faded, leaving Archie horrified by what he had seen and heard. He called out, wanting to hear her voice again, but it was too late. He was back in the darkness and she was gone.

*

'Are you all right?'

Han-Sin touched Archie's shoulder, feeling him shudder from the sudden contact. He opened his eyes and saw Richard getting to his feet, with Han-Sin staring at the two of them with a worried look.

'It's OK. I'm –'

'What's going on here? What are you boys doing up there?' shouted a croaking voice.

It was old Mankin the doorkeeper, obviously in a bad mood. Even with his poor hearing he had heard Archie's shouts from the stone as he hobbled across the quadrangle. He had been making his way back to the cubicle by the main doors, looking forward to a hot drink to relieve the night chill that had seeped into his bones, but now it looked as if he would have to deal with two boys who should have been fast asleep in their beds.

'I'm sorry, I should have seen that they were indoors by this time,' said Han-Sin, worried now that she could see lights coming on in the dormitories, with faces fast appearing at the windows to see what was causing the disturbance.

'Who are you, eh?' yelled Mankin, not realising he was contributing to the disturbance. He screwed up his eyes to take a closer look at the figure in front of him. 'What's a Lancer doing here at this hour?'

Han-Sin spent the next few minutes trying to pacify the old doorkeeper, but unfortunately, Major Ramstiff, wearing a military-style dressing gown and floppy leather slippers, and looking none too pleased behind his monocle, had arrived on the scene.

'Well, what do we have here? Why is it that I am not surprised that it is the Kinross boys who have half the college up out of their beds in the middle of the night, hmmm?' said Ramstiff, adjusting his monocle to see that Archie and Richard were looking decidedly uncomfortable under his gaze.

'I'm sorry, sir … but … but …'

Archie floundered as he tried to explain what they were doing on the stone.

'Enough! Both of you can report to me first thing this morning before classes begin. I will deal with you then!'

Chapter Twenty-Six

The Krippitz Test

Later that day, just after a lunch that neither of them had felt like eating, Archie and Richard sat on a highly polished oak bench outside Miss Harmsway's office, contemplating what was going to happen to them. Earlier that morning they had waited fifteen minutes to see Major Ramstiff before going to classes, but he had virtually ignored them. Instead, he had telephoned someone from his private office, and then advised Archie and Richard afterwards that they should report to Miss Harmsway directly after lunch.

'What do you think will happen to us?' asked Richard. His eyes were fixed on the office door, fully expecting it to burst open at any minute, with Miss Harmsway attired in her witch's-style robe, demanding that they enter her office to hear their fate. 'Do you think she'll expel us?'

'I don't know,' said Archie.

He was feeling pretty miserable. It was his fault, not Richard's, they were sitting here, and he wondered if things could get much worse than they had been that morning.

By now, the whole college had heard about their strange behaviour at the stone in the middle of the night, thanks mainly to Barron Cruet. Apparently, he had been sneaking back into the college at the same time, after spending an evening in Fort Temple procuring more contraband for his growing circle of clients.

'They're real weirdos, those two,' Cruet had said to anyone willing to listen to his version of what he'd seen in the quadrangle. 'They were sitting on that big stone in the dark, in the middle of the night, as if they were having a séance, and calling out to ghosts and all that crap. I tell you, those guys are seriously nuts!'

Archie groaned inwardly at what everybody must be thinking about them. Not that he was completely sorry. After all, they had got in touch with mum, and they'd found out where she was – but where the blazes was Copanatec and what should they do next?

And there was something else that he wondered about: mum had mentioned something called the Transkal stone. Was that the name of the stone in the quadrangle? Was that what they had discovered in the Yucatan jungle?

The office door opened and a small round head popped out. It was Mrs MacQueen, Miss Harmsway's secretary, a small chubby-faced Scotswoman and a second generation New Arrival, whose bright brown eyes and cheery smile made her a favourite with everyone. Unfortunately, her tendency to gossip was on a par with Finbar the Guide's, which made her a very useful source of information for anyone who might want to take advantage of it.

'Well boys, you'd better be getting in here. They're waiting, so let's be quick about it.'

She ushered them through her outer office towards Miss Harmsway's door.

Who could *they* be? Archie had thought that only Miss Harmsway would see them, but now he wondered who else would be sitting in judgement; probably Ramstiff ready to offer his opinion on what the punishment should be. He glanced behind and saw that Richard was nervously licking his lips as they stepped into Miss Harmsway's office.

Archie was surprised to see Benno Kozan sitting in an oversized leather armchair by the office window, smiling as they walked in. Miss Harmsway was seated behind a massive, carved Maroc desk that her grandfather had commissioned from the Rooters in the early days of the building of the college – and she wasn't smiling. She wore a fixed gaze that made Archie think that Richard's suspicion about being expelled from the college might not be far wrong.

'Come in! Come in – don't just stand there gawping at me!' ordered Miss Harmsway. 'I don't have all day to deal with this matter. Sit down there.' She pointed a long, bony finger at two plain wooden chairs placed directly in front of the desk. 'Mr Kozan wishes to speak to you about the nonsense that took place in the quadrangle last night, but before he does, I want to make it quite clear that neither of you are to engage in such behaviour again. I don't know what it is that seems to draw you to that stone, but I will *not* have the college disrupted in this way. Do you both understand?'

Miss Harmsway sitting behind her huge desk was intimidating, and Archie and Richard could only nod their heads, uncertain if they should say anything in their defence. Archie avoided her steely, green eyes by concentrating on the pearls in the black headband she wore, wondering what it was that Benno Kozan wanted to say to them.

'I'm going to leave you with Mr Kozan for a few minutes. I gather he wants to take you away for a day or two.' She shook her head in exasperation, looking from Kozan to the boys as if she had no say in the matter. 'I don't know why you two bothered coming to Harmsway College, as you seem to be more time away from it than in it!'

'My apologies, Miss Harmsway, for causing you so much inconvenience, but I can assure you that this business is of the utmost importance,' said Kozan. He gave her a disarming smile as they both stood up while she prepared to leave the office. 'I will not take up much more of your time. I just want to make an arrangement for the boys to attend the Evaluation Clinic.'

Miss Harmsway nodded, giving him a severe look before sweeping out of the office, her silver hair flowing in line with her black robe, saying she would be back in twenty minutes.

'I think that means she would like us out of here by then,' said Kozan. He winked at the boys, as she closed the door behind her.

'Is nothing going to happen to us?'

Richard looked over his shoulder suspiciously at the office door, half-expecting Miss Harmsway to dash back in again.

'Not this time, Richard, but we will all have to be very careful from now on, or Miss Harmsway might get really upset,' chuckled Kozan.

Archie shifted uneasily on his chair. He liked Benno Kozan, but he couldn't see what was so funny about causing Miss Harmsway to be upset with them. It could have been a lot worse, he supposed, and maybe they should thank him for that, but he hadn't explained yet what he meant by attending the clinic.

'What's going to happen at the clinic?' he asked. 'Has Dr Krippitz discovered something?'

'Not exactly, Archie,' said Kozan, more serious now, 'but before we get into that, I would like to know what happened in the quadrangle last night. When Major Ramstiff spoke to your uncle this morning, he mentioned reports of shouting. What was *that* all about?'

'That was me – I was trying to reach mum. I –'

'Archie can't speak to her,' interrupted Richard, 'and she couldn't hear him. It wasn't his fault!'

'I'm sure it wasn't,' said Kozan, 'but, please, take your time and tell me what happened.'

Archie told him about how he hadn't taken Richard's dreams or trances too seriously at first, but with his brother's first experience in the quadrangle on the stone, and after what Shaman-Sing had taught them about mind-control when they were with the Rooters, he'd had the idea of trying the stone again. Only this time both of them would use their minds together – and it had worked!

'Well, it sort of worked – I could only see and hear through Richard,' said Archie, 'and it must have been me who everyone heard shouting. I didn't mean to cause so much trouble …' he trailed off, feeling stupid again.

Kozan looked at the two of them, frowning, his hands clasped in front of him.

'Boys, I don't think you fully appreciate how much you have achieved. To communicate with someone in another world, and to do it at will, is incredible. You must understand that.'

'I don't know if we can do it all the time,' said Richard. 'It wasn't too bad, at first, getting in touch, but … but it wasn't easy to hold on.' He looked at Kozan, trying hard to make him understand. 'It was better than the other times – I think that was because Archie was there, but I still couldn't hold on …'

'Richard, I spoke to Shaman-Sing before I came here, and he told me you indeed do have an extraordinary power, but it will take time for it to mature. However, with Archie's help, and that of Dr Krippitz, who knows how much more you will achieve?'

'Is that why we're going to the clinic?' asked Archie.

'Yes, it is,' said Kozan. 'Dr Krippitz has just informed Dr Shah that, based on the previous tests he carried out with Richard and the installation of new equipment, provided by the new funding, he has devised a special test he wants to try with Richard. He has called it, modestly enough, "the Krippitz Test".'

Kozan's wide grin at the name of the new test made Archie laugh.

'Sir, have you heard of Copanatec, the place my mother mentioned?'

'No, Archie, I haven't. There is only one man I can think of who might know of such a place, and that is Father Jamarko at the monastery. He is a scholar who has spent many years researching the history of Amasia, and many other lands and worlds that most of us have never heard of.' Noting the look of disappointment on Archie's face, he added, 'What I would suggest, though, is that you go on one of the college's weekly visits to the monastery and speak to Father Jamarko yourself. He may be able to help. Would you like me to arrange it with Miss Harmsway?'

'Yes, sir, we would,' said Archie, looking at Richard, who shrugged his shoulders in agreement. 'I was supposed to go on one with Miss Peoples sometime. Maybe Richard could go as well.'

'I don't think that will be a problem. I will attend to it along with your trip to the clinic,' said Kozan, rising from his seat. 'I'm sure Miss Harmsway won't mind you spending an extra day at the monastery.'

*

Three days later, Archie and Richard found themselves sitting in a room at the Evaluation Clinic sharing soft drinks and chocolate biscuits with Shona and Krippitz. They were taking a break from the preliminary tests that had taken up the better part of the day, and were now waiting for Krippitz's decision to proceed with the main test.

'What exactly is the ... uh, Krippitz Test?'

Archie almost grinned as he asked the question, remembering Benno Kozan's reaction when he first mentioned the test, but he managed to keep a straight face.

'In simple terms, it's a measure of telepathic ability,' said Shona. 'It was after Richard's experience with the zimmerball force-field and his contact with the DONUT that I mentioned to Dr Krippitz what had happened, and I wondered if it would be possible to simulate the same conditions here at the clinic.'

'Yes, and I believe we have!' said Krippitz. 'After our meeting at the Gladden Plateau, Dr Shah told me privately that he didn't want to waste any more time, and that in spite of his earlier doubts about my work, he would support me in whatever it would take to bring this project to a successful conclusion! So, while you boys were at Maroc, I investigated the structure of the zimmerball force-field. Once I had verified the power levels at which the vallonium resonators energised the force-field, I was able to reproduce the same conditions in a special room where the Krippitz Test will take place.'

'Uh ... what does all that mean ... resonators and things?' asked Richard, eating another biscuit.

Ignoring Richard's question and the blank looks on the boy's faces, Krippitz continued, 'And thanks to the funds provided by the Elders I was able to build the room in record time!'

'But do you really think it will work?' asked Archie. 'I mean, how can you tell it'll work *here*?'

Richard didn't like being ignored, but he was ravenous and only half-listening to the conversation now. He had eaten the remaining chocolate biscuits and was only interested in obtaining a fresh supply.

'I'm starving!' he announced. 'Can we get something more to eat?'

Shona laughed.

'There's a clue! Richard's appetite and energy level increases when he's ready for a sighting!'

'I hope so,' said Krippitz, 'but to answer your question, Archie, although we cannot be one hundred per cent certain, everything is in place for a favourable result.'

He didn't see the necessity of telling them that, thanks to Emil Shah's intervention, both Brimstone and Targa the Vikantu had been persuaded to help him in designing new software to respond to the telepathic messages that were viewed on the monitors. Unfortunately, they'd had mixed results and only Richard's sightings would confirm whether he was on the right track or not.

They were interrupted by one of his assistants entering the restroom to tell them that Professor Strawbridge had just arrived. Archie and Richard stood up as their uncle walked in carrying what seemed to be a bulky office file under his right arm.

'Good afternoon, everyone, I hope I haven't kept you waiting,' said the professor, sounding a little out of breath, 'but I wanted to double-check some of my figures before we proceeded any further.'

He pulled up an old club armchair and plopped his large, slightly overweight, frame into it, complaining that the engineers at Mount Tengi were somewhat slower in compiling information than those at the Facility.

'It must be because they live longer here,' said the professor, with a touch of humour. 'Anyway, be that as it may, I am ready. How about you, Dr Krippitz?'

Krippitz nodded. Peering at the professor through the thick lenses of his heavy-framed glasses, he pushed them back from the tip of his nose and affirmed that he too, was ready.

'Perhaps you would brief Richard on what it is that you want him to do, Professor. Meantime, Shona and I will make the final preparations for the main test. Hopefully, we will commence the first sighting within the hour, eh, Richard?'

After Krippitz and Shona had left the restroom, the professor laid the file he was carrying on the coffee table before him. He extracted a couple of pages that were covered with hundreds of numbers and strange symbols.

'Richard, I want you to take a look at these pages; they will give you an idea of what we want to send to Chuck at the Facility.'

'But, Uncle John … I can't read this stuff!' protested Richard, his eyes widening as he surveyed the pages Uncle John handed him.

He looked at the little diagrams with all the lines of mathematical formulae scribbled in beside them, none of it making any sense whatsoever.

'You don't have to *read* the pages, Richard, you just have to *look* at them. Dr Krippitz's new test monitors will pick up the images in your mind, store them and then transmit them to the Facility.'

'What happens then?' asked Archie.

'Well, once Richard is in contact with the Facility we must tell Ed Hanks and the engineers that they have to build a timecrack chamber to link with the one here on Mount Tengi.'

'But how long will that take? Dr Shah said he worked on his chamber for years!' said Archie, beginning to think that it would take just as long to get back to Old Earth.

'Ah, but you must remember, Archie, we have the DONUT, which created the timecrack that brought us here. We can build the chamber *within* the DONUT in a fraction of the time!'

He saw the dawn of understanding flicker across his nephew's face. Like a newly lit candle in the corner of a dark room, he watched the gleam in Archie's eyes brighten as he realised that the power of the DONUT could be used to take them home.

'Yes ... *Yes*, Uncle John! I see! Do you really think it will work?'

'Yes I do, but it all depends on getting this information back to the Facility,' said the professor, noting Archie's sudden enthusiasm.

He knew how much Archie had been affected by the disappearance of Malcolm and Lucy in the Yucatan, even more so than Richard, strangely enough, but maybe that was because, in some inexplicable way, Richard had been able to keep in touch with his parents – although, at the time, nobody had really taken him seriously. The episode at the Harmsway stone, according to what Major Ramstiff had told him, also had something to do with it, and that coming on top of the Maroc business had worried him, but now was neither the time nor the place to delve into all that. If he was to get them out of danger and back to Old Earth safely then his absolute priority was to communicate with the engineers at the Facility and get the construction of the chamber underway as soon as possible.

'Right, boys, it's time we joined Dr Krippitz – he should be ready for us shortly.'

Gathering the loose pages into the file, the professor heaved himself out of the armchair and led the way into the long, brightly lit corridor that ran the length of the clinic. At the other end, the Krippitz Test room had been designed and built as a totally insulated unit, free from the influence of other equipment in adjacent rooms.

As Archie and Richard entered the room, crammed with machines glowing eerily in the dim light, they could see that two deep-padded chairs had been installed, with lines of connecting cables leading to the rows of monitors that completely covered one wall. The right and left sides of the chairs had extendable armrests that would enable them to touch each other.

'From what we have learned from the boys' time spent with Shaman-Sing, it seems desirable that we maintain a physical link between them to obtain the best results,' Krippitz explained to the professor.

Shona started fussing around the boys in a motherly no-nonsense fashion, all the time speaking quietly and soothingly, ensuring that they were fully relaxed as they settled into the chairs. She made the connections from the headsets to the monitors before fully extending the armrests that would allow Archie and Richard to hold hands during their transition into the trance mode. She continued to talk softly to Richard until she was certain that he was fully 'locked-in' to his trance, and then one final glance at Archie assured her that they were ready to proceed.

'Excellent, everything is running smoothly,' said Krippitz, to no-one in particular. He was standing close to the monitors, scanning the screens for any early signs of a sighting. 'Nothing yet, but it shouldn't be long before we see something. What is that? Look there! Yes, something *is* happening!'

He pointed excitedly to one of the screens where the professor saw nothing that made any sense. Confused, hazy-looking, greyish-purple scenes of vague figures and objects were appearing randomly on the screen, but none lasted more than a second or two, making it difficult to recognise what it was that Richard was actually seeing.

'Shona, I think we can take Richard to the next stage now,' said Krippitz.

Turning away from the monitors he spoke to the professor.

'You can give your papers to Shona. Once Richard makes contact with the Facility she will show a page to him and, hopefully, transmit it to your friends at the other end.'

The professor nodded in agreement and handed his file over to Shona. He showed her the numbered sequence of pages, but emphasised that she must send a coded page first.

'Otherwise they may not believe what they are seeing. It will confirm to Ed and Chuck Winters that we are who we say we are.'

Shona took the file and spoke to Richard, almost in a whisper.

'Richard, please concentrate. We want you to make contact with the Facility, just as you did before, but this time we want you to look at the page I'm holding and allow your friends at the DONUT to see it as well. Now open your eyes slowly and look at the page.' She turned to see if anything appeared on the monitors. After a few seconds several jumbled-up pictures flashed onto one of the screens, but disappeared just as quickly. 'Let's try again, Richard, but allow your mind to dwell on the Facility and their computer screens.'

After a few more attempts the broken images on the Krippitz Test monitors became more stable and less fragmented. Slowly at first, one of the screens began forming a picture of strange shapes and bright colours. Suddenly, the picture crystallised, displaying a view of a red-coated man running across a metal catwalk towards a row of computer monitors. Sitting in front of the monitors were several blue-coated women, one of them, waving a hand, was calling the man over to look at something on her screen.

'My God! It's the DONUT!' yelled the professor. 'And that's one of the engineers. Look! He sees the page!'

'Shoosh!' hissed Shona, angry at the interruption. 'We might break the link if there is too much noise.'

'Sorry, but I can't believe what we are seeing!' whispered the professor, putting a hand over his mouth.

'Professor Strawbridge, what is this coded page that your people are looking at?' asked Krippitz. He adjusted his glasses to get a better look at the screen.

'It's only two words, Dr Krippitz – "Amaterasu returns". It refers to an ancient legend in our world when Amaterasu, the Sun Goddess, in a fit of pique retired to a distant cave in Heaven, thus depriving the world of her power and plunging all the lands into darkness. One day, after the world had suffered long enough, the God of Force discovered the hiding place of Amaterasu, and through trickery he persuaded her to leave the cave, whereupon she was captured and her energy was restored to the world.

'I told Chuck Winters and Ed Hanks the story, during the early design stages at the Facility. I thought that we might call our energy processor Amaterasu, but the technicians had begun to call it the DONUT and it stuck. A more modern description, I suppose, but it seems to fit. More importantly though, the name will convince Chuck that it is me sending the message, and that it is genuine.'

They continued to watch as Shona fed Richard page after page from the professor's file while the technicians at the DONUT read and stored the information as it arrived on their screens.

'Well, Professor, I think we can safely say this part of the Krippitz Test has been highly successful,' said Krippitz, feeling very pleased with himself.

'Yes, it would seem so. Now it's up to my engineers to finish the job,' said the professor, thoughtfully.

Chapter Twenty-Seven

The Monastery

The following morning, while Archie and Richard waited at the clinic for Marjorie to collect them for their trip to the monastery, Anton Cosimo was planning a similar visit – but for an entirely different reason.

Anton was standing in the small cave opening that overlooked the wide expanse of Timeless Valley. Not far from where he stood, he could see the monks tending the stickleberry bushes on the wide terraces that ran all the way from the monastery wall to the lower slopes of the mountain. One of the monks was on his hands and knees keeping the paths between the bushes free of weeds, while others busied themselves cutting away some of the dead wood from the older bushes. As Anton watched, it pleased his orderly mind to see the effort made by the monks in maintaining the terraces; not like the disorder he had found in the Arnak training camp.

Lotane's men were passionate about the cause they believed in, but it was not enough. They lived like animals while in the camp, and their personal discipline and basic hygiene was appalling, but worse still, their attitude towards the handling and maintenance of their equipment and weapons, primitive as they were, bordered on the suicidal. Anton knew from the long years he and Sandan had spent fighting in the New European Wars that if ever these peasant farmers with their swords and lances, and the few guns and explosives they had managed to steal from the Lancer armouries, were going to retake the land of Hazaranet, it would take a great deal more than the sacrifice of a small boy.

Behind him, beyond the pile of fallen rocks, Lotane was in the centre of the cavern with several of his men, including that cowering idiot, Nitkin, preparing for the visit of the Harmsway boy to the monastery. Lotane's informant at the college had sent word earlier that morning that the boy and his brother would be attending the weekly guided history tour later that afternoon. Now he was putting his men in place and expecting Anton to take charge, but while Lotane plotted with his men what he was going to do with the boy, Anton was preparing to put his own plan into action.

For the past few weeks, Anton had paid lip service to Lotane's demands that when the time came – and according to Lotane that time would be celebrated by the offering of the Shamra child to Zamah – the Arnak rebels had to be ready to take over key positions in Fort Temple. It was nonsense, of course, but in his madness, Lotane was convinced that the Arnak citizens would rise up and join him. Anton had seen no evidence of any popular support for such an uprising. In fact, during his many visits to the Vallonium Institute and the vallonium mines, where he sought more information on the process of obtaining limitless energy, he had never met anyone who sympathised with the aims of the rebels.

He had even accompanied Nitkin on his spying trips into the city, including a drinking den known as Kelly's, where he seemed to glean much of his information. In that dark den where the ordinary Arnak citizens discussed their everyday business and politics, they very often ridiculed the rebels and their cause, but that was not the kind of information that Nitkin would ever pass on to Prince Lotane.

There was only one plan that was going to work – and that was his.

Ever since Elder Shah's announcement at the Meeting House that the Kinross boy held the key to making the timecrack chamber at Mount Tengi work successfully, rumours about how this might happen had abounded throughout Fort Temple. There was no doubt that the boy was a precious commodity, and Anton believed that Shah, at least, would pay any ransom, including the secret vallonium process, to keep the boy alive, for without the boy Shah's project might never work.

Anton knew that once he had obtained the secret he would have to hold the boy until he had negotiated a safe return to Old Earth for Sandan and himself. They would then return through the timecrack together with the boy, which would ensure that Shah and his friends did not try to trick him. After all, he had to be certain that they did not send him into another world, and only the boy could guarantee that.

He smiled grimly as he reflected on his plan. They would expect him to return the boy, of course, but once they were back on Old Earth he could readily dispose of the youth, leaving him free to pursue his aim of taking control of the Consortium and the mining camps.

His thoughts were suddenly interrupted as he heard his name echoing through the emptiness of the cavern.

'Anton!' called Lotane. 'Anton – join us, the men are leaving now!'

He left the cave and made his way through a break in the rubble of fallen rocks. He had cleared a rough path after his first visit to the cave opening with Lotane, feeling it was a private place where he could marshal his thoughts into a cohesive plan. Now he was ready to act, determined that Lotane and his halfwit followers would not impede him in any way.

'Prince Lotane,' said Anton obsequiously, feigning a respect that Lotane expected from his followers, 'I take it that the men are leaving for the monastery?'

Lotane looked closely at the dark narrow-set eyes of the black-haired New Arrival who towered above him. There was a sharpness, like that of a newly honed blade striking a log, in Anton Cosimo's voice, which disturbed him, but the man was undoubtedly a fierce warrior and a leader of men. If only he had an army of such men!

'Yes, Anton, our time has come!' His mouth and face still partly covered by the scarf he wore inside his cowl, Lotane's voice trembled with all the passion of a zealot on a fiery mission. 'And now I want you, and Sandan, to come with me. There is a hidden passageway which Sandan has already used that leads directly to a cellar in the monastery. There you will find a bolted door that will let you into the cellar and through to another door that leads to the kitchen. When you leave the kitchen, the corridor will take you to the main hallway. It is there that Father Jamarko greets the students and visitors who come to hear the history of the monastery.

'The boy will be with his brother and one of the tutors, and you must watch out for the Lancer escorting them. There will be visiting traders dressed like you, so you will not be conspicuous, but be careful not to arouse their suspicions, for the Lancer will be armed with a paragun and he will not hesitate to use it. Once you have the boy, bring him back through the cellar, and one of my men will secure the door behind you. Remember, Anton, we have little time left, so do not fail me!' Lotane's eyes blazed with a zeal that questioned his sanity. 'Bring the boy directly to me and my followers in the Sacred Temple, where all will be ready for the Ritual Sacrifice.'

*

'What is this place?' asked Anton.

He looked around the paved square, confused by the sight of several passageways as wide as streets, stretching away in different directions. Sandan and Lotane stood with him near the remains of a milky-coloured statue that lay broken in large chunks in the centre of the square.

'It looks as if this may have been a town a long time ago.'

'It is part of the upper city of Ka, which was destroyed when the mountain collapsed over four thousand years ago,' said Lotane. He pointed to the parallel scars in the paving stones below their feet. 'You can still see the tracks of the chariots that once travelled these streets and, Zamah willing, all this will be restored to us after the sacrifice.'

Anton shook his head unbelievingly, but said nothing. He followed Lotane across the square, looking over his shoulder to see Sandan standing still, studying the partly buried buildings, the doorways and windows filled with the rubble of the centuries. Very little of the town was now visible and it took a great deal of imagination to see it as the thriving community of men, women and children it once was before the mountain exploded crushing their fragile lives.

'Stop hanging back, Sandan!' urged Anton. 'We have no time to waste here!'

He looked at the squat figure of his brother whose eyes were searching and taking in every detail of the ruined buildings. Anton was troubled by Sandan's behaviour and obvious fascination for the Arnaks and their culture, for not once since their arrival in the cavern, had Sandan ventured out into the valley, seemingly content to stay put and explore the many ancient passageways that riddled the mountain. But he had to admit it had been useful, for Sandan had discovered old tombs, storerooms and other areas that not even Lotane knew about. One such place, he had decided, would be the Harmsway boy's prison until the ransom and his demands were met.

'Anton is right, Sandan, you must make haste,' called Lotane, now standing at the entrance to one of the passageways. 'This is the way to the cellar, and it will take you a little time to get there, so you must be on your way. I will leave you now, for I have much to attend to, but remember, I will be waiting for you in the temple!'

After Lotane had disappeared into one of the other passageways, Anton followed Sandan on their way to the cellar. They travelled nearly a mile through the mountain by the light of scattered vallonium seams before reaching the heavily studded wooden door of which Lotane had spoken. They went through and Anton saw that the door was well hidden behind rows of stacked Sticklejuice barrels. Scanning the room carefully he moved forward silently to another door at the far end of the cellar and opened it. Stone steps spiralled steeply upwards around a wooden hoist used for the transportation of the barrels to the upper floors. They climbed the steps to an unlocked door and stepped into a dimly lit corridor.

The loud buzz of voices, young and old, at the end of the corridor, caught their attention.

'That sounds like the visitors and the students gathering for the tour,' said Sandan.

'Yes,' said Anton, smiling and closing the cellar door behind them, 'and I have something here that should occupy their attention for a few minutes.'

'What do you mean?' asked Sandan warily.

He didn't like it when Anton suddenly came up with some unexpected plan or idea. It usually meant something dangerous.

'Simply this, Sandan,' said Anton, patting a small bulge at his waist below the robe. 'I have a device here that I've borrowed from our rebel friends, which will create a diversion, giving you time to grab the boy.'

'But —'

'Stop worrying. Just make sure you take him to the storeroom as we arranged, and Sandan …'

Anton's voice hardened as he gripped Sandan's shoulder.

'What?'

'Be *very* careful that Lotane does not find out what you have done with the boy.'

*

Marjorie pulled at Archie's sleeve as they mounted the wide granite steps that fronted the great brownstone building that seemed to spring up from the side of the mountain.

'Yes, Marjorie?'

'Archie, will you please make certain that you and Richard stay close to Han-Sin and me while we are in the monastery? I don't want the two of you getting lost in the crowd.'

They had just left the Freebus, and Marjorie was delighted to be back in the monastery again. It was her fourth trip with a group of students from Harmsway, and on each occasion the tranquillity of the place impressed her even more deeply than the last. This visit had been tainted with a warning from Professor Strawbridge that she keep an especially close watch on the boys. He hadn't said much, but she knew that something important was going on when Han-Sin was assigned to join them.

'OK, Marjorie', said Archie, watching Richard dash up the steps into the main hall. 'I'd better stay with him.'

He hurried inside and found Richard with several other students examining a large glass display case at the side of the hall. It contained a detailed scale model of the monastery and its position on the face of the mountain. Monks, like toy soldiers, were shown working at all the different tasks that went into the production of Amasia's favourite beverage: Sticklejuice.

'I'm glad to see our young visitors from Harmsway taking such an interest in our activities here at the monastery,' said a voice nearby.

Archie and the other students turned around to see a young monk descending a mahogany staircase that swept down one side of the hall.

'It's that Elder we saw at the Meeting House,' whispered Archie.

'My name is Father Haman and it is my pleasure to welcome you to the monastery,' said the monk. 'As many of you will already know, these tours are designed to spread the knowledge of our work here and, especially for the students, it is also an opportunity to hear from Father Jamarko more of the wonderful history of the monastery, and its relationship with Fort Temple and the rest of the valley. Now, if you will follow me, we will proceed to the library where Father Jamarko is waiting for us.'

Father Haman stepped down from the staircase and everyone fell in behind him as he led the way into a huge windowless room below the staircase where open shelves and glass-fronted bookcases, lined with all manner of books and ancient manuscripts, occupied every inch of wall space. There were plain wooden chairs arranged in rows in the middle of the room below a magnificent vallonium chandelier, and they were told to sit wherever they pleased. Archie and Richard managed to find seats at the back of the room while Marjorie and Han-Sin stood near the door.

Standing beside one of the bookcases, holding a large leather-bound volume entitled *The Life and Times of Nicolo Amasia,* was a very old monk with a long grey beard. His eyes were watery and his skin was like the faded yellow parchment of the book he now held open in front of his chest, but when he spoke, his voice was surprisingly strong and clear, and without any preamble whatsoever, he launched into a fascinating account of the discovery of Amasia.

He told them of the many trials and tribulations suffered by the founding father of Amasia, of the sickness and deaths suffered by his followers, of the vicious tribal wars he had fought and of the discovery of mysterious towns and cities that had been built by visitors from other worlds.

It was at this point, after listening to the old monk for nearly an hour, that Archie suddenly sat up and paid more attention. He was nearly asleep from sitting so long in one place, and his backside was beginning to ache, but when he heard Father Jamarko speak of mysterious cities and strange people that no one had ever heard of, he thought of the place his mother had mentioned. Without thinking, and to the surprise of the others in the room, he raised his arm.

'Sir, excuse me ...'

Father Jamarko was startled by the voice. He couldn't remember ever being interrupted in this way before. He closed his book and took a few shuffling steps towards Archie to get a better look.

'Yes, my boy – what is it?'

'It was just that ... well, I was wondering if you had ever heard of a place called Copanatec?'

'My, my, what an interesting thing to ask; I have not heard that name in such a long time. No, not for a very long time.'

'But you have heard of it?' asked Archie excitedly. 'You know where it is?'

'Oh, yes, I have heard of it, but as I say, it was a long time ago.' Father Jamarko placed the book on a small table by a bookcase and stroked his beard thoughtfully. 'It was believed to be a part of the southern continent of Amasia, but I can't tell you where it is – no one can.'

'But – why not?'

'Because it no longer exists – it vanished without trace during the time of the Great Flood.'

'But that can't be –'

At the precise moment when Archie was about to query what Father Jamarko had said, an explosion occurred and everyone heard a great *whoooosssh* outside the library door.

Marjorie had been listening to Father Jamarko, and wondering what Archie was driving at, when she felt the sudden rush of hot air touch her face.

'My God! What was that?'

'Get down!' cried Han-Sin. She grabbed Marjorie by the arm and pulled her to the floor just inside the doorway where they had been standing.

Someone in the room screamed '*Fire!*' causing students and visitors alike to panic as they stampeded towards the door past Han-Sin and Marjorie, pinning them against the wall.

'Stay here!' ordered Han-Sin. She left Marjorie and started to force her way through the crowd into the main hall.

She saw straightaway that the lower part of the staircase was missing and bright orange-red flames were licking their way along the banister towards the upper floor where a large tapestry was hanging at the top of the staircase.

Two monks were desperately throwing buckets of sand onto the flames, and in their anxiety they had overlooked the fire extinguisher on the wall beside them. Han-Sin rushed over and unhooked it, released the lever and directed the pressurised stream of water onto the banister near the tapestry. Within minutes the danger was over and soon they had the worst of the fire extinguished. The monks dropped the empty fire buckets and turned to Han-Sin still holding the fire extinguisher and thanked her profusely for her help.

'Well done, Han-Sin!' Marjorie was unhurt and was now pushing her way through the last of the crowd now streaming through the main door. She reached Han-Sin and looked at the damaged staircase. 'What do you think happened here?'

Han-Sin dropped the fire extinguisher onto the floor and got down on one knee to examine more closely what was left of the bottom of the staircase. She pulled a metal fragment away from the charred banister and held it towards Marjorie.

'It was an incendiary device,' she said. 'This was started deliberately – but why? It wasn't a big explosion, and why would anybody want to start a small fire here?'

She looked around and found Archie standing alone near them, when a very unpleasant thought crept into her head.

To cause a diversion!

'Archie, where's Richard?' cried Han-Sin.

'He's here,' said Archie, but he was wrong.

When he looked behind him, he saw that Richard was nowhere to be seen.

Chapter Twenty-Eight

Sandan's Dilemma

'*Aaahh*!' screamed Sandan.

He threw Richard down onto the rough earth floor of the passageway, glancing at his hand to see the little teeth marks where they had drawn blood.

'Look – I'm bleeding!'

'I don't care, you ugly brute!' yelled Richard. '*Let me out of here!*'

He stared at the squat hairy figure who had pulled him out of the main hall into the corridor and down into the tunnel. Rubbing his mouth with the back of his hand he tried to rid himself of the smell and taste of the man's coarse sweaty skin. During the fire, when he'd suddenly found himself being dragged away from behind Archie's back, he'd thought, at first, that someone was trying to help him. But when they reached the passageway the man had clamped a hand so tightly over his mouth he could hardly breathe. He'd resisted but the man had held him even tighter, until he bit him.

'Why have you brought me here? I haven't done anything to you!' he asked, trying not to show any fear.

Sandan sucked at the wound in his hand and spat some blood onto the ground near Richard.

'No – it's what we are going to do to you,' he growled. 'Now, get to your feet, and no more of your tricks or you'll feel my boot!'

'*Aaooww*! You're hurting me!' Richard yelped as Sandan yanked him savagely off the ground onto his feet.

Moving deeper into the tunnel he felt frightened and wondered what this horrible creature wanted with him.

The eerie blackness of the tunnel was broken only by the occasional vallonium seam, with its microscopic crystals flashing like millions of fireflies on a dark summer's evening. As they passed one of the thicker seams Richard felt a now familiar sensation pricking at his senses. An image was forming, a sighting of something, or someone, was taking shape; he could almost see it, like a passing cloud creating a picture in the imagination, but suddenly it was gone.

'Hurry up, we've no time to waste here,' snarled Sandan, tightening his grip on Richard's wrist whenever he felt the boy beginning to lag behind him. 'You have an appointment to keep, and the sooner the better as far as I'm concerned, so move!'

*

Not everyone had fled from the main hall. Some of the visitors, including two traders, offered their help to the monks now clearing some of the debris from the bottom of the staircase. They were thanked, but told it was not necessary, as the damage was slight.

Anton smiled politely and then waited with one of Lotane's followers until he was certain that Sandan and the boy were safely away. He needn't have worried: after placing the incendiary device, everything had gone like clockwork. People are so predictable, he thought. Just as he had planned, while everyone was rushing to get out of the building, or attending to the fire, Sandan had been able to snatch the boy without anyone noticing until it was too late.

Looking around to check that they were unobserved, Anton said to Lotane's man, 'I'm leaving now. Lock the cellar door to the tunnel behind me, but do not draw any attention to yourself, then report back to Prince Lotane that the boy is in our hands.'

But not yours, thought Anton. That was a problem that Lotane would have to deal with by himself. Sandan would explain that the boy had escaped and was now hiding somewhere in the labyrinth of old mining tunnels that criss-crossed the mountain behind the buried ruins of Ka. Meantime, he would contact Shah and make his demands. Secretly, of course, so as not to incur Lotane's wrath too soon.

Almost running, he made his way back to the town square they had passed through earlier. He had agreed with his half-brother they would meet there after the boy was locked in the storeroom that Sandan had discovered during his early exploration of the mountain passageways.

Arriving at the square he saw a slumped figure beside a large rock, holding his hand to his mouth and spitting on the ground.

'What is the matter with you, Sandan? Are you hurt?'

'Look at what the brat did to me.'

Sandan thrust out his hand for Anton to see. Anton inspected the small bite-mark, then threw back his head and laughed out loud.

'An interesting wound, but unless he's poisoned you, I think you'll live!'

'It's all very well for you to laugh –'

'Enough!' snapped Anton. 'I have no time for this. All I need to know is that the boy is safely secured while I move to the next stage of my plan.'

He stopped for a moment. Although he and Sandan were only half-brothers, they were close enough for Anton to realise that something was seriously wrong. Years of dealing with Sandan's moods, and his incompetence, had left him with little patience for his petty concerns, especially at a time like this, when every hour now counted.

'What is it, Sandan? What is it that has you in such a foul temper?'

Suddenly he had to step back as Sandan stood up and gripped him firmly by the front of his robe.

'Anton, what we are doing cannot be right – the boy must be handed over to Prince Lotane before he is thirteen!' Sandan was almost shouting, as if Anton could not hear him. 'He must be a Shamra child, otherwise the Ritual Sacrifice will mean nothing!'

Anton looked at him in astonishment, momentarily taken aback by his outburst.

'Lotane is mad, Sandan, and you must be out of your mind to believe such nonsense –'

'No! It isn't nonsense – look around you, this place is over four thousand years old. It is as real as you and I; and the Arnaks are real, and they are destined to have their land restored to them through the Ritual Sacrifice.'

'I should never have left you alone in this damnable place. You have been infected by Lotane's madness – and I blame myself for that – but hear this, and hear it well, Sandan,' said Anton. His cruel hawk-like eyes narrowed to mean slits as he gripped Sandan by the throat and slowly lifted him, almost dancing, onto his toes. 'I have not come all this way to be thwarted by superstitious primitives and their belief in some crazy ritual.' He brought his face close to Sandan's. 'And believe me: I will kill *anyone* who gets in my way.'

He threw Sandan to the ground and watched him slither to the rock, as if it might protect him from Anton's anger.

'Pull yourself together, and make sure you look after the boy. I have a message to send to our friend, Dr Shah, but I will be back soon.'

*

Marjorie and Archie left the main hall to go outside where they joined Father Haman and another monk at the entrance to the monastery. With their cowls cast back and hands clasped, their deep purple robes now covered in specks of grey ash from the fire, the monks were watching Teekoo's Spokestar coming in to land on the wide driveway in front of them.

Han-Sin climbed down, leaving Teekoo in the cockpit. Marjorie called anxiously to her.

'Is there any sign of Richard, Han-Sin?'

'I'm afraid not. We've checked everywhere from the monastery all the way down to and beyond the terraces and there isn't a trace of him.'

'This is terrible,' said Marjorie. She was visibly upset and beginning to panic, not knowing what to do next. 'Professor Strawbridge will be so angry that I let Richard out of my sight.'

'It is my responsibility and I will deal with it, Marjorie,' said Han-Sin abruptly. She was angry with herself for not staying close to Richard. She saw no point in Marjorie blaming herself when the Lancers had been appointed to protect the boys. 'We will go over the grounds again and this time we will widen the search, but he can't have gotten far in such a short space of time.'

'Please do not worry, Miss Peoples, I am sure the Lancers will search the area thoroughly,' said Father Haman. His hand touched Marjorie on her shoulder as if to reassure her. 'Brother Obay here, with the rest of our brothers, will comb the rest of the monastery. It may be that in the rush to get out of the building the boy has got himself locked in one of the rooms. Now, if you will excuse me, I will go and see what is happening.'

They went inside, leaving Marjorie and Archie to think about what to do next. Han-Sin also left, promising to let them know immediately if she and Teekoo saw any sign of Richard.

Marjorie was worried, but Archie didn't think she appreciated just how bad the situation might be. She hadn't witnessed how very determined the rebels were on the hoverrail to get their hands on Richard. Han-Sin had said the fire looked like a diversion, and now Richard had disappeared. It had to be the rebels, but why, and where would they have taken him?

Archie watched the Spokestar soar above the main monastery building and beyond the great brownstone towers towards the immense peaks of the Piranga mountain range. His eyes followed the treeline to where it was broken by a series of caves and a thundering waterfall that crashed down the mountainside to feed the river that coursed its way to the distant Amasian Sea. He couldn't help thinking that if Richard had disappeared into that wilderness the Lancers might never find him.

*

A long narrow break in the rock face behind the waterfall allowed daylight and fresh air into the room where Richard was now held captive. Large clay pots crowded most of the available space; some of them lined the walls on crude shelves cut out of the rock, while others lay shattered on the earthen floor. Thousands of years earlier the storeroom had been one of many used by the ancient traders of Ka to store a wide range of goods imported from all over Hazaranet, but now there was nothing, only mounds of dust and empty pots.

Richard sat huddled between two of the pots trying to stay warm and out of the way of the wind and spray that occasionally blustered through the opening in the rock face. Two nights had passed and he faced the prospect of a third without knowing what was going to happen to him. He was cold and hungry, having used up the last of the stale bread and jug of water the man had left him on the first day. It was getting dark again and he was dreading the thought of another night on his own, with no hope of escaping from this terrible place, although he had tried shortly after the man had left him alone.

Other than the bolted door, the only other way out was the opening to the waterfall, and that had proved to be a painful experience. Squeezing his head and shoulders into the break hadn't been such a good idea. He had become stuck and it had taken him ages to wriggle back into the room again, bumping his head and cutting his hands on the wet rock in the process.

Sleep didn't come easily; Richard was too cold and he kept waking up to the roar of the waterfall. As the long hours crept slowly by, he thought of Archie and Uncle John and Marjorie. They would be worried about him, and so would Han-Sin and Teekoo, and all the others who were depending on him to help Dr Shah to make the timecrack chamber work. He was sure Han-Sin would be looking for him, but how would she find him?

The night passed slowly and his thoughts kept turning to all the people he and Archie had met since their arrival in Timeless Valley. There was Aristo and Captain Hanki, and the Lancers and Brimstone, and Finbar and Targa and … Targa? What was it that Targa had told him the day they had met in the castle hallway? He tried to remember, but his mind was almost numb with cold and it was hard to concentrate.

It suddenly came to him when he formed a picture of the tall golden-haired man coming towards him. The thoughts were broken but now he remembered.

'We are Vikantus, master builders to the Castle Protector … You are both welcome here …. My name is Targa; please ask for my assistance if ever you need it.'

Targa had read his thoughts and he'd said he would help if ever he needed him. Could Targa help him now? Could he send Targa a message to tell Archie and Han-Sin where he was?

Excited by the idea, Richard sat up and leaned forwards with his elbows on his knees, his head supported between his hands while he tried to force a message from his mind to Targa. Nothing happened; he was trying too hard and nothing worked that way. He lay back against the wall again and remembered Shaman-Sing's advice that he had to relax and allow his mind to open up and become one with the universe. He wasn't sure what that meant, but after a while he felt his mind drifting as if he was about to fall asleep.

*

As he thought of Shaman-Sing and what he had said, Richard found himself sitting by the side of the riverbank in Maroc Forest. The sounds of the river gurgling over smooth stones and the whispering breeze passing through the high branches of the pine trees were soothing and restful.

He dwelt on the image of Targa. After a few moments he saw a tall, lone figure approach and then stop in front of him.

'Greetings, my young friend, I am pleased to hear from you again.'

319

'Uh .. Targa ... I'm ...' Words failed Richard, and Targa's voice began to fade. He could hear someone shouting from faraway. He tried to ignore it and concentrate on the image. 'I'm ...'

Quickly, Richard, we do not have long. I know you are in trouble and your friends are searching for you. Can you tell me what happened to you?

'A man – I don't know who he is – grabbed me in the monastery when the fire started and he forced me into a cellar. After that, he made me go with him into a tunnel ... it led to somewhere in the mountain.'

And where are you now, Richard?

'I'm not sure. He's locked me in a room – it's a sort of cave, and it's behind a waterfall.'

A waterfall?

'Yes, I think it's the big one near the monastery – the one that joins the river. Targa, I tried to get out, but I got stuck, and now I can't get out of here!'

Do not worry, Richard, we will come for you –

*

Targa's image disappeared and Richard was back in the storeroom again. Someone was shouting and shaking him roughly by the shoulder.

'Wake up, you little brat! You're coming with me!'

Sandan hauled Richard to his feet and pulled him by the arm to the door.

'Let me go! Where are you taking me?'

Richard lashed out with his foot, but he was too weak to make any impact.

'Stop kicking or I'll smash your face against the rock –'

'Leave him be! The boy must be unmarked, or you will answer to Prince Lotane for it. You know well enough how angry he is with you and your brother for the boy's disappearance,' sneered the voice.

It was Nitkin speaking, and he was enjoying Sandan's evident discomfort as he released the boy. He had no time for the Cosimos, and the sooner Prince Lotane disposed of them, the better. He pushed the boy through the doorway into the hands of one of his men in the tunnel.

'We will take him. We have no more time to waste,' said Nitkin, taking the lead as they left the storeroom.

Sandan grunted, but said nothing. He was frightened by the thought of what Anton would do when he found out that the boy was now in Prince Lotane's hands.

*

When Anton had thrown him to the ground and threatened him, Sandan had promised himself that it would never happen again. He had suffered years of abuse at the hands of his half-brother, but it had suited him to stay silent – what else could he do when there was no one left to whom he could turn? Anton had seen to that; turning every friend they ever had into an enemy, until even the dogs in the street ran from their presence.

But Sandan felt differently now, because Prince Lotane treated him as a friend and an equal – something that Anton had never done.

During his time in the cavern he had explored much of the ruins of the Arnak's ancient civilisation and he had come to know their history. It was their cause Sandan understood and believed in, like them, he had been an outcast for most of his life, and he knew the pain of rejection. Anton had made him betray the Arnaks, and for the past two days he had tortured himself about what he should do. In the end, his decision came easily enough.

But Prince Lotane's rage was so great that when he heard that Anton had disappeared as well as the boy, he vowed to kill Anton and Sandan if the boy was not found in time for the Ritual Sacrifice.

'Find him! He is somewhere in the mountain – find him, or the wrath of Zamah will fall on all of us!' he screamed at the Arnaks.

For two days they searched the passageways of the mountain and the rubble-filled buildings of Ka until Prince Lotane's anger could no longer be contained. He struck men down as he passed them and ordered others to be beaten when they could not meet his demands.

Sandan was so terrified he could no longer sleep or eat properly, worried that at any moment Prince Lotane might kill him if the boy was not found. Finally, he could stand it no longer, making up his mind to tell Lotane all that he knew, in the hope that the prince would protect him against Anton's undoubted vengeance.

'Forgive me, Prince Lotane, for not coming to you sooner.' Sandan cringed at the feet of the angry figure before him. 'Anton threatened to kill me if I revealed where the boy was, but now I know I was wrong not to come to you sooner.'

'And where is the boy now?' rasped Lotane, his eyes narrowing above the mask.

'He is in an old storeroom behind the waterfall. Anton wanted him held there until the Elders met his demands,' said Sandan, explaining what it was that Anton intended.

Lotane looked angrily at Sandan kneeling before him, hardly believing what he had just heard. No one had ever defied him in such a way before and his instinct was to break Sandan's neck and throw him to

322

one side like the pitiful dog that he was. But he realised it was Anton he would have to destroy. He would deal with both of them in due course, but for now he had to be certain of the boy's whereabouts.

'On your feet, Sandan,' said Lotane smoothly, seemingly calmer now that he knew where the boy was to be found. 'I want you to bring the child to me. My men will go with you in case you experience any more difficulties. Later, we will discuss your future here.'

*

They returned to the cavern with Richard. One of the rebel Arnaks, a fat scowling individual, half-carried, half-dragged him, kicking and screaming, while Nitkin kept a close watch on Sandan, who he suspected was capable of further treachery.

As they marched across the square towards the marble steps that led to the great golden doors of the temple, Sandan saw a strange forbidding figure carefully watching their approach. A golden cloak with the signs of the stone, richly embroidered with red and silver threads, adorned the figure. A tall golden headdress bearing the symbols of Ritual Sacrifice arose above a face that had been painted with black and green pigments, making those who knew its meaning shudder with apprehension at what was to come.

'My faithful followers, I welcome your return,' said the figure, gazing down on the small group before him. 'Is this the Shamra child for whom we have waited so long?'

Sandan was shocked. He recognised the voice as belonging to Prince Lotane, but it was the first time he had seen his face uncovered, although the black and green pigments revealed little of his features.

'It is, My Prince,' replied Nitkin, bowing before his master.

'Then take him and prepare him for his journey to Zamah, for it is written his time has come!'

Chapter Twenty-Nine

The Ritual Sacrifice

Anton looked around the storeroom, wondering if he had made a mistake. No, this was the place Sandan had shown him when he had made his plan to abduct the boy – but where were they?

The opening to the waterfall was too narrow for the boy to escape, and the only other way out was through the door he had found lying wide open. He bent down to examine the floor near the doorway: several pairs of feet had disturbed the earth, yet Sandan had assured him that no one ever came near this place. So, what had happened?

He cursed himself for depending on Sandan, but he'd had no choice if he was to pursue his plan, which had been straightforward enough. He had given the Vallonium Institute and the Elders, Kozan and Shah, seventy-two hours to meet his demands or he would kill the boy. They had to make their agreement known by publishing a code, included in his message, in the personal column of the *Amasian Chronicle*. It was an ultimatum that left no doubt as to his intentions.

With no guarantee that the postal system would deliver his letter on time, and with both Lotane's men and the Lancers searching for the boy, he knew he had no time to waste. It was a matter of finding a way to get the letter to the institute, without leaving a trace of its delivery. That had turned out to be remarkably easy, he had made the acquaintance of a blind man in Kelly's Tavern, and despite his blindness, it was said that he knew the city well. So for the price of a few drinks the man had, unknowingly, delivered Anton's ransom demand to the Vallonium Institute.

There was no possibility of the blind man identifying him, and as Anton still wore the trader's robe with the cowl hiding his face, no one else had paid any attention to him. He had spent the evenings in a cheap hostel where strangers were asked no awkward questions as long as they paid their bill in advance.

He had waited impatiently for the notice to appear in the *Amasian Chronicle* agreeing to his demand. His instructions had been clear, but for some reason the notice had not yet been published. Maybe they were stretching it out to the last minute, playing for time. Well, if that is the game they want to play, thought Anton, I will have to convince the institute of my intentions – an ear, or a finger, perhaps. Yes, he smiled grimly; the next letter would do the trick.

But now he had the added problem of finding the boy.

He kicked the earth angrily and proceeded to follow the tracks along the passageway that seemed to lead in the direction of the cavern. As he thought about what might have happened to the snotnose kid, he turned over in his mind the possibility that Sandan had betrayed him.

*

'Only a madman would send a letter like this,' said Dr Shah, sitting in his hoverchair at the end of a highly polished, oblong mahogany table that could seat twenty institute members at a time.

The letter lay on the table in front of him, the envelope alongside where Captain Hanki had left it. 'Do we have any idea yet who is behind this?'

'The security people say there are no clues,' said Hanki. 'It was written by an unknown hand on cheap paper that can be obtained anywhere. One of the reception staff thinks an old man with a walking stick left it, but she paid no attention to him, as they receive hundreds of letters every week. Usually they're just requests for information on vallonium products.'

'There *must* be something we can do. We can't just wait until something happens to Richard!' The professor's voice trembled as his hand slapped the table. He was still angry that between them, Marjorie, Han-Sin and Teekoo had been unable to protect Richard, especially after the events at Maroc had proven he was in danger. 'Can you not round-up these rebel Arnaks, as you call them? At least one of them could be forced to tell us where Richard is!'

'Professor Strawbridge, I share your concern, but we are not yet convinced that this is the work of the rebels,' said Hanki. 'It's not a tactic they have used before and, in my opinion, such a demand would indicate that a more ... shall we say, *devious* mind is involved.'

He hesitated to elaborate that in his opinion the rebels were a primitive lot, hardly capable of running a Sticklejuice party, let alone carrying out a kidnapping and a revolution. He knew his own competence and reputation were at stake here; and it didn't make it any easier that his own daughter, Han-Sin, had been in charge when the boy disappeared. His Lancers had searched the monastery grounds and the stretch of land all the way to the river, but after nearly three days there was not a trace of Richard to be found.

Looking at the others around the table, he continued.

'We are ready to place a notice in the *Amasian Chronicle* stating that we are prepared to negotiate.

Hopefully that will give us more time to develop a plan to find Richard.'

'Hopefully? I —'

Before the professor could give vent to another bout of table-thumping he felt his sleeve being pulled.

'Uncle John, maybe Richard is still *inside* the monastery somewhere,' said Archie.

Everyone sitting at the long table, Dr Shah, Benno Kozan, Captain Hanki and the professor, seemed surprised to hear Archie's voice. He'd hardly said a word since arriving at the institute with his uncle soon after they had received word of the ransom demand. It had been Kozan's suggestion that they use the institute's boardroom as a meeting place for those engaged in the efforts to find Richard, but so far they had nothing other than the letter to go on.

'What makes you think that, Archie?' asked the professor.

'I'm not sure. It's just that the Lancers said they'd checked everywhere outside the monastery straightaway and there was no sign of Richard. I asked some of the Harmsway students, who were hanging about after the fire, and none of them had seen him outside either. It all happened so quickly he *couldn't* have got very far. Even Father Haman said he might've been locked in one of the rooms. He *has* to be in there, Uncle John!'

Shah moved his hoverchair away from the table to a window overlooking Fort Temple and cast his gaze across the varied rooftops of the city skyline. Like the others he sat in silence for a moment, digesting what Archie had just said.

'Well, gentlemen,' said the professor, 'my nephew has obviously given this some thought, and I must admit what he says makes a lot of sense. Perhaps we should go into the monastery and turn it inside out until we find Richard.' He looked across to Shah at the window. 'What do you think, Emil?'

'I agree. Besides my concern for the timecrack project, Richard's safety is paramount, and every minute we waste puts him in further danger.'

Shah was also about to say that Archie was the only one who had said anything remotely sensible so far, when he heard a knock on the boardroom door.

A thin-faced Salakin woman in a plain grey dress entered the room. It was Benno Kozan's secretary, clutching a radiocom as she approached the table.

'What is it, Creena, I thought we were not to be disturbed?' said Kozan, sounding unusually irritated.

'I'm sorry, Benno Kozan, but I have an urgent message for Captain Hanki. The caller says it is vital he speaks to him –'

'I'll take it,' said Hanki, jumping up from his chair and snatching the radiocom from Creena's outstretched hand.

He held the device to his ear and walked the length of the room without saying a word, listening carefully. After a couple of minutes he handed the radiocom back to Creena, who quickly left the room. He faced the others around the table, a huge smile creasing his face.

'Well, some good news at last – we've received a message from Richard!'

'What!' exploded the professor, leaping to his feet 'Where is he?'

Archie nearly fell backwards out of his chair as his uncle pushed his way past him to stand in front of Captain Hanki.

'That was Brimstone. He says that Richard sent a message to Targa the Vikantu a short time ago. It seems that he is being held in the mountain near the monastery,' said Hanki.

'How did he get into the mountain? Who's holding him?'

'I don't know, Professor, but we will soon find out. My Lancers are on their way to join Brimstone and Targa at the mountain. I'm going there now.'

'We're going with you,' said the professor, his voice brooking no refusal.

'I'm going too!' insisted Archie, fearing that he might be left behind.

The professor smiled down at him.

'You certainly are – I'm not taking any chances that you might disappear too!'

*

Anton stiffened as he heard his name echo throughout the huge cavern. In spite of the manic shriek that accompanied it, he recognised Lotane's voice, angry and shrill.

He was crouching behind a pile of fallen rock, near the passageway he had just left. Raising his head slowly until he could command a better view of the Sacred Temple, he saw that Sandan was at the bottom of the marble steps, on his knees between two of the rebels, with his head bent low as if in prayer.

'Get on your feet! It is Anton I want, not your feeble excuses,' snarled Lotane. 'If I find that you *did* betray me, then you will pay for it.'

'It was Anton – he forced me to hold the boy! He – *aahhh*!'

Sandan fell to the ground clutching the side of his head where one of the men had struck him with the flat of his sword. At a signal from Lotane the men dragged him to the top of the steps where he lay curled up in a corner, frightened that they would hit him again.

'Leave him there where you can keep an eye on him,' said Lotane, turning away from them. 'I will deal with him later.'

They talk of betrayal, thought Anton bitterly, *but what about me, Sandan, what about me?*

Shafts of broken light entered the cavern through breaks in the rock above, making it difficult for Anton to hide from the straying eyes of the rebels now making their way to the front of the temple. He crouched low, slipping from one pile of rocks to another, until he found himself in a position to see more clearly what was happening inside the temple.

There was no sign of the boy, but he could see several women dressed in long, purple-hemmed white robes assembling around the stone – the priestesses, he realised.

Then he saw Lotane, dressed in a brilliant robe and headdress – *ah, now he is playing the part of the High Priest,* thought Anton. He had heard enough from the stories repeated by Sandan, to realise what was happening here. Lotane's face was uncovered, painted in black and green pigments, lending him a sinister appearance in keeping with the act he was about to carry out. Strangely, the face seemed all too familiar to Anton, but for the moment he couldn't place it.

Anton waited, shifting his position occasionally to ease the ache in his bent knees, calculating what he would do when the boy appeared. It was unlike him, for he had no plan other than to take advantage of the rebels' distraction while they waited for the Ritual Sacrifice to commence. His immediate thoughts were to overpower the two men nearest him and seize their weapons. Having trained many of them, he knew their limitations as warriors; he could deal with them easily enough. The rebels usually carried swords, but these two had acquired long-guns of the type that had been used on Old Earth long before his time. They were primitive weapons, probably carried through a timecrack by their owners, but still effective enough in the right hands.

After that, shock and surprise would be on his side, enabling him to grab the boy and dash for one of the tunnels before they realised what had happened. The odds were against him, he knew, but if he could kill Lotane it might stop the rebels in their tracks before they gathered their wits.

Suddenly, Lotane stepped forward, arms spread out before him, calling out to his followers. Two of the priestesses walked behind him, supporting a small figure between them.

'Arnaks, behold the Shamra child!' cried Lotane, stepping aside to show his followers the sacrifice that Zamah demanded.

Cheers and shouts of approval erupted from the rebels as they moved forwards to see better, waving and shaking fists tight with weapons above their heads.

Lotane gestured to them to be still.

'My brothers, our time has come! As soon as Zamah has accepted the Shamra child you will go from this place and reclaim the land of Hazaranet!'

More rebels, old and young, had arrived in the cavern, and now they stood in little groups, awestruck by Prince Lotane's words, hardly believing they were about to witness the ancient tradition of Ritual Sacrifice that their forefathers had practised so long ago.

They watched silently as their leader, now in the role of High Priest, turned away from them and pointed through the golden doors to the stone. Since its removal from the square, the people could no longer see it from where they stood, but they knew well enough what would happen to the Shamra child in the next few minutes.

As the two priestesses led the boy to the trough in the centre of the stone, Anton ran unnoticed to another pile of rocks, bringing him closer to the men with the long-guns at the side of the temple. He could see that the boy was unsteady on his feet; probably drugged with some herbal potion or other, he guessed. If he ever managed to get to him, it would make their escape more hazardous.

Lifting a small sharp rock to use as a weapon, Anton cursed his brother.

'Damn you, Sandan. Damn you for your treachery.'

*

Richard struggled to release himself from the grip of the priestesses, each of them holding an arm as they pushed him firmly into the gold trough. It was no good; he didn't seem to have the strength to resist as they forced him to lie on his back, one of them ripping open his shirt to expose his chest to the other priestesses now forming a circle around the edge of the stone.

He lay there, confused and uncertain by what was happening to him. His eyes were unable to focus properly and his mouth was bitter with the aftertaste of the foul potion they'd made him drink earlier. He tried to speak, but he couldn't form the words.

Ghostly images began to appear before him, swirling around the great stone, staring at him with hollow eyes as black as pitch, their chests scarred by the signs of sacrifice. They floated in and out of the thin grey mist that accompanied them, as if they were waiting for Richard to join them in some unearthly game. He was horrified by what he saw and he wanted to leave this terrible place, but he couldn't move – not a finger, not a muscle.

The trough was getting warm, its deceptive deathly embrace lulling him into a dark silent place where he knew he shouldn't go. He fought the feeling of sleep that threatened to overtake him, afraid that he might never wake up. He couldn't move as he tried to push the images back into the mist that now covered the stone. Slowly, the faces of everyone he'd ever known or met came to him in a long continuous stream, like a great uncoiling snake arising out of the darkness. They faded away again, but one face remained, its thoughts trying to reach and probe into his mind until, at last, it gained access, now able to see what Richard could see.

It was Targa, trying to communicate with him, but before he could respond, he suddenly felt something cold and sharp pricking his skin.

The mist and the faces vanished, revealing the grotesque features of a green and black painted face staring down at him. It was the High Priest, surrounded by the priestesses chanting in a strange tongue, tracing the point of the sword in a ritual pattern across Richard's chest. As the High Priest raised the sword above his headdress Richard screamed, but it was a silent scream and no one could hear him. A frightening chill coursed through Richard's body, for the face of the High Priest was a face he'd seen before.

It belonged to Father Haman.

Chapter Thirty

The Cave

The Bonebreaker shuddered as Aristo brought it to a stop in front of the monastery. He lowered the landing-pads, creating little clouds of gravel dust that swirled around the nose of the huge machine, obscuring his vision for a moment.

He spotted Archie and his uncle, waving as they ran through the dust cloud towards him. They climbed up the metal rungs into the cockpit and took the seats in the front beside him.

'Good to see you again, Professor Strawbridge,' said Aristo, 'and you too, Archie.'

'Thank you, Aristo.' The professor sighed heavily as he sat back in the seat and wiped some of the dust from his face. 'I'm afraid I'm not as fit as I thought I was, but I'm glad you got here so quickly.'

'You can thank Dr Shah for that. He contacted me to put the Bonebreaker at your disposal as soon as he heard about Richard.' Aristo thumbed over his shoulder to the rear where Brimstone and Targa were sitting with four of Captain Hanki's Lancers. 'Brimstone did the rest.'

'Has Targa heard anything more from Richard?' asked Archie, squeezing past the bulk of his uncle's large frame to take the seat beside Aristo.

'I don't think so, Archie. You'd better ask Brimstone, he's the only one – besides your brother – who can understand the Vikantus.'

When Brimstone heard his name mentioned again, he spun his head ninety degrees to face the cockpit.

'No, Archie, Targa has had no contact with Richard since the first message, but his mind is open and he may find him the closer we get to the mountain.'

'Well, the sooner we get there the better,' growled the professor. 'He's been inside that mountain long enough!'

Aristo nodded.

'I agree, Professor. Hold on tight and I'll get us up there as quickly as I can.'

He engaged the propulsion system and retracted the landing-pads. The Bonebreaker rose slowly, almost reluctantly at first, and then gained speed as he pointed the huge nose fender in the direction of the waterfall.

Archie was worried. Ever since Captain Hanki had received the message that Richard was a prisoner in a cell somewhere in the mountain, he'd had the uneasy feeling that something terrible was going to happen to him. They had flown with Captain Hanki and his Lancers directly to the monastery to wait for Aristo, but Archie wondered if they would find Richard in time.

*

It didn't take them long to reach the waterfall. Aristo brought the Bonebreaker in as close as he could, ignoring the spray falling on them as he cruised slowly from one side of the waterfall to the other, searching for the break in the rock that Richard had mentioned to Targa.

'Can you see anything?' Aristo had to shout to make himself heard above the roar of the water cascading down the mountainside. 'Is there a cave there?'

'No, I don't think so,' Archie yelled back. 'There's a big crack behind the waterfall, but it's not wide enough for anything to get through.'

He was standing on the seat, his uncle holding his legs, resting his hands on the windscreen frame and leaning forward to get a better look. Columns of water bounced off the fender's huge steel plates as Aristo took the Bonebreaker in as far as he dared without being flooded. His upper body was soaked as he stood halfway out of the cockpit.

'That's enough, Archie. Get back down here.' The professor hauled him back into his seat, handing him a handkerchief. 'Here, wipe your face with that. It's not much, but it'll have to do.'

'It looks as if there's no way through here,' yelled Aristo. 'I'm going to take a look at the caves farther along.'

He pulled away from the waterfall and headed for the rock face where he'd spotted another opening. Targa had told Brimstone that Richard had said he was locked in a cave or a room behind the waterfall, and that he'd been taken there through a tunnel. If he assumed that the tunnel was on a level with the break behind the waterfall, and if he maintained the same height, then he might find a cave that would get them inside.

Aristo cruised slowly, with all of them – except Targa, who had his eyes closed – scanning the mountainside, hoping to see an opening big enough for one of the Lancers to enter.

Hanki had been emphatic: if they found a way in, the armed Lancers had to go in first, in case they ran into trouble. Aristo had no argument with that; from what he'd heard about the rebels recently, he was not about to take any chances with Archie and the professor aboard.

'*Look!*'

Aristo's thoughts were interrupted by Archie's shout. He was pointing farther up the mountain to where a Spokestar was weaving in and out of a ring of pine trees that circled a group of small caves. Above it, another Spokestar was hovering near a large, flat jutting rock well beyond the trees.

'I see them, Archie,' said Aristo. 'Including the men here, Captain Hanki has virtually the whole squadron out scouring the mountain.'

Aristo felt a hand touch his shoulder. He looked round to see Brimstone standing in the short passageway between the cockpit and the rear of the Bonebreaker.

'Is there something wrong, Brimstone?'

Aristo pulled a lever and engaged the hover position to enable him to concentrate on what the androt had to say. Brimstone pointed to one of the Spokestars.

'One of the Lancers with us has received a radiocom message from the Spokestar at the flat rock. They have found an opening large enough for us to explore.'

The professor, Archie and Aristo immediately cast their eyes upwards to the Spokestars above them, but there was little they could see from their present position.

Aristo moved to disengage the hover lever, but Brimstone stopped him.

'Wait – there is something else. Targa senses that Richard is nearby. He sees something strange happening within the mountain, but he cannot tell what it is yet.'

'Well, until he can, I propose we go to that opening and see where it leads us,' said the professor impatiently.

'Yes! We *have* to go,' cried Archie. He still had the uneasy feeling nibbling at the edge of his mind that they would be too late to save Richard. '*Please*, Aristo, let's go there *now*!'

'OK, Archie, we're on our way.'

Aristo disengaged the hover lever and steered in the direction of the two Spokestars. As they approached, the Spokestar at the flat rock backed off, allowing Aristo room to manoeuvre in front of the cave, giving all the occupants in the Bonebreaker a better view. The cave had by far the largest opening yet. As Aristo hovered with the entrance directly ahead of him he could see that it was almost big enough to accommodate the Bonebreaker.

'Aristo! We must move quickly!'

It was Brimstone again, the unusual urgency in his voice attracting everyone's attention.

'What is it?' demanded the professor.

'Targa has seen the sword of Zamah – we must act now!' demanded Brimstone.

'What in heaven's name are you talking about?'

The professor had heaved himself out of his seat and was looking back into the rear at Targa, trying to understand what it was the mysterious Vikantu had seen, but Targa was sitting quietly with his eyes closed.

'What is this … sword of Zamah?'

'It is part of the Ritual Sacrifice to Zamah. Richard is in great danger, Professor Strawbridge, we must get to him *now*,' said Brimstone. Turning to Aristo, he pointed to the cave opening. 'We have no other choice. We must enter here.'

*

When Lotane raised the sword above the boy lying in the mouth of the gold trough, Anton knew he had to act immediately. The circle of priestesses obstructed his view, and he could only catch glimpses of Lotane between their bodies, but he took aim and threw the stone with all the force he could muster, hoping that he would hit Lotane's head or outstretched arms.

He missed.

The sharp edge of the stone struck one of the priestesses on the back of the head, splitting her skull with a dull crack. She fell with her arms flung outwards, across the trough, her body protecting Richard from the sword that plunged into her back.

The other priestesses screamed at the sight of their blood-spattered sister as she fell across the Shamra child. They fled panic-stricken, leaving Lotane dumbfounded, unable to comprehend what had happened. He stepped back from the body of the dead priestess, staring at the stone sword protruding from her back. It was jerking back and forth as the Shamra child tried, frantically, to extricate himself from under the dead body. Pushing, shoving, and with his chest and arms covered in blood, the boy crawled out of the trough. Shakily, he rose to his feet.

Horrified that the Ritual Sacrifice to Almighty Zamah had been desecrated by the death of the priestess, Lotane was shocked by the sudden turn of events; and now the Shamra child was about to escape.

'*No*! You will not leave this place!' Lotane screamed, scrambling to pull the sword from the priestess's body.

Richard had begun to shake off some of the effects of the drug and was staggering, trying desperately to stay on his feet to reach the temple doors before Lotane could stop him.

Outside in the square, the priestesses had caused widespread confusion by their hysterical accusations that the High Priest had killed one of their sisters, and now the rebels stood leaderless, arguing amongst themselves what this unexpected act of killing a priestess meant to them.

Behind them, Sandan had been left unguarded and was standing beside the temple doors when Richard came running through, almost into his arms.

At the same time, Anton arrived from the other side of the temple carrying a long-gun he had taken from one of the two rebels he had disposed of with another rock.

'Sandan, give me the boy!' yelled Anton.

He ran forward, but was stopped in his tracks by the fearful sight of the High Priest, his face twisted with hate, and clutching a bloody sword in his right hand, appearing through the temple doorway.

'You – Lotane! You are the Elder … *Father Haman*!' Anton raised the long-gun to aim at the crazed figure in front of him. 'That explains a great deal – '

'No, Anton, don't shoot!' cried Sandan. 'He must have the boy –'

Just as Anton was contemplating shooting the two of them, a distant rumble distracted him. It came from the direction of the cave he used to stand in, the one overlooking the valley.

What the devil is that?

He had spun round to see an amazing sight. A huge metal nose had appeared out of nowhere scattering rocks like pebbles across the cavern floor. Behind it, a tank-like machine dropped its spider-like legs as it came to a halt on the other side of the chasm. Almost immediately, armed Lancers jumped from the rear of the machine to hunt down a group of rebels running from the pillar bridge that spanned the chasm.

Behind him, Anton heard Lotane yelling. He turned to see Sandan running down the steps and realised, with a flush of anger, that the idiot had let the boy get away and was now chasing him.

Chapter Thirty-One

Zamah's Revenge

The cave opening was large enough for the Bonebreaker to enter, but it narrowed abruptly a short distance in, forcing Aristo to stop.

'Hold on tight,' he warned, 'I'm going to shift some of this stuff.'

He reversed the Bonebreaker about twenty feet, and then slowly raised the fender until it was level with the cockpit, virtually blocking his view of the rest of the cave. With a sudden burst of power, he drove the fender into the walls on either side of the cave, tearing great chunks of rock away until he forced a passage through to the edge of the cavern. He stopped for a moment, lowering the fender to take a look at what he had done. There was one last barrier, a pile of boulders directly ahead, but above and beyond he could see a vast open space lit by beams of light streaming in from the outside. He looked over his shoulder and saw that the two Spokestars had followed him in, but were keeping a safe distance while he smashed a way through.

'OK, here we go,' yelled Aristo, this time keeping the fender below eye-level, making certain he held the Bonebreaker in a direct line with the boulders. 'One more push should do it!'

Archie felt a tremendous surge of energy vibrate through the Bonebreaker as Aristo powered it for another massive push. They burst through into the cavern, scattering the last of the boulders in a cloud of dust before coming to a halt near the edge of a deep chasm.

Archie stood up in the cockpit to get a better look, but a sudden pinging sound off the fender made him duck instinctively without knowing what it was.

'Get down, Archie, I think someone's shooting at us!'

The professor pulled him back down into his seat as Brimstone joined them in the cockpit.

'Targa says Richard is very near, but he is still in great danger –'

Another shot rang out; this time ripping through the shoulder of Brimstone's tunic, striking his metal skin.

'Brimstone – are you hurt?' gasped Archie, looking at the small round hole that had just appeared in the tunic.

'Do not concern yourself, Archie. Their weapons will do me no harm.'

While Brimstone stood defiantly in the cockpit, more shots rang out, echoing through the deep spaces of the cavern. Above him, one of the Spokestars took a position directly over the chasm. It returned fire with its lance, bright orange tracers splitting a boulder into smithereens from behind which a rebel had been firing a long-gun. The second Spokestar flew to the other side of the cavern chasing a group of rebels, armed only with swords, seeking to escape into the sanctuary of the tunnels. Meanwhile, the four Lancers had leaped over the sides of the Bonebreaker to chase rebels they had spotted running into the ruins of a building near the chasm.

'Uncle John – I see Richard!'

They had ducked down as low as they could in the cockpit to avoid being shot, but Archie had raised his head to have a look across the gaping mouth of the chasm that had split the ancient streets of the city thousands of years earlier. The remains of a paved road, its jutting slabs broken and uneven, ran past the ruins towards a large square dominated by a wide set of marble steps. The steps approached a row of collapsed columns that once graced the front of a mighty temple.

'Look – over there!'

The professor, Aristo and Brimstone followed Archie's pointing finger to where they saw Richard running down the steps away from three men. A short, squat dark-haired man was chasing him, while on the top step a horrifying figure dressed in a golden cloak and headdress, wielding a sword above his head, confronted another man carrying a long-gun.

'I see him,' said the professor. 'They must be the men who were holding him, but there seems to be trouble brewing between them.'

'I've got to help him!' said Archie.

Before they could stop him, he had pushed past his uncle and climbed over the side of the cockpit onto the metal rungs.

'Get back in here, you'll get yourself killed out there!' shouted the professor, but it was too late.

Archie had jumped and landed beside one of the landing-pads. He skirted around it and ran like mad towards the bridge that crossed the chasm.

*

'*Stop him, he must not escape*!' screamed Lotane.

Sandan had been distracted by the arrival of the Bonebreaker and for a moment had relaxed his grip on the boy. Now he was stumbling down the steps as fast as his short stumpy legs would allow him.

'Come back here, you little brat!' he yelled.

Richard had also seen the Bonebreaker and he knew it was his only hope of getting out of the cavern. He'd recovered from whatever drug they had given him and now he was running for his life. He glanced over his

344

shoulder to see that the man who had held him captive in the storeroom, was chasing after him. His mouth dry with fear and his heart thumped so hard he thought it would burst through his chest, Richard pounded across the square past the priestesses still gathered there. One of them, terrified and confused like her sister priestesses by the events in the temple and the arrival of the Lancers, made a tentative grab to stop him when she heard the High Priest shouting, but he easily brushed past her. He ran even faster to get to the far side of the square to a road that seemed to lead in the direction of the Bonebreaker.

Just before he reached the road, Richard chanced one more look behind him. The man chasing him had burst through the priestesses, flailing his arms about him like a madman, snarling at them to get out of the way.

He turned into the road, partly covered in rubble from a building that had collapsed nearby, to discover two rebels running towards him. They were being pursued by a Spokestar that fired its lance at a spot a few feet ahead of them, as a warning for them to surrender. The unexpected explosion in the road in front of him threw Richard to the ground. He was unhurt, but it gave his pursuer a chance to catch up with him.

'Got you!'

'*Aaaoow*!'

Richard cried out as he heard the cruel voice again and the familiar savage grip on his arm. He tried to wrench himself free, but the man increased his hold by twisting Richard's arm behind his back.

*

'Zamah will destroy you, Cosimo.' The eyes, small and dark, peered out at Anton from behind the green and black painted face. 'You have dared to interfere with the Ritual Sacrifice, and for that you will surely die.'

'You are mad, Lotane – or Haman, or whatever your name is. Your business here is finished; look around you – the Lancers are everywhere and the boy's gone.'

'No! Sandan will bring the boy to me and Zamah will have his Shamra child!'

It was the change in Lotane's hate-filled eyes that warned Anton a split second before he ducked and threw himself to one side. The sword swept over his head as he fired the long-gun, but it was unwieldy and he had no room to aim. The shot went wild and as he regained his balance he saw Lotane dash through the golden doors into the temple.

Anton was in no mood to go after him. He needed to get his hands on the boy, and there was no better time than now. With Lotane hiding in the temple and the rebels panicking in disarray before the Lancers, all he had to do was find the boy – with or without Sandan – and disappear into the tunnels.

He looked across the square, but there was no sign of them; only the stupid priestesses wailing and screaming like banshees at no one in particular.

Suddenly there was something else.

Anton tilted his head back, straining to hear the faint threatening rumble slowly getting louder. He looked to the huge machine on the far side of the cavern that had smashed its way through the cave, but it was still there, unmoving, parked on the far side of the chasm.

A sudden shudder beneath his feet made him look down to observe a spider-like web of cracks appearing in the marble, alerting him that something was seriously wrong. One of the remaining upright temple columns was trembling, sending out little clouds of dust into a beam of daylight streaming into the cavern through an opening in the mountainside.

Rocks from an ancient landslide began to fall on the steps, forcing Anton to step inside the temple doors as a terrible roar erupted above him. Everything around him seemed to be falling apart: a section of the temple wall crashed down onto the stone, splitting it in two. The marble floor heaved like a giant wave, throwing part of the broken stone against one of the golden doors, tearing it from its hinges.

'No, Zamah! No! The Shamra child is –'

Inside the temple, Prince Lotane, the last of his line, never had a chance to utter another word. It was as if Almighty Zamah had decided to finish the task of destroying the temple that had been started four thousand years earlier. The scream died in his throat as the mountain exploded above him, bringing down thousands of tons of rock, burying the temple so completely it would never be seen again.

Anton was hurled through the doors over the steps and across the square. He lay stunned for a few moments before picking himself up, feeling his arms and legs to see if he had incurred any injuries. He felt sore and shaken; otherwise he seemed to be alright.

Rocks were still falling onto the square, filling the air with throat-choking dust. Coughing and spitting, he rubbed his eyes and looked around the square. The place was deserted, except for two bodies lying still beside several large chunks of masonry from the temple. They were obviously dead priestesses, unlucky enough not to have escaped with their sisters and the rebel Arnaks into the tunnels.

Anton looked up as more rocks fell, warning him of the danger he still faced. More openings had appeared in the cavern roof, casting laser-like beams of daylight through the dust-laden air, illuminating what was left of the ancient city and the road where he had last seen Sandan with the boy. He cursed as he stumbled on the hem of his robe as he made his way across the rest of the square to the road. He glanced down and saw that a torn remnant of the robe was trailing on the ground. Angrily, he pulled it over his head and threw it to the ground, revealing the black crew overall he had worn on the space station.

Damn Sandan. If it hadn't been for his brother's infatuation with Lotane's superstitious nonsense, he would have the boy in his hands and in a safer place than this. Now he had to find them before the Lancers got to them, and if Sandan tried to interfere again, he would have to deal with him – permanently.

*

Archie stared hard at the other side, forcing himself not to look down. He knew if he did, he might not make it. He wasn't good with heights, but this was much worse than anything he had experienced before: it was a black abyss, an unknown void trying to suck him off the edge of the bridge and down into a bottomless pit.

It wasn't a proper bridge, just a long, flat narrow pillar no more three feet wide, which had fallen away from a nearby building when it collapsed across the opening of the chasm centuries earlier. The chasm had divided the cavern, leaving only the bridge to connect the two areas.

Suddenly an explosive roar from the mountain as it tore itself apart shook the bridge making him lose his balance. He dropped to his hands and knees, terrified that he would go over the edge. It seemed an eternity before the bridge stopped shaking, although it was only moments. He got to his feet, and without thinking what lay below him, dashed to the other side.

He didn't stop running until he reached the approach to the paved road that led to the square where he had seen Richard running from the men on the temple steps. At the other end he saw two robed figures trying to evade a Spokestar hovering above them. The Spokestar fired its lance in front of the figures and they dived in panic into the ruins at the side of the road, disappearing before the Lancers could fire again.

It was then that Archie saw Richard. He had broken free from the man holding him and was now running towards him.

'Richard!' Archie yelled, and waved his arm as he sprinted down the road, skipping between the shattered slabs to avoid tripping. 'I'm over here!'

The mountain erupted again, throwing tons of rocks across the cavern; an angry giant now fully awake, intent on finishing its job of utter destruction.

The Spokestar received a direct hit from a rock that split the canopy. It came crashing down in the middle of the road where it flipped over, with the Lancers still inside. It skidded to a halt twenty feet away from Richard, but he didn't stop. He just kept running as fast as he could towards Archie.

*

Sandan was petrified. The thunderous, deafening roar that reverberated throughout the cavern, the falling rocks and the Spokestar crashing in front of him, had made him relax his grip on the boy, letting him escape again. Now Anton was bearing down on him, looking as if he might kill him.

'Sandan, you bloody fool – stop him before he gets away!' Anton grabbed Sandan by the throat as part of the cavern roof caved in onto the square behind them.

'There's no way out back there now, we have to go after the boy.'

'The temple – it's gone,' gasped Sandan, choking under Anton's fierce grip.

He couldn't believe his eyes as he watched the remaining part of the square disappear under the heaving onslaught of rocks and dirt.

'Yes, and Lotane with it,' sneered Anton, releasing his grip, his black eyes hooded and burning with anger, forcing Sandan to cringe and turn away. 'So, let's not hear any more nonsense about the restoration of the temple and the land of Hazaranet being returned to the Arnaks. It's not going to happen. Now, get after the boy before I am reminded again of your treachery.'

Anton shoved Sandan savagely towards the road, making him stumble onto his knees.

'Get moving, you idiot, before we're trapped here,' he yelled.

*

Inch wide cracks were appearing in the road as Archie raced to reach Richard before the men got to him. The ground was trembling, with cracks spreading out in every direction, getting wider every second and pushing the old slabs of paving upwards like tombstones.

He reached Richard as the mountain beyond the vanished temple roared again.

'Archie, they're trying to kill me! That man is still after me –'

'I know, Richard, I know. There are two of them chasing you. We have to get back to the Bonebreaker before this place blows up. C'mon, let's go.'

Archie pulled Richard by the arm as they ran back towards the bridge over the chasm. The noise was horrendous as more cracks opened up, forcing them to hop and skip every few feet. A sudden whiplash of sound gave Richard little warning as the ground opened up below his feet. He fell back, pulling Archie with him, his feet slithering down the side of a widening crack.

'Archie! I'm falling –'

'Hang on, Richard, I've got you.'

Archie fell flat on the ground to spread his weight evenly, allowing him to reach over the edge of the crack to hold onto Richard's wrist with both of his hands. Richard scrambled frantically with his feet to find a foothold and just managed to get his right foot onto a small ledge, making it easier for Archie to pull him up.

Just as they got back onto their feet they heard one of the men shouting a short distance away.

'Catch him, Sandan – don't let him escape!'

Richard looked over his shoulder, and saw that it was the ugly squat man with another taller figure close behind.

'It's him, Archie. He's the one –'

'Forget it. Let's get to the Bonebreaker – look, there it is!'

They reached the bridge and started to cross to where Aristo had brought the Bonebreaker to a stop on the far side of the chasm. The huge machine was a cumbersome thing to fly and Aristo was wary of getting too close to the remaining walls of the ruins that were now shaking and threatening to collapse on top of them at any moment. They were surrounded by pyramids of rubble that made it difficult for him to manoeuvre safely without causing more damage. He had decided against forcing a way through and had raised the angled blades of the huge fender to deflect the falling rocks away from the cockpit where the professor and Targa were now seated beside him. Brimstone had lowered himself onto the metal ladder below the cockpit ready to help if needed.

'Get them on board fast,' shouted Aristo. 'We've got to get out of here before the whole place caves in on top of us!'

Carefully, he turned the machine round to face the way they had come, ready to make a quick exit.

Down on the bridge, Archie and Richard were over halfway across when a deep rumbling sound roared up from the bowels of the chasm below them. Rocks fell away from the edges near the bridge as it started to shake.

'We're going to fall!' screamed Richard, dropping to his knees in front of Archie.

'Keep going — those men are right behind us,' warned Archie. He was trying to keep his balance as the bridge started to slip away from the edge behind them.

Suddenly Brimstone's voice echoed across the chasm.

'Richard, come to me. Do not be afraid. I will hold the bridge until you are both safely across.'

Brimstone had jumped down from the Bonebreaker and was using his enormous strength to press the end of the bridge firmly into the ground.

'Go, Richard, I'll be right behind you,' encouraged Archie, looking behind to see the ugly man starting to work his way, unsteadily, across the bridge.

Richard got to his feet and, without looking down, kept his eyes locked on Brimstone until he reached the other side. He scrambled off the bridge and fell to his knees behind Brimstone. Archie followed slowly, his heart thumping wildly as he tried to ignore the horrible groaning sounds coming up from the chasm below. Just as he prepared to take the last few steps to reach

Brimstone, he felt something touch his leg. It was the ugly man's hand grabbing at him, trying to hold him back.

'Archie, take my hand,' called Brimstone, taking his own hands away from the end of the bridge.

Immediately, the bridge – without Brimstone holding it – lurched to one side, trembling violently as it drifted away from the edge. Archie shook himself loose from the man trying to hold him and threw himself forward onto Brimstone's outstretched hands as the bridge suddenly fell away from below his feet.

Brimstone retreated quickly from the edge to lift Archie onto the Bonebreaker's ladder. The boys climbed into the cockpit where the professor hugged the two of them close to his chest.

'Well, you two certainly know how to keep me on my toes,' said the professor, a wide smile of relief spreading across his face.

*

Anton had hardly ventured onto the bridge when it suddenly bucked upwards like an angry stallion trying to throw its rider. He hurled himself backwards onto the ground away from the bridge and then rolled away as the chasm widened, roaring and belching clouds of stone and dirt into the air. He rose to his feet and watched helplessly as Sandan was tossed about like a rag doll in the hot gases, before falling out of sight into the fiery depths below.

The boy had escaped, and now Sandan was gone. He felt no sorrow or pity for his half-brother, only deep contempt for his stupidity and treachery. Sandan deserved his fate and he would weep no tears for him. But his anger grew as he realised that the boy was now beyond his reach.

He looked up at the roof of the cavern as huge slabs of the mountain surrounding the temple crashed into the square. The Bonebreaker rose into the air, its spider-like landing-pads retracting into the underside, gathering speed as Aristo pointed it towards the cave opening that would take them out of the cavern and over the terraces where the monks collected the stickleberries.

Chapter Thirty-Two

Marjorie's Decision

Nearly three months after the events in the cavern, Archie and Richard were ushered into the outer office by Mrs MacQueen and directed to sit on the large leather armchairs near Miss Harmsway's door.

'You'll have to wait for a few minutes, boys. Father Jamarko's still in there, but they shouldn't be too long now,' said Mrs MacQueen, straightening her tartan skirt and sitting down behind an old-fashioned wooden desk that supported a modern computer monitor, so large that she almost disappeared behind it.

Behind her, Archie's gaze drifted to the oak panelled wall that held a very ornate, gold embossed frame displaying the portrait of a silver haired, stout-looking figure, resplendent in gold and purple robes, and holding on his lap what looked to Archie suspiciously like a very thick cane. It was Samuel Harmsway, the founder of Harmsway College, and he stared back at Archie, making him feel restless and out of place.

'I wish they'd hurry up,' said Archie, in a low voice that Mrs MacQueen wouldn't hear. 'I can't wait to get out of here.'

He was itching to get away, but it was their last day at Harmsway and they had to see Miss Harmsway first, before Aristo arrived with Marjorie to take them to Mount Tengi.

'I dunno, I'm sort of sorry to be going back,' said Richard, almost whispering, trying to ignore the surprised look on Archie's face.

'*What*! After everything that has happened here?' Archie started to raise his voice, but when Mrs MacQueen stared at him, he quickly lowered it. 'Have you forgotten what nearly happened to you in the cavern? I thought after that you couldn't wait to get back home.'

'No, I haven't forgotten,' said Richard, 'it's just that I've got used to being here, I suppose. And what it's going to be like when we do get back home? I mean ... how are we going to explain where we've been?'

'I don't know, Richard, but what you've got to remember, is that it's important we get back if we're ever going to find out what happened to mum and dad.'

'I suppose so, but it's going to feel strange going back to Grimshaws after being away for so long.'

'I feel the same,' said Archie, 'but then we haven't been here too often either.'

It was true. On quite a few occasions during the past few weeks, they had been to Mount Tengi to help Uncle John and Dr Shah establish the link they needed to make with the engineers at the DONUT, and now it was finished.

Today was the day they were going back to Old Earth.

They had Richard to thank for making the link, but Shaman-Sing (who had been invited by Benno Kozan to join the Mount Tengi research group) had warned Krippitz not to depend entirely on Richard's power. He explained that it was unpredictable and might suddenly leave Richard at any time (just as he had described the loss of his own power to the boys when they were in Maroc). Krippitz said he understood, but emphasised that once the link was established they would no longer need Richard.

Funnily enough, though, Archie had noticed that Richard didn't mention his dreams now, and he hardly spoke of the trances. He had mentioned it to Shaman-Sing and thought it was because, subconsciously, Richard had learned to control his power; but for how long, no one could tell. The more he thought about it, Archie couldn't escape the feeling that, somehow, Richard had been affected by all that had happened to them in Timeless Valley, in some strange way that he couldn't explain.

Archie's thoughts were disturbed as Miss Harmsway's office door opened.

'Ah, the Kinross boys. What an unexpected pleasure to actually see you both here at Harmsway.'

Miss Harmsway entered the outer office, followed by Father Jamarko a few steps behind. She stared at Richard as he and Archie jumped to their feet.

'Especially you, young man. You have been quite a stranger to this college, but I gather from Dr Shah that your efforts at Mount Tengi have been very successful.' She smiled unexpectedly, her green eyes twinkling, 'You needn't look so surprised. I don't always bite. I'm only sorry I couldn't have seen more of the two of you during your time here.'

'Is this the boy I've heard so much about?' queried a quiet voice behind Miss Harmsway.

It was Father Jamarko. The old monk took a shaky step forwards to take a closer look at Richard. His eyes were weak, but they still glistened with interest.

'Your name is Richard?'

Richard nodded.

'My, you are very young to have been involved in so much danger – but then it was inevitable, wasn't it?'

'Inevitable? Whatever do you mean, Father Jamarko?' snapped Miss Harmsway. She was beginning to wonder if other Harmsway students might be in danger. 'Why should –'

'Miss Harmsway, I know you have little time for myths and legends, but I can assure you that even today, in this enlightened age of ours, a large number of

Arnaks take these stories very seriously indeed – especially that of the Shamra child.'

Miss Harmsway's eyes widened in astonishment; she was not used to being interrupted so abruptly.

'And what *exactly* is a Shamra child?'

The old monk moved, unsteadily, to a padded leather seat near Mrs MacQueen's desk, indicating he needed to sit down before continuing.

'I'm afraid my legs are a little weaker today,' he said, making himself comfortable as he sank into the soft leather. 'Ah, that's much better – much better indeed. Now, Miss Harmsway, to your question, but first I must repeat what I told you in your office earlier: that your students are very welcome to return to the monastery at any time. I do not want what has happened to act as a barrier between us. Now that Father Haman has gone ...' He hesitated for a moment, shaking his head disbelievingly as he thought of the monk who had worked with him for so long, and yet had caused so much trouble. '... there should be no need for concern.'

'That may be so, Father, but what is this business about a Shamra child?' said Miss Harmsway impatiently.

'Yes, yes, of course. Well, it was believed in ancient times – by the Salakins as well as the Arnaks – that a boy with the power to see other worlds must be a son of Almighty Zamah. In times of war or natural disaster, or when the Sacred Temple priests were greatly troubled, it was believed that such a child who had not yet reached thirteen years would appease Zamah by means of the Ritual Sacrifice. A primitive practice, I know, but in Richard's case, Father Haman – or in his true identity as Prince Lotane – sincerely believed that through such a sacrifice the Arnaks would regain the land of Hazaranet.'

'So that meant Richard had to be younger than thirteen?' asked Archie.

'Yes. It was considered by the ancient tribes that only such a boy would be acceptable to Zamah: at thirteen he becomes a man.'

'But ...' Archie struggled with a thought that now raced through his mind, 'but Richard was already thirteen when he was captured.'

The old monk, stroked his chin slowly as he caressed the few wisps of long grey beard left to him. 'I don't know if the age difference would affect the sacrifice, but if was essential to the ritual, it could explain why Zamah – provided you believe in such things – destroyed the temple. After all, we should remember that the legend says he visited his anger on the temple over four thousand years ago when his people displeased him.'

'It would seem they have angered him again,' said Miss Harmsway, raising her eyes in disbelief, making it painfully obvious that she had little time for myth and legend. A few more minutes of polite discussion brought her to her feet, indicating that their meeting had come to an end and that she had other matters to attend to.

After saying goodbye to Miss Harmsway, Archie and Richard left the office with Father Jamarko and made their way to the quadrangle to meet Marjorie and Aristo.

'Not so quick, young man,' said Father Jamarko, 'these old legs of mine are not as nimble as they used to be.'

'Sorry,' said Archie, grabbing Richard by the shoulder to slow him down. 'I wasn't thinking.'

'No, it is I who should be sorry for holding you back, but tell me, aren't you the young man at the monastery who asked me about Copanatec?'

'Yes,' said Archie, looking surprised. In the excitement of all that had happened, he had forgotten that he had asked the old monk about the mysterious island city. 'You said something about a Great Flood, and that the city no longer existed, but ... well, I don't know what to think now.'

Archie's thoughts were confused as he tried to remember what he and Richard had witnessed when they were on the Harmsway stone. Everything they had seen seemed so real – as real as they were now – but if the city no longer existed, how could it be real?

'What is it, Archie? What is it that troubles you?' asked Father Jamarko.

They had reached the quadrangle, where Archie stopped and pointed to the stone. He described everything that happened that night when Han-Sin had let them visit the stone in the middle of the night.

'I could see the people and the buildings and I ... I mean, we ... heard our mother, and then Richard spoke to her. Didn't you?' said Archie, suddenly turning to Richard for support.

'Yes, I did,' said Richard, recalling what had happened. 'Mum said they were in a place called Copanatec. I don't know what she meant, but I think they're being held in some sort of prison.'

'It is very strange,' said Father Jamarko, 'but it may be that your power has allowed you to see things in a place that was thought to have disappeared below the waters a long time ago.'

'What do you mean? What happened to Copanatec?' asked Archie, anxious to know more.

'Little is known. The ancient books tell us that a magnificent city and its people were destroyed when a great earthquake, near what is now the coast of Central Amasia, caused the sea to rise and cover the land.'

Father Jamarko looked up as someone called to them. It was Aristo and Marjorie walking across the quadrangle towards them.

'Ah, I see your friends have come to collect you.'

'But isn't there anything else you can tell us?' urged Archie, desperate now that they were leaving, for any scrap of information that might lead them to their parents.

'No, my son,' said Father Jamarko, resting an affectionate hand on Archie's shoulder. 'All I can say to you is that you should go to the place where your parents were last seen. Perhaps there, Richard may be able to use his power to find what you seek.'

*

They left Harmsway College for the last time, with Aristo swooping low over the blue zimmerball bounce-pitch, giving Archie and Richard one more chance to take a look at the grounds and buildings that had been their home for the past few months.

Below them, several players hovered above the bounce-pitch as they prepared for practice. Archie felt a sudden pang of regret as he looked down and thought of Jules Stein, who had tried to teach him how to use Zap boots, and the basics of zimmerball. He hadn't seen Jules since he had been shot by Slashface in the railcar at Maroc Forest, but apparently he had made a full recovery and was staying with his father at Sitanga.

As they left Harmsway, Archie thought about what Richard had said about leaving, and wondered if they would ever see Jules or any of their new friends again. But, as always, his thoughts turned to his parents: where were they, and how he was going to find them.

His thoughts were interrupted by Captain Hanki, as he described the aftermath of the events in the cavern to Richard.

'I believe we managed to capture most of the rebel Arnaks, and all of them say that their leader died in the temple; but the New Arrival – probably the killer of Suntee – may have escaped into the tunnels. If so, you can be sure that we will find him.'

'I saw him on the far side of the chasm when the other guy who was chasing us, fell into it,' said Archie. He shuddered as he remembered the horrible screams as the man fell into the abyss. 'But I don't know where he went after that.'

'Do not worry, Archie,' said Hanki, 'we have his description from Lotane's followers – it is only a matter of time until we catch him.'

'Were they followers of Lotane as well?' asked Richard.

'We know now that after killing Suntee they escaped into the mountain and it was there they joined forces with Lotane. The rebels sheltered them, and in turn they agreed to help the Arnaks in their cause. We think it was the New Arrivals who sent the ransom note.'

'But why?' asked Archie.

'Apparently, they wanted the vallonium process. For what purpose, we have yet to discover.'

They sat quietly for a few moments, each with their own thoughts about the recent events they had experienced. Suddenly Hanki smiled. He turned towards the cockpit. 'It would seem our friend Aristo is very happy today!'

'He loves flying the Bonebreaker,' said Archie. 'He told me it's the next best thing to travelling through a timecrack.'

'Perhaps, but I think there is more to it than that.' said Hanki.

Archie looked at him curiously, but before he could ask what he meant, Aristo called to them that they were approaching Mount Tengi.

Ahead of them lay a great lump of a mountain reaching into the sky like a giant haystack. Its flat top was dominated by a grid of massive black pillars connected to each other by a network of metal cables. Suspended by more cables in the middle of the grid was a large, shiny silver sphere, its surface reflecting so much light it was difficult to see its shape. Thick power lines drawing energy from the vallonium deposits deep in the heart of the mountain snaked up each of the pillars and into the sphere. As big as a house, the timecrack chamber was almost impossible to look at directly without being blinded.

The passengers in the Bonebreaker raised their hands to protect their eyes as Aristo turned away from the chamber and made his approach to the landing field. They passed through two greyish-black outcrops of rock that formed a natural entrance to the TRU complex.

Before they landed, Aristo passed out sunglasses to everyone.

'You'll need these until we get into the TRU building. Dr Shah is drawing power from the mountain to charge the chamber, so it will get much brighter. Please don't take them off until we get inside.'

They left the Bonebreaker parked near a row of Spokestars, and Captain Hanki went to see some of his Lancers, saying he would watch their departure later.

'Archie,' said Richard, nudging Archie's arm and pointing to Aristo and Marjorie walking in front of them towards a long, low stone building that stood directly underneath the timecrack chamber. 'Look, he's holding her hand!'

Archie had been looking up at the chamber and not really paying attention to anything else, but Richard was right: Marjorie and Aristo were holding hands. Surprised, he followed them into the TRU building past two Lancer guards who nodded in recognition as Aristo spoke to them. He saw Uncle John waiting for them in the spacious hallway beside a lift door.

'Welcome, everyone, it's good to see you here,' said the professor, a broad smile on his face. 'Well, this is a big day for us. It has been a long time coming but now we are ready to go home.' He stopped for a moment, looking at Marjorie as if she might say something. 'Except for you, Marjorie, unless you have changed your mind?'

'No, Professor, I haven't. I talked it over with Aristo this morning and I've decided to stay.'

'What! But ... but why ...?' spluttered Archie.

'Marjorie ... you're not really staying, are you?' Richard stared at her, his voice almost a whisper.

Richard looked so serious that Marjorie felt sorry for him. She reached out, put her arm around his shoulders and hugged him.

'Yes, Richard, I am staying. I'm sorry I didn't tell you sooner, but I did mention it to your uncle last week that I was thinking of staying on at Harmsway.' She hugged Richard tighter. 'It's hard to explain what it is I feel for this place. I've loved it since the day we arrived, but it was only this morning that I finally made up my mind to stay.' She grinned at Aristo and said, 'Aristo can be quite persuasive, but I didn't need much persuading.'

Archie and Richard quizzed her if she really knew what she was doing, hardly believing she had made such an incredible decision. But after a while it was plain that Marjorie had made up her mind that her future lay in Timeless Valley.

*

The professor pressed the button for the lift and they followed him in. They dropped several levels below ground to enter the main observation and control room where Shah was examining a strange-looking metal capsule. It was about the size of a telephone kiosk, and Krippitz was sitting inside it studying a monitor as a series of colour bars popped up and down on the screen.

'Dr Shah calls it the Parasite, because it feeds off the main timecrack chamber, but it's properly known as MUCS, a multi-universe communication system,' said Krippitz, turning to face them. 'There is an identical one on Old Earth, and it will have a communicator sitting in it replicating exactly the same information we have here during a traveller's journey. Each communicator will keep a log to keep us informed at all times of the traveller's condition. With the final pieces of equipment in place we are now ready whenever the travellers are ready to go.'

'I hope so, Carl. The Elders, especially Julius Stein, will have my guts if we ask for any more development money,' grumbled Shah, turning his hoverchair to face Archie and Richard. He studied their faces for a moment and then asked, 'Are you ready to go home, boys?'

'Yes, we are, Dr Shah,' said Archie.

He shifted his feet nervously, hoping that nobody would notice how uneasy he was beginning to feel now that they were so close to entering the chamber. He glanced quickly at Richard, wondering how he felt, but his brother had started to poke his nose into the

Parasite, taking a look at how it worked, seemingly not bothered by their imminent journey.

'Good. Everything is ready for all of you. You will go with the assistants to the preparation room and change into the tracker suits, check them out and then you will be ready to leave,' said Shah. 'A big improvement on our original suits, isn't that so, Aristo?'

'Yes, sir, very much so,' agreed Aristo, winking at Archie reassuringly, as if he'd guessed that Archie was having last minute butterflies in his stomach.

'Excellent. You and Professor Strawbridge will enter the chamber first and we will monitor you from here. As soon as Carl receives your communication that you have arrived safely, the boys will go next. Any questions?'

'Aristo is going back with us?' asked Archie, wondering what other surprises he was going to hear.

'Yes, Archie, he is taking Miss Peoples' place – a last minute change of plan but one that we should have considered before this,' said Shah. 'You see, we hadn't planned for a return journey, but Aristo pointed out that we needed to test the chamber in both directions, and I had to agree with him. He is travelling with your uncle, and after they confirm their safe arrival you and Richard will go next.'

For the next hour, Shah and one of his assistants went over the required procedure for entering the chamber and what to expect when the timecrack was initiated. Two assistants then escorted the professor and Aristo to the preparation room where they helped them change into the tracker suits. They checked that everything was functioning properly and then walked with them to the lift shaft that would take them directly to a hatch in the side of the chamber.

Finally, they entered the chamber and the hatch was sealed.

*

In the control room, Archie and Richard sat with Marjorie, watching apprehensively as they waited to hear from Krippitz in the Parasite the news that they were next. High above them the timecrack had come and gone, but deep in the mountain they hadn't heard or felt a thing. Their only clue to what was happening was the behaviour of the assistants, along with Krippitz and Shah attending to their respective tasks.

Time seemed to pass slowly and after twenty minutes, with nobody saying anything, Archie felt he wouldn't be able to stand the silence any longer. He felt ready to explode. Why was it taking so long? Had Uncle John and Aristo landed somewhere else? Would they ever hear from them again?

Suddenly he heard a yell.

'Emil! Emil – they have arrived! Their signal has just come through!'

Krippitz almost fell out of the Parasite in his excitement to tell everyone the good news. His large glasses slipped to the end of his nose as he dashed across the room to Shah's hoverchair.

'We've done it, Emil! They have reached Old Earth exactly at the time and place we planned!'

'Well done, Carl,' said Shah, guiding his hoverchair towards Archie and Richard, waiting on the other side of the control room. Krippitz hurried alongside to keep up with him. 'But we still have the task of sending two young men to the same place – and getting Aristo back safely to Mount Tengi.'

Chapter Thirty-Three

Amaterasu

'*Hey*! Get off me – your elbow's in my ear!' yelled Richard, shoving Archie aside.

'Sorry,' said Archie. He was having a problem with his balance as he struggled to stay on his feet.

He pushed the headband filter up from his eyes, and looked at their surroundings. The blinding yellow light had disappeared, and only wisps of the blue mist that had filled the chamber when the timecrack arrived, remained.

The grey padded floor and slightly curved walls that had cushioned their arrival reminded Archie of the bouncy castles they used to play in at the fairground, when they were much younger. It was similar to the chamber at Mount Tengi they had just left: there were no windows or doors, only the concealed strip lighting above them and the humming sound of the energy resonators in the background.

'Is this it? Are we back?' Richard was on his knees, looking around the room. 'Maybe we never left. Maybe we've ended up somewhere else – '

But before Richard's fertile imagination started to conjure up endless possibilities of where they might be, they suddenly heard a strange humming sound, like a refrigerator switching on. Archie turned quickly to face one of the curved walls where a crack had started to appear. Slowly the crack got wider and he realised it was a hidden door, its outline disguised by the ribbed padding that made up the walls and floor of the room.

Two men appeared in the open doorway. One of them, a small man wearing a red overall, was Ed Hanks the chief engineer. The other, tall and with deeply tanned skin and a thick drooping moustache, stared at them for a couple of seconds and then laughed out loud.

'Welcome back, pardners. I hope you enjoyed the ride.'

'Chuck! Richard, it's Chuck!' cried Archie, pulling Richard up onto his feet.

It was Chuck Winters, head of the security team at the Facility. He stepped inside the chamber as the boys rushed to meet him, but in his excitement, Archie tripped on the ribbed floor and fell to his knees with Richard falling on top of him.

'Whoa, take it easy, pardners. We don't want you breaking a leg now that we've managed to get you back here in one piece,' said Chuck.

He helped them off the floor and led them to the door, while Ed stood outside and scribbled notes on a clipboard.

They left the padded chamber and walked along a metal catwalk towards a lift cage. Archie looked up at the huge tyre-shaped cylinder that surrounded them, suddenly realising where they were.

'We're in the middle of the DONUT, aren't we, Chuck?'

'That's right, Archie. When we received the plans from Dr Shah and your uncle to build the timecrack chamber, *Amaterasu* – that's the name your uncle wanted when we first built the DONUT – we decided to place it where the original timecracks kept occurring. Pretty obvious, when you think about it. But we still have more work to do to finish the transmitting part of the chamber, if we're going to send your friend Aristo back.'

The lift cage transported them to one of the upper catwalks leading to the terrace where Archie and Richard had first seen the inside of the Facility. The professor and Aristo were waiting for them and like

Archie and Richard, they were still wearing their tracker suits.

'Well done, boys,' said the professor, stretching out his arms to greet them. 'Except for Marjorie, we're all back safe and sound.'

He was smiling, but his face didn't reveal the concern that had preyed on his mind over the dangers of the incredible journey they had just completed. Thank God they had made it. Now they were safely home he felt he could relax, but there was still so much more to do.

Amaterasu had to be finished to get Aristo back to Mount Tengi. After that there would be ongoing development between the two timecrack chambers to help other travellers reach their destinations. Beyond that, the professor realised, they could only speculate what lay ahead.

But more immediately, there was the problem of his sister, Lucy, and her husband Malcolm. He had listened carefully to the boys' strange tale about a lost city called Copanatec, a place where Lucy and Malcolm were supposedly being held prisoner. He didn't know what to make of such a bizarre story, but one thing he did know: The boys – especially Archie – would never rest until they'd found the answer to their parents' whereabouts. He only hoped they were still alive.

Richard had been instrumental in getting them home, but finding Lucy and Malcolm, what would that entail? He knew it was a task that might take a very long time and all the resources he could command.

As they left the catwalk for the terrace he gripped his old friend by the shoulder.

'You'll have to bring me up to date on all that's been happening here, Chuck. We've been away nearly six months and we have a lot to catch up on, but first I need to attend to making arrangements to get the boys back to Grimshaws.' He grinned as he heard Richard groan. 'And Miss Peoples is no longer with us – I'll explain why later – so I'm leaving everything in your hands.'

'Sure, whatever you say, Professor,' said Chuck. He removed the white Stetson he habitually wore and scratched his head, a frown creasing his brow. 'Ed here will look after Aristo, and I'll see to Archie and Richard, but there's one thing I don't quite get.'

'What's that?'

'Well, it's just that you haven't been away six months. It's more like eighteen months since you all disappeared off that catwalk.'

'What! What are you saying?' The professor came to a sudden halt. He looked at Chuck as if he had just said something crazy, something utterly outrageous, but then he smiled and clutched his beard. 'Of course, how could I be so stupid? I'd completely forgotten about the time differential!'

Archie looked curiously at his uncle and Chuck as they stared at each other in astonishment. Then it suddenly dawned on him what it was they were talking about: because of the time differential they had lost a year and a half of their lives on Old Earth!

He felt Richard pulling at his sleeve and turned to look at him.

'What?'

'I'm confused,' said Richard. 'What age does that make me now?'

The story continues...

Coming Soon

Copanatec

Chapter One

Captured

Malcolm thought they had landed in the middle of a nightmare – but he was wrong.

This was for real.

He was standing beside Lucy in the middle of a village compound, the air thick with burning smoke from burning huts on every side. Dark-skinned men and women, dragging children behind them, were running in every direction, screaming and yelling in fear for their lives. One of the men fell near them. Trying to save himself, he reached out a hand towards Lucy for support. Instead, he grabbed at her shirt, ripping it away from the shoulder, exposing part of her arm and back.

Lucy screamed. The man lay at her feet, the bolt from a crossbow protruding from his back.

'What's happening?' she cried. 'Where are we?'

'God only knows, Lucy, but by the look of things around here we'd better make ourselves scarce!'

Malcolm grabbed Lucy by the arm, pulling her close to his side as he looked for a way to escape. It seemed only a short time ago that they had been trapped by the sudden storm floods on the flat of a large stone, near the edge of the dig they had been excavating. The mysterious blue cloud close to the pyramid they had been watching had descended rapidly, sucking them into its core, a tunnel of intense yellow light that must have transported them, somehow, to this strange place. A place with people he didn't recognise, and seemingly under attack.

His best guess, as far-fetched as it sounded, was that they had been caught up in some sort of freak tornado and then dumped somewhere else in the Yucatan. But the blue cloud that had swept over them was unlike any tornado he had seen before. Nothing like the tornado he and Lucy had witnessed a couple of years earlier off the coast of Playa del Carmen, when they had been waiting for a ferry to the island of Cozumel.

It had all happened so quickly; he remembered little of what it was like in the cloud, except the feeling of weightlessness and tumbling through space. And none of the madness going on around them made any sense – but it was obvious they were in danger and that they had to find somewhere safe.

Ignoring the pain in his knee, Malcolm tried to move quickly, but it was no good. He had lost his walking stick in the blue cloud and now he found it difficult to take more than a few steps at a time without it. As they made their way past one of the burning huts towards a rocky ridge and a clump of trees on a height behind the village, Malcolm winced with pain, coming to a sudden halt.

'Please, Malcolm, don't stop,' pleaded Lucy. Her eyes were red-rimmed with tears as the thick, acrid smoke choked the air around them. 'We have to get out of here.'

'I'm sorry – it's this damned knee. I need to find a stick or something to support it.'

The fear in her voice unsettled him. He was beginning to dread what might happen to them, but before he could utter another word they were confronted by a group of men – and a more, ugly, dangerous lot, Malcolm couldn't imagine.

Four guards, swarthy and squat, with heavy brows over slit eyes, pug noses and broad yellowish features, were driving some of the village men towards them. They cracked vicious-looking, metal-tipped whips above the heads of the men while two more guards marched in front, armed with short bronze and silver coloured crossbows held across their chests.

'Haggh! Haggh!' The men with the crossbows called out, or so it sounded to Malcolm.

The strange words of the language were unknown to Malcolm; unlike Spanish, or Mayan, and certainly not English, the meaning was very clear: a warning to stay where they were, which in the face of the weapons they carried, seemed to be their only option. He put his arm around Lucy's shoulders, drawing her close to his side.

'Stay calm, Lucy,' he whispered. 'Let's see what they want.'

One of the men; Malcolm assumed they were some sort of guard, stepped forward and flicked his whip, threateningly, near Malcolm's face, the metal tips almost touching his skin.

His heart thumping wildly, Malcolm shouted at him, first in Spanish, and then in the few words of Yucatec Maya he knew, and finally in English, hoping the ugly devil would understand.

'What do you want with us? We have done you no harm!'

The guard lowered his whip and looked curiously at Malcolm. Like the other guards, he was dressed in brown leather leggings and calf-length boots. A belted, dark-red tunic open from neck to waist exposed a thick, hairy chest. He stared for a moment, and then turned his gaze to Lucy, inspecting her a little too closely for Malcolm's liking. He seemed to make up his mind about something, and without saying a word he strode across the compound towards another group of villagers and guards.

Malcolm watched as the group parted to allow the guard to approach a man clutching a long black rod, about four feet in length, who was herding several terrified male villagers into a long, narrow mesh cage at the rear of what appeared to be some sort of tracked vehicle. He was much taller than the guards or the villagers and his face was decorated with little tattooed feathers. With long black hair reaching to his shoulders he had the appearance of a fierce-looking bird ready to descend on its prey. He wore a close fitting yellow robe, tied at the waist with a black sash, and like the guards, he wore leather calf boots.

'What are they doing with those people?' whispered Lucy.

Malcolm felt Lucy shiver, through cold or fear, he wasn't sure. He gave her a reassuring hug, but as he did so, he tried to shake the terrible thought that was beginning to form in his mind.

Were these men slave traffickers? God, surely not!

He looked around at what was left of the village. All the huts had been destroyed, the smouldering remains a pathetic reminder of what had apparently been a small village community in the middle of the jungle. Several bodies lay on the ground, including women and children, alongside several dogs and goats, all of them showing evidence of indiscriminate butchery. Only the men had been taken and were now being driven towards the cage.

The guard pointed with his whip towards the prisoners when speaking to the tall man. But when the guard returned with him to the group, it was clear that the tall man's eyes were fixed on Malcolm and Lucy.

Malcolm experienced an icy chill course through his blood as he wondered if their fate was about to be decided.

The tall man stopped in front of Lucy, his piercing grey eyes examining her from head to toe, like a horse breeder considering the merits of a new pony. He walked slowly around her, taking in the contours of her body, while Malcolm seethed with anger at the indignity of their treatment. Despite the condition of her muddy clothes as a result of the flood at the pyramid, the tall man nodded approvingly. Suddenly, he stopped to look more closely at Lucy's shoulder where her shirt had been torn. His fingers reached out to trace a pattern on her skin.

Lucy screamed and tried to pull away from him. Malcolm swung her round to place his body between Lucy and the tall man, but as he did so, an excruciating pain shot through his body. He fell to the ground, hardly able to move a muscle.

'Stay there, alien,' barked a voice above him. 'Do not move.'

Malcolm did move and the pain returned, more intense than before, forcing him into a foetal position. After a moment, he managed to look up to see the tall man standing over him, holding the black rod, ready to strike again.

Bloody hell, thought Malcolm, *it must be some sort of electronic cattle prod.*

The pain eased and he managed to gasp, 'Who are you?' hoping the rod wouldn't be used again.

'I am Talon of Copanatec,' said the tall man, 'and who are you?'

'You speak English?'

'I speak all languages, alien. I ask again, who are you?' said Talon, pointing the black rod closer to Malcolm's chest.

'You don't need to use that thing,' said Malcolm, raising a hand to protect himself. 'My name is Malcolm Kinross and my wife's name is –' He stopped and rose to his knees, looking around to see what had happened to Lucy. 'Where is my wife? What have you done with her?'

'She is a chosen one and will serve at the temple,' said Talon, smiling for the first time at Malcolm's confusion. 'Do not concern yourself, alien. She will serve us well ... and so will you, if we let you live.'

'What the hell are you talking about, you crazy butcher?' shouted Malcom, getting to his feet. 'Bring my wife back –'

He felt the rod prod him forcefully in the chest. This time pain and shock overcame him and he fell unconscious at Talon's feet.

*

Malcolm woke up to find he was crushed together with twenty, or so, of the village men in what he took to be the cage he had seen earlier. From what he could see through the wire mesh on his side, they were now on the open deck of what appeared to be a very large craft, and they were powering through a turbulent sea to an unknown destination!

Behind them, in the fading light of nightfall, he could see the outline of a rocky coast and wreckage-strewn beach. Beyond the beach was the jungle they had just left, but he recognised none of it as part of the Yucatan he had worked in for so long.

As he stared at the rapidly retreating coast, Malcolm was aware of something unpleasant in the air around him. He realised it was the stench of fear, and men being sick where they lay. It was overpowering, but worse than that, was the fear at what might have happened to Lucy.

My God, he thought, *how did we end up in this nightmare?*

Copanatec
will be published by
New Generation Publishing

William Long was born in Belfast on 6 June 1939.

After a long and varied career in sales and marketing, including running his own business designing and producing branded goods for a number of high profile companies as well as smaller organisations, he retired and devoted several years to a men's hostel for the homeless.

When diagnosed with prostate cancer he wrote the story of his experience, and along with a selection of his own Irish short stories, published them as a collection in *An Unexpected Diagnosis*, available as an eBook on Amazon.

He now concentrates on writing and travelling.

Timecrack is the first of a series of novels about two young brothers, Archie and Richard Kinross, and their adventures in other dimensions.

Lightning Source UK Ltd.
Milton Keynes UK
UKOW03f0425160914

238636UK00001B/56/P